THE NICANDER CHRONICLES

BOOK ONE

OF PAST AND PRESENT

By Tom Jackson

Copyright @ 2023 by Tom Jackson

All rights reserved. No part of this book may be reproduced, distributed, or transmitted in any form or by any means, including photocopying, recording, or other electronic or mechanical methods, without the prior written permission of the author/publisher, except in the case of brief quotations embodied in book reviews and certain other noncommercial uses permitted by copyright law.

For Shainy

Table of Contents

Chapter one 6

Part One.. 22

Chapter two 23
Chapter three 31
Chapter four 38
Chapter five 45
Chapter six 52
Chapter seven 55
Chapter eight 68
Chapter nine 74
Chapter ten 81
Chapter eleven 90
Chapter twelve 100
Chapter thirteen 106
Chapter fourteen 114

Part Two... 123

Chapter fifteen 124
Chapter sixteen 130
Chapter seventeen 136
Chapter eighteen 143
Chapter nineteen 150
Chapter twenty 157

Chapter twenty-one 169
Chapter twenty-two 175
Chapter twenty-three 190

Part Three *203*

Chapter twenty-four 204
Chapter twenty-five 218
Chapter twenty-six 228
Chapter twenty-seven 232
Chapter twenty-eight 250
Chapter twenty-nine 254
Chapter thirty 266
Chapter thirty-one 274

Part Four *288*

Chapter thirty-two 289
Chapter thirty-three 304
Chapter thirty-four 315
Chapter thirty-five 321
Chapter thirty-six 324
Chapter thirty-seven 334
Chapter thirty-eight 339
Chapter thirty-nine 344
Chapter forty 352
Epilogue 363

Chapter one

Liverpool, England, UK
Eight years ago

Merchant's Lodge had been abandoned for some time.

There was a loneliness in the soul of the place that felt somehow deliberate, as though it had always been that way.

Ari Nicander pulled up outside, killed the engine of his 1965 Triumph Bonneville motorcycle, and flicked out the kickstand. He swung his leg over the back of the bike until his boots met with gravel, then flipped the visor on his helmet and took in the outer wall.

The gate guarding the abandoned mansion was as unremarkable as it was large, a simple design of dark oakwood with black-iron fittings and a hefty deadbolt in the middle. A note from the local council in a stained plastic wallet explained that the building was due to be demolished and trespassers should stay off the land. Another couple of posters doubled down on that warning.

Ari looked back along Grove Street, the cul-de-sac where several such Victorian mansions stood forgotten. He squinted into the glare of the mid-morning sun.

It was hard to believe that the hubbub of Liverpool's city centre lay only around the bend, where a never-ending roar of traffic and seemingly endless throng of people flocked toward its busy high streets.

Grove Street, however, was silent, wrapped in cellophane.

Ari took a deep breath. Not a cloud threatened the blue sky of the spring air, and a cool, calming breeze gently lapped at his exposed ankles, where the material of his light blue jeans was cut short.

He pulled off his helmet and propped it on the seat of his motorcycle. He wore a brown leather jacket, a close-fitting black t-shirt, and the same pair of worn-looking Chelsea boots that he had owned for as long as he could remember.

Ari stepped back a few paces to get a clearer view beyond the gate.

He could see a meandering driveway, which snaked for some distance, covered by overgrown trees that had come together over the path to form a passage. In parts, the sunlight penetrated the canopy like pins through paper, and little blobs of light pockmarked the dirt.

Merchant's Lodge had an imposing circular turret on one side, built with washed-out grey stone that had faded and started to turn brown in parts. Ari could see that some of the roof had started to crumble, falling in on itself like a collapsing star. If he had cared to think about it, Ari would have said that it was a shame to have to demolish the buildings of Grove Street, all of which were, for better or worse, part of Liverpool's history.

An engine banged, drawing Ari's attention.

A flash of mint green paintwork dazzled across his line of sight as a second 1965 Bonneville was brought around, the rider turning his handlebars inwards as he came to a stop and killed his engine too, but not before pointlessly revving the throttle a couple of times. He slid off the bike with experienced grace.

'Marius,' the man said, muffled beneath his helmet.

He had a thick Eastern European accent, and he over pronounced the "oos" at the end of Ari's full name - as he always did.

Ari's boss and mentor, Ondrej, removed his helmet to reveal a pair of cerulean eyes, letting go a mane of long, silver hair. His face was rounded, though not from corpulence, and his pronounced forehead sat proudly above a prominent nose and puckered lips. He had a tattoo of a small bird behind his ear, the signature of his gang, the Bluebirds.

'It'd better be here,' Ondrej said plainly. The Czech took a battered Golden Virginia tobacco tin from an inside pocket of his heavy-duty duster jacket and lit a pre-rolled cigarette with a match.

'You doubt me?' Ari asked, unable to hide a trace of annoyance.

'I never doubt the men who work for me,' Ondrej said simply. For a split second, Ari felt his stomach go tense, but his boss did not press the issue.

'What I doubt,' Ondrej continued, 'is that the families who used to live here would have left this house to fall into disrepair without first burning every fucking shred of evidence,' he said.

Ari shrugged, 'only one way to find out.'

'If you say so,' he grunted. 'Get the gate open. I'll be waiting.'

***

Up close, Merchant's Lodge was impressive but decrepit beyond repair. Every nook of its four floors was covered in a green moss that had grown in the absence of proper maintenance, and every crevice was darkened as though coloured with charcoal.

A wooden trellis sprawled unevenly upon its off-white walls, and behind the windows lay darkened rooms with no trace of life; no curtains hung in the windows, no lights flickered.

The door to the house was unnecessarily huge and came to a point at the top. It looked heavy, but it was also wooden, and the weather had slowly eroded it to the point that some of the panels had begun to fall away. There was no glass left in any of the large window frames, and of the four chimneys that Ari counted, only one remained unimpaired.

Ondrej made to step through.

'Wait!' Ari called out. Ondrej stopped.

'What?' he asked, obviously annoyed.

'Look at this place!' Ari exclaimed, stepping toward his boss and dragging him back out on to the driveway. 'It's clearly about to come down, and your life is worth more than mine,' Ari said, simply. 'To the Bluebirds, to everyone.'

Ondrej grunted in response.

'And anyway,' Ari added. 'You don't know what you're looking for,' he said with a wink, then ducked into a hole in the door.

The foyer must have once, surely, been a magisterial sight.

A grand, ornate staircase ran along the wall on the left-hand side, sweeping around to meet an open landing on the second story above him. The wooden banister, which had small, white-marble cubes running up the length of the beam had started to fall away, and the olive-green tiles on the floor of the foyer were chipped and dusty.

And yet, there was beauty in the interior where there wasn't outside. As though Ari could look past the disrepair and see the tapestry of time written into the decoration of the walls, where outside he only saw discoloured bricks and a building ready for demolition.

Across the foyer, flanked by a disused Grandfather clock on one side and a coat stand on the other, was a small square door.

He smiled to himself. *Just like my contact said,* Ari mused.

'Ondrej?' he called over his shoulder. 'Wait there and just... keep an eye out,' Ari said.

'Why? Are we expecting... *company?*' he asked with a snarl.

Ari pictured his boss' Bowie knife, which he always kept about his person. Instinctively, Ari touched his own, stored in a custom-made holster on the inside of his brown-leather duster jacket. He was yet to use it and hoped he would never need to.

'Just keep an eye out, boss. I'll be back as quickly as I can,' Ari replied.

He crossed the foyer and approached the square door. He tried the handle, which he knew would be locked, and instead turned his attention to the Grandfather clock.

It was a full head taller than Ari's six-foot frame and was again decorated with white-marble cubes in each of the four corners of the otherwise-plain face.

Henry Tate, the original owner of the house, was a man of the ruling class by virtue of his sugar cube empire, and he had kept prestigious company throughout his long life, which had lasted for most of the nineteenth century.

According to Ari's contact, at some point Tate had been made aware of the whereabouts of the infamous Loch Arkaig Treasure; a lost shipment of French gold sent to Scotland to aid a political uprising in 1745 CE.

After the uprising in Scotland had failed and its leader, "Bonny" Prince Charlie, had fled to Europe, the gold was no longer required to serve the rebellion. And at that point, knowledge of the whereabouts of the treasure was extinguished, much like the fire for violent rebellion in Scotland, which became part of the United Kingdom shortly afterwards.

And then, as was so often the case, the Loch Arkaig treasure miraculously popped up in history once more, this time at the door of Tate's business empire. In his haste to hide it away from prying eyes, Tate had secured his house. Built large walls around the mansion and placed guards at every entrance until, eventually, he had died, the money ran out, and the people who had been chasing the treasure had given up or died too. With them the trail of the Loch Arkaig treasure went cold.

Ari's contact had told him that since Tate had died with no obvious heir and his house had lain empty after his death, it was *possible* that the treasure was still there. Or at least a clue to its whereabouts. At Merchant's Lodge.

The story turned in Ari's mind as he reached up and placed a finger on the larger of the two hands of the Grandfather clock, which he spun until it sat at the quarter to the hour mark. Slowly, delicately, Ari moved the smaller hand up past twelve o'clock.

He directed it round and down, where it clicked into place just shy of the six o'clock mark. There was a sudden commotion that disturbed the silence.

Ari jumped backwards as the clock began to chime, and he watched in amazement as its door opened to reveal its inner workings, the components within whirring and ticking together, spinning in different directions as the chiming got louder and louder. Until eventually, it chimed a final time with a deafening blow, and the hands stopped quite abruptly, both pointing to twelve.

Ari spun around to see Ondrej had entered the foyer. The noise had stopped, and there was no apparent change to the room.

'What the hell was that?' Ondrej asked, his Bowie knife drawn. *Typical,* Ari thought. *The man wants to fight a clock.*

'It was an alarm,' Ari replied calmly.

'And it's activated through the clock?' Ondrej asked, sheathing his knife back inside his jacket and replacing it with another hand-rolled cigarette from his tin.

'Yes, you set the hands to a quarter to six,' Ari said, 'and this door should open,' he added, pointing to the white cube handle of the small square door underneath the stairs.

'Hidden in plain sight,' Ondrej said. 'Why a quarter to six?'

Ari replied with a smirk. '17:45. The year Bonny Prince Charlie landed in Scotland,' he said.

'These fucking English pricks,' Ondrej burst out in response, with genuine venom and anger in his voice. It took Ari by surprise. 'Too pompous for their own good. If he had chosen a normal password, it might have stayed hidden forever!'

Ari nodded in agreement, then put his hand on the white-marble cube handle of the small door, which clicked and opened now and revealed a small room that was painted in all red. There were cobwebs everywhere he looked, and the only light came from the foyer behind him.

An overwhelming stench of damp was released, and Ari held his breath as he squeezed his head inside. There was a chest, but it was small.

'What's in there, kid?' Ondrej asked.

'Not the treasure,' Ari replied, knowing in his heart that he wasn't looking at a chest filled with ancient gold.

Ari crouched down and ran his hands along the surface and edges of the small casket, looking for a release mechanism, which he found under the left-hand lip. The lid swung open and, inside, the chest was decorated with the same red velvet fabric as the walls of the room. It was empty, apart from a small, handwritten note.

'Well? What does it say?' Ondrej asked impatiently. 'Doesn't look like fucking gold to me,' he spat.

'No, it's not,' Ari said as he stood up. 'It says: from darkness comes sweetness,' Ari said with a sigh. 'My contact warned me about this. It's the slogan from a rival confectionery company which was in business at the same time as Henry Tate. The rival must have broken in here after Tate had died and-'

Ari cut himself short.

'What is it?' Ondrej asked. Ari frowned at nothing in particular. His face was scrunched up as though he were straining.

'Do you hear that?' he asked his boss, lowering his voice.

'You know I don't,' Ondrej said, gesturing toward his ears as if to indicate their ineffectiveness.

Ari closed his eyes and listened intently, his focus far away from the room his body occupied.

'The end of the drive. There are people there. Four of them, I think,' he said. He opened his eyes and gave Ondrej a stern look. 'They know we're here,' he added.

'Well obviously! The bikes are out there!' Ondrej said, drawing his Bowie knife once more. 'Who are they?'

Ari closed his eyes again and focused his mind on the voices.

'Come on, like we practised,' Ondrej added, more gently.

Ari's mind cleared, and the sounds of the voices filled his head like water pouring into a glass, displacing all other noise until, eventually, despite the distance, he could hear every word. He remained in this meditative state for a few moments, then brought himself back to the room.

'Sounds like Ocean Pearl,' he said gravely. 'I am going to *kill* that contact!'

'Ha!' Ondrej barked. 'Kid, I don't know why you can do the things that you can do – but I'm damn glad we spent all those hours training you.'

Ari smiled unattractively, but it seemed like they had more pressing matters at hand. 'I appreciate the compliment, but how do we play this?' he asked.

Ondrej only laughed with a sardonic candour.

Ari closed the square door to the room with the chest and tried to shut the face of the Grandfather clock, but the mechanism was complex, and he couldn't work out how to do it.

Instead, Ari picked up a nearby brick and smashed it unceremoniously into the clockface a few times, damaging it beyond repair. He felt a pang of guilt.

'Smart move,' Ondrej said.

'Perhaps we should try to move through the house?' Ari asked, trying to get his boss to focus on coming up with a plan. Ondrej shook his head.

'Let's just surprise them,' he whispered. Ari rolled his eyes. On the face of it, it seemed like a terrible idea. There were four Ocean Pearl agents, and Ondrej knew as well as Ari did that they would put up a damn good fight.

But there was no stopping the Bluebird boss once he had made his mind up.

Moments later, one by one, three of the four Ocean Pearl agents appeared through the doorway. Ari gave them a quizzical look up and down, as each of them wore a suit with an odd, midnight-blue sheen that looked like plastic.

'Nice wetsuits,' Ondrej said, flashing the trio a grin.

'What are *you* doing here?' one of the agents asked. He was tall and had longish hair that fell loosely around his face. He had an athletic build and angular features, the kind that makes a person look immediately untrustworthy.

'Ha!' Ondrej barked again. 'Hear that, kid? These guys want to know why *we're* here, as if *they're* not here for the same damn reason!' he snapped, taking a step forward.

The agent seemed to step back a little but recovered himself quickly.

'This is an Ocean Pearl site,' he said flatly. 'You can't be here.'

Ari felt Ondrej's arm twitch next to him.

In a flash, the Bluebird boss stepped forward from his front leg and brought his right fist up in a curving arc, driving hard into the agent's chin. There was a sickening crunch as he went down, falling backwards into the oakwood front door, which was sufficiently damaged that it gave way under his weight, and the agent went crashing into the driveway outside.

'Shit!' Ari exclaimed as he hurled himself into the fray. Adrenaline took control, and Ari felt himself enter a frenzy. He was swinging his fists and blindly kicking out at the agents until, eventually, they were down, and he and Ondrej stood panting with their knees on their hands.

'Jesus, boss,' Ari said, trying to catch his breath.

'Give me a break,' Ondrej said. He spat on the floor. 'There's four of them, no? Let's find the last one.'

'My contact must have really needed the money to have given the same information to both us and them,' Ari said bitterly.

With a final glance at the broken clock, he and Ondrej headed left and passed through a room that contained a mountain of covered furniture, which led to another long, well-lit corridor, lined on either side with closed doors and ended with a large window that showed a long stretch of garden at the back.

'This place,' Ondrej muttered. 'Seems to go on forever.' Ari said nothing and found himself reflecting on the strangeness of his situation, creeping around with his boss, a renowned gang leader-cum-treasure-hunter, having followed a two-hundred-year-old trail of clues that had led him there. But his train of thought was interrupted by a shuffling noise from behind one of the doors. He stopped dead.

Ondrej had kept walking.

Ari made a hissing noise to try to get him to stop. His boss turned, and Ari motioned with his head toward the door to indicate there was someone behind it. Ondrej raised an eyebrow, then set himself in the corridor, knife and fists raised in a pugilistic stance. In a seamless motion, Ari kicked the door hard, which swung inwards.

Ondrej burst past Ari into the room.

For a moment, nothing happened. Ondrej half-shrugged and turned as if to tell Ari it was a false alarm when, in a flash, a figure dropped from above and landed hard on top of Ondrej, who crumpled and went down with a groan.

'Jesus!' Ari cried out.

He could see there was already blood on the floor. The attacker had broad shoulders and fists, which he was now bringing down in a barrage upon Ondrej, who was unable to move or retaliate.

Ari sprung forward, but the agent aimed an elbow backwards which caught Ari sharply underneath his ribs. He bent double, wheezing, but managed to recover, the sound of Ondrej's gargling cries spurring him on.

He came again, but this time, the Ocean Pearl agent stood and rounded on Ari, who was now faced with another man who was thirty or so, fair skinned with a strong jawline and a hint of grey dashed into his otherwise dark hair.

The agent snarled and aimed a right hook, which clattered against Ari's left eye. Ari recoiled and saw more blood on the floor. The Ocean Pearl agent turned his attention back to Ondrej, who had been battling to sit back up, but was quickly buried underneath another flurry of blows.

And, before Ari even really knew what he was doing, his hand found his Bowie knife.

He stepped forward, his left eye already swelling. The blade seemed heavy.

Ari gripped it tightly, took a quick step forward and leapt into the air, landing on the agent's back. He felt the knife pierce the man's suit. And flesh.

The agent cried out in agony and rolled away. Ari watched him for a moment, wiping the blood away from his face. In a trance, Ari knelt down by his boss, whose face was a constellation of bruises, cuts, and blood.

'Boss?' Ari asked, timidly. 'Ondrej?'

His boss cracked a bloody smile, then looked weakly over at the Ocean Pearl agent, who had gone quiet. Ari wondered whether the man's life was seeping away. In an instant, Ondrej's smile evaporated as the gravity of the situation descended upon him. He looked out at Ari with a stern countenance.

'The knife,' Ondrej gargled, then produced a cough that sprayed blood all over the floor next to him. Ari frowned at him, puzzled.

'Take my fucking knife,' he said. 'And give me yours.'

Ari's eyes widened. He looked over at the dying Ocean Pearl agent, then back at his boss, recognising the gesture Ondrej was making to him.

'Boss,' he said. 'You can't-'

Ondrej started to cough again. 'Don't be an idiot,' he said, harshly. 'Give me your knife, and you take mine. I'll survive this, but Ocean Pearl would hunt you down and kill you. There's no need for them to know you were here.'

Ari sniffed. He wanted to turn back the clock. He had been rash and had panicked, despite everything he had supposedly learned. He should have hit him with something blunt, knocked him out. Not stabbed him. Not this.

'I protect my own,' Ondrej said in his thick, Czech accent. Slowly, Ari leaned over his boss, picked up his knife and swapped it with his own.

'The agents outside... They saw me...'

Ondrej coughed more vociferously this time. 'You leave those fuckers to me. Now go, Ari, get out of here.

You do understand what this means?' he asked. Ari blinked.

'You'll need to disappear,' Ondrej said, closing his eyes and letting out a long breath. To Ari's amazement, his boss managed to gingerly sit himself up. He looked Ari squarely in his remaining, open eye.

'More than that,' Ondrej continued. 'You can never come back here. To Liverpool. Never mention my name. You must never tangle with Ocean Pearl again. And that means you can't hunt the Loch Arkaig treasure. Hell, you can't hunt *any* treasure,' he said. 'Ocean Pearl, they're involved in everything, you know that. Don't give these fuckers a reason to go looking for you. You are gifted, Ari, and they will seek to exploit that,' he said.

He coughed again. It sounded wet.

'Now go!' Ondrej exclaimed propping himself up on one knee now, preparing himself to do what was necessary. 'Go!'

'Thank you,' Ari managed to squeeze out through clipped breath.

Then, with one last glance at Ondrej who was nearly standing now, a maniacal look in his eye and his unkempt, blood-matted silver hair dangling around his face, Ari backed out of the corridor and took off toward the garden.

He dived through a glassless window and out onto the grass, then ran all the way around the grounds, not stopping to look back. By the time he reached the end of the snake-like driveway, the iron gate and his motorcycle which – mercifully – the agents didn't seem to have touched, he was sobbing uncontrollably, and he spent a full minute heaving great breaths of sorrow before he eventually managed to calm himself.

He swung his leg over his bike and donned his helmet, then allowed himself a final moment of reflection.

He muttered another solemn thanks to Ondrej, then brought the engine to life and revved. With a twist of his wrist, he took off, roaring back into the traffic lanes and away from Grove Street, away from Merchant's Lodge.

As though he had never been there at all.

***

Tom Jackson

PART ONE

Chapter two

Liverpool, Merseyside, UK
Present day

Ari knew he was running late.

He threw some money at his cab driver, fumbled out of the car and bowled up the stairs at the entrance of the Fruit Exchange, flashing his invitation card at the security guards.

Inside, he heard a muffled cry of an auctioneer shout, '*sold!*' followed by the punch of gavel-on-wood and an uproarious gaggle of punters.

Ari strode up an ornate staircase four steps at a time, paying almost no attention to the wonder of the décor or mastery of the artwork on display. He blasted through the double doors at the top.

'All right, all right!' the auctioneer was saying, leaning into the mic. 'I mean come on, is this an auction house or an ale house?!' he asked, gesticulating with the gavel. The crowd dissolved into a frenzy.

With that, the lights went up, and the band broke out into a cover of *Help* by The Beatles.

Ari lingered near the door, looking out over the scene before him.

The Fruit Exchange was an ideal forum for an auction; a large, heptagon-shaped exchange hall with steeply tiered seating and timber benches with fixed backs, each with end armrests that curved round to face a large, raised podium and a hollowed-out space underneath for the band. The flat roof in the central area of the ceiling boasted a colossal domed skylight, and there were four smaller skylights in the corners of the room. It reminded Ari of a planetarium.

The disused fruit sellers' marketplace had fallen into disrepair sometime after modern retailers had entered the high streets of England. Ari thought the investors who had reopened it might have come up with a more imaginative name, but he conceded that at least they had kept it as an auction house, as opposed to the hotel they had originally planned.

Although, Ari thought, *that was probably a planning permission problem.* Either way, when the Exchange had reopened, someone had thrown alcohol and swanky cocktail waiters into the mix, and the result was a trend-setting venue; a nightclub-cum-auction-hall.

The idea was a little strange, Ari mused as he scanned the room for his seat, granted, but blended experiences such as these were becoming increasingly popular with younger crowds, and on any given weekend there would be no shortage of trendsetters in attendance, as much out for the kitsch items on sale as they were the booze.

Ari spotted his pre-booked booth halfway across the hall to the left-hand side of the stage. His date, Melissa, was already sitting there. She must have been eyeing the door, as she noticed him too. Now, she found herself under pressure to break the awkwardness of the moment as their eyes locked.

She elected to do so by standing with a bottle of champagne in her hand, mouthing "it's free!" silently to him. He smiled to himself. *These tickets cost me a damn fortune,* he thought.

Ari fanned his thick, dark hair backwards and headed down toward her. He liked to imagine how he must have appeared to onlookers, his tall frame, tight-fitting black chinos, white polo shirt and blazer gliding across the room. He gave a wry look to another attendee who caught his eye, then checked himself, having fleetingly forgotten his need to remain inconspicuous. He bowed his head and hastily made his way through the rest of the aisles.

'This place is amazing,' Melissa said as he approached. She had remained standing the entire time he had walked toward her, and they hugged awkwardly when he arrived. Ari brushed her cheek with his mouth, but she turned her face at the same time, and he sort of managed to kiss her ear.

She laughed nervously.

She had made an effort for the occasion. She wore a fairly short, chic-red dress and had applied a healthy dose of thick makeup to her pale complexion, giving her skin a warm, blushed tone.

'Never been?' Ari asked, trying to act casual. 'Thought this might be up your street.'

'Never had reason to come until you asked me,' she said. 'I don't really get asked on many dates-,' then stopped herself short, '...anyway, no. I've never been. It's incredible though. I love the skylights,' she said, looking up. Ari followed her gaze.

'Yes,' he said despondently.

And there ended the extent of his plan.

Make it into the Exchange, sit down with his "date" and watch the auction. It hadn't occurred to him that she might actually expect some conversation.

'Do you think they make a lot of money here?' she asked. Ari was already starting very much to wish he had come alone. The profile on Melissa's dating site read:

> *Bit of a history geek, copywriter for an interior design company and - honestly - a little shy.*

Ideal.

Ari had presumed she would sit quietly, enjoy the auction and go home happily afterwards, all the while serving to present him as part of an unassuming couple, simply out for an evening to attend an auction. And that was exactly how she had come across in their message exchange leading up to the date.

But, he suspected, in anticipation of this – an intimate evening with a VIP guest list –Melissa had indulged in a bit of Dutch Courage, so to speak. *Irritating.*

'No idea,' he said, motioning to the waiter for a glass of Dom Perignon which, as Melissa had pointed out, was "free".

In answer to her question about the venue's profitability, he in fact thought the *Exchange* was probably something of a gold mine; the more the punters drank, the more asinine they were likely to become with their bids.

Couple that with the online auctions the Exchange held and the collectors' conventions, the place must have brought in a pretty penny. But he didn't verbalise these thoughts for the sake of conversation with his date who, admirably, tried again,

'Oh, where are they going?' Melissa asked.

Ari looked over to where she had pointed. A large part of the crowd was being ushered out slowly, and he realised he really had arrived just in time.

The drunken purchase of Lot Fifty-Eight - a small but elegant Victorian broach - marked the end of the public event and the start of the ticketed ballots he was here to see.

'They're being escorted out before the VIP event begins,' he replied.

He couldn't help the smile that set in as he watched the throng of people snake toward the exit, laughing, lingering, trying to get a last swig of prosecco in. Life was hard for many people in the North-West of England. Liverpool had, for a time, been sucked dry by London politicians and, although it had been some years since Ari had visited, he still felt a rush of inspiration that emanated from his home city, a kindling of optimism that might at any time spark an explosion of success.

It was in that moment that the weight of longing he felt for his childhood neighbourhood, a place he could no longer show his face, and concurrently the feeling of the recklessness of his decision to return to Liverpool struck him like a punch in the guts. He felt his heart rate begin to increase, and a pool of sweat began to form under his arms. He knew he would be turning red. He closed his eyes. *Calm your nerves, don't let it consume you. Just like we practised,* he could almost hear Ondrej, his old friend and mentor, saying.

A tap on his shoulder startled him back to the real world. Ari turned.

'Alright there, lad?' an usher said in a slow, scouse drawl, his eyes bloodshot, his accent strong. Ari let out a long breath and recovered his face.

'Fine, thanks,' Ari said, trying to smile.

'Need to see your ticket, lad,' the usher said in response.

Ari produced his VIP passes and waited while they were looked over. The band seemed to be wrapping up - they had just finished a cover of *Tainted Love*, one of the single most annoying songs in human history, or so Ari thought - and didn't seem to be restarting. The hall was distinctly quieter, the background music replaced by the audible squeak of leather, the clinking of glasses and the humdrum of low, anticipatory chatter, like the soothing grumble of an engine.

The usher handed back Ari and Melissa's passes and moved on. As the humdrum settled, Melissa started to ask Ari a question about how his week had been, but Ari had zoned out.

Having only just recovered, he found himself being drawn into a new state of panic. His heart rate rose again, and his leg started to bounce involuntarily, uncontrollably. He breathed as heavily as he could manage.

Down to his left, nearer to the stage, a group of young, well-groomed men and women, clearly at ease, laughing and joking as they were shown to their seats on the front row had entered through a set of doors that were not accessible by the public.

It was them. Ocean Pearl.

Again, the urge to flee overcame him. Unable to control himself, Ari stood up and started fumbling to get out of the booth.

'Ari?!' she hissed. 'People are *staring*,' she said. He shot back into his seat.

'Sorry,' he muttered. 'Thought I saw someone,' he said. Melissa didn't respond, and instead signalled for a bottle of champagne, this time telling the waiter to leave it there. Ari had to force himself to withdraw his arrested gaze from the Ocean Pearl group.

'*Ladies and gentlemen,*' a female voice announced unexpectedly, bouncing around from the wall speakers. Ari jumped up as though a gunshot had rung off. *Never should've come here,* he thought to himself.

'*Bidding on our first ticketed item of the evening will start in... FIVE!*'

He frowned at the podium above the stage as the lights went down and the spotlight drew to the centre. It was dark now, and Ari shuffled to the edge of the sofa - away from Melissa.

Where do I know that voice? he thought to himself as a pre-recorded countdown took over. The red curtain covering the length of the back of the stage began to rise, and the host of the event appeared from behind it.

Ari's mouth hung open. His childhood friend. *Fliss.*

From his booth, Ari could see that she had dressed well for the occasion: an aquamarine dress, a deep rouge chiffon and tall, dark heels. Around her neck she had draped what looked to be a faux-fur scarf, and he could easily make out a pair of large, hooped silver earrings. Her short, ash-blonde hair was pulled into a tight

29

ponytail, and she sported deep purple lipstick which accentuated her mouth against her fair skin.

He watched in disbelief as she approached the microphone slowly, and wondered how they had grown so far apart that he hadn't even known she would be there that evening. How, despite never spending more than a few days apart during their formative years, it had been some eight years since they had had any contact. And now, she was there, a host for the Fruit Exchange VIP auction.

This spectacle, Fliss' own voice from the speakers counting down while she walked purposefully toward the mic, must have been performed at the start of every VIP event, Ari decided. Once his initial surprise had worn off, he saw that the routine was slick, well-rehearsed, and Fliss looked very comfortable as she took her well-timed steps, flashing a bright-white smile around the room as she did so. *Not your first time*, he thought.

And yet, he also sensed that she seemed on edge. Doubtless, she possessed a natural grace and effortless style, but she was betrayed by a little bounce between her steps, and a twitch in her fingers, as though she were itching to get on with the evening.

And rightly so. For that evening, there was a very special item on the ballot indeed.

The item Ari was there to see.

The Grandfather clock Ari thought he had destroyed some eight years previously.

***

Chapter three

James Prince was across the street in an Ocean Pearl safehouse while he waited for his target to arrive at the Fruit Exchange.

He knew the VIP ballot was about to begin, and the dim light on his wristwatch told him it was right on schedule, *22:00*. Prince winced as he lifted himself onto his knees. He stayed on all fours for a second, then hoisted himself up, shaking out his legs.

He caught a glimpse of his reflection, the dark of the outside offering a distorted view of his salt and pepper hair in the window. *Damn,* he thought to himself, *I'm too old for this shit.*

The Ocean Pearl Corporation, his employer, had spent the last two centuries building an Empire out of ancient treasures, monetising and monopolising that market with great success.

Nowadays, you could scarcely visit a museum in Rome, a lost city in the Americas, an ancient temple in Sri Lanka or any other historical attraction without encountering the infamous Ocean Pearl logo: a gleaming, gold and red *labarum* set upon a black background with a gold Chi Rho, a kind of long *P* with an *X* through the stalk, meant to symbolise protection against hostility.

Ocean Pearl owned safehouses in lots of different cities that their agents could use, and it just so happened that this one, a third and fourth floor maisonette occupying the Eastern corner of an old Georgian building on Castle Street in Liverpool, lay directly opposite the Fruit Exchange. The exact location Prince had lured his target to on this, a brisk October evening.

He had arrived earlier in the afternoon, accessing the apartment using a fingerprint reader disguised as a doorbell. He had set up his bits of equipment near the window: a high-powered night-vision telescope, sound-amplifying microphone and speakers, face recognition software; all gear routinely supplied by Ocean Pearl which, over the years, Prince had acquired and kept with him.

He was part of an older breed of agent who refused to "check in" his equipment after an assignment, instead preferring to have his own.

His PearlTECH Vantablack suit, for example.

Vantablack was a material originally developed by NASA to keep errant light from entering its telescopes. The Vantablack was cultivated and *grown* into the suit, like flowers in a bed of soil; a dense forest of light-conducting tubes weaved into the material, the resulting effect being that nearly one hundred per cent of the light that shined upon it was trapped as opposed to bouncing off.

The all-body suits allowed an agent to undertake the most covert of operations while ensuring maximum protection. The material itself was like neoprene - soft and supple allowing for full range of motion, but padded with bullet and force-proof shock absorbers which meant an impact such as a fall from a great height could be taken without inflicting lasting damage.

Probably its most useful feature, however, was its ability to literally move *through* his clothing to become the outermost layer, then change colour to match its surroundings allowing him to blend in with his environment or, in the dark, disappear entirely.

One of the boys back at Ocean Pearl's lab had told him that the design was based on the anatomy of a cephalopod. Prince could hardly have been less interested, and yet was now stuck with the knowledge that some species of squid were able to camouflage themselves by changing their skin to blend in with their surroundings, despite themselves being colour-blind.

And it was in this PearlTECH Vantablack suit that he sat, waiting. He picked up his laptop. Marius Nicander, or Ari, had proven himself a slippery bastard, James Prince reflected as he punched in his password.

Ari had come back under Ocean Pearl's microscope after he had been implicated in some particularly nasty business involving the Bluebirds, but had subsequently dropped off their radar. Sometime later, Ocean Pearl discovered he was the author behind a number of forgeries of ancient artefacts and treasures, which he produced to an extraordinarily high degree of verisimilitude.

Near-facsimile, Ari's products were only really detected as fakes by the sheer volume sold rather than any identifying feature in the items themselves. He had sold too many too quickly, and that had made him vulnerable.

Auctioneers up and down the country began to report a sudden deluge of Romano-British artefacts in their halls without reports of any substantial finds to go along with them, which had aroused suspicions within Ocean Pearl. Yet, even once they had identified a few items they thought had come from Ari's hand, it had still taken a whole team of technicians to identify them as fakes, and no one had been willing to put it in writing.

In fact, they had tested the fakes with dozens of experts across the world, all of whom had sworn the coins were legitimate. Most of them had said that they were some of the best specimens they had ever come across. And therein lay the second doubtable element to the sales. They were *too* good. Too pure, too clean. Ari had made the mistake of getting creative, dreaming up his own inventions.

When Ari made copies of real Finds, he copied the impurities. When he made his own, he couldn't deviate from his own perfectness. His downfall was his exceptional talent.

James Prince was sifting through the case notes that he had compiled over the last few months. Ocean Pearl were generally happy to have a certain number of fakes in the market, especially ones of a high degree of quality which, in his early days as an agent, Prince had found difficult to understand.

'Why don't we just shut these guys down?' he remembered asking Ironmonger, the name given to the rank above his, an agent, at Ocean Pearl.

'Firstly, Prince, we're not the police,' Ironmonger had said in her traditional clipped, caterwauling tone. 'We must remain clandestine in such matters; we cannot go removing every upstart with a metal detector from the market just because we don't like them. People would talk. We can only "shut people down," as you put it, when we have leverage enough to be certain that the individual cannot - or would not dare - expose us.'

'Right,' he had said, not fully on board.

'Prince,' she'd said, curtly. 'If someone is producing fakes, that is palatable to a degree. If we crushed every single forger as soon as they started out, you might consider that to be rather like dropping an anvil on a feather. *I* give the orders, and I choose when to drop the anvil. It is reserved for those who give us real trouble, and, let me assure you, there are plenty of those.'

And at some stage, Ari had crossed that line. Probably when he had progressed to selling some fairly major items and passing them off as his own, Prince mused. When the lie began to seam with the truth and Ocean Pearl were at risk of losing sight of him.

In Ironmonger's terms: it was time to prep the anvil.

Ocean Pearl advertised themselves as treasure hunters, but that wasn't really the case anymore. They had started out that way under the British Empire, sure, but the days of swashbuckling adventurers sailing off to distant lands to liberate a country of its most valued possessions were long gone.

No, now they operated a fairly rudimentary, transactional business; they bought treasure off unsuspecting Finders who were perfectly happy to make a profit, then sold whatever had been discovered at private auction for huge sums. It was as elegant as it was simple.

These days, Ocean Pearl only entered a "cold" archaeological site - one without a previous lead - if they thought what might lay there was really worth it.

And so the majority of the work of an agent was prying these Finds and discoveries from the real Finders.

More often than not, a local Coroner (a Government employee tasked with dedicating treasure) would contact them at the point of discovery, knowing they would be able to take a cut later down the line. This was in fact probably the company's biggest overhead: keeping people paid.

Once Ocean Pearl had acquired the treasure or taken over a site, then they would start the publicity. This was also costly, but it was estimated that a true "Big Find", to use Marketing parlance, could be worth in excess of one hundred million pounds to the company. Between family excursions, merchandising, television series, books, educational resources for schools, Government interest in national heritage, research grants, hell, sometimes even *prize money*, a Find was big business, and big business for Ocean Pearl meant big bonuses for the agent (or sometimes agents) who had helped to acquire it.

'You gonna need us tonight boss?' Prince heard Tennant say through his earpiece.

Tennant was also an Ocean Pearl agent, his colleague and right-hand-man of more than twenty years, although he had never really displayed the intuition needed to make a name for himself.

Unlike Prince, who had once been a rising star in the company.

Prince had made a big splash in his early twenties when he had excavated *Aquae Sulis* – a Roman bath house in Bath, Somerset - but the lack of a Big Find during that excavation had cast doubt on his talents. His subsequent engagements had, somehow, never quite lived up to the hype, and he had quite quickly found himself only working on cases that involved tracking small-fry forgeries such as this.

But there was something about Ari Nicander that intrigued him.

Something that seemed different, and when Prince looked back out over the road at the Exchange, he felt a small twinge of optimism gnawing at his subconscious.

'I doubt it,' Prince said out loud, replying to Tennant after watching the street a few seconds longer. *'Any more of us will only spook him, only problem is he's not arrived at the Exchange yet-'*

Prince cut himself short, then smiled.

'Scratch that, he's here. Knock off for the evening.'

Tennant didn't need telling twice.

Prince almost felt sorry for Ari, who really was an exceptionally gifted fraudster. He imagined Ari's excitement at having been accepted to attend the event that evening, when the reality, of course, was that he had been lured there to be intercepted.

'Should have stayed away, kid,' Prince muttered out loud.

***

Chapter four

Ari sensed the auction was beginning to draw to a conclusion.

He'd pulled his collar down, his hair was a little frizzy from the heat, and there was a palpable air of tension in the Exchange. They had just seen Lot Thirteen - a fine and complete copy of the first collected edition of Shakespeare's plays, edited in 1630 - sold for just shy of £9,500, one of the cheaper but more sentimental items of the evening in the VIP ballot.

And now, finally, Lot Fourteen had been announced. This was the ticket item Ari had come to see.

His date Melissa had, "nipped out for some fresh air" somewhere around Lot Eleven and Ari hadn't seen her since. He hadn't been very good company, he reflected, and the splendour and wonder of the occasion had been lost as people took more time over their bids and made more considered purchases.

By Lot Six she had chosen to stare out of the skylight rather than watch the auction, and by Lot Nine she had been outright ignoring the whole event, instead playing a game on her mobile phone. Perhaps the earlier auction, selling cheaper items to the tune of the band, when the booze flowed and the music thumped, might have made a good atmosphere for a first date. This, the serious event, was basically like inviting someone round to watch other people put bids on super expensive eBay.

Although admittedly, Ari thought, *from the comfort of a very luxurious chair.*

Fliss was on stage telling a story about Lot Thirteen, a quite magnificent set of bronze-age coins. In the spotlight, the coins were an iridescent, shimmery array of stars.

Twenty, in total. Fliss was telling how, quite by accident, near Fakenham, North Norfolk, an Ocean Pearl employee had been out walking his dog and had unearthed a dream come true. Really, she said, the hero of the hour was Chump the inquisitive Staffordshire Bull Terrier, who had gone digging through the soil and overturned the first of the items. The rest, as they say, was history: Mr Davies - the dog's owner - had contacted the local council's Treasure Coroner, and in the short dig that followed, they had found a further nineteen coins, all of which were dated to mid-way through the first century BCE, minted by the *Iceni* tribe who had occupied East Anglia during this period. Shortly after their discovery, the coins were declared a priceless treasure.

Or at least, this was the story that Ocean Pearl put out.

Ari had kept one eye on Ocean Pearl's group of smarmy individuals in the booth down to his left throughout the auction. Fortunately, the overwhelming feeling of emotion that had threatened to overcome him earlier had passed as time had gone on, as Ari had decided that they weren't paying him any attention, and didn't seem to be interested in anyone except themselves.

There was something characteristically sneering about the way they uncorked their champagne; they oozed a certain imitative class which put outsiders on edge. A veil of nastiness and an unnerving, unignorable presence.

Ocean Pearl agents were generally dismissive of anyone outside of their circle. And yet, Ari thought by the way her eyes cast over their booth, Fliss seemed to be superbly envious that she wasn't there with them.

And they had good reason to celebrate.

The Treasure Coroner from the story of the Fakenham coins was, of course, in Ocean Pearl's pocket - as was everyone else in the business - and as soon as the Coroner made Ocean Pearl aware of the Find, they would have been out in a flash, cheque book in hand.

The real Finders would have been paid to hand over their treasure and made to sign an NDA, but only given a fraction of the true value. Which, for the most part, the Finder would never know. It was, after all, a private auction.

But most people in attendance wouldn't have known any of this. Ari had struggled for a long time to make his way as someone who operated outside of the reaches of Ocean Pearl. And he had been fairly successful in the eight years since he had left Liverpool, before he had vowed to never return. But his curiosity had gotten the better of him this time.

Fliss had paused now, and Ari returned his gaze to her. She looked directly back at him.

'Lot Fourteen,' she said flatly.

***

The auction finished, Ari walked out of the Fruit Exchange building onto Victoria Street with something of a swagger. Not drunk, but euphoric. He had been foolish to come to Liverpool, he knew, but it was worth it. Seeing Lot Fourteen - the mangled remains of the Grandfather Clock he had all but destroyed eight years ago - told him that Ondrej, his old mentor and friend, had survived after all.

He must have done, Ari thought.

After all, the clock was a legendary part of treasure hunting history; it had been the clue that had in the intervening years led to the discovery of the *Loch Arkaig* treasure, which had been announced as Found by Ocean Pearl shortly afterwards.

Ari had suspected then that Ondrej had been the real Finder, and that it must have been him who had given *Arkaig* to Ocean Pearl; the bargaining chip that surely saved Ondrej's life. He wondered whether it was Ondrej or Ocean Pearl who sold the clock in the Exchange tonight, but he suspected that the celebratory atmosphere emanating from their booth answered that question for him.

As he stood, both a little warm from the alcohol and cold from the crisp October air, he smiled as he imagined finally putting that chapter of his life to rest. For the first time in eight years, he felt free of the shackles of guilt that had wracked him. He would never know whether he had killed the agent he'd stabbed, or whether Ondrej had finished him off afterwards, but Ari had long made peace with that conundrum, deciding that, in the end, it didn't matter. The outcome is the same.

Ari propped himself up on the corner of the Exchange building and looked on as friends in small groups meandered toward the city centre and different bars. Ari, alone and unnoticed, watched as a couple of girls walking past shot him an awkward glance, and he tried to rearrange his face to look a little more mysterious. He felt the wheels that had turned his life begin to grease, and the grinding cogs of shame and regret began to churn. His thoughts passed by his Mother. Perhaps he would visit her. He could travel again.

Lot Fourteen had paid any part of the debt that still belonged to him, he was sure of it.

Ari flipped his phone to the front-facing camera and started to fan his hair back across his head when, quite abruptly, he was interrupted. Grabbed roughly by the shoulder, he was pulled around the corner into an alleyway.

Instinctively, his hands went up to guard his face and his weight shifted to his back leg. A fighter's stance.

'Ari?'

'*Fliss,*' he breathed with genuine relief, letting his guard down.

She had changed from her auctioneer's outfit into a jacket that was too slight for the weather, but the neck was pulled up high, and the hood pulled over, obscuring her face. All Ari could see was her eyes, nose and a portion of her fringe, which hung from under the hood in its unmistakable shade of ash blonde. She wore matching tracksuit bottoms and a pair of white Nike Air-Max. They looked new. He tried to hug her, but she pushed him away.

'*Follow me,*' she said, an urgency in her voice.

'What?' he replied, unable to keep the surprise from his tone.

'For God's sake Ari you are in terrible danger. Now *follow me*,' she said, enunciating the last two words. He felt his heart quicken and glanced over his shoulder expecting to see a pack of Ocean Pearl agents. Fliss let out a sigh of exasperation, turned face and set off up the alleyway at a half-run, toward Matthew's Street, home of Liverpool's infamous Cavern Club.

Ari followed but kept glancing back behind him, trying to see what had spooked her. The alley was tight, and the walls on either side stretched up seven or eight floors, giving the illusion that it was getting thinner as they ran.

The pair burst onto Matthew's Street just as the cobbled streets began to change colour with a speckling of rain. Fliss grabbed his arm and jerked him onward.

In contrast to the vacuum of the alley, Matthew's Street was a cacophonous humdrum of mirth, where people gathered outside bars sung loudly, orders were barked out to people in queues in takeaways, groups huddled in doorways and smoked furiously, talking overzealously. Groups of girls took selfies with buskers who were spaced not ten feet apart, each belting out a different song to the next, and the scene was cast in a greenish hue from the seemingly never-ending series of pubs and bars which ran the length of the street.

The noise was incredible, and if they had ever been in need of somewhere to lose someone – whoever that someone was - this seemed to be it. With each door they passed, walking hurriedly away from the Cavern Club, toward the Liverpool History Museum, Lime Street Station and beyond, Ari became more and more sure that Fliss was bound to duck in through one of the doors at any second.

He stopped.

'Fliss!' he shouted over the noise of a neighbouring cocktail bar. 'Where the hell are we going?' he asked, incredulous. She tried simply ushering him forward once more, but this time he wouldn't move. It was the only time he could remember feeling uneasy in her presence. She turned and made an exasperated noise like a car screeching to a halt. From behind her snood and hood, he saw genuine fear in her eyes, and she gesticulated wildly as she spoke,

'Didn't you *see* what was happening tonight, Ari?' she asked hoarsely, straying her voice between a whisper and a shout.

'Obviously not!' he said, confused as to why she sounded so agitated.

'Well that makes a bloody first,' she said, irritably. 'It's Ocean Pearl, Ari, and they know you're here!'

***

Chapter five

Fliss dragged him for a good while longer after that; all the way past St George's Hall, through a near-deserted Lime Street Station and out the other side, heading toward Upper Parliament Street.

Ari had thought they might have been aiming for the Anglican cathedral, where they could hide in the darkness of the grounds, shaded from the moonlight by its century-old russet walls. But quite suddenly he found himself being hurled through a small gap in a fence, yelping as his clothes caught on the wood on the way through.

'Where are we?' he asked, scanning his surroundings for a second before it dawned on him. He was stood in a dimly-lit courtyard. On three sides were what looked like the backs of terraced houses, but on the fourth side was a long, glass door.

'Christ, Fliss. Really?!'

She wasn't listening to him. She had already pushed the back gate of the terraced house nearest to the glass wall open, then flashed him a glance and slipped inside. Ari groaned and followed her, pushing through the gate into the tiny garden. The wall on the left-hand side was covered with ivy, and as Ari came through the gate, Fliss seemed to have disappeared into it.

'What the hell?' Ari said out loud, then realised she had slipped through a door behind the ivy, which neatly obscured a sign that read FIRE EXIT. Ari followed her in, and she closed the door behind him.

'Been broken for years,' she muttered.

'I'm not sure this was a good idea, Fliss,' he whispered.

The pair stood in a gloomy, poorly-lit, redbrick tunnel. It somehow sounded damp and smelt vaguely of sawdust. It was comfortably wide and tall enough for the two of them to stand and walk in, at least.

'Well, we haven't been followed, have we?' she snapped.

They began to walk downward, heading underground. The clip-clop of Ari's boots reverberated noisily as they descended, and after a while the slim tunnel opened out into a large cavern.

'The Williamson Tunnels,' Ari said. 'You remember the school trip?'

'I remember,' she said, distractedly.

'Then you'll also remember that they were used for some pretty unconventional reasons,' he said, wrinkling his nose.

Joseph Williamson had been an eighteenth-century Liverpudlian philanthropist, much-loved by the community until it was posthumously revealed that he had used his money and influence to build what was, in effect, a series of dungeons linked by these tunnels.

Ari and Fliss made it to the so-called "banqueting hall", which was in fact nothing other than a place to hold prisoners and slaves for Williamson and his patrician friends.

Now, though, the walls of the room were adorned with scaffolding which, at best, Ari thought looked flimsy. At worst, like the whole thing might fall on them imminently. There were tools, workbenches generators and halogen lights dotted about. *Could have at least hung a painting,* Ari thought to himself.

'What even made you think to come all the way across town anyway?' he asked.

'I don't think they will find us down here,' she said, simply.

'"They" being Ocean Pearl?' he asked. She ignored him. 'Also,' Ari continued, 'I assume it's not lost on you that the only way out of this place is the way we came in?'

Involuntarily, he found himself reflecting on the vulnerability of his situation, cursing himself for having been led so easily. The nausea, panic and urge to flee that he had felt in the Fruit Exchange when he had seen Ocean Pearl's table was beginning to set back in, and his claustrophobia threatened to overcome him. He breathed for a moment and, for the second time that evening, found himself listening to Ondrej telling him to calm himself.

Fliss, on the other hand, seemed to have relaxed. She had removed her hood and unzipped her jacket to reveal her ash-blonde hair in full, and perched delicately on one of the workbenches.

Ari couldn't help but notice that she had become unmistakably attractive in the years since he had last seen her. Where before she had looked a bit drab and bookish, now her face was more angular than it had been during the pudginess of youth, and she held an air of confidence that he didn't recall she had ever possessed before. It was reflected in her stylish clothes and the way she held herself. He wondered what had happened.

'I have questions,' he said, bluntly.

'Well?' she said, drolly.

'OK... For a start, how do you know Ocean Pearl were after me tonight?' he asked, figuring out the answer before she had even given it.

'Christ Ari. I'm the VIP auctioneer at the Fruit Exchange, I see Ocean Pearl Agents week-in-week-out. But anyway, who said anyone was "coming at us"?' she asked.

'I assumed that's why you dragged me away!' he retorted.

Fliss raised an eyebrow. She pursed her lips and gave him a look which implied a tone of voice so venomous he was glad she hadn't vocalised her feelings on the matter. It dissipated, and she waved a hand with a scoff.

'You really haven't changed, have you?' she asked, walking a few paces away from him. 'You may have super senses-'

'*Heightened* senses,' he corrected her.

'Oh whatever,' she spat. 'You may have *heightened* hearing and *heightened* vision, Ari, but you're as blind as the Finders who sold their treasures to Ocean Pearl for a fraction of their worth before tonight's auction.'

It was strange to hear someone else talk about his "abilities". Ari looked at her with genuine bemusement.

'Fliss, what on Earth are you talking about?' he asked. 'We haven't seen each other for years, and you drag me—'

'They know, Ari,' she said flatly.

'They? Who? Know what?'

Fliss blew the air from her nostrils.

'Them! Ocean Pearl!' she exclaimed. 'They, as I do, know that you've been manufacturing "ancient" artefacts and selling them all over the country.' Ari began to protest, but she continued, 'attending auctions, making sales, writing articles, "making a name for yourself"...Sound about right?'

Ari said nothing.

'You really think it was a coincidence that your name was pulled from the ballot to attend tonight?' she asked. 'They came to me a week or so ago asking if I had heard of you, and whether I thought I could lure you to the auction,' she said. 'Must have looked at my old pictures on social media or something.'

He looked aghast.

'Of course, I told them no,' she said, explaining the answer to the question he hadn't asked. 'That you and I aren't in contact anymore. I chased it up with them the next night and they told me that, as luck would have it, you had applied for a ticket for the event tonight, and the problem was solved; you had effectively volunteered yourself to them. Then earlier today, while we were setting up for the auction, I overheard one of them talking about "intercepting a target". I put two and two together. I knew that if you attended, the only reason they had allowed you to be there that night was to grab you at some point and gently... "convince" you to stop producing your counterfeits. I've seen it happen to others. There wasn't much I could have done if they had gotten to you during the event, but when I saw you were still sitting in your booth at the end, when Lot Fourteen was drawn, I figured they must have someone waiting outside. You never would have made it home.'

He looked away from her, turning it over in his mind. *Is it possible?* He thought to himself. He eyed his friend with a penetrating gaze. If she was lying, her face didn't show it.

Fliss sighed.

'What *happened* to you, Ari?' she asked, changing tack. 'After I went to university... You just... disappeared. Do you know what that felt like? For me, for your Father? How long do you think it took us to realise that you had gone? How many unanswered calls does it take before someone starts to get worried?' she asked.

'I had to leave. I had to get away. Ocean Pearl-'

'Save it, Ari. I don't want to know. You were involved in some shady shit with that thug, *Ondrej*,' she said his name as though it left a physically unpleasurable taste in her mouth. 'No doubt you crossed a line, stepped on the wrong toe, and he told you to skip town and to stay out of Ocean Pearl's way forever. Sound about right?' she asked, raising an eyebrow. 'Well, you failed, Ari. Pretty damn spectacularly. Couldn't keep away, could you? As always, your arrogance is unrivalled. You thought because you hadn't been caught making and selling your fakes you wouldn't be caught if you came back here. To Liverpool, your old turf. Every day that passed, your confidence that Ocean Pearl had forgotten all about you grew and grew. Well guess what? You were wrong. Again,' she said, flatly.

Ari said nothing, but Fliss sighed a sigh of true sadness, laced with the kind of disappointment usually reserved by parents for their children.

'Ari,' she said. 'Eventually Ocean Pearl gets them all. Those agents they use. They're tenacious and dangerous. They'll do anything to get a Find, or to win favour within the company ranks. They'll hunt a treasure until the end, and they don't care who gets hurt along the way. And they can't have counterfeiters out there flooding their market with fakes. It's just bad for business,' she said. 'Now usually they would just convince the person to stop. Threaten to expose them. But you? You've been rattling the cage for a long damn time, and they finally decided it was time to lock you in. Whatever you did with Ondrej hasn't been forgotten. Your number's up,' she said.

Despite the chill of the underground tunnel, Ari felt himself begin to sweat once more.

***

Chapter six

Where is he?! James Prince asked himself as he stood panting on the corner of Upper Parliament Street.

The outline of a century-old cathedral dominated his view, the bright light of the full moon bathing its rust-red stone in a milky blue. This part of town was deserted, the cathedral being the only real attraction in the area, and Prince stood in the cold, alone.

For all Prince could tell, Ari had simply vanished when he had left the Exchange. One moment he was there, the next he was gone, lost among the crowd of punters. Prince had raced across the street to look for him, drawing a few suspicious looks, and had been fortunate to catch a glimpse of his target's heels as he rounded the corner toward an alleyway that led to Matthew's Street, accompanied by some hooded figure – a girl, he presumed based on their height – in a full shell-suit.

From there, he had followed the pair along Matthew's Street all the way to Lime Street Station and out the other side, where he had managed to tail them to the cathedral, then lost them again. Prince had assumed them to be in the cathedral grounds, although for what reason he was less sure. A quick turn about the yard had revealed no one, save a security guard, who he had hidden from by switching his PearlTECH suit to Vantablack mode.

Now, he had lost them. He groaned out loud. *What's Ironmonger going to say?*

If he could possibly avoid it, he didn't want to get Ocean Pearl involved tonight. There would be plenty of other opportunities to intercept Ari, but people who get rich stay that way by squeezing tight to every penny in their grasp, and this assignment had only been budgeted to run up until that evening.

If Ari escaped, Prince would have to ask for additional resources, probably invite Ari to another auction, use another safe house and keep Tennant on standby. It would also mean that Ari could continue producing unchecked forgeries for longer, and Prince's reputation would be damaged even further.

And so it was with a heavy heart that he dialled Ironmonger's name on his phone. He was about to call when he noticed a brown street sign.

Williamson Tunnels.

He dismissed the phone call, entertaining another possibility. He keyed in a few commands on his phone, and within a few seconds, he was looking at a map of his exact location. A map that looked very different to any normal land survey.

He could see the outline of the cathedral, its massive structure lit up orange, all of its features, nooks and crevices displayed in sinewy detail. He could see himself, outlined like the buildings around him, and if he moved his arm, the little orange line representing his arm on the screen moved in real-time.

The image was produced using a technique called remote sensing, which worked by overlaying hundreds of aerial-view satellite images on top of one another to give the user an idea of their immediate surroundings.

This technology had been developed by Ocean Pearl to give them a read of any landscape around them, and at any one time they had hundreds of their own satellites in space sending data back about the Earth below. Importantly, the technology showed underground structures too, by using depth-perception technology embedded into the satellite relay.

It was actually this technological development that had dramatically increased Ocean Pearl's ability to make new Big Finds in more recent years – and some of their most profitable. Generally speaking, a large underground space meant a temple, a vault full of treasure, the wreckage of the hull of a ship, all of which were easily marketable and good business for the company.

And it was in real-time that Prince saw a bird's eye view of his own location, as well as what lay beneath his feet, emerging before his eyes in the view of his map, the warren of the Williamson Tunnels flicking out in different directions like a crack in a car windscreen. Two orange dots flickered.

'Hmm,' Prince mumbled out loud. 'Gotcha.'

***

Chapter seven

Fliss couldn't have seemed less interested in Ari's quarter-life crisis if she tried. She slid off the bench, a blasé look pasted across her face, and glided over toward him.

'Look,' she offered, softly. 'There's no point in worrying about it now. What's done is done. We can hang out here for the night, and then in the morning you can leave again. And this time, make sure you stay out of Ocean Pearl's way,' she said, warningly. Ari grunted in response as he struggled to comprehend the vastness of his own naivety. *How could I have been so reckless?* he asked himself.

There was a chill in the tunnel, and he pulled his coat up closer around his face. *Ocean Pearl manipulated me so easily.*

He closed his eyes, and in that moment he genuinely believed that Fliss was right. Tomorrow, he would leave Liverpool again, and stay out of Ocean Pearl's way. No more forgeries, no more auctions. *No more treasure.*

'Anyway, in the meantime,' Fliss said, breaking his train of thought. 'Look at this.'

Fliss thrust her phone in from of him. It displayed a photograph of a battered-up piece of lead. An *old* battered-up piece of lead. Misshapen, a bit like the state of Texas. Ari was hardly in the mood and wondered whether he was already breaking the vow he had made not seconds before. He squinted one eye.

'There's writing on it... Middle English?' he asked, knowing the answer. 'Looks medieval to me. I can read it, but it'll take me a second.'

'No need,' she said. 'I've known what it says for years. *-never be found. VLSM,*' she quoted. 'Then on that other bit that sticks out at the bottom, it says *-ENR*'. He looked back at the image.

'Yeah,' he said, absent-mindedly. 'And is it medieval?'

'Yes. Somewhere around 1100 CE, give or take a century.'

Ari brushed his hair over toward the back of his head and breathed in deeply. The smell of sawdust lingered.

'Fliss,' he started, looking up from the phone. She was perched back on the workbench, watching him curiously. 'What the hell are you showing me this for?' he asked, his voice rising a little. 'I've literally only just escaped the clutches of Ocean Pearl, do you have to immediately put me back in their firing line?' he demanded.

There was a slight tremor in his voice as he spoke, the kind you hear on the news when someone isn't used to public speaking. The feeling of uneasiness he felt in his stomach had grown into a knot. Sweat pooled around his underarms.

'Wait,' he added, struck by a sudden thought. 'Was there even anyone following us? Why couldn't you have just emailed this to me?!' he demanded.

'Unbelievable,' she said, her eyebrows raised. Ari stepped backwards, stumbling over a yellow hazard sign as he did so. Fliss' hair had come loose from the bobby pin that had clipped it back, and her bangs fell loosely about her forehead, covering her eyes and nose.

'Ari, the crowd you had fallen in with, and the rumours about your sudden leave of absence... until last week I didn't even know if you were still alive, let alone whether you had an email address,' she said flatly. 'So don't get pissy with me!' she snapped. 'The thing in the picture? It's yours. You gave it to me when we were kids.' Ari looked at the image on the phone again and frowned. He didn't recognise it. If she was telling the truth, he didn't recall the exchange. 'And yes, someone was following us. I'm as sure as I can be that you would have been "intercepted" by Ocean Pearl outside the Exchange tonight, had I not-

'Shut up,' Ari said, quite abruptly.

'Oh charming-' she started to say.

'Seriously, shut up.'

She stopped.

'What is it?'

'Someone's just pushed the fire exit open.'

'*Shit,*' Fliss said, much more quietly this time. 'I forget you can do that.' In a flash, she whipped her hood and zip back up, covering her face once more. 'The last thing I need is to be recognised and this gets back to my boss,' she said by way of explanation, her voice barely more than a whisper. 'Anyway, it might be the security guard,' she offered meekly.

Ari ignored her and, without speaking, signalled to her to follow him, setting off in the direction of the only light source in the room; a bright, halogen lamp.

'Where are we going?' Fliss whispered.

'Let's find out if whoever it is can see in the dark,' he said.

The base of the lamp was a mess of wires, like vines in an olive grove. Ari frowned, trying to follow the one linked to the light, but too late; Fliss had picked up a saw from a nearby workbench and was on her knees, cutting at random.

'Fliss!' Ari said in a hushed tone. The lights went off with a fizz, and, in the absence of any windows, a total and complete darkness collapsed around them.

Ari's vision changed.

'Is anyone coming?' she whispered, although she needn't have bothered. The tunnel leading to the hall was illuminated now by the dim light of a torch, which slowly came closer and brighter as whoever was carrying it headed in their direction.

'If this goes bad,' Ari whispered, 'cause a distraction. Nod if you understand.' He saw the white outline of her head move up and down.

Ari had been able to see in the dark like this for as long as he could remember. He looked around the room, and the outlines of the objects around him appeared as white lines pencilled in on a blue background. It still amazed and surprised him.

He and Fliss had spent countless hours in their youth in the dead of night, her throwing things to him and him catching them, or him telling her how many fingers she was holding up. This had, inevitably, resulted in sneaking into all sorts of places they probably shouldn't have been in the dead of night, and he was suddenly struck by the feeling that they were back on one of those midnight misadventures once again.

Fliss pulled Ari back underneath the scaffolding that ran around the wall of the entire room. She gave him a meaningful look as the beam from a flashlight appeared, sweeping the room, then moved off, passing underneath the scaffolding on the opposite side. *Whoever it is, they're looking for someone*, Ari thought.

Ari took Fliss' hand and stood up, creeping as softly as he could out from their hiding place, heading in the opposite direction to the figure with the flashlight. They moved away from the exit at first, keeping to the wall, Ari flitting between looking at the scene in front of him and what the torch was doing.

After a short distance, he stopped Fliss and crouched down again. He supposed it must have been a strange sensation for her, being blindly led across the room in total darkness, the light of the torch only illuminating a corridor of light a few metres ahead of its carrier.

Ari couldn't remember what darkness looked like.

He rose slowly, taking Fliss' hand once more, and changed course, edging toward the ramp and the exit. Ari's breathing eased a little. The intruder was still poking about underneath the scaffolding behind them, while Ari and Fliss only needed a few more paces and they could make a dash up to the surface.

Then the lights came up.

Slowly at first, but within a second or so they were beaming at full power, and the gentle chug of a backup generator could be heard.

'Mr Nicander, I believe?' James Prince said. Ari stopped and turned slowly to face the voice. Fliss immediately ducked behind Ari, and pulled her hood and snood back up, concealing her face.

'Who's your friend?' he asked, not unkindly. Fliss didn't reveal herself. There was a rasping quality to his voice.

He had a distinguished yet scruffy look, and was older than Ari by maybe ten years. He gave off a classic "bored at school" vibe. His long-ish black hair was pushed back behind his head and he sported a fashionable stubble which followed the edge of his jawline. Small wrinkles threatened the corners of his eyes and mouth, and he had a hungry look in his eye.

The midnight-blue suit he wore bore an odd, plastic-y sheen, as though it had been glazed with sugar. The kind of suit Ari hadn't seen for eight years. *A wetsuit,* he thought, thinking of Ondrej. Definitely Ocean Pearl.

'I'll get right to it,' Prince said. 'I represent an organisation that is very interested in your... talents.'

Instinctively, Ari touched the breast of his jacket for his Bowie knife. Well, Ondrej's Bowie knife. It wasn't there, of course.

Does this guy know about Merchant's Lodge? Ari thought.

'An organisation? You mean Ocean Pearl,' Ari responded flatly. He scanned the room as best he could in his periphery. If he was right, the backup generator wasn't too far away, and if they could kill it, the lights would go out again and he could lead them back outside in the dark.

It was a weak plan, but it was all he had.

'Why the harsh tone?' Prince asked. 'You're quite gifted, Ari,' Prince said smoothly. Ari did not flinch at the use of his first name, though he did wonder how much these people truly knew about him. Then, sickeningly, his thoughts turned to wonder whether this was all another rouse to draw him in. Lull him into a false sense of security and then, when he least expected it, take their revenge for his involvement eight years ago. Ari resolved himself not to let them get their chance.

'My name is James Prince, and I've been watching you for some time now,' he said, slowly taking a step toward the pair. Ari shuffled backwards in return.

'In fact, I've followed you up and down the country, and I have been extremely impressed with your work. Truly, I have.'

'If you want to buy something from me, I'll be auctioning-'

'Tsk,' Prince said, impatiently. 'I don't wish to *buy* anything from you. You have created nothing that we couldn't replicate.' Ari saw that as a lie, but allowed the agent to continue. 'But, as I have said, you are talented, and I don't doubt you could be of great value to my company.'

'If you can replicate my work, why don't you?' Ari asked, goadingly. Prince raised an eyebrow.

'What do you know about Ocean Pearl, Ari?' Prince asked.

'I know that you call yourselves treasure hunters,' Ari said. Any anger he had harboured toward Ocean Pearl seemed to be growing inside him, as though it had been bubbling under the surface, reaching boiling point but never quite achieving it. Ari had to be careful not to allow it to explode all over the man in front of him which would, surely, create more problems than it solved. 'I know that you make money by selling items at auction, and I know precisely why you're here,' Ari said.

'Pray tell,' Prince said.

'You're here because you think I'm getting too big for my boots. You're here because you don't want your precious company to be undermined by an amateur,' Ari said, standing a little straighter.

'You don't want the public to know what you do, what you've been doing for years. You don't want them to know that the heritage sites they visit all over the world have been largely stolen and wrongfully claimed. You don't want people to see the legal battles, the bitter rivalries that go on behind the scenes, the life's work ruined or the activities your so-called "agents" get up to on foreign soil. From Tutankhamun to Saqqara, you've been doing the same thing for a century; stealing history from its rightful owners - the people.' Prince stood unflinchingly still.

'Finished?' the agent asked, sarcastically. 'We have survived all sorts of so-called "scandals," and as much as I enjoy standing in disused tunnels debating moral philosophy, in this instance, I am simply here to make you the offer of a job.'

Ari stared at him. He felt Fliss shuffle behind his back.

'A job?' he asked, blinking.

'Yes. A job. As I said earlier, someone with your talents could be highly valuable to us. I have seen the extraordinary quality of the fakes you produce - and they are fakes, don't bother trying,' Prince said, perhaps sensing Ari was about to interject, 'you know, we sent your specimens to experts all around the world. They proved to be quite the head-scratcher. We had one Peruvian scholar willing to fly to England to testify in court on your behalf that those "gold staters" you sold in Amsterdam - sold to us, by the way. You know the ones... *The bust of Artemis with bow and quiver on one side,*

Nike driving fast biga on the other, bidding will start at £3,500,' he said, mimicking an auctioneer's voice.

Prince scoffed. 'Ha! The man was ready to stake his reputation that they were real and insisted we stopped calling into question the integrity of the Finder... Because that's what you are Ari, right? A *Finder.* And you *find* yourself now considering my offer fairly seriously, don't you?'

In fact, all Ari could consider, over and over, was one word: *Amsterdam.*

That auction had taken place nearly *two years* ago. All the moves he made, the long hours spent, the time travelling to auctions all over the world, building his reputation as a - well, as Prince put it - a Finder. *Could they possibly know about it all?*

Prince laughed again, filling the room. Across his face, a broad, disconcertingly genuine smile appeared. Fliss nudged Ari in the back. He had nearly forgotten she was there. *Right,* he thought to himself, collecting his thoughts: *focus on escaping this nightmare.* He could address his existential crisis... well, existentially, but right now in the here and present he needed to execute an escape plan, for which he was relying on Fliss' distraction being the same as the one he had in mind.

'Yes, Ari, we know you quite well. You say we have stripped the people of the history that belongs to them, I say we have *given* the people more history than they could have possibly enjoyed without us!'

Prince took one step forward.

'Take Saqqara, which you brought up, what was there before we started digging? A cliff-side? A lot of sand? It was only because one of *our* agents happened to be holidaying in the region and someone had approached him in a bar after he had been shouting his mouth off about being a treasure hunter, that they had told him they had something he would be highly interested in learning about. And from there, boom! No other company in the world would have committed so fiercely to what was essentially a hunch, and a drunken one at that. Three tombs and counting, over nine thousand artefacts found, all of which will be displayed at the Antiquities Museum of Cairo-'

'And where is the man in the bar in your headlines?' Ari asked. 'Where does his story come into this? All I seem to remember are glossy TV adverts telling me to visit the historic site. Hand over a small fortune and I could take a journey like no other, *given* to me - as you put it - by Ocean Pearl, but I don't remember any damn mention of a guy who is actually descended from the people buried there who found the place. He deserves the fame, hell he probably would have forgone any monetary offering,' Ari said.

'Are you so naive?' Prince spat, angrily now, taking another step. *Come on, damnit. One more.* Ari thought to himself, the knot in his stomach growing tenser.

'No one "forgoes" money. He would have taken everything offered to him with arms wide open-'

'At least he would have deserved it!'

'And where is the "honour" in your line of work? You deceive exactly the same as we do!' Prince said, more shrill than before.

'No one gets hurt doing what I do!' Ari retorted, although he knew it wasn't a particularly strong argument.

'You wouldn't call losing twenty grand being hurt? All they have bought is the value of the gold!'

Ari struggled to deny him, and so chose instead to deflect.

'Look, at the end of it all, you are nothing more than...' Ari paused a moment and nudged Fliss gently with his left elbow. 'In fact,' he spat, feeling Fliss rise slightly, ready to move. 'That's what you are,' he said. 'I can't believe I've never thought of this before. You're a parasite. And to answer your earlier question: there's no way in hell I would consider working for you.'

And that, it seemed, was all Prince needed to hear. It happened extremely quickly. Fliss sprung out from behind Ari, sure to keep her face covered, and made a beeline for the emergency generator that Prince had left unattended. Prince watched her move, snarled and came at Ari, fists up. Ari stepped forward, ready to engage.

He knew there was a very real possibility that he would be beaten to a bloody pulp. Prince was upon him now, and with such speed, the first blow surely about to land.

Ari stood firm, hands raised, his face, fighting with all his might the urge to bend double and cower. Then there was a fizz, and the lights went out on cue with the sound of the emergency generator failing. Ari's vision changed instantly, and he watched as the white silhouette of the Ocean Pearl agent faltered against the inky blue background. Ari didn't miss his opportunity.

He sprung forward, kicking out as hard as he could at Prince's knee, which buckled and sent the agent tumbling to the ground with a loud cry. Ari didn't stop his stride, bounding over the limp figure on the floor. He ran at the scaffolding at the back of the room and aimed a flying kick at one of the flimsy-looking joists supporting the massive structure.

It seemed to work. The leg of the scaffold bent in on itself, and slowly the rest of the structure groaned as it began to teeter away from the wall, falling in the direction of Prince, who Ari hoped was still rooted in position.

Ari ran toward the exit, calling out Fliss' name from the other side of the room.

'Start running!' he shouted. She had positioned herself well in the newly-dark room, and as she set off ahead of him he could see she was on the right track to make it to the exit. Ari pumped everything he had into his running, and as he hurled himself up onto the exit ramp, he heard the last of the scaffolding give way, and the din of metal clattering against metal rang out like the bells of the Anglican cathedral. He didn't slow his pace.

Outside, Fliss was waiting for him. She had her hands on her knees, recovering her breath, but Ari didn't stop as he came flying through the doors.

'Come on!' he shouted as he ran past her. She rallied and followed suit, and the pair headed out of the fenced-off entrance to the Williamson tunnels. Ari had never been so glad as to see a Night Bus approaching.

'There!' he said, sprinting across the deserted road toward the bus stop.

The driver gave them a funny look but allowed them to board.

They sat down on the lower deck, and Fliss kept her hood and zip up to obscure her face. They were both panting, unable to speak. The bus was well-lit, and Ari knew if more Ocean Pearl agents were in the area they wouldn't have too much difficulty recognising them. The man hadn't seen Fliss' face, but it would have been fairly obvious; they were filthy.

Ari couldn't tear his eyes away from the entrance to the tunnel. The bus sat idling for an agonisingly long time before, eventually, the doors closed and it limbered up to move away. Ari reflected that a bus, much like a Williamson Tunnel, only had one exit. Ari craned his neck to watch the tunnel disappear from view as the bus ambled toward the city centre, unable to shake the feeling that he had indeed seen the silhouette of a man appear just as they left.

Ari breathed hard and sat back in his seat.

'That was... well. That was something,' Fliss said, her breathing becoming less aggravated. Ari didn't say anything. He was looking at his own reflection in the window of the bus, and all he could think was: *they know.*

***

Chapter eight

Ari's eyes snapped open.

He didn't remember falling asleep, but his face was pressed uncomfortably against the cold glass of the Night Bus window which trundled lazily through Chinatown.

He sighed heavily and rubbed the tiredness from his eyes. When he looked back from the window was surprised to find Fliss staring at him.

'What now?' she asked, expectantly. Ari frowned. *She can't be serious.*

'What now?' he repeated, groggily. 'I'm going home, I suppose,' he said.

Fliss' expression did not soften.

'You-bloody-well-will-not-go-home you sack of shit!' she said at break-neck speed. 'I rescue you from the jaws of Ocean Pearl, put my career on the line, my *life* on the line, and you think you can just "go home"?! Well wouldn't that be bloody rosy, Ari. Let's all just "go home". Head on back to our cosy little lives and pretend like none of it happened,' she said, flashing him a look that, in other circumstances, might have turned him to stone.

'Well? What would you have me do, Fliss?' he asked, rising to match her impudence. 'In case you hadn't noticed I've just been hunted down by an *agent* who said he's been "following me" for years!' he said, slamming back into his chair petulantly, turning his gaze toward the window. 'Clearly they're not happy with what I've been doing these past few years, and for all I know they know about-'

He stopped himself abruptly.

'Know about what?' Fliss asked. When he didn't answer, she repeated herself almost hysterically. Ari said nothing, and he heard Fliss let out a long breath.

Outside, Chinatown melted into the distance, and the bus stopped outside St Luke's, a church that had been hollowed out when it was bombed in the Second World War.

The walls remained standing but there was no roof, and over time it had evolved into an events venue. Ari must have walked past its imposing, gothic-looking structure a thousand times when he had lived in Liverpool, running jobs for Ondrej as part of his gang, but this was the first time he had ever truly appreciated the adventitious nature of the site, a symbol of religious fortitude and resilience, imposing itself on a busy junction at the top of Bold Street. *The walls are standing but the roof has caved,* Ari thought to himself. *Not a bad metaphor.*

'Ari,' Fliss said to the back of his head as though she had sensed his thoughts. 'The past is the past. That part of your life is over. I mean really, who the hell have you been selling to? Attracting the attention of Ocean Pearl. Did you not think it would happen?'

She was right, of course, Ari reflected bitterly. On both counts. He had been selling too voluminously and had gotten too greedy, and he hadn't "thought" at all. He had encountered Ocean Pearl, sure, they were at most big auctions. But never could he have guessed they had put in place such control over his life and, at some point, had taken over the reins entirely. Somewhere along the way, Ondrej's warning that he should get out of the treasure-hunting business had become more of a nagging worry than a present danger. He had started to believe that they had forgotten about him. Or perhaps, never known about him in the first place.

Clearly, he had been very, very wrong.

'But you can't "go home",' she said, 'wherever that is for you now. I think you should come with me,' she said, unexpectedly.

Ari turned from the window to look at her. If she was joking, her face didn't show it.

'Come with you?' Ari said, repeating her.

'That's what I said. Come with me. The picture of the old lead thing I showed you earlier,'

'Never be found, VLSM. ENR,' Ari quoted.

'Yes. I want to know what it means. And it's part of your life. You gave it to me, after all,' she said with a shrug. Ari gave her a quizzical look.

'It's just a piece of lead, Fliss. I don't even remember it ever being in my possession. It's just something I probably nicked off my Dad then gave to you,' he said.

'Everything happens for a reason, Ari,' she said. Ari scoffed. People were always using determinism to imply that some event - usually negative - was "meant" to happen, somehow part of a plan.

Fliss had never been that kind of person before, and he wondered now what had happened in the intervening years to turn her into one.

Shit happens, and we invent the reasons, he thought solemnly.

'So now you're a what, treasure hunter?' he asked.

'No,' she started, slowly. 'I'm just going to take... take a break. Get out of here for a while and decide what comes next for me. I'm not so sure about the Exchange any more.'

'Hm. Wonder what put you off?' he asked sarcastically, which she acknowledged with a weary smile.

'I just want to get out of Liverpool,' she said.

Ari took a moment to process what she was saying.

'OK... let's just *say* I come with you and, as you imagine, we find the rest of your piece of lead. So what? We'd just have another battered-up old piece of junk and a complete statement.'

'Not all treasure is valuable in a monetary sense, Ari,' she said. 'It might be good to have some purpose that doesn't involve pissing off Ocean Pearl.'

The bus stopped and let a single passenger on, who headed upstairs, stumbling as he did so.

'What am I even saying,' Ari said. '"find the rest," there is no finding to be done! We wouldn't even know where to start.' Fliss shuffled uncomfortably.

'Well, I do,' she said, a little sheepishly. 'It came from *Aquae Sulis*. The Roman baths, in Bath.'

'*Aquae Sulis*,' Ari repeated, incredulous. 'Talk about not pissing off Ocean Pearl! I mean, they gutted the place in the mid-nineties, found everything there was to find, and it's been theirs ever since!' he said.

It had taken Ari some time to be able to talk about Ocean Pearl at all. To even speak their name. It wasn't so much fear that he felt toward the memory, more like a sense that they were ever-present. A panoptic company with agents everywhere. Ridiculous, of course, but he had witnessed first-hand that evening that he hadn't been entirely wrong.

Whenever their name was mentioned or something reminded him of them, which happened frequently, he felt his Bowie knife plunging into that agent's squishy flesh. He felt the blade go all the way through. It was a sort of persistent nervousness which would evaporate quite instantly without him even realising. He came back to reality when he realised Fliss was talking again,

'I know it probably sounds ridiculous. But I've been reading up on these "pieces of lead," as you put it; in Latin they're called *tabula desfixonis* - curse tablets, and-'

Ari shot her a meaningful look that implied: *not here.*

'Sorry,' she said quietly, 'you're right. And, of course this isn't some kind of destiny, and we probably won't find anything... But whoever wrote this thing certainly had something to hide. "Never be found," they wrote, and *you'll* never be a Finder if you don't bloody well *try* to at least find things when they are so obviously presented to you as lost, rather than simply forging things for profit,' she said. 'So will you come?'

The noise of the bus's idling engine at the traffic lights near Lime Street Train Station was a fair approximation of Ari's state of mind. He was still going, still ticking over, but he certainly wasn't moving, and he wouldn't be getting anywhere particularly quickly, either.

He rested his head against the window and looked at the impressive St George's Hall, and surrounding sandy beige cobbled streets in view and once again he thought of his Father.

This is where it all started, he mused. *All that time ago, when Dad became the curator at the museum here.* This is where he had met Ondrej, and Ocean Pearl had become more than just a name he knew from the television.

Perhaps it would be good to get away from Liverpool for a while, Ari reasoned, to lay low while the dust settled on their adventure. And perhaps they might even find something interesting, even if it wasn't financially valuable, as Fliss had said. Maybe then he could call himself a Finder. Maybe the newly inescapable feeling of failure would fade. Maybe this one, tiny shred of purpose would allow him to complete something genuine for the first time in years.

He sighed and looked back at Fliss, who seemed quite exhausted all of a sudden. Despite himself, he simply replied:

'Yes, I'll come.'

***

Chapter nine

Ari stood inside Liverpool Lime Street Train Station at 04:15 AM waiting for the first train to Bath Spa, not departing until 05:26 AM.

His hands were wrapped around a large, puce-coloured coffee cup, and the steam from the liquid inside warmed his face. Simultaneously, he was working his way through a bacon and sausage sandwich which he had smothered in HP sauce.

As he ate and drank, Ari watched the Departures board with a fixed fascination that he could only put down to extreme fatigue. The large, airy concourse was bookended by two double doors, which opened periodically and doused the passengers within with freezing cold air from outside. On the board, each little orange platform number, destination and associated departure time flickered and changed, like lights in a cityscape.

'£90.26 each for standard, or £112.50 for First Class,' an attendant said, breaking his reverie. Ari nearly choked on his sandwich and seemed to be preparing for an argument, but Fliss had pushed in front of him and paid the fee before he could even begin his tirade.

First Class, too.

He and Fliss had been surprised that the earliest departure was that early at all. He had secretly hoped to be able to slope off back to his rented apartment to grab a shower and a change of clothes, but Fliss had told him fairly unequivocally that if he missed the train she would murder him, assuming Ocean Pearl didn't get there first. She had seemed serious too.

'Cheers,' he muttered as she pushed his train ticket into his hand before making off into some shop or other while Ari waited near the turnstile. When she reappeared, she seemed to be coming around to his way of thinking on the train station prices.

'*Nineteen quid,*' she said incredulously as she approached carrying a handful of items. Ari burst out laughing.

The pair meandered nonchalantly around toward Platform One, taking care not to seem as though they were trying to avoid being seen, until eventually, they stood alone in front of the closed train doors, having passed through the ticket barriers unhindered.

It was colder out in the open near the tracks, and Ari still only wore his satin-blue barber and black chinos. His Chelsea boots looked even more battered than they had done already.

He knew if he bothered to look his hair would be a mess but, fastidious as he usually was, in that moment all he could think about was getting on board, knowing he would have the luxury of a seat to himself in First Class, the conductor would give him a ludicrously-thin blanket, and he could sleep.

Fliss, on the other hand, seemed to have other ideas and was already poring over one of the newspapers she had bought.

'What could you possibly be looking for?' he asked.

'Sometimes there's an article on the sale at the Exchange,' she said, without looking up. 'And this is today's paper.'

Ari pursed his lips.

Eventually they were allowed to board and find their seats, and Ari was grateful for the blanket after all; the air-con seemed to be stuck and was blowing directly onto his face, drying out his eyes. He considered asking to switch seats, but realised that, as it was only the two of them in the compartment, it seemed unlikely he would need permission once the train started moving.

The First Class coach was at the front of the train, so their long, slender carriage only had doors at one end - the rear. Each side of the slim aisle was decked with chairs upholstered in a way that belied their uncomfortableness, with wood-finished plastic tables topped with little green reading lights in between.

The maroon walls contrasted garishly with an off-white ceiling and worn-looking blue carpet, a colour scheme that - he assumed - was meant to mirror the Union Jack. On one wall was a poster boasting, "stunning views!" for the duration of the journey. *And a good job too*, Ari mused, *you couldn't spend half a day in this rattly old cage with nothing to distract you.*

Fliss didn't seem to have noticed any of this even though their seats were facing each other, she hadn't lowered the newspaper from her face yet. They were still waiting for the train to pull out of the station having been allowed to board fifteen minutes before departure, when someone else stepped onto the carriage.

Ari's heart dropped into his stomach.

The man was in his mid-thirties, sported a sharp, short haircut, and an almost undetectable trace of stubble. He stopped dead as soon as he entered, and his eyes narrowed as they landed on Ari, then moved away.

Ari attracted Fliss' attention by aiming a hard kick at her shins underneath the table. Her newspaper shot down with a crumpled flurry, and the face that appeared in its place was quite enraged.

'What are you doing?!' she spat. He nodded over her shoulder at the stranger, who was still standing in the doorway, now typing on his phone. She peered out around the seat, then shot back a millisecond later.

'*Ocean Pearl,*' she mouthed, silently, her eyes wide open in fear. Ari's reaction must have been similar to hers, because the man was looking at him again with renewed interest. He looked back at Fliss and gave her an imploring look, as if to say "you're sure?"

She nodded slowly. Ari held up a finger; the man had turned away and placed his phone against his ear.

'He's making a call!' Ari said in a hushed whisper.

'Will you be able to hear him?' Fliss asked.

Ari's heightened sense of hearing had begun somewhere around the same time he had developed his ability to see in the dark, which in itself was linked to generally superlative vision. He had only actually realised his hearing was "heightened" at all when he got to secondary school, having previously assumed that his fellow classmates were also distracted by the noise of the internal whirring of the electronics of older models of mobile phones, or a bird making its nest in a tree near the classroom window.

At the time, he had been too young to be taken seriously, and his complaints were dismissed as fantasy. He had been diagnosed with all sorts of conditions: ADHD, aphasia, dyslexia, dyspraxia; basically anything which affected his ability to concentrate, but he had never really felt like any of the descriptions fully fit with his symptoms - if they could be called "symptoms" at all. Fliss had always said he had "powers," but he preferred to think of it as simply being highly tuned, as though he had been fuelled with ninety-nine octane fuel versus the bog-standard ninety-five.

Fliss had been the first person really willing to listen to him and to try to help him to understand, his grades had steadily improved once he had learned to *focus* his hearing and sight on what he wanted to listen to or see.

His night vision, of course, was never switched off. And in the absence of competing noise he could hear far better than the average person over a much greater distance, but generally speaking, he had to pick and choose what he wanted to focus on. And he had gained this control through hours of practice with his friend, who sat opposite him now.

The same friend who now relied on these "powers" to keep them out of potentially serious harm, in the same way, she had in the tunnel when he had heard the fire exit open, and his ability to see in the dark had all but ensured their escape.

'Shouldn't be a problem-' he said, but was interrupted at that moment by a loud *BONG*. 'No!' Ari said out loud.

'GOOD MORNING LADIES AND GENTLEMEN. WELCOME TO THE 05:26 PENDOLINO SERVICE TO BATH SPA,' the announcer said in an inordinately loud voice.

'*Yes, I think it's-*' Ari heard the man say, in between the gaps in the announcement, straining to hear.

'*THE SHOP CAN BE FOUND IN COACH C, WHERE YOU'LL FIND A RANGE OF ON-BOARD SNACKS INCLUDING BREAKFAST ROLLS-*'

'*It's him.*'

'*...NEWSPAPERS AND HOT DRINKS-*'

'*Can't see her face, but it must be the girl.*'

'*THIS TRAIN WILL BE CALLING AT THE FOLLOWING PRINCIPAL STATIONS:*'

'*-intercept?*'

Ari was dismayed.

'He knows it's us. Well, me. He hasn't seen you,' Ari said, without looking away from the man. 'He's waiting for confirmation as to whether he should "intercept" us or not.'

'*Shit!*' Fliss said, probably more loudly than intended, but indistinguishable over the announcer who was now telling them where their nearest emergency exits were. She started to stand, fussing with her newspaper and knocking over several items on the table as she did so.

'Wait!' Ari said, raising a hand. She had been about to move into the aisle to grab their bags from the overhead shelves, but the man had adopted a look of deep consternation. 'Wait,' Ari repeated more softly. Mercifully, the announcer had stopped talking, and the man in the suit spoke quietly, but Ari could hear comfortably when he focused his hearing on their conversation.

'You're sure?' Ari heard him say, noting the tone of surprise in the man's voice. *'Boss they're... yes I'm still on the train... OK! No need to yell,'* was the last thing Ari heard him say before he spun on one heel without so much as a second glance and stepped out the train door, and back onto the platform. Seconds later, the sound of three beeps in quick succession followed by the hiss of the sliding doors told Ari that it was 05:26 AM, and the train was due to depart.

Sure enough, it pulled lazily out of the station, and Ari could just about see through the window of the train doors that the man was back at the ticket barrier, in conversation with the attendant, probably explaining why he needed to get back through to the concourse.

Ari let out a slow breath. Damp sweat had pooled underneath his arms.

'He's gone?' Fliss asked, lowering herself back into her seat.

'He's gone,' Ari repeated, blinking. 'Anyone you recognised from the Exchange?' Ari asked.

'No, but definitely Ocean Pearl... Anyway, I wonder whether they'll serve breakfast,' she asked, cheerily changing tack.

Ari simply stared at her.

'What?' she asked, rhetorically. 'We're in First Class, after all,' she said with a mischievous smirk.

Ari didn't share her uplifted mood but smiled nonetheless.

***

Chapter ten

Ari awoke from his slumber with a start. His head was sore, and it took him a moment to remember where he was.

The rattle of the train as it ripped through the English countryside was gently comforting, and he closed his eyes again to see if he could compel his mind and body back to sleep.

Giving up, he sat up straight having bent over to rest his head between his folded arms on the table in front of him and stretched, the tension in his shoulders undoing itself, like unlacing a knot on a pair of trainers.

Fliss wasn't in her seat, but she had left an empty coffee cup and the remnants of something called a "Breakfast Box," so Ari assumed she hadn't gone far. He pulled the window blind up to reveal a crisp, sunny autumn morning. It was October, shortly before the clocks were due to change, and dawn had broken a few hours ago.

Ari thought that Bath couldn't have been far away; the countryside was different in the South of England compared with the North, somehow. Equally, though, he wasn't particularly keen on hearing another of the announcer's messages, and so was happy for their location to remain a secret for a while longer. He reflected on the tranquillity of his current surroundings compared with the events of the night previously.

He didn't have his watch on, but his phone told him it was 09:30 AM, so he reckoned he had managed about three hours' sleep. He checked his emails on his phone, most of which were junk, and one from the Exchange asking him to "rate his experience". In spite of everything that had happened, he couldn't help but smile at the thought of what he would write:

Comfort: five stars

Entertainment: five stars

Murderous intent: five stars

Value for money: costly, in lots of ways.

Fliss returned and, despite wearing the same clothing as she had been when he had fallen asleep, looked as though she had just been for a spa treatment at a fancy hotel. She smiled at Ari.

'Nice hair,' she said. He grimaced and tried – unsuccessfully - to push it back across his head and into some kind of style.

'I was asleep a while,' he stated.

'Yes. We're about an hour away from Bath Spa, I think. No more stations either, Birmingham New Street was the last one.'

'Any more, ahem, *visitors?*' he asked. She shook her head, and he sat back in the seat, relaxed. They remained the only ones in the carriage, save for one gentleman a few rows down, of whom Ari could only see the back of his head above the top of the seat. He nodded in that direction,

'And him?'

'Nah,' Fliss said, 'I've walked past a few times just to make sure, but he's been asleep the whole time. I don't recognise him, and he doesn't strike me as the type.'

'Good,' Ari said.

They fell into silence. He and Fliss hadn't seen each other for a long time. Some seven years, and the last time they had they had both been too angry to do or say anything that didn't cause the other to overreact.

Last night, being hunted down by Ocean Pearl and hiding in the tunnel, Ari had imagined they were children again, being chased off a field by a farmer or away from a fishery by the landowner.

Now, in the cold light of day, faced with the decision to travel to *Aquae Sulis* which they had taken together when adrenaline had been flowing through them after evading what seemed like some sort of kidnapping - or worse - Ari realised he didn't have the faintest idea about what he should say to her.

Fortunately, Fliss filled the silence.

'Thanks for coming,' she said, simply.

'You didn't give me much of a choice,' he said, 'but you always had a good hunch.' She smiled at him and looked out of the window.

'Why didn't that guy "intercept" us do you reckon?' she asked. He shrugged.

'Hard to say. Too public? I mean we would have made a scene.'

She hummed her agreement, but Ari suspected she wasn't entirely convinced.

'So how *did* you end up fixed so squarely in their sights?' she asked. Ari raised an eyebrow.

'I thought you had it all figured out?' he asked sarcastically, remembering their conversion in the Williamson Tunnel.

'Come on,' she said. 'I only know that Ocean Pearl were after you, which usually means you have entered their turf, so to speak. They don't go after just anyone, as far as I've seen.' Ari once again felt the odd sense of pride he had enjoyed when Prince had complimented his work.

'I was producing fakes: coins, artefacts, inscriptions, parchments, texts... you name it, I copied and sold it,' he said. Fliss locked her gaze with his.

'OK... and you were getting too big?' she asked.

'Too good, I reckon,' Ari said. 'That agent in the tunnel, "James Prince",' he said, miming quotation marks with his fingers. 'He was there to offer me a *job*. I'm obviously doing something they've not been able to replicate.'

He briefly explained to Fliss how his progression from creating and selling small items at auction had started, then how he had moved on to those which fetched higher fees, and how he had begun to develop stories for his Finds, moving on from simply copying things to deriving his own creations with their own backstories and Finders.

Fliss still stared at him unblinkingly.

'And the equipment?'

Ari shrugged. 'Didn't need it. Anything a machine can do, I can do by eye,' he said. '"Powers", remember?' he said and winked at her.

Fliss' eyes narrowed as though she were going to scold him, then at the last moment seemed to instead choose to gaze out the window and remain silent, watching as the white-silver glimmer of the frosted dew on the grassy hills disappeared into the distance behind them, only to be replaced by new ones, seemingly indefinite and forever.

'You must think I'm an idiot if you expect me to believe that's even half the story,' she said after a while, coldly.

'Quite the contrary,' he said. Fliss rolled her eyes.

'I didn't "leave you," you know,' Ari said.

'Well I don't exactly remember you leaving a phone number,' she said, curtly. He didn't particularly want to argue with her again.

'Not everything is so black and white, Fliss. I needed time, space to think and to find new experiences. I couldn't handle the risks I was taking any more. I couldn't live day to day not knowing where the next pay cheque was coming from, waking up on sofas in strange houses not remembering how I got there, going to dodgy, black-market auctions and helping those awful people. I had made a big mistake,' he said. 'And I needed to work through what kind of person I wanted to be.'

'Pft,' she scoffed. 'Come on, don't give me that crap. "You didn't like who you were involved with." Absolute nonsense. You were flying high. I heard your name in all sorts of-'

Ari held up a hand to cut her off.

'Can we just agree to disagree here? Please?' he asked through gritted teeth. 'You shouldn't pretend to know how I felt... but raking this up won't help. It was years ago, and it's different now. We don't need to have this argument,' he said.

Fliss chewed her bottom lip. 'Fine,' she said, coolly.

At that moment, a train attendant came by with the food and drinks trolley, from which Ari ordered another latte and another round of sausage sandwiches.

Once it was poured and he had paid his outrageous fee, he said to Fliss,

'Show me the picture again. Of the inscribed lead,' holding out his hand.

'The tablet,' she corrected him. Fliss rummaged through her bag, found her phone and loaded the image.

'Here,' she said, sliding it across the table. He turned the screen brightness up to maximum. He *focused* his vision on different parts of the lead, which brought some things into sharper detail than others. He could see – with ease – where minuscule knicks had been taken as the carver had made the inscription and, although it was worn, he saw the fine layer of dust that sat on its surface. He could even make out the remnants of a fading fingerprint in one corner – although most of it was missing.

He widened his vision, allowing as much light as possible into his pupils, which dilated to an unconventionally large size. He saw it even more clearly, as though it were under a microscope, but it bore nothing of note.

He wished she had brought the actual piece with her.

'Where is it? This... what did you call it?'

'*Tabula desfixiones,*' she said. 'It's Latin for "curse tablet". And it's at home,' she added, simply. He went back to studying the image, which he struggled to understand the significance of, or why Fliss thought it might be somehow special.

'As I said in the Williamson Tunnel, the only thing I can think that separates this piece from the presumably thousands of others like it is the fact that it is written in Middle English, and dates from somewhere around the eleventh century,' he said, matter-of-factly, speaking as though he were reviewing it's worth. 'And I'm assuming that a "curse tablet" is not something any medieval God-fearing Christian is likely to have employed, or even known about,' he said. 'So it must be pagan,' he said. 'But that seems very odd for the time. Christianity was very much dominant by the eleventh century, and it had spent a long time carefully culling rival deities to the point of extinction,' he said. 'Unless there were other pagan artefacts lying about around then?'

'I doubt it,' Fliss answered. 'And you're right, it was the anachronism that first caught my interest. Of course, examples of curse tablets have been found in their thousands from all across modern-day Europe as remnants of Hellenistic, Viking and Roman culture, and some older examples of cuneiform tablets from ancient Mesopotamia. But they were *particularly* common at the Roman Baths – *Aquae Sulis* - in Bath. In Britain. The pagan Goddess worshipped there would be asked to cast a curse upon someone who had committed some kind of wrongdoing in the eyes of the worshipper,' she said. 'It was like a bargain; people would usually present an offering while also committing themselves to a vow to live a certain way or build a shrine in her honour in exchange for her help.'

'A votive offering,' Ari said.

'Yes. But this thing,' Fliss continued, returning to the present. 'This might be the latest example of a curse tablet *ever* discovered. Paganism was well and truly dead by this point. I know you're only usually meant to get excited by the oldest examples of things, but I think it's the relative youth of this object that makes it unique.' Ari simply hummed his agreement.

'And,' she said, snatching the phone back off him and leaning in, pointing at the screen, 'not only that, but whoever wrote this has made a total hash of it. - *VSLM* is a Latin abbreviation which loosely translates as, "discharges the vow freely, as is deserved," and is supposed to signify that the person writing has done their part - that their part of the vow has been fulfilled and the Goddess should exact the curse. *Do ut des* - I give that you might give - that's the *pax* - the pact. But this person? *ENR?* All they have done is ask the Goddess to make sure something is "never found," without promising to do anything in return,' she said, a little excitedly.

'Well as I said,' Ari replied in a reasoned tone, 'they were writing a long time after this type of practice had died out, perhaps they didn't know they were meant to do something for this Goddess and were just trying to call on some divine goodwill,' he said, not particularly sharing in her enthusiasm. She seemed deflated. 'I wouldn't get your hopes up, Fliss. The headline is: "Person gets pagan practice slightly wrong." It seems very normal. Cool, sure. But I doubt we'll find anything "connected" to it.'

She pursed her lips.

'Person gets ancient pagan practice *seriously* wrong, at a time when you could be executed for heresy,' she corrected him. 'The writer has missed the whole premise altogether. And they're clearly desperate if they're asking some random pagan Goddess for help. There's something interesting here, I'm sure of it. Perhaps not valuable,' she warned him again, as she had on the Night Bus, 'but interesting.'

Ari eyed his old friend, who was displaying the same determination she would sometimes treat him and his parents to as a teenager when she particularly wanted to do something or go somewhere.

'Fine,' he said, 'we'll follow up. But I'm only there for a visit, to have a break and get away from Ocean Pearl. I don't want to do anything stupid for a hunch, no matter how good yours used to be.' Fliss was silent for a moment.

'Still is,' she murmured.

There was another almighty *BONG* that made them both jump.

'LADIES AND GENTLEMEN, WE WILL SOON BE ARRIVING AT BATH SPA, WHERE THIS TRAIN WILL TERMINATE.'

***

Chapter eleven

Ari and Fliss' arrived at Bath Spa train station somewhere around 11:00 AM. Nestled in the countryside of South-West England, the city of Bath dated back some two millennia, to Roman Britain. As the train pulled in the city sort of appeared, like objects adjusting to a frame rate in a video game.

First, the aqueduct rose from the thick treeline like a stone monolith in a jungle of nature. Then, decked into the hills, rows of houses became visible among trees which, in early October, were a wonderful mix of silky browns, mauves, yellows and oranges. It was hard to imagine that there was a sprawling city somewhere in amongst all the greenery, but when Ari and Fliss disembarked and left the train station, they were met with all the usual amenities that could be expected of a bustling and vibrant place, all constructed in wonderful honey-coloured limestone.

They managed to source some breakfast (croissants from an open-front artisan baker van outside the station) before heading off to explore their surroundings.

Bath was, by all accounts, fairly small. Ari was sure he had visited as a child but didn't have much recollection of the place. He had always found that returning to places as an adult was never the same as the image from childhood.

Perhaps his brain did it on purpose, to allow the memory to be stored even if inaccurately, but it all seemed very new to him as he traipsed around the unique cobbled streets and warren of alleyways.

Having meandered fairly aimlessly for a while, taking in the neoclassical-Roman architectural blend and enjoying looking at some of the spectacularly old buildings and places, Fliss eventually suggested they go for a look around the museum of the Roman baths to get an idea of what was there already. Ari was hesitant but agreed.

He was still struggling to understand why they hadn't been intercepted at Lime Street station, and wondered whether showing their hand to Ocean Pearl immediately was the best idea. But, he equally agreed they had exhausted the city centre in the few short hours they had spent there, and they had, after all, come to look at the collection of curse tablets held by *Aquae Sulis.*

Ari hadn't voiced his concerns as they had handed over their forty-something quid and been admitted to the baths, but Fliss must have sensed something.

She stopped him in the atrium as they set up their audio guide - which looked like a GameBoy he had owned in the early nineties - to ask if he was feeling OK, by which point he had donned his over-ear headphones. He flashed her a toothy grin and gave her the thumbs up.

Her reaction was difficult to read, as she wore a baseball cap that she had pulled low and a scarf high to her nose, concealing her face as she had in the Williamson Tunnel. They had decided it would be too conspicuous for Ari to do the same thing and conceded that Ocean Pearl already knew his identity, but for as long as they could keep Fliss hidden from them, the better.

Since leaving Liverpool and arriving in Bath they hadn't seen anything to suggest that Ocean Pearl were still watching them, but *Aquae Sulis* was Ocean Pearl territory, marked on almost every corner by the iconic red and gold *laburum*, and Ari couldn't shake the feeling that they were trespassing, observed from the panopticon of unseen Ocean Pearl presence.

Fliss finished fiddling with her own headphones and the pair left the atrium, heading into the museum, their audio guide talking at them robotically as they snaked around the exhibits.

The baths - or *thermae* -, were something of a natural wonder. The Romans, who worshipped a large set of pagan Gods in a practice known as polytheism, thought the *thermae* were the work of those Gods and Goddesses.

Or more specifically, one Goddess; the Romano-British Goddess known as *Sulis Minerva*, to whom they had dedicated a great temple right at the site of the *thermae*. The attraction of the temple had given rise to the Roman name for the modern-day city of Bath - *Aquae Sulis*, translated as, "the waters of *Sulis*". *Sulis* who, at some point in history, had merged with the Celtic Goddess *Minerva*, birthing the hybrid - *Sulis Minerva*.

Of course, modern scientists now understood that the warm water flowing into the *thermae* was not the work of *Sulis Minerva*, but was heated underground thanks to a process of enhanced geothermal warming, then rose through fissures in the rock up to the surface. Somewhat surprisingly, Ari also learned that these were the only naturally occurring hot springs in the whole of the United Kingdom.

Even during the great days of the Roman Empire, the audio guide told him, there had been nowhere quite like the *thermae* of *Aquae Sulis*. People of nobility would have travelled from across the Empire to bathe in its waters and give an offering at the Sacred Spring, the largest of the pools.

It was slightly unclear as to how, but the people of the time conceived of the Goddess *Sulis Minerva* as both a life-giving Mother, and simultaneously an effective agent of executing "curses" at the behest of those who felt they had been wronged. This seemed somewhat contradictory to Ari, and Fliss raised her eyebrows when they were told about it.

'See,' she said quietly. '*Votive offerings!*' she whispered.

Soon, they found themselves in a room full of these so-called votive offerings. Most looked exactly like the picture on Fliss' phone, albeit eight hundred years older, and written in Latin as opposed to Middle English.

The collapse of the Roman Empire in the fifth century ushered in a long period of intellectual stagnation for the Britons, known colloquially as the Dark Ages, and Ari couldn't deny that Fliss' curse tablet was an enigma. Paganism was long gone by the eleventh century, Christianity had taken hold, and as she had pointed out, the person who had written it was asking *Sulis Minerva* to make sure some treasure or other stayed hidden, which wasn't the point of these types of curse tablets.

But really all the exhibit at the museum told them, Ari thought, was that the stuff she had looked up online was correct; that the *thermae* at Bath was famous for these types of relics.

And while they gave great insight to a historian interested in Romano-British life, they told Ari nothing about the prospect that *Sulis Minerva* might have watched over anything other than a dilapidated old bathhouse. And he wasn't particularly interested in the Goddesses' divine ability to deprive a local grain salesman of sleep because the buyer felt he had undercut him at market, as was the curse inscribed on a liver-shaped piece of lead that Ari found himself looking at as he mulled over the timeline.

In fact, and he dare not voice this opinion, but he found the inscribed tablets to be quite boring. They barely even told stories, and most were punctual and concise.

They detailed what had happened to the writer, who had wronged them, what was being offered to the Goddess and how the curse should be exacted against the perceived perpetrator in return, which more often than not was just an ask that they "pay with their life," although there were other examples.

The only thing that piqued his interest was that, apparently, in an attempt to maintain anonymity, many of the messages were written in a kind of code. Some had words or letters written backwards, others had lines alternating between left to right and right to left.

'I hope our tablet isn't like that,' he said to Fliss quietly as they studied one such example; a man asking the Goddess to "curse" a family with no sons after a land dispute, but written with some letters swapped out for numerals.

'We could figure out the code?' she asked, speculatively.

'Yes,' Ari replied quietly, 'but not if we only have half the tablet.'

They spent some time examining the remaining examples on display but found nothing that matched their half, nor any written in any language other than Latin. Ari even focused his vision on a few to see whether he could discern any detail, but all he saw was ancient text on an old piece of lead or stone and, after a time, Ari suggested they move on with the tour.

Each new section they entered brought new, alien names that yet bore resemblance to their modern names - the *Caldarium, tepidarium, frigidarium*, as well as changing rooms, saunas; the remains of all of which were quite clearly marked out for visitors to see.

Some were no more than a few stones on the floor, where Ari felt somewhat at the mercy of his audio guide, while others were extraordinarily-well preserved, and Ari had a sense that he was connected to the ancient past in a way he had never truly been before.

But even here, everything was covered in Ocean Pearl branding, the gold *laburum* printed everywhere he looked. That said, the poor condition of the audio guide unit and the faded, dated images and signs told him that the site probably hadn't seen much investment since they had taken it over in the nineties.

Ari wondered whether that wasn't just another indication that they had already found everything there was to be found of any value at *Aquae Sulis*, deepening his resolve that he and Fliss would find nothing new.

They made their way into the Great Bath, which was the size of a large swimming pool. The water was a teal-green colour, clearly unused, and the whole place

95

smelled stagnant. On all four sides, there were shallow stairs where bathers would have entered the pool, and each edge was lined with evenly spaced, corrugated stone pillars that stretched some twenty metres into the air. It was easy to imagine the barrel-vaulted roof that would have once covered the whole thing and the majesty that the room would have commanded.

Most of the stonework in this section was reconstructed later, the audio guide told him, but the limestone used to create these newer, magnificent carvings were, in Ari's opinion, worthy of their Roman ancestry.

Everything he saw in *Aquae Sulis* made him feel quite sombre as he thought about the countless number of people, societies, and civilisations that had gone before. Somehow, there was a sadness he couldn't shake.

The final part of the exhibition lay in the courtyard of a once-great temple, the Temple of *Sulis Minerva*, which for a long time would have dominated the ancient city's landscape. There was a 3D video reconstruction showing how the entrance to the baths would have faced the front of the temple facade, which was raised and accessed by a set of deep stairs. There were digitised British-Romans milling about the courtyard on an uncharacteristically sunny day, and although Ari was not inclined to believe the scene would have been so tranquil in real life, the model did help to give context to what would have otherwise simply looked like a large broken floor.

But it was the artefact raised on a towering plinth, surveying the temple courtyard with piercingly dark eyes that drew Ari's attention.

He moved closer, and saw it was an almost fully-preserved, two-thousand year-old gilt bronze head of *Sulis Minerva.* She was unsmiling yet kindly, her hair tied up tight to her head, and she had a distinctly divine look, Ari thought.

Certainly not beautiful; quite the opposite in fact, but she possessed a certain Motherly look that put him at ease. He wondered how, given her maternal countenance, she had ended up renowned by the people for fulfilling curses. *Never judge a book by its cover,* he mused.

Ari focused his vision in on the detail, his heightened senses giving him a zoomed view. He could see the intricacies of the gilt, where the gilder had misapplied or misjudged with his hammer, leaving small dents and bruises, like a fingerprint all over the work. When he looked again, unfocused, they were gone.

Ari imagined himself standing near the temple steps, delivering news to the *plebians* from Rome, of games taking place and senators visiting Britain in the coming days and months.

After a time, Fliss suggested that they move on, and as the walkway guided them out of the temple courtyard, they queued in a single file. He had no way of seeing what was around the corner, but remembering the map, they would soon be met with a fork. They could either head left, toward the gift shop and exit, or right, down a small corridor to the entrance to the Great Drain, which had been built by the ancient Romans to carry waste water all the way to the River Avon.

As the queue shuffled along, Ari stopped dead.

On the wall, among other Ocean Pearl propaganda, hung the unmistakable face of the Ocean Pearl agent he had stabbed in *Merchant's House*, some eight years previously.

Ari felt his heart-rate jump, and immediately he placed a hand on the wall next to him, hoping Fliss hadn't noticed his sudden turmoil. He stared into the face, wishing he could make it sentient, but it only stared back from its water-coloured grave with a measured countenance: his jawline long and strong, his hair clipped short as it had been then.

There was a small notice underneath which didn't include the man's name, but did mention that he was an Ocean Pearl agent and that he had worked at *Aquae Sulis* when it had first been excavated in the nineties.

It also informed the reader that he had been back to re-designate the site in the name of Ocean Pearl two years prior.

Two years ago.

Still rooted to the spot, Ari tried to calm himself.

He survived.

Ari rolled his eyes to the heavens, almost succumbing to the emotion of his private revelation. Having once, not twenty four hours earlier, thought he could let go of the guilt of not knowing whether he had delivered a fatal wound only to be thrown back into turmoil, here was definitive proof that the man had survived. It was almost too much. Ari found his heart rate was increasing as he began to panic, and something in his stomach pushed up toward his heart like a balloon.

Then Fliss grabbed his arm.

'What's with all the scaffolding behind there?' Fliss asked him quietly. Without realising it had happened, the queue had moved on, and Ari found himself staring into the small, crimson-rock opening that the Romans had called the Great Drain. Ari acknowledged the significance, but couldn't respond.

'Ocean Pearl were clearly interested in something in that tunnel,' Fliss said. 'Are you OK?' Fliss asked him quietly, sensing something was wrong. Ari snapped back to reality, feeling a little green. He smiled at her as warmly as he could manage.

'No,' he said honestly.

***

Chapter twelve

They exited the museum into a brightly-lit courtyard, the imposing fascia of the front of Bath cathedral to their right and a row of quaint shops in front of them, mostly selling Roman gift-shop-esque souvenirs.

Fliss was clutching a copy of *Aquae Sulis: Roman Britain*, which she had insisted on buying. Ari wasn't sure what she thought she was going to gain from re-reading the guidebook, but he hadn't made any remonstrations.

It felt good to be outside, and the light breeze cooled his sticky skin where he had sweated lightly through his undershirt. He noted he was *still* wearing the same clothes as the previous night, and resolved to buy a new outfit that afternoon. And his Chelsea boots still needed a good clean.

'Where to?' he asked, as breezily as he could manage. She didn't answer him immediately, but looked him up and down, her eyes slit suspiciously.

'What happened in there?' she asked.

Ari breathed hard and tried to act casually. In the end, despite his wobble, he felt he had done quite well to make it to the entrance to the Drain, where the hole in the rock revealed a large amount of scaffolding and other construction equipment in the Drain itself, as though something had been erected down there.

'Just a bit warm,' he said, unconvincingly. 'What do you reckon was in that Drain?' he asked, changing the subject. Fliss hummed in response.

'Clearly something Ocean Pearl thinks is worth investigating. Or at least they did, at one time,' she said with a sigh.

'It was always a long shot,' he said. 'That we would find the other half of the tablet here.'

'Yes,' she replied absently.

She had pulled out her phone and was typing furiously. 'Yes,' she repeated, a little more definitely, looking up at him. 'But the absence of evidence is sometimes evidence itself. The fact the other half is missing tells us one of a few things: they never found it, they did find it and sold it, or - I think most likely - they found it but don't understand it. Who knows what is referenced on the tablet as "*never being found*"' she said.

'Fliss,' Ari asked again, not wishing to be drawn on the subject in the middle of the street. 'Do we have a plan?' he asked, with a trace of exasperation. He still felt haunted by the image from his past in the picture frame, and it once more made him feel as though Ocean Pearl were somehow watching their every move. He wanted to get away from *Aquae Sulis* as swiftly as possible, and preferably somewhere they could be confident they weren't being listened to.

'Sorry,' she mumbled. 'Come on, we're meeting someone,' she said, pocketing her phone. Ari shot her a look. 'Don't worry,' she said, 'you can trust him. It's Benny.'

'As in Uncle Benny?!'

'The very same,' she said.

It was only a short walk to Pulteney Bridge, where she said she had arranged to meet her uncle. The drizzle of the morning had broken into a clear autumn afternoon.

'Have you seen him recently?' Ari asked as they walked.

'No,' she said. 'But Mum has.'

Fliss didn't have much family, but Ari remembered Uncle Benny popping up from time to time to take her on a day out or buy her a present. Benny was actually a collector of some sort himself, or at least was when Ari had last seen him as a teenager.

On the train, before Ari slept, Ari and Fliss had caught up a little about the rest of their families. He had told her how his Father had moved to Oxford to take a position in the faculty at the University there, while his Mother had taken on consultancy work somewhere in the Middle East.

Despite having not spoken more than a few words to either of his parents since the incident in Merchant's Lodge, some eight years ago, he at least benefited from the fact that although he wasn't with or in contact with them, he could be generally confident that they were doing OK.

Fliss could not share in that luxury.

Even as childhood friends, she rarely spoke about her family life. Her Mother had fallen into alcoholism and a cycle of self-destructive habits in Fliss' teenage years, which was in part how she had ended up spending so much time with the Nicanders. But she could hardly be blamed; her husband, Fliss' father, had vanished into thin air from a seemingly happy marriage, abandoning his young family never to resurface again.

In the whole time he had known her, she had mentioned the man perhaps twice. Once in simple passing conversation when she had referenced his fondness for Cuban cigars, and another when they were a little older.

They were teenagers and had snuck into Ari's Father's alcohol cabinet, mixing all kinds of spirits into a deadly concoction. That evening, drunk, she had cried and said she, "missed her Dad sometimes, despite having never really known him." She had gone on to lament the difficulties in being expected to miss someone she wouldn't even recognise, and felt somehow obliged to do so, as though someone was keeping tabs on her grief.

Shortly after that, she'd fallen soundly asleep on Ari's sofa and had only awoken when she had decided it was time she should vomit. She had never revealed as much again, and as they rounded the final corner and the water of the Avon came into view, Ari found himself thinking about his own Father again. Most of the time when he did that, all he heard was the venom in his voice when Ari had joined Ondrej's gang and started working for him.

He remembered the betrayal his Father had felt. He also remembered feeling distinctly unconcerned. Still, the image of his Father in his mind's eye soothed his conscience after seeing the portrait, and by the time they reached Pulteney Bridge, he felt much calmer. Probably calmer than he had felt since before he had left for the Fruit Exchange, in fact.

I still can't believe he survived, Ari thought, his emotions so mixed with relief and regret that he could hardly process it.

The River Avon was wild despite the relatively calm weather. Pulteney Bridge ran its entire breadth and consisted of a row of uniform-looking windows: two-high and twelve across, six-a-side, with a larger, taller window in the centre. A promenade of shops and a road sat atop three evenly-spaced, large stone arches, through which the swirling river water danced away into the distance. It was an austere-looking thing, and Ari couldn't decide whether he liked the design or not.

As they approached, he was struck by the entrance to an old Arcade that came up on their left, the kind he had imagined as a child would possess all sorts of treasures just waiting to be found. He stopped outside the door to peer in at the market stalls. The reality, sadly, was that they were often deserted save the staff.

'Benny!' Fliss said quite unexpectedly, drawing him away.

She stepped out across the road, and Ari turned to watch her cross to the other side of the pavement and hug a complete stranger. Or so it seemed.

Ari hadn't recognised him at first, namely because Benny had grown so large he wouldn't have looked out of place if he were painted black and white and thrown in a cowshed. Ari crossed the road too, marvelling at Benny's exorbitant midriff as he came closer.

'Hiya Benny, long time,' he said as casually as he could manage as he approached. He wondered whether his face gave away his surprise. Benny stuck out a huge hand, which Ari grasped weakly. It was clammy.

'Marius Nicander!' Benny said, loudly. Either Fliss hadn't passed on the message that they were trying to remain inconspicuous, or Benny didn't care. He turned his attention back to his niece. 'How *are* you my girl?' he asked.

'Tough question Ben, do you have somewhere we can go?' she asked.

He must have sensed a certain gravity in her voice because he had hailed a passing taxi before she had finished her sentence.

'Get in,' he ordered. 'It's not far to the house,' he said, 'but I'm not walking.'

Walking? I'm surprised you're breathing, Ari thought to himself as he climbed into the back of the black cab.

***

Chapter thirteen

Benny, as it turned out, was an extraordinarily wealthy man, or so his house would suggest.

'Benny,' Ari said as they sat down in the living room on the ground floor. 'This place is...'

'Glorious, eh? I've got the only residential one left on the row. I must have had a thousand offers to sell up at this point, but I never will,' he said resolutely, as though Ari had just asked to see the title deeds.

Benny set down a small tea set on the coffee table in the middle of the room, while simultaneously taking up the last of the remaining free space on a large, green-leather armchair. It squeaked its protest as Benny's massive frame settled in.

The Royal Crescent, Benny told them briefly, was nearly two hundred and fifty years old. A row of thirty terraced houses laid out in a crescent, sweeping imposingly across the city's landscape. It was one of the most sought-after areas in the whole of the county, and Benny occupied one of the largest; an end-terrace with views over the hill, and down over the rural city below.

The living room was large, with a set of three bay windows that faced a spacious back garden. The sunny afternoon spilt into the room, illuminating the oakwood floor and off-white walls, as well as all sorts of bric-a-brac that Benny had clearly accumulated during his time as a collector. There were hip-height piles of books in every nook, paintings on every part of the walls and oddly-shaped objects on every inch of every surface: ashtrays, toys, kitchen utensils, vinyl records. Benny's living room looked like an antique shop.

Ari at last had a chance to properly survey the massive man sitting before him. The first thing Ari thought about him was that his face, at least, was extraordinarily well-groomed. His greying goatee beard was trimmed short to his chin, and his moustache was well-groomed, which gave his inhumanly large head something of a shape. His spectacles were pushed high up to his face, and his hair was sort of spiked up at the top, although Ari wondered whether he would be capable of holding his arm above his head for long enough to try anything that might be considered a style.

'Well,' Benny said, leaning forward with some difficulty to pour the tea. 'Have you heard from your Mother, Fliss?' evidently, she hadn't been anticipating the question, and found herself fumbling with her words. Benny seemed to have heard all he needed to. 'Understandable,' he said with a deprecatory wave. There was a moment of true awkwardness that followed, as both Ari and Fliss knew Benny was toying with asking whether she had heard from her Father. Instead, he said:

'Tell me everything!'

With some relief, Fliss explained briefly about the Fruit Exchange and the auction, and how she had been working as the compere there for some time. He said he was surprised he hadn't heard, but conceded he hadn't actually attended an auction for some years, instead preferring to buy his items online.

Mercifully, she glossed over the details of Ari and his goings-on in the preceding decade, instead saying he had "fallen into some hot water" with Ocean Pearl.

She did, however, tell him about Ari's fake products, why Ari was so valuable to them, and about their entanglement in the Williamson Tunnel and subsequent escape on the early-morning train. Ari held his breath, but she didn't go into any great detail about his abilities and omitted the second Ocean Pearl agent from the train. The mention of the company seemed to spark an almost visceral reaction in her uncle that neither of them expected.

'Ocean Pearl. Charlatans! Call themselves treasure hunters!' he exclaimed when she was finished. The pair had expected Benny to elaborate, but when he didn't, Fliss continued, telling him about the curse tablet. How it came from *Aquae Sulis*, its date from the eleventh century and the strange - but partial – inscription asking for something to be protected. She pulled out her phone to show him the picture, then informed him that they had been to the museum but found nothing.

'And so, in a bid to help me to "lay low" from Ocean Pearl for a while, your niece suggested I come with her here, to Bath, to find the other half of the tablet,' Ari added when she was finished.

Benny was silent for a moment. He closed his eyes for slightly longer than was perhaps normal, but Ari had noticed that everything he did had a distinctly cumbersome quality to it.

'Perhaps for the best,' he said after a time, his eyes still closed. 'That you found nothing at the museum,' he said. Ari exchanged a glance with Fliss.

'You two need to be careful. What you're getting into could be extremely dangerous if that gang of pirates is involved. Hell, it's already been dangerous!' he said. Ari couldn't deny him that.

'So you think I'm right, then?' Fliss asked. Ari gave her a quizzical look, unsure how Benny's warning had led to the inference that he sided with her. 'You think this curse tablet could mean something?' she added, eagerly.

Benny made a grunting noise and shuffled in his seat.

'Anything is possible! I hear your scepticism, Ari, but you need to realise that if Ocean Pearl are interested in it -'

'But we don't know that they are,' he cut in. 'We don't even know if they know the tablet exists,' he said. Ari's mind flashed back to the agent at Lime Street. *Why did they let us go?*

'There's treasure and *money* involved, Ari. They know about it,' Benny said, unblinkingly. 'I've been living here for the best part of thirty years, and let me tell you, they have uncovered some glorious ancient Roman sites in the area. But the *Aquae Sulis* excavation... They put *so* many resources into it, and the treasure they found there was worth a pretty penny. But there has always been a feeling among the Collectors that they missed... *something*. A site of that size, not to uncover a vast treasure? It's almost unheard of.

'Every month it seems they uncover a new "Big Find", as they call them, all around the world, and everyone expected to receive the same news at *Aquae*. But it never came, save the few items they found in the Great Drain,' he said, eyeing Ari. 'They approached me, you know, when I was the Treasure Coroner for the council,' Benny said heavily, taking a long sip from his tea.

At that moment, Ari was startled by a large, orange cat that leapt onto the arm of the sofa. Seemingly unperturbed by the commotion, the cat yawned, then folded itself into a pose that made it look rectangular, tucking its legs in underneath its body.

Fliss and Benny were giggling.

'Sorry if he gave you a fright,' Benny said, still laughing.

'I can't believe Cicero is still alive,' Fliss said, clearly delighted. She crossed the room and sat next to the cat, offering her hand, which he accepted. Soon, he was purring loudly as Fliss rubbed his head, and the trio listened to the cat in a trance.

'Anyway,' Ari said after a time. 'You were saying you were a Treasure Coroner?' he asked.

'Right, yeah. I had no idea,' Fliss said. 'You mean one of those people who authenticates treasure?'

'The very same. Each county has their own, and I was Somerset's for a long time. I was collecting back then but not as I am now... ha!' he barked, causing Ari to jump again. 'I held this naive notion that history belongs to the people.'

Ari cringed as he was reminded of his argument with James Prince in the Williamson Tunnel.

'I thought the work I was doing was as important as that of a surgeon. I felt history, intrigue, mystery... could save lives, bind communities and families together... But I have since learned otherwise. History belongs only to Ocean Pearl,' he said with some venom.

'I remember once they contacted me to ask me to certify a treasure - which was my job after all - so I gladly obliged. It was a significant piece; some weaponry and a few rare pottery fragments they had found at the quarry, so I set about contacting the university here in Bath. Everything seemed perfectly normal. The items sold for a fair amount, a few hundred thousand in the end if memory serves, and everyone was happy.'

Benny paused, Ari thought, for dramatic effect. 'Until I bumped into a mate of mine, Ruaridh McIntosh, shortly afterwards.

'His eyes quite literally widened with fear when he saw me. He tried crossing the road, but I was slimmer back then, so I managed to catch up to him. He was a wreck, poor guy. It had seemed that the sight of me had brought about his sudden turn. It really took some convincing that my intentions were benign, but I eventually calmed him down and brought him here, where he apologised and explained that he had run from me because he had assumed I was "one of their people."

'To cut a long story short, I plied him with fine whiskey until he told me the truth. It was *he*, not Ocean Pearl, that had found the weaponry and the pottery pieces - and Ruaridh knew his stuff. He had recognised immediately it was a damn good find, and its approximate value at auction. So he phoned my office and spoke to my secretary at the time, Jane Groutson. Heh. The look on her face when I confronted her,' Benny said, misty-eyed.

'It took a while of course, but I eventually tracked the leak. She was "on the take," so the expression goes. Ocean Pearl were paying her to siphon information about valuable finds to them before they went to auction. So Ruaridh, having taken what he'd found home, was approached and asked if he would accept a nominal fee for the find, hand over the treasure and sign a Non-Disclosure Agreement. He refused-'

'And they forced him,' Fliss finished the sentence.

'They certainly did. Killed his dog in the end,' Benny said, almost nonchalantly. 'Said his mother would be next.' He let the words linger for a while. Ari's face must have shown his dismay.

'An empty threat? Perhaps,' Benny continued. 'But who is taking that chance? You wouldn't guess at the lengths these people have gone to and will go to protect their interests. All anyone sees is a big company that puts on fun days out for families and finds lots of old shit. No one *thinks* about how they have gained that monopoly... Because nobody cares. And why should they? A lot of the time the Finder is happy with their fee from Ocean Pearl. Sure, they exploit a few people, bully a farmer who finds a stone circle in his field to turn the land over to them, kill the odd dog, whatever,' Benny said, flippantly. 'This stuff doesn't cause a big enough splash for it to be in the public eye particularly, but it goes on. They're dangerous,' Benny said, repeating his earlier assertion. 'And I'm not happy that you're in their sights,' he said, nodding at Ari. 'Nor am I happy that you have gotten yourself mixed up in this,' he added, directing his gaze at Fliss.

The sheer pace of the events of the last twenty-four hours hadn't really allowed Ari to process much, but Benny's story made him sure of one thing now: if he and Fliss decided to proceed, to go digging around at an Ocean Pearl site, they would need to be damn sure it was worth it.

Ari was no longer in Bath for a "break," it seemed. And the fact that they had been to *Aquae Sulis* already was, in hindsight, incredibly foolish. Ari felt the beginning of a gnawing suspicion as to why they had not been intercepted on the train.

'And your friend, Ruaridh, he thought you were an Ocean Pearl man? That's why he ran?' Fliss asked, breaking Ari's concentration.

'Oh yes,' Benny said. 'I should have explained. He assumed it was me who had passed his information to Ocean Pearl, and he had wanted to stay well away. It was at that point that I realised I wasn't the only one with a dodgy secretary, or an ulterior motive of my own. I did a little more digging and discovered that Ocean Pearl has pretty much everyone you can think of when it comes to treasure hunting in their pocket. All of them. Anywhere there is money to be made from a Find, they are all over it. I suspect those who are paid to pass the information don't see it as a particularly massive deal. A moral grey area, perhaps. But it's an established system, and they get a reward from it. What's more, in their eyes, it's a victimless crime. My secretary Jane Groutson never knew about Ruaridh's dead dog.'

Benny tailed off, then, quite abruptly said, 'I want to show you something,' raising a massive arm.

Fliss jumped up to help him out of the chair. He stood with all the grace that could be expected of a man of his size and shuffled off down the corridor, beckoning the pair to follow. Ari and Fliss fell in line, allowing Benny to lead them.

***

Chapter fourteen

Ari didn't know what he should have expected of the library of a prolific collector, but nothing could have prepared him for what fell upon his gaze now.

The huge room had a "classic" library look about it; a hideous, mauve and rouge floral carpet, walls lined with ceiling-high wooden shelves, each with a railing at the top and an access ladder.

The windows had been bricked up to allow space for more shelves, and so the room was dark save for the lighting, which was attached strategically at the ends of evenly-spaced aisles.

At some point, Benny had had wooden archways installed, six in total, to allow for more shelving units to be placed in the spandrels. In the middle was a reading and writing desk which was raised on a podium. It was the only thing in the room that wasn't a book, and it was there that Benny sat himself now.

'Fliss, be a lamb and fetch this for me?' he asked, jotting down a series of numbers. She took it without a word and glided off, disappearing into the labyrinth. Ari expected it would take her a few minutes to find whatever it was Benny had asked her for.

'So,' Benny said. 'How is she?'

Not a question Ari had been expecting.

'She's well, I think. You understand we haven't seen each other for some time before yesterday?' Ari asked.

'Doesn't matter, son. You know her better than anyone. I remember you both as children. So I ask again, how is she?'

It wasn't a topic Ari had given any real consideration to. Fliss had practically begged him to come on with him to Bath. She had been hot-headed and angry when he had suggested he wouldn't join her, and she was adamant that there was something to find here. *Why?* Ari thought to himself for the first time. *Why did she need this to be a treasure so badly?*

Perhaps she was down and out on her luck too? Maybe she was in debt and needed money... If that were the case, she would be vulnerable, and easy to manipulate. Benny's gaze levelled at him as though he were reading his mind. He raised a massive eyebrow.

'I'll help you find what you're looking for, son. But for the love of God, be careful. Be careful with her.'

At that moment, Fliss came scurrying back around the corner with a collection of papers. Ari had been hoping for something a little more dramatic as he was left pondering Benny's warning. Fliss approached and put the papers down on the table.

'Talking about me?' she asked with a smile. Benny ignored her.

'Thank you,' he said as he took the papers from her and began rifling through.

'I wanted to show you... yes, this is it. I wanted to show you what you're dealing with in Ocean Pearl. How their methods are intrinsic to the core of the company.'

He pulled out a single sheet of paper and put it down on the desk in front of the pair, who stood opposite. He spun the light around and shone it directly onto the document in order to illuminate the text, which had faded dramatically with age. It bore a tea-stained look that indicated it was a good number of decades old, but the title gave it away:

November 5, 1924.

The date rang a bell in the back of Ari's mind. The writing was tiny, and scrawled across the page like ivy on a trellis, although Ari could read it perfectly well when he focused his vision. Fliss, though, asked for a magnifying glass, which Benny obliged, pulling one from the top drawer of the writing desk. She immediately bent down, poring over the text and blocking Ari's view.

'*Jesus,*' she exclaimed when she was finished, stepping away and giving Benny a grave look. 'Here,' she said, moving to let Ari in. She offered him the magnifying glass, which he took and pretended to use. Ari focused on the writing which went from illegible to clear in a click. It opened with:

That bastard's coming for me.

Ari looked up and made to open his mouth, but Benny hissed at him to keep reading.

That bastard's coming for me. I curse the day I was foolhardy enough to get into business with such swine! Alas, what choice did I have? I wish to detail events never made public here in this diary, so that the truth may be known in the coming years. From the discovery of Tutankhamun exactly two years hence.

That's where I know the date from, Ari thought to himself. *This is Howard Carter's journal!*

Carter was the lead archaeologist who uncovered Tutankhamun in the early twentieth century. He was adored by many, but based on what he had written in his journal, someone had clearly wronged him. It continued:

I, nay, we, discovered the Boy King Tutankhamun on 5 November 1922. The world rejoiced, and we were overnight made famous. I have never been as joyous, nor known another to experience such mirth. I, we, had achieved a lifelong ambition. But success, as usual, begets jealousy. And jealousy begets foul play. The untimely and most unfortunate death of my dear friend Lord Carnarvon proved to be catastrophic in ways he simply could not have foreseen, for in the absence of a benefactor, the excavation dried up for some months. In fact, from that date until the intervention of Lord Salaco in June, there was no work carried out at the site. The most exciting archaeological prospect lay underground, held up by Government red tape and arguments over funding. Even Stanley hadn't been of assistance.

Ari raised an eyebrow. *Stanley Baldwin,* he thought to himself. *Prime Minister in 1923. Friends in high places.*

Of course, when Lord Horatio Salaco offered to help, who was I to say no? The prospect of renewed finance meant digging would resume. I put on record here this day that the eighteen months hence have been the worst I have experienced. I should have seen it coming, but I don't possess that keen sense of character that Lord Canarvon seemed to employ so effortlessly.

Of course he, Salaco, wanted to claim the dig for himself. Clearly he had only involved himself in order to create a dynasty bearing his family name. He had not banked on the good name of Lord Canarvon, though. For all I read in the newspapers was praise for my late friend and, dare I say, my own good name mentioned in connection with the find. Salaco felt snubbed. He felt he was our "saviour," and he was mightily arrogant about it too, God be forgiving. Lord Canarvon worked for a love of Egyptology, and for the progression of the understanding of the human condition; I did not take kindly to profiteering. There was a fight and, I am ashamed to admit, I directed considerable slander toward Salaco, after which he fled the site. I have not seen him since.

It has now been eight months since the first death in my team. Solomon, my foreman, his Father a foreman before him, drowned while his rowboat was in the Nile. Abdullah, one of my archaeologists, he died next, stabbed on his way home from work. There have so far been six more, all of them essential personnel at the site of the dig. There is talk of a curse on the tomb. People are starting to ask whether we should never have entered, and perhaps we are punished for stripping Tutankhamun of his treasures. I cannot prove it, and yet am resolute in my belief that there is but one curse placed upon this site, and that curse has a name and sports a moustache. Lord Horatio Salaco.

And he is coming for me next.

Ari blew the air from his cheeks and looked up at Fliss and Benny, who both reflected his grave expression.

'Ocean Pearl?' he asked. 'Salaco?'

'Yes. Its founder. Long dead, of course.'

So Ocean Pearl really was built on blood.

'Salaco never did manage to disassociate the names of Howard Carter or Lord Canarvon with Tutankhamun,' Benny said.

'Ironically enough, it was this type of behaviour that forced Ocean Pearl to become a more clandestine outfit than Salaco had ever envisaged. But he achieved his goal, of sorts. I kept digging. If anything, the "curse" ended up serving the site well, because it added more intrigue and mystery. This page had been missing from Carter's diary for some time. Even this is only a copy; I suspect the original is closely guarded by Ocean Pearl, if not destroyed. It wasn't until a friend of mine in Cairo reached out to me to let me know he had it that I learned the truth.

'We should go to the press!' Ari said.

'Have you been listening to anything I have said to you today at all, Ari?' Benny snapped. 'No one cares! This "story" would be a one-pager, three quarters of the way through a handful of tabloids and a feature in *History Today* magazine. Nothing would happen. There's no way to prove any of these murders, now so long ago, and they have been operating outside of the law for so long that I doubt they even regard what they're doing as illegal any more.'

Ari was silent for a moment and thought about his own dealings with them. Benny was right. Even Ari, as someone who had relatively regular interaction with them, gave them very little consideration. He had always known they were immoral, a large, faceless corporation that paid no tax and exploited real people for their own gain. And he knew they would engage in some underhand tactics to get what they wanted, but the fact their founder actively murdered six people... Seven, if he was the one who got to Carter?

'But if we could prove that they're still-' Benny waved him away.

'Perhaps now you realise why I'm so hell-bent on getting one over on them, Ari,' Fliss interjected. Ari exchanged a fleeting look with Benny. 'There *must* be something we can find at *Aquae Sulis* that they don't know about yet,' she said exasperatedly.

'And we have a clue. I feel this is *something*. I have been watching them for months at the Fruit Exchange. They're sneery and condescending and they think they can just take whatever they want. I want to take something from *them*.'

It dawned on him that Fliss had never truly considered this to be a simple "getaway" from Liverpool, and had probably been concealing her true intentions from the beginning. Whether she knew Benny would have such damning evidence or not he couldn't be sure, but one thing was certain: she had taken over the role of orchestrator in his game of destiny. He didn't see he had much choice but to stay along for the ride. He sighed audibly.

'I'm still highly sceptical that we'll find anything,' Ari said bluntly. 'And I should really stay out of their way...' he said, his thoughts lingering on the face of the Ocean Pearl agent in the picture frame at *Aquae Sulis*. And yet, he found himself drawn to the idea like nothing else he could recently recall.

'But... perhaps we could try,' he said, a hint of determination in his voice. 'Although,' he admitted with a falter, 'I don't know where we should start. The baths told us nothing, and we have no idea where the other half of the tablet might be.'

Benny cleared his throat. 'No, but what you did see was that the things found at *Aquae Sulis* are kept there. It's a unique type of history where the objects are tethered to their place of discovery. So, if it has been found... it's in there somewhere. Do you think Ocean Pearl would display it for all to see if they hadn't yet understood its meaning?'

'No,' Ari and Fliss said in unison.

'And,' Fliss added, 'I've been thinking about why they didn't pick us up on the train.' Benny shot her a look of concern, which she ignored. Clearly she had forgotten she had omitted that part of the story. 'They want to know what we know.'

'I agree,' Ari said. He was relieved to hear that it had been playing on her mind as much as it had his. 'The moment that agent told his boss where we were heading, the boss' immediate thought must have been, "why?" ...why would we be coming to Bath at six in the morning?'

'Yes. It was silly of us to come straight here. We should have gone via a different route. But why not just pick us up and bully it out of us? It hardly seems as though they would be averse, based on what we have learned,' Fliss said, nodding toward Benny.

'Perhaps they don't think we would tell them? I mean they can't kill everyone who slightly irks them, not these days. This isn't a movie. They would be shut down immediately!' he said.

'Yes... It's a little tenuous,' she admitted. Ari nodded. 'I mean, to my knowledge neither of us have any particular connection to this place,' she said in a way that made it sound like a question.

'I certainly don't,' Ari lied, all the while the face of the agent on the wall in his mind. *Although, it wasn't a connection I knew about until today,* he reasoned with himself.

'Hmm,' Fliss said, seemingly content. 'We know they value you and your work. Perhaps they want to see if your talent for finding treasure matches that of your forgeries.'

At that point, Benny cleared his throat and said, 'I think this is verging on too much information. I don't need to know the ins and outs of your dealings in the last ten years, I just wanted to tell you these stories and show you what I had found to test your resolve. To check you understood the danger of the adversary you face...'

'Is this going somewhere, Uncle?' Fliss asked, jokingly. Benny smiled.

'Being a former Coroner and well-known collector seldom comes with advantages,' he said. 'But I reckon organising an after-hours trip to *Aquae Sulis* should be pretty doable.'

They were both looking at Ari, who looked down at his coat, remembering the promise he had made to himself earlier in the day. Suddenly, he was exhausted.

'I'll need a change of clothes,' he said.

***

PART TWO

Chapter fifteen

Aquae Sulis, Somerset, UK
Present day

On York Street, James Prince sat in an alleyway in the driver's seat of a black SUV, his gaze firmly fixed toward the end of the street, tucked away behind the back outer wall of *Aquae Sulis* in Bath.

The engine idled quietly, and all the lights were down, other than those on the dash. In the passenger seat was Tennant, Prince's right-hand man. In the back sat an Ocean Pearl agent called Aurora, who normally had a posting in Egypt. Prince hadn't worked with her before, but he had begrudgingly accepted her help when Ironmonger had offered.

'Sure you're up for this?' he asked, catching Aurora's eye in the rear-view mirror. She smiled derisorily.

'I should be the one asking you that, old timer,' she said in a thick, middle-Eastern sounding accent. Despite the joke, her demeanour did not change from one of heavy seriousness.

Dark-skinned, dizzying black hair, and piercing brown eyes, he pictured her with some envy in Egypt, at Saqqara, fending off thieves at night and doing back-room deals with Arabic men over treasure. Prowling the weekend markets, all the while keeping her ears pinned to the floor for any word that there was another tomb, another Big Find.

In a lot of ways, Egypt was considered the holy grail of modern-day treasure hunting. Despite being two millennia older in some instances, their tombs somehow remained more intact compared with Roman or Greek structures. Prince often found himself spending entire days looking over remote-sensing images rather than out looking for gold, which wasn't necessary in Egypt because the buildings were already visible.

Not that the British Isles were without their treasure. *Aquae Sulis* was a prime example, and he was sure that the secret to why Ari had high-tailed it down to Bath as soon as he had the chance lay within the ancient *thermae's* walls.

It had taken the Ocean Pearl trio of agents a little time to track Ari down and establish their next move.

Prince's entanglement with Ari and his mysterious girlfriend in the Williamson Tunnel hadn't been Prince's finest twenty-four hours as an Ocean Pearl agent, and his humiliation was only compounded by the fact that his assailants were a couple of amateurs who should really never have gotten the better of him.

But he *was* still an Ocean Pearl agent – just.

After a while under the fallen scaffold, he had managed to send a message to Tennant to ask for a rescue, with a plea that he refrain from immediately reporting the incident to Ironmonger.

Shortly afterwards, the on-call team had arrived to rescue Prince and, through some detective work, Tennant had figured out that Ari and the girl had probably come out of the tunnel at around the same time a Night Bus headed for Lime Street was due.

Back at the safehouse opposite the Fruit Exchange, trying to work out what he would say to Ironmonger, Tennant had called with news.

A rare half-*tabula* – a stone tablet - that had originated from *Aquae Sulis* had been due to be sold at the Fruit Exchange a few days ago but had been stolen before it could be auctioned.

Tennant had been at Lime Street where, sure enough, he had found the pair heading for the early-morning train to Bath, the home of *Aquae Sulis*. Prince had immediately instructed Tennant not to intercept.

'Run the plan by me again, boss?' Tennant asked, sheepishly. Aurora laughed, as she did at most things Tennant said.

'Jesus,' Prince muttered. 'After everything we've been through together Lawrence Tennant, it's a wonder I've managed to get by without punching you. It's very simple. The Target, Ari. He's the one from the Williamson Tunnel, and you saw him on the train, remember?' Prince asked in a mocking tone.

'Yes,' Tennant said, unwilling to speak any more than was absolutely necessary. Aurora, it seemed, couldn't help but chime in.

'And you think he can... see in the dark?' she asked, barely able to stifle a giggle.

'Must be a right handful, old Carrots,' Tennant said, turning to flash Aurora a grin who managed to compose herself.

Prince sighed deeply.

Ari had managed to guide him and his female accomplice to safety in total darkness. And in the aftermath of their altercation in the Williamson Tunnel, how he had managed it still gnawed at Prince's mind.

'I'm not saying he's some kind of super-human, but... Look, in the Williamson Tunnel, for example, he had heard me coming when I opened the fire exit. He must have, in order to turn the lights off before I'd arrived – because the only other explanation is that they'd been sitting in the dark the whole time.'

'Or maybe,' Aurora said, 'just maybe they had a torch?'

Tennant barked out a laugh.

'That doesn't explain how he could still see after the generator had gone out. We were underground. No windows. No light in or out. And as he escaped he somehow managed to avoid the falling scaffolding and make his way to the exit! I don't understand it either, but it was pitch black down there.' he said.

In the mirror, Prince saw Aurora raise an eyebrow in the back seat.

And there's no way he could have escaped me like that without some kind of advantage, Prince added mentally, although he managed to stop himself from saying it out loud.

'OK, boss,' Tennant said, no longer smiling. 'I believe you.' Prince nodded his approval.

'You don't, I assume?' he asked Aurora, catching her eye in the rear-view mirror. She hesitated for a moment.

'Prince,' she said matter-of-factly, 'in my short time with Ocean Pearl I have been sent on all sorts of assignments. I have heard the bizarre language spoken by the Pirahã tribe in the Amazon rainforest, observed the sacrificial practices of the Kuru, had a near-death run-in with the Patagones in the City of the Caesars,' she said.

'If you're grandstanding,' Prince said, 'you needn't bother. I've seen your CV, I know you've been given some of the best assignments,' he said.

'You are missing my point. I have seen things that I couldn't describe to you in Arabic or English. So I am willing to believe that this man can see in the dark.'

Prince gave Tennant a triumphant look, then said,

'Listen, whatever this guy is, he is just that. A guy. Whether he has supervision, X-Ray vision and can fly, none of that will protect him in the long run.'

'I still don't understand why you didn't just let me bring them in on the train,' Tennant said. Aurora sat forward too now, apparently her interest piqued sufficiently to actually pay attention - or at least feign it. And there it was. His *modus operandi* laid bare.

'They're here at *Aquae Sulis* for a reason, these two,' Prince said. 'And I want to know what that reason is. No doubt it is connected to the stolen tablet, and no doubt they think they can find what it means.'

And Prince had, so far, been proven right.

As he had suspected, Ari and his girlfriend had visited *Aquae Sulis* almost immediately upon arrival. This smacked of an amateurish treasure hunter who, when in danger, immediately went to protect his most precious haul. The smart move would have been to leave it well alone. But according to Ocean Pearl's surveillance team, Ari's trip to *Aquae Sulis* during the day had been uneventful, and neither he nor the girl had shown any sign that they knew the location of some great treasure.

And that, to Prince, meant that the pair had something to *find*, not protect, which placed Ari as the prime suspect in the case of the tablet stolen from the auction.

And if they had something to find, they would need time to look. So Prince had wagered they would make their move on *Aquae Sulis* any time after dark. He was convinced Ari had stolen the tablet, convinced he had a reason for visiting *Aquae*, and – most importantly – he was convinced that reason would involve some kind of *treasure*.

Prince didn't much care how he broke free from the lowly intellection he held among his peers; if following this fraudster for a few days before intercepting him led to a Big Find, he would take it.

If only the surveillance people hadn't lost him after he had left Aquae yesterday, Prince reflected bitterly.

'And what makes you so confident that they will be here tonight?' Aurora asked, interrupting Prince's train of thought.

'Well for a start,' he replied coolly, 'that's them.' He pointed down the alleyway where, in the distance, three people glided across the entrance. Tennant was smiling at his boss.

'You were right!' he said excitedly.

Prince felt somewhat vindicated.

***

Chapter sixteen

A short while later, all three of the Ocean Pearl agents had set their suits to Vantablack mode as they made their way toward the back wall of *Aquae*, making them almost invisible in the gloom.

The rain slid off them like hot wax, and the street was silent, save the clip-clop of Aurora's *Doc Martin's* echoing around the cobbled street.

It was possible that Ari had already figured out they were on his tail; in the brief glimpse Prince had managed to get of them, it looked as though the girl had her face covered, as it had been when they had visited *Aquae* the day prior. As to her identity, he was still unclear. No one had yet managed to get an ID, and there were no clues in Ari's case file; he had never attended an auction with anyone else, and there was no mention of a girlfriend.

But it didn't matter particularly, he knew he wouldn't need to wait long. Once they had discovered whatever Ari was looking for, he would be intercepted and the girl would be identified.

As they walked, Prince considered the stakes he had in the mission. It had become something more to him than simply stopping forgeries from entering the market. Now, he knew if he could deliver treasure for his employers, his mishap in the Williamson Tunnel would be forgotten, and all that would be remembered would be whatever he found as a result. His failure at *Aquae Sulis* in the nineties would be consigned to history, and he could finally concentrate on moving up.

He tried to calm himself.

As they approached the end of York Street, Prince nodded at Tennant who headed off toward the main entrance of *Aquae Sulis*, while he and Aurora were left staring at the outer wall, over which lay the largest of the *thermae*, the warm pools of water.

When Ocean Pearl had acquired the site in the late eighties, the wall had been no higher than twelve feet. Someone quite tall could probably have stood back and got a free view themselves. One of Ocean Pearl's first acts as the site owner had been to triple it in height and add the red *laburum*, which was the sight that greeted the pair now.

The plan was simple. He and Aurora as Ocean Pearl agents could access a live feed of any of the security cameras at any Ocean Pearl site, so he had tuned into *Aquae Sulis* on his phone, and was watching as Ari and the girl were shown through the door by a gangly-looking teenager.

The cameras were old because the site itself was relatively old, but it was in colour, and Prince could see clearly that Ari was in all black. He quickly recorded an image and sent it off to Ocean Pearl's tech guys, who came back with a positive ID in a matter of seconds.

Prince let out a grunt of satisfaction when it returned a match with Marius Nicander.

'Girl's covered her face again,' he muttered out loud to Aurora, who was setting up a grappling hook. She didn't respond, and her mood seemed to have shifted from disinterested to vaguely annoyed. Prince found himself wondering whether he would be able to rely on her during the mission. But he dismissed the thought.

Ocean Pearl had paid a lot of money to have her in England, and she had accepted the assignment. She would be professional.

The CCTV image on Prince's phone flicked from one screen to the next, following Ari and the mystery girl across the atrium. *Who are you?* Prince asked himself. He zoomed in and sent another image off to the Ocean Pearl tech lab of the partial view of her face but, as he suspected, there wasn't enough for a match.

'I'm in position, boss,' Prince heard Tennant say in his ear, interrupting his thought. Tennant's task had been to enter the museum and take place by the door. Ideally, he would also get rid of whoever it was who had let Ari and Fliss into the museum, in as inconspicuous a manner as he could.

'Any problems?' Prince asked, a little tentatively. To a bystander, it would have seemed as though had spoken into thin air.

There was some shuffling noise in the background of the audio in Prince's ear, and Aurora looked up for the first time.

'Sorry, just pulling the uniform on,' he heard Tennant say a second later. *'Nah, flashed my badge and told the kid he could go home. Said it was orders from Ocean Pearl. He was overjoyed.'*

Prince nodded at Aurora, who took that to mean that they were good to go. She went back to her grapple hook, which looked as though it was nearly ready.

The assortment of metal and plastic she had pulled from her duffle bag a few moments ago now resembled a cannon of sorts, which stood on an adjustable stand and had a large, pointy arrow protruding from the end. They had agreed to allow Ari and the girl enough time inside the museum to see if they could glean what they were looking for before they intercepted, the idea being that they would surprise them just as they made their discovery, hence the clandestine entrance.

Prince flicked the video feed on his phone back to the CCTV, cycling through the cameras until he found the pair.

'OK, they're in the museum... They're studying the curse tablets,' he said to Aurora. He wiped the image away. 'So it was him who stole it,' he said, definitively.

Aurora stood back, looking at the grapple hook with pride. She was still only fairly new to the company, and it was possible, Prince thought, that some of her bravado was more bluster than anything else.

'Do you have eyes on them, Tennant?' Prince asked.

'Got them on the camera system at the main desk,' came the reply. Prince dropped his own visual feed and wondered whether there was anything he had missed, something he hadn't accounted for. He, Aurora and Tennant had played out a number of scenarios, up to and including the death - accidental or otherwise - of any or multiple members of either group.

He gave Aurora the thumbs up, who crouched and dialled a few buttons on the side of the grappling hook. The angle of its position had been calculated to perfection, and it shot its metal arrowhead up and over the wall, then zipped automatically to attach itself to the nearest horizontal surface. The rope made a fizzing sound, then went tight. The cannon doubled as a handle, which Aurora grabbed onto. She winked at Prince and engaged the motor. The magnetised handle shot upwards, taking her with it. She reached the top in a few seconds.

Prince watched on as she dangled for a moment, then swung her legs up and perched herself at the top, sending the handle back down the wire for Prince, who repeated her steps exactly.

Once at the top, Prince looked down over the Great Bath on the lower level. The water was suffused by bright lighting around the edges, and the different colours of the patchwork floor gave it the look of a picnic blanket. The *hippocampus* mosaic stared back at him. He glanced at Aurora who, for the first time, seemed impressed. Prince raised an eyebrow and she immediately reset herself.

'It has nothing on Saqqara,' she muttered. Prince rolled his eyes as they both dropped off the wall, landing with a practised *thud*, the shock absorbers in the padding of their PearlTECH suits allowing them to take the fall with relative ease.

But as soon as their boots touched the floor, they both swore loudly in unison. The alarm had been set off.

Prince hadn't accounted for the possibility that in the intervening years since he had owned the site, Ocean Pearl had invested in more security. He cursed himself mercilessly as the wailing siren blared out. Clearly the alarms inside the museum had been disabled, but those on the grounds remained active. There was a mechanical sound, and both his and Aurora's gaze was drawn upwards where a retractable roof slowly glided across the hole vacated by the ancient ceiling. *Aquae Sulis* was being locked down.

'*Boss?!*' Prince heard Tennant say. '*All the bloody doors have just bolted themselves, I'm stuck in the atrium!*'

Prince put his head in his hands and rubbed his eyes furiously.

'*Find the override, Tennant! Get on to Ironmonger and get these bloody doors open, then man the exit in case either of them makes a break for it!*' he yelled over the impossibly loud wailing of the siren. Aurora was smiling maddeningly.

'Come on!' he shouted to her. 'I've lost the CCTV feed, must be the security system. When Tennant gets those doors open, we make a dash for them. Forget why they're here, let's just get them back to the Safehouse and take it from there!'

But Aurora wasn't looking at Prince. Her gaze was locked over his shoulder, at the centre of the upper wall, where the roof slowly slid toward the centre.

She pointed upward at the ceiling, and Prince swivelled around, eyes glowing red with rage.

There, clear as day, a hand had appeared over the wall.

***

Chapter seventeen

It had taken a few days to organise but, true to his word, Benny had managed to get an after-hours, unescorted trip to *Aquae Sulis* for Ari and Fliss.

On the eve of their mission, the trio sat in Benny's dining room waiting for their chaperone to collect them. The dining room was the size of some people's entire ground floor, with maps, books, scrolls, left-over takeaway boxes and a few empty bottles of beer strewn haphazardly across his massive, twelve-seater dining table.

Percival, Benny's budgerigar, hopped around joyfully on the table, pecking at crumbs of food and giving Ari the occasional quizzical, head-tilting look as if to say, "hmm?"

Cicero, the massive orange cat, seemed thoroughly bored.

Ari, Fliss and Benny had spent the last few days planning their outing.

Ari had been tasked with anything that involved going outside: checking out the CCTV cameras around the streets of *Aquae*, buying radio equipment, kitting them out with dark clothing, packing bags in case they had to make a quick getaway, checking local bus routes and scoping out hiding places.

Between them, they had decided on this approach as, although Ari was the real target, Ocean Pearl still hadn't seen Fliss' face, and they figured it best to keep her identity concealed for as long as possible. Moreover, the longer Ari was out in the open and they knew where he was - which he was certain they did - without "intercepting" him, the more credence was added to their theory that they really did want to know what he and Fliss were up to. On the one hand, Ari felt that it was unwise to be seen to be goading them, but in equal measure, couldn't really help himself from doing so.

He was struggling to come to terms with the fact that everything he had done had only happened because it had been "allowed," so to speak. He felt juvenile, as though Ocean Pearl were his parents who had decided that playtime was over, and now he should spend some time on the naughty step. And over the last few days, he had hardened his resolve to get some payback. This company had ruled his life for over a decade, and it was time to play them at their own game.

With Ari doing the outdoor activities, Benny and Fliss had locked themselves in the library, and had undertaken a voluminous amount of research on all things *Aquae Sulis*.

Romano-Celtic Gods and Goddesses, the origins of the *thermae, Desfixionis* – curse tablets - Roman Britain - basically anything that could be connected to their tablet - and what Ocean Pearl had done there in the nineties.

Each evening over the last few days, they had given Ari a download of the research they had carried out and what they had unfurled that day, and each time Ari left feeling more and more convinced that they were somehow destined to uncover some vast treasure that had been hidden at *Aquae Sulis* after it had been abandoned in the Medieval age. Benny and Fliss, on the other hand, were less enthusiastic.

The less their research revealed about the evidence of a treasure, the less they were inclined to believe it existed.

The very fact that there were almost no recorded uses of a curse tablet after the Roman Empire fell was, according to Fliss, all the more reason to think that their tablet wasn't even real. Perhaps it had been thrown into the pool by a student of Middle English at some point in the much more recent past, she suggested. Or, if it was written in the twelfth century, just an example used to give locals an idea of the practices that had come before. That seemed less likely; there was no evidence that people from that time period were particularly interested in local history, but it was a possibility.

Ari, on the other hand, saw the lack of evidence as a sign that someone had simply hidden it well.

'They say so in the tablet itself,' he had argued. '*-never be found.*' Whatever "it" is or was.'

Fliss and Benny had exchanged concerned glances which hadn't gone unnoticed by Ari.

It was his belief that Benny had given Fliss a similar pep talk to the one he had given Ari in the library. That Fliss should think about why he – Ari - was really there. Perhaps her uncle had, all along, been trying to dissuade them from going to *Aquae Sulis* at all, hoping the trip he had organised would be abandoned.

As a consequence, their stay in Benny's house together had grown to be more than a little tense.

The deeper Fliss fell into her research and began to adopt a more realistic outlook at the possibility of treasure to be found, in equal measure, Ari had clung to his notion that there *was* something to be found, and that he would keep looking until he found what it was. No matter how much he reminded her that she had reversed her position completely in just a few short days, she was intractable, and she simply reminded him that he had done the same.

There had been a series of arguments which usually ended in Benny wearily declaring he was going to bed, and Fliss would depart too, leaving Ari to stew alone in the massive dining room with Percival and Cicero.

He had found he had more stimulating conversations with the bird and cat than he did with the people in the house.

The arguments about the existence of a treasure had devolved into disagreements about pretty much everything, not least the way they should approach their mission that evening.

So, as they sat waiting for their escort to pick them up and take them to *Aquae*, there was a frosty atmosphere between the three. Benny was evidently sick of the pair's constant bickering, the pair sick of each other, and a wholly rotten mood hung in the air, palpable in the quiet. Benny blew air from his massive cheeks.

'Ready?' he asked, glancing at the clock on his wall. Ten minutes to go. Both Ari and Fliss were reluctant to answer, but eventually Ari said,

'Ready for what? We're not doing anything.'

Benny closed his eyes, clearly regretting having broken the silence. Fliss shot him a look then picked up one of the books on the table, pretending to read.

'What?' Ari asked rhetorically, 'we're not,' he said idly, tapping a pen absent-mindedly on the table.

'Would you stop that?' Fliss snapped. Ari kept going and stared directly at her. 'You're a child,' she added.

'Yeah. Says the one who's afraid of the dark,' Ari retorted. Benny put his head in his hands.

'Good God, how many times do we have to have this bloody conversation?' Fliss asked, exasperated. 'I get that you want to go marauding round an English heritage site, I get that you think your "heightened" senses might uncover something that Ocean Pearl missed the last time, and Lord *knows* I get that you think this all a big waste of time.'

Ari snorted. 'You can say that again.'

'But as I - and Benny - have told you on countless occasions: IT. IS. NOT. WORTH. THE. RISK.' She stopped, and Ari could see she seemed genuinely quite upset. He stood and started to pace.

'If an opportunity presents itself, I'm going in,' Ari said flatly. This caused exactly the uproar he had expected.

Two days ago, he had suggested that the place they should be looking was in the Great Drain, near the picture of the Ocean Pearl agent he thought he had mortally wounded, where they could see the scaffolding behind the opening in the rock almost teasing them to come inside.

The more they read and researched about the site, about where Ocean Pearl had managed to find treasure, the more it seemed the only plausible place for them to find anything. And that scaffolding confirmed they had been looking for something, at some point.

'We saw that they had built something behind there,' Ari said. 'We know that was where the majority of any treasure that was there was discovered, and we *know* there's nothing more to find in that damn curse tablet exhibition!' he exclaimed.

'It's the only place we haven't looked! And tonight is the perfect opportunity to do so... Think what you like about my arrogance, but the fact remains that I *am* the only one who might actually be able to find something they missed!' Ari said. 'What are we going to find just by looking at the curse tablets again? We're risking getting caught by Ocean Pearl for no reason!' he exclaimed.

'Son,' Benny said, his voice filled with a mix of melancholy and exhaustion. 'All the evidence suggests that there is no treasure attached to this tablet. We have found nothing... not even a whisper of a rumour of a treasure buried here. No one is so adept at covering up that they leave no traces whatsoever-'

'We have a trace!' Ari said.

'No, we have something which *might* be half of a trace. And we don't know what it might be half of a trace of a clue to finding. Fliss is right. I've been clear about this all along. You're only going into the Drain if the risk seemed worth it. I want to pull a fast one on Ocean Pearl as much as you do, Ari, but we can't do it if you're in prison because Ocean Pearl has caught you and exposed your fakes. Which, incidentally, I'm surprised they haven't done already.'

'And so,' Benny added in a tone of finality. 'You're not risking anything. Ocean Pearl won't be expecting you to arrive at *Aquae Sulis* at midnight, but if you break into their Drain and they find out, they'll intercept you tomorrow. And as it stands,' he said, looking at Ari in a way that reminded him of his father, 'there's nothing worth taking any risks for. I said I would help, but this tour will only go ahead if you give me my word that you will not engage in anything other than what we have discussed already. If not, I will call it off.' He picked up his phone, as if to ask whether he needed to make a phone call.

Ari sighed deeply and gave Fliss one more imploring look. She didn't avert her eyes from Percival.

'Fine,' he said, moodily. 'You have my word.'

'Good,' Benny said. 'Because your chaperone is here.'

Once more, Ari's thoughts lingered on the face of the Ocean Pearl agent in the portrait near the Drain.

***

Chapter eighteen

Aquae Sulis was eerie at night.

It didn't look any different from the outside particularly, but Ari couldn't shake the feeling that despite being empty, it felt oddly full. Benny's "chaperone" was a greasy-haired teenager called Kenny, who was employed at *Aquae Sulis* and, evidently, wasn't particularly bothered whether he kept his job or not.

Kenny had the kind of unhealthy look that some teens get when they spend too long indoors, pale as a sheet and thin as a rake. He didn't have his work uniform on as he "didn't have one washed in time," and so instead wore an oversized black Greenday hoodie with the words "*Bullet in a Bible*" splashed tastelessly in bright red across the front.

Fliss wore a merino icebreaker so as to disguise her face from the cameras, but was otherwise dressed identically to Ari; black tracksuits and boots. They must have looked as though they were there to rob the place, but Ari had thought that if Ocean Pearl showed up, they could try the same trick as last time; turn the lights off and make a quick escape.

They had studied the blueprint of *Aquae* in considerable detail and knew all the quickest routes to get back to the atrium which, according to Kenny, was the only way out.

Not strictly true, Ari thought, his mind once again on the Great Drain, which he knew led to the river Avon.

Uncle Benny wasn't going with them on the tour. His size and general inability to move made him a liability, but *Aquae Sulis* had a live camera feed on its website that allowed visitors to watch the goings-on at the site, which Benny could follow and radio ahead to Ari and Fliss if Ocean Pearl showed up, assuming Ari didn't hear them.

The live feed was probably an older one having been installed in the early days of Ocean Pearl's activity at *Aquae*, when there was actually something to find. Ari had also managed to get hold of some old radio equipment that had once been used by a theatre company, and they had tested out its range when Ari had gone to buy the clothing. The sound quality was patchy at best, and the earpieces were clunky and quite obvious, but it would have to do.

Kenny didn't have much to say once he had let them into the atrium, other than they weren't allowed to actually get in the water of any of the baths, and that they should stay inside the museum as the alarm was still activated in the courtyard. Ari couldn't help but think of the teenager in a similar way to that of a substitute teacher.

Ari and Fliss shrugged at one another, then headed straight to the museum exhibition containing the other curse tablets, but not before asking Kenny if they could have the keys to the display cabinets, to "get a proper look," as Ari had put it. The lad handed them over without blinking, and Ari was again struck by the fact that Ocean Pearl really must have lost all faith in *Aquae Sulis* to have employed someone like him. Ari looked at the keys, each bore a small engraved *laburum* and a small tag that read "Curses".

The Nicander Chronicles: *Of past and present*

The distinctive smell of the water from the *thermae* returned, and Ari soon found himself face-to-face with the *desfixionis* – the curse tablets.

'Open the cabinets then, let's have a look. But if we don't find anything, we're leaving,' she said, nodding at the camera in the ceiling corner. 'They know we're here,' she added in a cautionary tone.

He didn't respond, but silently followed her instruction, using the small key to open the cabinets dotted around the room, exposing the ancient *tabulae* to the elements.

'You start over there,' he said, sending Fliss to the opposite side of the room in the hope that some physical distance would prevent them from arguing.

Ari started his investigations and set about focusing his vision on each tablet at his end. Nothing new in particular revealed itself. One example, written in the third person, read:

> *Docimedis has lost two gloves and asks that the thief responsible should lose their minds and eyes in the goddess' temple.*

But even in his heightened field of view, all Ari saw were those words. He could see the marks where the inscriber had missed with his stone slightly and could make out the whole message where another might only be able to see it in part given how it had faded, but nothing told him that it was in any way related to their mysterious Middle English tablet. He moved on to the next, some of which was missing:

> ...so long as someone, whether slave or free, keeps silent or knows anything about it, he...

...may be accursed in blood, and eyes and every limb and even have all intestines...

...quite eaten away if he has stolen the ring or been privy...

Ari literally rolled his eyes.

Fliss was poking about in one of the other cabinets, but he could see she wasn't fully invested. She was drawing out the evening to appease him, and clearly wanted to leave before Ocean Pearl showed up. She must have noticed him watching her, because in that moment she bent over in fake concentration, pretending to study something. She even made an audible "hmm," sound before moving on to the next.

Ari couldn't contain himself any longer.

'This is pointless,' he snapped. Fliss didn't answer, but he jumped when Benny said,

'Keep looking,' in his ear, having almost forgotten that Fliss' uncle was on the other end of the radio.

He sighed and wondered about some of the other displays, opening them lazily and re-reading the inscriptions. At one point, he stuck his fingers up to the CCTV cameras and heard Benny chortle.

'What are you two up to?' Fliss said as she spun on her heel, unamused.

'Nothing, chill,' Ari responded.

She went back to her work with a harumph. After not much time at all, they had looked through all of the cabinets.

They stood, hands on hips, looking around the room as though something obvious would present itself to them. It struck Ari that Fliss looked fairly exhausted. Ari didn't doubt for a second that his own appearance was similarly haggard. He smoothed his hair back across his head.

'There's nothing here,' she said, stating the obvious. Ari rubbed his eyes with his hands.

'I know what you're going to suggest, but we agreed,' she warned, reading his mind. In between buying clothes and radio equipment, he had been reading up about Ocean Pearl and their excavation techniques. In some of Benny's choicier texts, he discovered that the company had found some fairly extraordinary places. Cities thought long lost, cave networks that previously only existed in fantasy, entire *islands* sunk under oceans, inlets and peninsulas broken away from the mainland, hanging waterfalls and hidden vaults.

As he had read, annoyingly, he was impressed. But, it had occurred to him that not *all* those finds could have been stolen from other people, and indeed he was correct. Ocean Pearl had made a lot of their Finds employing a technology known as remote-sensing, which Ari's surprise, was a fairly simple but quite ingenious practice that involved overlaying a series of satellite images on top of one another to get the read of a landscape.

Although the technique had clearly served them well, Ari thought it simply couldn't have been the case that it was infallible, especially in the nineties the last time Ocean Pearl had been here. Perhaps the Great Drain underneath *Aquae Sulis* had been "remote sensed" multiple times and nothing had ever shown on their scans, and so in the absence of a vaster treasure hidden here than what they had already found they had simply neglected to do further digging.

And he was desperate to get down there to find out.

He hadn't shared his research with Benny and Fliss, largely because he knew it would only serve their argument: if Ocean Pearl had remote-sensed the site and found nothing, then there was nothing to find. Ari wondered whether Benny had ever read that particular article himself, but was drawn back to reality when Fliss said:

'I think we should just go-'

'There's someone here!' Benny said suddenly. The pair froze in horror, staring at each other. An eternity of silence passed until Benny spoke again,

'Oh boy, this isn't good. Someone has entered the atrium and sent Kenny home.'

'What does he look like?!' Ari and Fliss asked in unison. Benny described a man in his mid-thirties, clean-shaven, well-dressed with a nasty-looking expression, wearing a funny, black suit.

'Shit,' Ari muttered.

'The man from the train?' she asked quietly.

'Or Prince,' he said. 'Either way, we're in trouble now.' They had discussed this scenario at length and had decided that Benny to call the police and raise a concern for their safety.

In the meantime, Ari and Fliss shouldn't have too much of a problem in hiding somewhere in the museum, as long as they turned the lights down to avoid the CCTV.

Although, as Ari had reflected, they shouldn't lose sight of the fact that this was Ocean Pearl's site, and they had home-field advantage. With a look that implied they had nothing to lose, Fliss headed over to where a control panel - that Ari had scouted in the previous days - was affixed to the wall.

She pulled it open and looked at the switches. The label next to the large one in the centre read "Museum Lighting," and she guessed it was likely to have the most effect. With a shrug, she flicked the switch.

Both she and Ari jumped out of their skin when the alarm started blaring and the door back to the atrium slammed shut. The lights did go off, but they were replaced with the emergency low lights, which flashed on and off slowly, intermittently casting their surroundings in a reddish hue.

'What did you do?!' Ari screamed over the sound of the alarm, furious.

'I just hit the lights!' she shouted back, visibly confused. The sound of her voice against the alarm hit Ari's heightened hearing like the bang of a bass drum, and he recoiled in pain at the sound.

'DON'T SHOUT!' he yelled at her. She held her hands up apologetically. Ari stood planted for a moment, as though he were between two decisions. The atrium door did not look as though it would reopen easily. He grabbed Fliss' hand.

'Come on!' he said.

'Where are we going?!' she asked. He pulled the earpiece out of his ear, not wanting Benny to interrupt him.

'There are two ways out of here!' he yelled.

***

Chapter nineteen

Alarm blaring, heart soaring, sweat dripping, Ari dragged Fliss from the *tabula* exhibit in the museum, sprinting as quickly as he could. *Aquae Sulis* was by no means large, but it was a warren of small corridors, sharp twists and turns.

'This was a mistake!' Fliss screamed between breaths. Ari ignored her and kept running until they came to a small hallway. To the right, a closed door that blocked a path back to the exit. It seemed as though the security system was putting *Aquae Sulis* into some kind of lockdown.

To the left, another closed door, this one much more heavy-duty; it usually would have led outside to the Great Bath which, if anywhere, is where an intruder would probably have entered, and Ari remembered Kenny telling them not to go outside.

Directly in front was a corridor flanked by windows on either side. Outside to the right, a view of the Sacred Spring and entrance to the overspill pipe. And the Great Drain. Fliss stopped at the entrance to the corridor, as though it were a line she was unwilling to cross.

'Absolutely not!' she shouted over the sound of the alarm. 'I'm not going into the Great Drain!'

Ari grimaced.

'We've no choice, Fliss!' he yelled back. 'All the doors have closed... Look out there!' he said, pointing through the window on the left. Fliss took a few steps forward, edging closer, her snood pulled high around her mouth and nose, her face still covered.

For Ari, it was easy to see. The window was grimy, and the lights were low, but when he focused on the scene through the window, his pupils dilated wide and let him view the Great Bath outside. And its occupants. Fliss had to get right up close and press her face up to the glass. She recoiled.

'It's Prince!' she said. 'He's fighting someone!'

Ari remained focused on the scene outside; he saw the dimly lit pool flanked on all sides by ancient columns, he saw the benches that ran around all four sides and the uneven stones made up of centuries of history.

And he also saw Ondrej.

His old boss and mentor was unmistakable; silvery hair, bomber jacket, *Bowie knife*.

It was the first sight Ari had had of his old boss since Merchant's Lodge, and he felt an odd sense of *déjà vu*, Ondrej fighting Ocean Pearl agents now as he had been then. A pang of guilt crossed his chest as he saw that Ondrej's left eye seemed to be permanently closed.

In his mind, he pictured the Ocean Pearl agent from the portrait straddling Ondrej, raining down blows, showing no sign of stopping. Ari instinctively reached for his Bowie knife. It wasn't there.

'Who is that?!' Fliss asked, breaking Ari's reverie. He didn't look away from the window. Ondrej seemed to be locked in battle with Prince, fighting fiercely. The Bluebirds boss was a skilled martial artist having mastered multiple disciplines, but Prince had the technological advantage. Those wetsuits they wore seemed to be padded, and he was able to eat the blows that Ondrej aimed at his stomach and kidneys unharmed, while returning with punches of his own.

There was another skirmish between a female Ocean Pearl agent, or so he assumed, and two of Ondrej's Bluebird gang members, but it didn't seem like it was going to last much longer. She was clearly superior to the pair of street brawlers, and she was tying them in knots. Ari vaguely recognised the men from his time running with the Bluebirds, but he couldn't place their names.

He looked at Fliss with a grave expression.

'Who is it?!' she shouted again.

'Someone we don't want to see,' Ari said. Fliss looked at him with an intensity that made him blush.

'Ondrej?!' she asked.

Ari nodded, then pressed his face back to the glass, a move he regretted almost immediately, as he and Ondrej locked gaze for a split second across the Great Bath.

'Shit!' Ari screamed. 'They've seen me! Fliss, *come on,*' he urged. 'It's the only way out!'

The split was visible on her face, clearly torn between the plan she absolutely did not wish to execute and one she thought would probably lead nowhere. Still, her gaze lingered on the door through which they had arrived at the corridor.

'There's no point!' Ari shouted, sensing her thinking. 'If you go back up there, the doors are locked, and they'll only open when Prince gets this system lockdown reversed! By which point it'll be too late; he'll be in here with us!'

Still, she hesitated. She was clearly dead set against entering the Great Drain, but Ari wasn't going to wait any longer. If the door to the Great Bath opened, he knew that Prince, Ondrej and the rest of them would be shortly behind.

'For God's *sake*, Ari!' she said.

He took that to mean she was on board and set off down the corridor, sprinting as quickly as he could. He glanced over his shoulder and saw Fliss a pace behind him, her brow furrowed and set straight ahead, concentrating. They rounded a corner which led to another corridor, then another, and eventually brought them all the way to the entrance to the Great Drain.

Ari nearly ran headfirst into the large, grated shutter that had been brought down in front of its entrance. Clearly it too was part of the lockdown.

He and Fliss stood with their hands on their knees, breathing hard from the running, the alarm still beating into his head like a steel-drum band.

'Great plan!' she said.

'Yeah, sarcasm will save us!' he screamed back.

'What now?' she asked. He recovered his breath and tried to focus on various aspects of his surroundings to see if he could establish a way of opening the gate. He knew it was futile. The security system was controlled from the central desk at the atrium - Kenny had told them as much - and there was no way of accessing it.

Even if there were, Benny had already informed them that there was an Ocean Pearl man covering that exit.

Their other option was to wait for the alarm to stop, at which point the shutter would presumably open. But Ari had a gnawing feeling that if they did that, Prince would somehow find a way to leave the grill over the Drain entrance closed. Cover all exits.

He saw only one possibility.

He stared at the fire extinguisher attached to the wall for a long moment. Fliss gave him a deploring look, but he had made up his mind. In an instant, he turned and pulled the extinguisher from the wall. It was old and surprisingly heavy.

'Wait!' she shouted. Too late.

Ari had heaved the extinguisher over his shoulder and launched it like a shot-put. It crashed through the window sending shards of glass flying outwards, which landed in the water of the Sacred Spring outside with a splash. Somehow, the noise of the alarm doubled in its intensity, and it seemed now to be bashing against Ari's very soul. The cold air from the night outside blasted through the window, whipping him like an icy lasso.

The extinguisher had left a fair-sized hole in the window. He kicked through a few other shards of glass to be sure, motioning to Fliss to do the same. His sweat turned cold, and he had ripped the sleeve of his black shell suit on the glass as they worked. A trickle of blood ran down his arm.

When they were done, the pane stood completely empty, and Ari nodded at Fliss, whose entire expression screamed unwillingness. Ari steeled himself as he struck a runner's pose, as though he were on the starting block. He put his head down near his left knee and focused on his breathing for a moment.

He breathed deeply. Somewhere, in the depths of the background noise, he managed to make out the gentle tick of Fliss' beating heart. It was fast, same as his own, but he focused on it hard, until eventually, the blaring of the alarm was no more, entircly replaced by a steady thud. The sound consumed him, and the fear he clung to evaporated.

Thud. Thud. Thud.

He opened his eyes, took three paces and leapt.

When he hit the water, he had forgotten it would be warm. Somehow, it embraced him, as though he were a welcome guest. He knew where the pipe that carried water from the Sacred Spring to the Great Drain was from having studied the plan of *Aquae* in great detail, but he also felt as though he were being pulled toward it, which made sense. It was a functioning Drain, after all.

He suspected he wasn't the first person to have evaded capture or death in these waters, and that many people of Roman Britain had done the same. Some, perhaps, with the same idea as him: sneak in overnight to plunder treasures lost to the Great Drain then wash up on the riverbank and escape, unseen. *Wonder how many of them died,* he thought as he bobbed in the water waiting for Fliss.

She stood in the window looking down at the water which changed from red to black, red to black as the light of the alarm flickered on and off.

'Come on!' he called out. She seemed to visibly fix in place.

'I'm not going down there, Ari!' she called back. 'I told you already!'

Ari was treading water and having to swim against the swell from the Drain, which gently tugged at his ankles. He knew if he stopped resisting, he would float toward its entrance.

'Don't be an idiot!' he called back. 'Get in!'

But Fliss had already stepped away from the window. She shot him an apologetic look, then walked away at a brisk pace, back in the direction from which they had arrived.

'Fine!' he called after her as she disappeared. 'Fine! Have it your own way!' he shouted.

He dove underwater.

He stayed there for a moment and allowed himself to calm. When he popped back up, Fliss was still gone. *Shit*.

He hadn't meant to shout at her. He was in two minds about whether to go back up and get her. As they had discussed, he was Prince's target, not her, and despite her and Benny's remonstrations, he still believed he was the best chance they had of finding something in the baths. But he resolved himself, muttered an apology to the heavens, and then dove back under.

It was impossible to see. Even when he tried to focus. The water was clean - he could smell the chlorine - but it was murky. He swam a few metres toward where he knew the entrance to the pipe that led to the Great Drain was. He popped up for air and glanced back at the window for a second time, secretly hoping Fliss would be back, ready to join him.

When she wasn't, he turned and reached down near his thighs, running his hand along the wall. Where it broke, he could feel a light pull as water was swept through a grill, which was mercifully just large enough for him to slip through. He took the deepest breath he could muster, put his whole body underneath the warm water, and disappeared into the pipe.

***

Chapter twenty

Ari landed with a grunt.

He had travelled a fair distance, underestimating the length of the pipe. It was small and reminded him a little of a water slide at a water park he had visited as a child, but full of water. He knew roughly how long it was based on the size of *Aquae Sulis* and where it was leading him, but it had been difficult to judge while he was actually sliding.

Of course, the pipe he had used wasn't really part of the Great Drain at all. Ocean Pearl had installed a much newer system, one less prone to collapse that had allowed them to excavate the Great Drain without the water from the *thermae*. That had shown up in the newer plans of the structure, and he found himself extremely thankful for the time they had spent studying the floor plan.

When he opened his eyes, it was dark. Pitch black, in fact. He could tell by the white lines outlining his surroundings that were almost phosphorous, and the deep, navy backdrop seemed ebony, offering him a particularly clear view. Paradoxically, the darker his environment, the better he could see. He rubbed the water from his eyes and ran his hand through his warm hair.

Gingerly, he got to his feet.

The water from the pipe behind him continued to pour out at some velocity. In front of him, there was a large, crescent-shaped archway. The water ran through it and off to the left, which must have been the way to the river. He knew there was another outlet built into the Drain a little further down, and he focused on the different sounds he could hear until he eventually picked out the distant running water. That, however, was not where he was headed. He entered the main body of the Great Drain and turned right, toward the old entrance, where forty feet above he had been stood on the surface with Fliss not five minutes previously.

The tunnel was cramped and tight, and in parts, he had to turn his body to squeeze through the slim gap between the brick archways. On more than one occasion, he stumbled on a loose piece of brick or stone, invisible even to him underneath the slow-moving, shallow trickle of water that flowed toward him.

The incline was only very slight as opposed to the drain he had just slid down, and he guessed the sheer length of this waterway didn't call for a particularly steep gradient. Above his head, the tunnel was perhaps twice the height of his six feet, but it grew taller the further he progressed.

Eventually, he reached the head of the Great Drain. By this point, the tunnel had opened out into a wide, expansive space, and he had to step stepping up onto a raised stone-circle platform.

It had become slightly lighter as he approached, which he could tell by the change in his vision, and he found himself face-to-face with a huge wall, which was covered in the scaffolding they had previously seen from the other side. Forty feet above him, he could see the entrance to the Drain at the top, the source of the weak light.

Ari found that he was surprisingly calm, perhaps comforted by the fact that he knew the Drain was damned, and that the water level would not rise higher than the few inches it reached now. He listened to the echoey trickle that emanated around him for a moment and breathed in deeply. The serenity of the space contrasted starkly with the blaring alarm and panicked escape he had just endured.

The warren of scaffolding fixed to the massive wall before him climbed like an ivy trellis all the way to the top, and as he stood in the middle of the stone circle, craning his neck upwards, he followed each level of scaffold to try to work out why the hell it was there. *Whatever the reason,* Ari thought. *They didn't build it for nothing.*

To Ari's mind, it was more evidence of there being something further to find, something missed by Ocean Pearl. More evidence that surely would not have brought Fliss and Benny around to his way of thinking.

His thoughts turned to Fliss for a moment, and he wondered what had happened to her, and why she had been so desperate not to enter the Drain. He felt as fine as it was possible to feel in his current circumstances, and he was sure she would have been too. He worried for her but steeled himself.

She had made her decision, and all he could do now was hope that she had made it out without being intercepted, although he was unsure how that could have been possible; the entrance back to the atrium was presumably still blocked when she had left, and as soon as the alarms had stopped James Prince and Ondrej would have found their way through.

And they would spare no time in hunting her down.

Best hurry this up, Ari thought to himself. His vision tracked across the second level of the scaffold from left to right as he tried to read the wall behind, looking for something that explained why Ocean Pearl had built here. Nothing. He reached the end, then followed the trail up to the third, and kept going, back and forth over each level, until he had scanned nearly half of the wall.

He was beginning to abandon hope when, *wait.*

He looked back down.

His focused vision worked just well in the dark as it did in the daylight, it just looked different. It had taken him a little practice to get good at discerning what sometimes looked like nothing more than a big ball of white lines, but he had eventually learned to recognise different shapes. Once he had done that, he had been able to pick out distinct shapes, then he had practised that skill until he could see everything there was to see during the day.

And now, he saw the shape of a small opening in the rock, tucked away in the far corner of the ninth level of the scaffolding. Man-made, but haphazard. And submerged in darkness. Whoever had put it there had done so to avoid it being seen.

Ari smiled triumphantly.

He made short work of the climb, his nimble fingers pulling his body weight up the cold scaffold poles with relative ease. He landed on the eighth platform, just one below where he needed to be, and muttered a silent thanks to his years in the gym.

He jumped and hooked his legs up over the bar, then hung for a moment, clinging to the scaffold like a sloth might hang from a branch. He looked to his right, down the throat of the Great Drain, then set his sights on the underneath of the wooden plank in front of him, hoisted himself up and crouched low on the ninth platform.

He was right.

At the end of the scaffold was a manmade passageway, the entrance to which formed a hole that was smaller than it had seemed from afar. He walked to it, then had to crawl to get through the opening.

When he emerged, he stood in a small, stone tunnel. He pressed his hands against one side of the brick wall and edged forward, creeping for a short distance. The tunnel narrowed to the point that he had to turn on his side in order to squeeze through, but eventually, it opened into a bigger space.

He stepped through into the cavern and stretched his arms and back as he took in his surroundings. The "room," if it could be described as such, was large, and red brick, the same colour as the walls of the Great Drain. Ari could see from their pristine white outlines that these bricks were much better preserved than the ones in the Drain itself, presumably sheltered from the water entirely. Ari reasoned that it must have been built at the same time as the Drain, though, as Ari couldn't fathom a reason why anyone would go in and add it at a later date.

The longer he stood, the more absurd it seemed. *Who builds a secret room in a sewage pipe?* Ari thought to himself.

He could also see on the walls that there were tiny inscriptions dotted neatly around, all at the same level, and when he focused his vision, he could see that there were sections where the dirt had been disturbed, as though something had sat there for an extraordinarily long time.

Ari paced around and read a few of the inscriptions. The more he looked, the more he saw, and he slowly realised that the wall was covered in scratchings, each of which chronicled a different artefact that had once stood there. *A treasure vault,* Ari thought to himself. He punched the air in celebration, unseen by anyone save the darkness.

Why did Ocean Pearl never publicise this?!

He felt vindicated in as much as he had found something, and something none of the others could, but as he studied the strange inscriptions, he realised that the vault must have been abandoned for some time.

"It was always thought that they had missed something," Ari heard Benny's words a few days previously.

Well, they hadn't missed this room.

A chill washed over Ari all of a sudden, and he realised his teeth were chattering. For the first time since he had come into the Great Drain, he was aware that he was sopping wet. He ran his fingers through his hair and found his mind wandering again to the surface, Fliss and the Ocean Pearl agents.

He resolved to look more quickly, although he wasn't exactly sure what he was looking for. At first glance, the place had been thoroughly gutted and was now little more than a cave. None of the walls gave anything away. He wondered for a moment whether he shouldn't just turn around and get out of there altogether, but somehow he felt obligated to stay.

Not so that Fliss and Benny would be happy, more so that he could say "I told you so," which, he reflected, probably wasn't a good attitude.

Nevertheless, he was determined.

He needed a different method of exploration.

Dotted around the room were desks with drawings of *Aquae Sulis* and equipment that bore the words "PearlTECH," although some of it was clearly old.

There were laptops there from the early noughties, models that Ari was fairly convinced he had used when he was in secondary school. Otherwise, there were a few folders filled with invoices, logs of some of the items found and catalogued by Ocean Pearl and a collection of other, unbranded equipment.

Drilling equipment.

He sidled over to one of the desks and began flicking through some papers that sat upon it, reading the white-outlined words in the darkness, looking for a clue as to how the room was used.

One file was simply titled: *Aquae Sulis*, and the case handler was listed as James Prince. Ari's heart skipped a beat. *No wonder he followed us here,* Ari thought, but he shrugged the coincidence off and opened the folder, which immediately showed him a 3D map of *Aquae Sulis,* with the treasure room he was currently in marked out in red biro.

He suspected it was an image captured using remote sensing technology, and closed his eyes as he tried to imagine where the room he currently occupied was situated. On the map, it showed him as underneath the Temple of Sulis, the room where the *Haruspex* stone and head of *Sulis Minerva* bookended the room above.

He flicked through a few more pages until he found an inventory, which showed that the room was definitely full when they found it. Heaped with the treasure given to the goddess *Sulis Minerva* in exchange for exacting a curse, in fact. Ari read on and came to a chapter which hypothesised about the room's purpose.

Ocean Pearl seemed to think that, much like the Great Drain itself, the room was something of an overspill. A place where, when the Temple became too crowded with offerings, the *Haruspex* priest would have the treasure moved underground.

Would it have added to *Sulis Minerva's* veneer of divinity, if she was able to make treasure disappear overnight, as if she had taken it from whoever had left it? Perhaps.

Maybe it was a sign that a curse had been carried out, a way for the Temple to continue to receive offerings. In fact, Ari reasoned, the fact that the room was housed at the end of a tunnel was probably specifically in order to allow it to be situated underneath the Temple, for that very purpose. This meant there must be another passage through which the offerings could be passed, and that passage must lead to the surface.

He put the file down and studied the ceiling, frowning hard as he focused on every inch of its small surface.

Ari's mind turned to the inscription on the tablet.

"Never be found."

If whoever wrote those words wanted something hidden, this seemed as fair a hiding place as any. But then, if you *truly* wanted to hide something, Ari thought, this room might have been known by a fair number of people, was it possible that there was somewhere else?

If discovered, the illusion would have been broken, and the temple might have lost its primary source of income.

He moved back to the desk and picked up the 3D image once more, visualising the layout of *Aquae Sulis* above him in an attempt to judge how far the little tunnel he had walked through to get to the abandoned treasure room had taken him. He suspected he was quite close to the front of the Temple, and so if there was anything else to be found, it would surely be on the back wall.

But when he looked, save the markings left by the ancient Romans who had marked receiving the offerings, he was certain there was nothing there.

Alone, in the dark, cold and shivering, Ari closed his eyes and began to whistle.

Not any tune in particular, just a high-pitched, constant whistle, that he modulated to be louder and quieter as he began to pace up and down in the room, stopping every so often to listen, then resuming.

Echolocation was a talent usually reserved for dolphins, bats and selected other animals, but it was something Ari had learned - and adapted - in the years since he and Fliss had parted.

Much like echolocation, as he whistled he listened to the sound that came back, which helped him to determine objects in his immediate surroundings. Perhaps not very useful for someone with heightened vision that can see in the dark, but Ari had taken the skill a step further. He had learned that if he changed the pitch of the whistle, the frequency of the sound that came back to him gave him an impression of the depth of the space *behind* the object.

Ari couldn't see through walls, but he could get a damn good sense of what might lay past one if he had a few moments of quiet. The first time he had tried it, in his apartment, the overwhelming noise that reverberated had caused him to vomit. Bats, he had researched, were able to turn off their "middle ear" before they echolocate to protect themselves from the volume of the sound, which was a luxury not extended to Ari by his human physiology.

It had taken him some time to hone this craft and be able to focus on the sound to a degree that allowed him to listen without being overwhelmed.

The picture that Ari picked up from behind the wall in front of him now was one of solid rock, with the exception of a small fissure centre-left of middle. He raised an eyebrow.

It could be another tunnel, like the one that had led him to this room, or it could just be a natural gap caused by the geothermal process that pumped water into *Aquae Sulis.*

Only one way to find out, he told himself. He cast an eye over the objects that lay strewn across the cave. There were lots of tools that probably would have served if he had more time, but lying underneath a table, half covered in tarpaulin, he recognised the corkscrew of an auger drill.

It was an older model, but the word PearlTECH was clearly visible along the edge.

He picked it up and tested it. Ocean Pearl had, for all their faults, done some incredible work in advancing archaeological technology far past its means; as the auger vibrated in his hands causing his whole body to shake, Ari realised it wasn't connected to a power source. He frowned and turned the drill over in his hands, which was about the same size as a cricket bat, and felt along the edge for a battery. Nothing.

He didn't question it for long, offering the drill to the wall where the fissure lay. More than likely, this type of work should usually be carried out with a hard hat and steel-capped boots, but he would have to make do with his sopping wet tracksuit and Chelsea boots. After a solid ten minutes of work, Ari had managed to gouge a hole just small enough to look through.

Often, Ari forgot that he was in total darkness, and he reflected that if he had come down here without his heightened senses, he would never have made this discovery.

What he saw through the hole caused his heart rate to quicken. His eyes widened, and he immediately picked the auger back up and began drilling once more.

The integrity of the rock was damaged, the hole seemed to widen more quickly, and with every passing second Ari made more headway. He was concerned about the noise he was making but decided that he didn't have much choice. If an Ocean Pearl agent followed him into the Great Drain, they would know where he was heading anyway. A few more minutes passed as he drilled hard into the rock face, and eventually, he threw the auger aside and stood back to admire his handiwork.

He had created an opening just wide enough to crawl through.

The seam that had existed between the fissure and the outer wall had proved completely imperceptible to Ari, and yet he had just drilled through into another, smaller tunnel.

He wondered whether he hadn't just found the second clue that there had been activity at *Aquae Sulis* in the medieval ages.

That type of work would have required a skilled hand, and he was quite sure that even the master builders of the Roman Empire, famed for their ability though they were, wouldn't have been able to reseal a misshapen hole to the extent that it had lain unnoticed for further fifteen hundred years.

He took a deep breath and squeezed himself through the new opening, and only when he looked back, did he realise that the tunnel had been sealed from the inside. It had been put back in brick-by-brick, then sealed with cement, and the outside seam smoothed over with a plaster of some kind.

In that moment, Ari suddenly felt quite detached from his body. His wet clothes clung to his skin, but he didn't feel their uncomfortableness. He had uncovered an ancient tunnel, but he felt no excitement.

All he could think of was the person who had worked on sealing the chamber from the inside, brick-by-brick, who must have known they were trapping themselves inside.

The image of the Merchant's Lodge agent in the portrait swam in his mind's eye.

***

Chapter twenty-one

Ari realised fairly quickly why Ocean Pearl hadn't managed to find the chamber.

To his surprise, the hole in the wall had led him up a tiny set of stairs which spiralled in on themselves, leading to a new room, which he thought probably sat atop the larger treasure room underneath. This new room was extremely small, and he suspected that the hole in its ceiling would have led him out into part of the temple of *Sulis Minerva* currently buried beneath the modern road outside the museum.

He also suspected that the remote sensing technology Ocean Pearl used to determine the blueprint of a structure had simply overlooked this middle space, given the larger space directly below it, and the lack of physical evidence of a door must have caused them not to look any further.

Now, Ari stood in a room which he presumed hadn't been entered since its entrance was bricked in at the fall of the Roman Empire.

Despite its miniature size, each wall of the room was adorned with high shelves, some of which had dusty boxes on them but, in general, were empty. Ari could see the white outline of a trap door on the ceiling which led up to the surface, and there were also the remnants of an old pulley system, much of which had since fallen to the floor. A thick rope lay curled at Ari's feet like a large snake, and a rudimentary container used to haul items was broken in half, the other dangling precariously from a shelf above him.

So the person inside didn't die in here, he realised.

He bent down and inspected the half-box on the floor. *Empty.* He looked above him. The room was cramped enough that he could lift his arms above his head, but little else. He wanted to inspect the other half of the box, but couldn't quite reach it. He was maybe six inches away. He put his foot on the lowest shelf and tested whether it would take his weight which, incredibly, it did. He hopped slightly and, in doing so, managed to bat the box off the shelf, which fell to the floor with a crack - as did Ari.

The shelf gave out beneath him, and he landed painfully in a heap, taking his body weight on his left wrist. He yelped, then clutched at it and sucked air in through his teeth, an agonising grimace pasted across his face. Tears formed in his eyes which he swatted away, then thought about standing. He removed some of the debris that lay around him with his good arm and, from the other half of the wooden box, something came loose.

In complete darkness, he watched its white outline fall to the floor and land softly on the sandy floor. Immediately he scooped it up. It had writing on it.

Will no one rid me of this turbulent priest? Sulis-

Beneath, where the signature was, the letters *H*, a gap where it was broken, and a *Y*. Ari could scarcely believe it. The missing half of Fliss' tablet.

The pain from his wrist momentarily forgotten, he celebrated silently, punching the air, then filled in the full message with the new parts from memory:

Will no one rid me of this turbulent priest? Sulis, let it never be found. Henry.

At that moment, a loud boom echoed around the chamber. Some loose dust fell from the ceiling, and the shelving rattled menacingly.

Startled, Ari jammed the newly-discovered half of the tablet into the soggy inside pocket of his black tracksuit jacket. He swore out loud, then stood up with some difficulty, trying not to hold his weight on his wrist. He strained and focused his hearing.

In the distance, he heard two Ocean Pearl agents making their way into the Great Drain, and realised that the time he had to enjoy his discovery was over.

'This place is weird,' Ari heard a heavily-accented woman's voice say, presumably the same person Ari and Fliss had seen fighting outside the door with Prince earlier on. Ari gathered that the melee was over, and seemingly – somehow – the agents had come out on top.

'Yeah, well you know what? Weird is our speciality, so just get down there,' he heard the other respond.

James Prince.

'Who *were* those guys?' Aurora asked.

'Old friends of Ocean Pearl that we are trying to leave behind. Dangerous and bloodthirsty men. I don't know how or why they're tangled up in this, but we need to get moving before they figure out how to get inside,' James Prince said.

'Fine. How do we even know this "Marius" is down here?' the woman asked.

'There's no other way out. And this is where we found most of our treasure. If he's here looking for something, he's either in the treasure vault or he's already left it. Now come on!' Ari heard James Prince respond.

I need to move, Ari thought to himself.

He fancied himself to escape from a one-on-one situation against Prince - especially in the dark - as he had done before, but not with a sprained wrist. He didn't think he would have much choice but to try to walk down the Great Drain to wherever it led. He wouldn't be able to get back up the pipe he had slid down earlier, and the route back to the surface via the scaffolding was blocked by the Ocean Pearl agents who were now descending.

He gave the room a final sweep, surveying the white outlines of the shelving for a final time, knowing that the next people to see its contents would likely be Ocean Pearl. It pained him to have to leave behind whatever treasures lay in the other containers, but was consoled by the fact that he had achieved what he had set out to.

He squeezed back down the narrow passageway into the other, larger room, desperately trying to stay quiet so as to avoid alerting James Prince and his accomplice to his presence. He stopped for a moment, alone in the darkness, and listened to the drip of the tunnel. From what he could hear, he guessed that the agents were on the level above, which would lead them to the tunnel and the room he now occupied. He picked up the pace and crept back along the passageway.

When he reached the end of the scaffold platform, he looked above him. He saw the boots of the agents gliding above him, the illumination of a flashlight or head torch sprawled in front of them. Ari steeled himself and skipped across to the ladder, where he began to descend, the adrenaline overcoming the pain in his wrist. Less than halfway down, he thought he heard something down the tunnel. *Are they blocking me off down there, too?!* he asked himself, feeling his heart begin to pump even harder.

He glanced over his shoulder from the ladder for a moment, frowning at the white outlines of the throat of the tunnel, then looked back up at the agents on the level above. They couldn't see him, but they would know he had been there once they reached their treasure room; it would be quickly obvious that he had used the auger to bore through the wall.

Before he could move, there was a sudden light, and he was illuminated as though he were on stage. He shielded his eyes against the impossibly bright beam, holding the ladder with his good arm. The second he had taken to investigate the phantom noise had made all the difference.

He made to speak, but was cut off.

'You'll pay for bringing that thug here to protect you!' James Prince said menacingly, pulling down a pair of expensive-looking goggles.

'But I didn't-'

'*Do it now,*' Prince said before Ari could reply, seemingly speaking into thin air.

He and his accomplice grabbed a hold of a railing which appeared to be bolted to the wall. Panicked, Ari tried to descend the ladder in a hurry. But there was no time.

The belly of the Great Drain made a hungry rumbling sound, then gurgled like a kitchen sink. Ari heard the sound of gushing water. Then, quite explosively, the wall behind the scaffolding burst in a thousand places, and before Ari could react he was flipped upside down and inside out, and the last thing he remembered was a fleeting feeling of hopelessness, and the flash of the head torches growing distant as he was swept away like a pebble in a stream.

A blow to the head knocked any further conscious thought from his mind.

***

Chapter twenty-two

Ari awoke, coughing in the midnight air.

His first thought was not of the tablet but of his Bowie knife. He clawed at his chest for it, as though if it were there it might save him.

Of course, it wasn't there.

He was dripping wet, lying on a cold stone ground. His head felt as though it had been cleaved in two, and the pain from the blow he had taken shimmered back into his mind. His brain exploded with agony, and he tried to sit up to combat the feeling of dizziness.

And he had definitely done some damage to his wrist.

He lay motionless for a while, his eyes closed.

After a time, he gingerly tested his eyes against the evening and found he could open them well enough to make out his surroundings.

He looked around his immediate vicinity and could see that some of the stone had been dyed blood red. He let out a gasp, and his head fell back against the stone.

It felt like some time before he awoke again, although it was still dark.

His head felt clearer this time, and the nausea seemed to have passed. He realised that he was lying underneath one of the arches of the Pulteney Bridge, where he and Fliss had met Benny earlier. A shallowing in the water of the Avon had revealed the stony riverbed below. A few feet in front of him, the torrent of the river rushed past him, a thousand galloping horses moving in unison making a deafening sound, and only now did he notice the noise that reverberated all around the underside of the bridge.

He wasn't sure if anyone would be able to see him from the street, and it occurred to him that he would need to try to move at some point. Like a patient coming round from an anaesthesia, he laboriously dragged his limbs to a sitting position, each pained action seemed to take ten times the amount of concentration as it would usually. Nevertheless, he found he was able to stand and, gingerly, move about the small space he occupied underneath the bridge.

How could I have been so stupid? he asked himself.

He hadn't really taken the threat of Ocean Pearl seriously. Nor had he heeded Ondrej's warning from eight years ago to stay away. But now, he knew. For Ondrej to be personally involved, he clearly had stakes in whatever it was they were trying to achieve.

Benny and Fliss had been right: Ocean Pearl were no joke, and he had been naive to assume that he would be able to evade them unscathed a second time.

He peered out from under the bridge, trying to get a view of the road above.

'Get *up* here,' he heard someone say.

Fliss!

Miraculously, blurrily, he made out the shape of her silhouette against the night sky, leaning out from over the bridge.

'I'm hurt,' he replied simply.

'Surprise surprise,' she responded dryly. 'Too hurt to climb a simple set of stairs?' she asked rhetorically, then disappeared.

Ari turned in a stupor and found himself face-to-face with his friend. On the other side of the stony platform, a short set of stone stairs led them back onto the road, and the pair soon found themselves heading blindly across the city of Bath, the night pulling them along. Ari couldn't move his left wrist, and he suspected it was broken. Fliss didn't seem to be feeling much sympathy.

'Come on,' she said sharply, dragging him down an alley. Despite his limited cognitive function, he was aware that they had come around in a loop but allowed himself to be led.

Periodically, Fliss stopped to check the coast was clear before rounding a corner or exiting a street, and would occasionally press her ear, presumably listening to Benny. Ari put a hand to his own ear, but the earpiece was gone, lost in the Great Drain.

After a time, Fliss came to a stop near a large set of doors. She took a set of jangling keys from her pocket and pushed them into a wooden back door.

'In here,' she murmured. Ari shuffled through into darkness, his vision taking a second to adjust, but the unmistakable white outlines of market stalls, winding corridors and bric-a-brac shops fizzled into clear view. They were in some kind of bazaar. Fliss flicked a switch, and the lights made a crackling sound as they came on. Not a bazaar, but an Arcade. The same Arcade he had looked at with such fondness when they had first arrived in Bath.

'Bloody hell Fliss, this is right next to *Aquae Sulis*!' he said, his thoughts suddenly a little more coherent. Ari's wet clothes clung to his skin, and he found his teeth were chattering.

He grabbed a hoodie from one of the nearby marketplace stalls and threw it over his head, leaving the left sleeve hanging limply, his sore wrist resting on his lap.

He noted the hoodie seemed to be in the same style as the one Kenny had been wearing earlier.

Kenny.

He had almost forgotten. Ari hoped the boy wouldn't get into too much trouble. Fliss was pacing. Her tracksuit was ripped in several places, but it was the torn expression she wore on her face that concerned Ari most greatly. He wasn't sure whether to interject or not, and so instead opted for silence while she worked through her thoughts.

'You look ridiculous,' she said. Ari pictured his image, a full tracksuit with Chelsea boots, sopping wet, pathetically clutching his wrist. He said nothing.

'That was... intense,' she added. Ari gave her a "you could say that," look.

'How's your arm?' she asked. He held up his left wrist and tried to move it, but recoiled quickly.

'Sore,' he said.

'Broken?'

'Hmm,' he replied. 'Not sure. I'm... I'm sorry,' he mumbled. She seemed too dejected to be truly angry.

'Doesn't matter, it's done now,' she replied. 'I can't believe they pulled the plug on you,' she said.

'Me neither. Do you know what happened?' he asked.

She sighed and turned toward the stall nearest to them which, among an infinite number of other things, sold camping chairs. She pulled a couple out and set them up in the middle of the corridor. They sat down, and Fliss removed her earpiece.

'I think we should stay here for a little while, to make sure no one followed us in. Then we'll take a cab back to Benny's,' Ari agreed without saying it aloud. 'and we'll use a fake name,' she added.

Ari wanted nothing more than to curl up in bed and rest his wrist but knew it would be unwise to leave when Ocean Pearl could still be out there looking for them. Instead, he settled into his camping chair – which was surprisingly comfortable – and propped his wrist on its arm.

'Where did you get the keys to this place?' Ari asked.

'Benny gave them to me,' she said distractedly. 'In case we needed to hide. Sorry, I forgot to mention,' she said. There was more silence.

'Well?' he asked after a short time. 'What happened?'

Fliss closed her eyes for a moment, as though she was struggling to remember.

'After you went into the pool, I headed back up the corridor, to see if I could get back into the atrium.'

'Why?' he asked in an accusatory tone. 'Why didn't you follow me?'

'*Don't* accuse me of anything, Ari,' she snapped, suddenly more cognizant than she had been since they had sat down. 'I'm not in the mood. But if you must know the exact details of my thinking, I knew that Ocean Pearl would head to the Great Drain as soon as they realised the other exits were blocked, and if we were both down there, we wouldn't be able to distract them on the surface,' she said.

'Why didn't you tell me!' he asked, momentarily forgetting the pain in his wrist and trying to rise, wincing as he did so. He settled and sunk back down, defeated.

'Because there's no way in hell you would have gone along with that plan,' she said. 'I wanted to be up there to try to hamper their progress as much as I could. I only hesitated because we had seen that other man. Ondrej, or whatever you called him,' she said.

Ari had almost forgotten seeing the old Bluebird fighting in the courtyard of the Great Bath.

'Plus,' Fliss said. She stalled for a moment, then took a breath. 'I... I wanted you to go into the Drain.'

Ari gave her a look of genuine puzzlement.

'You have spent the last three days trying to convince me *not* to go into the Drain,' he said.

'Yes, and I'm sorry about that, but... Look, I had to bring you on board, Ari. Cast your mind back to three days ago. You may also remember that you didn't believe there was anything to be found in *Aquae,* and that we were only here for a holiday,' she said. 'I had to reverse that position somehow, in order to get you to be willing to take a *risk*,' she said, emphasising the final word in a menacing tone. So I did what I have been able to do to you since we were teenagers... I pushed your buttons.'

Ari scoffed. 'Leave off,' he said.

'Sorry Ari, but it's true. I started by just generally rubbing you up the wrong way - so to speak - then graduated to actively taking an opposing stance to yours on pretty much anything, including the work we were doing. The more intractable my position – that there was nothing to find at *Aquae* - the more convinced you were that I was wrong, and slowly you began to polarise. You've always been the same,' she said, sheepishly. 'You don't trust my instincts.'

Ari rubbed his eyes. Manipulated. Again. But this time, by his friend.

'I told you not a week ago,' he said through gritted teeth, 'that you had always had a good hunch.'

She smiled gently.

'But only when you already agree with me,' she said, softly. 'Anyway, how we got here is irrelevant,' she said, although Ari vowed silently to bring it up with her again when he had the chance. The lights in the arcade flickered, and the pair stopped talking for a moment, starting at one another.

'It's nothing,' Ari said after a short pause. 'We're feeling jumpy.' Fliss closed her eyes.

'Anyway,' she continued, 'you went in the pool, and I went back to the exhibit with the door that led to the atrium. The alarm eventually stopped, and I stayed hidden just in case the two agents who came in from outside decided to split up. Fortunately, they headed straight for the entrance to the Great Drain.'

'Did you see Ondrej?' Ari asked, trying to sound unconcerned.

'No. I don't know how they managed to get rid of him, but they did,' she said. 'And I also don't know what happened to the security system, but they clearly had some trouble getting in as I heard them arguing between themselves as to the best way to remove the grill over the Great Drain. Evidently,' she said, 'they opted for the no-nonsense approach and blew the thing up.' Ari pursed his lips.

'Right,' he said, as the sound of the explosion and the falling dust in the treasure room replayed in his mind.

'The door to the atrium opened when the alarm subsided, so I made my way up there. There was an agent – the guy from the train – but I don't think he was expecting company, because he was pretty distracted, trying to talk on the phone to, I presume, someone at Ocean Pearl, to figure out how to drain the Great Bath of its water. That's when I realised you were in pretty serious danger,' she said.

'Well, you put me there,' he said, abruptly. She made a shushing noise.

'I told you not to accuse me of anything,' she replied, much calmer now. 'Not two minutes ago you believed you put yourself there, so don't get on your high horse. Deceit or not, you still went against your word. You promised Benny you wouldn't enter that Drain before we left. And now he knows you can't be trusted,' she said.

'Trust!' Ari exclaimed. 'You've been manipulating me into risking my life to find your treasure!'

Fliss smiled. 'Then I guess none of us should trust the other,' she said.

Ari shook his head, exasperated.

'So, as I was saying,' Fliss continued breezily. 'I knew you were in danger. I didn't think I would be able to stop them from emptying the Great Bath and flooding the Drain if he was stood right there next to the controls, but I was also certain that if I simply left and went to warn you, I would be washed down there too, and he would be there to intercept us both.'

'The means really justify the end in this story, huh,' Ari said, massaging his left wrist theatrically. Fliss ignored him.

'So, I thought I would retreat back down the corridor, to try to get him away from the control panel. I certainly didn't want to *fight* this guy, so I wanted to draw him into the museum where I might be able to use some kind of weapon. Unfortunately, he spotted me. I'd only just got back to the exhibit when he appeared in the doorway and, well, I was... overpowered fairly quickly.'

'Overpowered?' Ari asked.

'He picked me up over his shoulder. I had underestimated his size, he was huge.' Ari couldn't help an escaping laugh.

'Sorry,' he muttered. 'Mortal danger and all that. Go on.' She gave him a rankled look.

'*Fortunately*,' she said, pointedly, 'that was the moment that his mates chose to blow up the entrance to the Drain. They must have forgotten to turn off their headsets, or however it is they communicate with each other,' Ari remembered Prince giving an instruction into thin air, 'because my guy jumped out of his skin, and dropped me to the ground.'

'Jesus,' was all Ari could say.

'So I grabbed the nearest heavy object, a brass pewter, probably fifteen hundred years old and worth about fifty grand... and smacked him over the head with it,' she said, proudly. This time Ari did laugh.

'And how did he feel about that?' he asked.

'It seemed to just annoy him more than anything, because he stood up and pushed me backwards into the wall which, to both our surprise, I fell through. Then I blacked out. Something must have happened, because when I came round, he was gone, and I was still on the floor.'

'He got the order to empty the Bath and flood the Great Drain. I watched Prince do it,' Ari said.

'Ah. Perhaps. I think the plan was for him to drain the water and then go and pick you up from underneath the bridge, where I found you. Maybe he didn't have time to deal with me, knowing he would need to get there pretty sharply.'

Ari hummed his agreement.

'So I found myself lying on the floor in a room that you can't see from the normal exhibition, you know, having had to fall through a wall to find it... and above me, I saw the gilded head of *Sulis Minerva.*'

Ari gave her a quizzical look.

'Had it been moved?' Ari asked. He pictured the head, with its motherly countenance, as he had seen it in the temple courtyard room with the *haruspex* stone when they had visited.

'No,' she said cryptically.

'Then what?! Ari asked, irritated.

'Well... it's a second head,' she said with a slight shrug. 'More than that, in fact... I suspect the other one is a copy.'

'I focused on that thing when we were there pretty carefully,' he said. 'But a second head... why did they hide the first one?'

'I'll show you,' she said. She pulled out her phone and loaded an image, handing it to him to inspect. 'Took this before I left.'

As she had described, it was a picture of the head of *Sulis Minerva,* identical to the one in the temple courtyard. Save for a single - yet obvious - detail.

'What is *that?*' he asked, focusing his vision on the left eye of the Goddess. 'Hang on... Surely not?'

'Yep,' she said before he could finish. 'It's three Cornish Choughs.'

Fliss was no ornithologist, but he was certain she was right about these particular birds.

'The coat of arms of Canterbury?! What happened next?!' he asked, his mind swimming with possibilities.

'It was quite simple from there, really. When I arrived in the atrium the agent was bent over some access panel on the floor, jabbing at the buttons in an uncoordinated fashion,'

'He managed to accomplish his goal, though,' Ari said bitterly. 'He drained the water.'

'Yes, I must have just missed him, but as I say he was still crouched so I ran across the atrium and, without stopping, aimed a flying knee at his face,' she said, candidly. 'He stayed down that time,' she added, even prouder than before.

'You didn't!' Ari exclaimed gleefully.

'I did... then I just sort of, kept running,' she said with another shrug.

'Out the main entrance and into the street. The doors had opened when the alarms stopped. As I rounded the corner, I heard sirens behind me, so Benny must have called the police as we agreed he would. I knew we would probably be safe, then, as it would take some smoothing over on the part of the agents. Better safe than sorry, though, I thought we should come here rather than go straight back to Benny's.' Ari was impressed, but he didn't show it. He still had mixed feelings about his friend's subterfuge. 'What happened to you?' she asked.

In the excitement of Fliss' tale, he had almost forgotten his own. Ari filled her in on sliding through the pipe, emerging in the dark, the treasure room with the auger and the second vault. At the end of it all, her mouth was wide open.

'How didn't they know that room was there!' she asked excitedly.

'Beats me,' Ari said. 'It was extremely well hidden, and it was sealed in a way that makes me think it happened much later than the Roman era. I can only assume that in the nineties the remote sensing tech Ocean Pearl used was less reliable. That room sits between the larger treasure vault and the temple courtyard; perhaps when they created a scan of the underground structure it was lost to the sight of the images, sandwiched between two much larger spaces.'

'Incredible... so you found it?' she asked, quietly, disbelievingly. 'Why didn't you lead with that!' she said. 'What does it say? Where is it?'

A sinking feeling sagged Ari into his chair and, for the first time, the realisation that he must have lost the tablet really hit him. He knew it wasn't there from the moment he came round underneath the bridge.

'I... I don't have it,' he said. 'I lost it when they flooded the Drain... But I know what it says,' he said, slowly.

'Well?' she demanded.

He looked her dead in the eye. He was too tired to tell whether he was still angry with her, but he wasn't feeling particularly trusting. He hesitated. She must have sensed his reluctance, because she softened her tone and added, 'we'll do it together this time. No manipulation. I promise.'

His exhaustion had come on quite quickly, and he found himself craving the spare bed in Benny's massive residence.

'In full, the message says:

Will no one rid me of this turbulent priest?

Sulis, let it never be found.

Henry,'

Ari recited from memory. He could almost hear Fliss' brain working behind her eyes. She narrowed her eyes to near-slits.

'Where do I know that quote from?' she asked.

'It's King Henry II. They're the words that are supposed to have led-

'- to the death of Thomas Becket,' Fliss finished the sentence. 'Thomas Becket,' she repeated.

'The very same.'

'The archbishop of Canterbury. The Cornish Choughs. Ari, what *is* this?' she asked, rhetorically.

Ari closed his eyes. 'I think we can safely assume that this tablet is of at least some importance after all, and that someone has gone to great lengths to conceal the links between *Aquae Sulis*, King Henry II and Thomas Becket the martyred archbishop of Canterbury.'

A pagan treasure, hoarded by a King of England and guarded by a Roman Goddess and, somehow, involving the most famous archbishop in living history.

Ari's mind reeled until Fliss filled the silence.

'So... the tablet was written by King Henry, or someone purporting to be him... and he is asking for help from a *pagan* Goddess in order to hide something from his archbishop: Thomas Becket?' she asked.

'That seems to be the rub of it,' Ari said.

'And the coat of arms in the head of *Sulis Minerva?*'

'I wasn't hundred per cent certain until I heard that. But it seems that someone, somewhere down the line, wanted to try to expose whatever has been concealed.'

'You think the second head is... a clue?' she asked, still a little incredulously.

'It's not even a clue, Fliss. It's a simple direction. To Canterbury. And the tablet is a direction specifically to Canterbury cathedral.' The pair were silent for a short while.

Through the frosted window, he could see the sky had brightened ever so slightly.

'We'd best call that cab,' he said, standing with some difficulty from his camping chair, only able to use one arm. Fliss continued to stare at the floor, her brow furrowed, deep in concentration. Ari wondered whether all she could see was the maniacal look on Ondrej's face, too.

***

Chapter twenty-three

Ari was trapped in a cage underwater, as though he were shark diving. He was screaming, rattling the bars, unable to move or escape. Paralysis weighed him down like a log on his chest. James Prince's face was maddeningly close to his own, the Ocean Pearl agent grinning like a Cheshire Cat. Prince extended two huge, fiery arms and wrapped them around Ari's torso, then squeezed, forcing the air from Ari's lungs as he struggled for breath.

Tighter and tighter, his breath became shorter until it eventually failed him entirely, and with his last gasp, he called out for help.

Which woke him up.

He sat up in the huge bed in Benny's spare room. The sheets were soaked with sweat, and his head felt fuzzy, as though he had a hangover. He smelled like a river.

He rubbed the sleep from his eyes and frowned at nothing in particular, watching as millions of particles of dust danced in the stream of light that shot across the room from the gap in the massive curtains.

Slowly, he recalled the events of the previous evening, not least his left wrist, which was wrapped in a homemade bandage. His head hurt, and he allowed himself to flop back onto the sheets.

The bedroom was painted in an emerald-green colour with a high ceiling and an old wooden floor. The tall, north-facing bay window had a large sill that doubled as a sofa, and only now did Ari notice Cicero, Benny's massive orange cat, stretched out across it. He got up and crossed the room, pulling the curtains open with his good arm. Cicero opened one eye, then closed it again.

Ari pulled on a dressing gown and some slippers that Benny had left out for him, which he wore over the jogging bottoms and t-shirt that he had slept in. From somewhere downstairs he could smell coffee, and he followed his nose down the ornate staircase to the kitchen which, like all the other rooms of the house, was huge.

The kitchen put Ari in mind of an antique shop; colours of brown and rusty red met his gaze as he took in the scene, which was more than a little chaotic.

The mahogany-topped island which dominated much of the open space was now covered with the same books and files as had been on the dining table the night before, complete with Percival, the bird, who was pecking at the corner of a particularly delicate-looking and old textbook.

Fliss had her back to Ari. She was standing, leaning over the counter, her head in a book, while Benny was shouting and banging around indeterminately from somewhere outside. The most unexpected person in attendance was Kenny, their gangly chaperone from the night prior, who sat at a highchair around the island, headphones on, fully engrossed in whatever was occupying the screen of his phone.

'Morning,' Ari said to Fliss' back, yawning. 'I see we gained a houseguest,' he said, nodding to Kenny. Fliss looked around and murmured a response, then back at her book. 'Reading anything interesting?' he asked.

'Yes, I'm trying to get this recipe right,' she said, moving away from the kitchen counter to reveal a view of the hob, which had a number of pans simmering simultaneously. Ari wandered over and lifted a pot of coffee from the cafetiere, peering over the stove and inhaling deeply.

'What is that smell?' he asked.

'It could be any number of things, but probably the ginger. It's quite potent,' she said, ushering him out of the way so that she could go back to cooking.

'And what is the ginger being used to make?'

'Ramen,' she said. 'And it's quite tricky, so if you wouldn't mind keeping Percival entertained until I'm finished, I'd be quite grateful. Stupid bird keeps trying to eat my crushed cashew nuts,' she looked back over her shoulder at the island, where Percival had turned his attention to the white cable attached to Kenny's headphones. 'Wonder which of them would win in a game of chess?' she asked with a faint smile. Ari smiled back.

'Wait,' he asked. 'What time is it? Ramen, for breakf-' he was cut off by a loud bang that came from somewhere beyond the kitchen, outside the back door. The noise made him wince.

'Is that Benny? What's up with him?' Ari asked.

'Ah. Well. He's not exactly pleased. With either of us really. I told him about my plan to get you into the Drain, and that you always intended to go back on your word. He's feeling a little... used,' she said.

A moment hung between the pair, as though Ari were teetering on making a comment or letting it slide.

'Used? He's not the only one,' Ari said, unable to resist.

Ari headed out the back door into the glaring sunlight. He hadn't found out the time, but the autumn sun was past its highest point, so he assumed it was early afternoon. He had taken some fairly strong painkillers for his wrist when he got back in the early hours of the morning, which must have knocked him out.

As he crossed the small patioed courtyard, he sipped his warm, black coffee and felt the caffeine course through his whole body, eventually reaching his brain and putting his mind into gear for the first time that day.

Benny's shouting, as it turned out, was coming from a small food store. The garden of the house was surprisingly modest in comparison to its otherwise gargantuan size, but spare land was at a premium in the middle of the city centre. Ari entered the food store which, not unlike the library, was lined with shelves, only the books were swapped for long-life foods. Benny was wrestling with some boxes.

'Morning Benny,' Ari said, trying not to sound sheepish. 'Struggling?' he asked. Benny didn't look up. 'Thanks for your help last night,' Ari ventured. 'You bought us valuable time when that agent showed up.' Benny grunted in response. Ari rolled his eyes and moved to help him with the boxes.

'Don't bother,' Benny said unceremoniously. 'I've told Fliss already. Once your wrist is healed, I want you out.' He looked down at Ari's arm and the makeshift bandage he had applied. 'And it's looking better already,' he added, ominously.

'Come on, Ben,' Ari said, trying not to sound desperate. The previous night's revelations had only settled Ari's resolve more firmly overnight and, although in pain, he had awoken with a new-found clarity and purpose that wouldn't be easily set aside. 'You're not going to throw us out, surely. We're in more danger than ever.'

'And whose fault is that?' Benny spat, throwing the box aside. Ari felt a flutter of trepidation. He didn't think Benny would hurt him, but his size was so vast that if he tried, he could probably do some lasting damage. 'You two... conniving little shits... concocting your own plans... you lied to my damn face!' he said, venomously.

'I didn't mean to, Benny. I swear. If that alarm hadn't gone off-'

'Save it, Ari,' Benny said. 'You swore you wouldn't go down there into that Drain, but you did. And you nearly died in the process.'

'But Benny, if I hadn't gone down there, we would have been caught. Fliss' identity would have been exposed.'

'It was exposed anyway!' he retorted. 'She told me so herself this morning.' *She didn't mention that in the Arcade,* Ari reflected, wondering how she had omitted such a crucial detail from her account.

'That guy she punched saw her face when she fell through the wall,' Benny continued. 'She was put in harm's way, and you've fractured your wrist. I had to bring Kenny here for fear that Ocean Pearl would want to question him, which has also put me in danger. And somehow, separately, you managed to reach the same conclusion. Between your lack of planning and her goading, you ended up in that Drain.'

'But we found-'

Benny raised a massive hand and, in that moment, he looked all of his sixty-plus years.

'I don't care what you found, Ari. And I certainly don't want to know about it, it'll only put me - and you - in yet more danger if *I'm* ever questioned by Ocean Pearl. You can stay tonight, use the kitchen and the library, but after that, we're done. I've told Fliss,' he repeated.

Ari lingered.

'You know, on the day we arrived here, you told me that I should question the reason that Fliss had brought me here,' he said. 'Well, I guess we both know now. She did want me to find whatever was hidden at *Aquae* after all. In a strange way, she believed there was something to find, and believed in me to do it. Her methods were wrong, but her heart was in the right place. And this afternoon, we're going to go over every single detail of what we know and what has happened so far. She has given me more purpose in the last few days than I have had for years. And I think,' Ari said, pausing for a second. 'That is exactly what you have been lacking in your life for some time, Benny. A little purpose.'

With that, Ari turned from the food store and marched back into the kitchen, leaving Benny among the boxes.

***

Ari and Fliss were in the kitchen, at the island. It was dark now, the daylight having collapsed into dusk some hours ago. The leftover ramen was cooling on the stove behind them, filling the kitchen with a spicy aroma that Ari found to be immensely comforting.

Kenny was, quite remarkably, still playing on his phone.

Occasionally, Ari had waved his hand in front of the boy's face to check he hadn't entered some kind of vegetative state. He was yet to be convinced one way or the other.

Percival and Cicero were nowhere to be seen, and Benny, still in his mood, was also absent. Fliss said he would come round, but Ari wasn't so sure.

Ari and Fliss had spent the last few hours researching anything that they thought might be relevant to *Aquae Sulis,* Thomas Becket, King Henry, pagan treasure or Canterbury cathedral, which had proven both valuable and frustrating in equal measure.

Ari was confident that whatever the curse tablet and Cornish Choughs were pointing to at Canterbury cathedral hadn't already been discovered by Ocean Pearl previously; they had never had the full tablet that led them to the cathedral specifically and, even if they had, the cathedral had been notoriously resistant to Ocean Pearl influence over the years.

Content that they weren't searching for a treasure that had already been discovered, they had slowly started to construct a narrative about what might have been going on between King Henry and Becket.

In the 12th Century, King Henry II was fighting numerous wars on all fronts. He faced a lifetime of war and revolt, undertook military campaigns to bring the nations of the British Isles under single rule, and at a later time, his sons rebelled against him for power. Fighting these wars would have required financing, but the England that King Henry II inherited was – monetarily speaking – in dire straits.

Perhaps, they had mused, the King was told of the existence of the treasure at *Aquae Sulis,* pagan offerings left untouched since the days of the Roman Empire, and wanted to use it to finance his campaigns.

Dreaming up uses for the vast hoard of gold and silver, but knowing his Christian archbishop – who was also Chancellor, in charge of the country's finances - would never allow the use of a *pagan* treasure to finance his conquests, he became increasingly desperate to find a way to do so.

Perhaps, Fliss had suggested, this led the King to expel his current archbishop-cum-Chancellor – Theobold de Bec, and appoint his old friend and adviser Thomas Becket to the role. It was surely the King's hope that Becket would turn a blind eye to the use of pagan silver, allow it to be sold and finance the King's conquests.

But maybe Henry was wrong. Maybe Becket put his calling to the Church above matters of State upon assuming the archbishopship.

And unable to reconcile this rift, over time a bitter Political feud between the two ensued, ultimately ending with the archbishop's murder at Canterbury cathedral, an event that shocked the medieval world, turning the archbishop into a martyr and symbol of Christianity the world over.

But even if this picture was accurate, none of this answered for Ari and Fliss, the crucial question: what happened to the pagan treasure?

'It *must* have been moved somewhere at some point,' Fliss said. It was later in the evening now, and they had been over the same points multiple times. 'You heard Benny saying that there had always been a feeling of missed opportunity at *Aquae*, and the room you found was virtually empty... If the temple there was receiving offerings from Roman citizens on a daily basis, that had lain hidden after the fall of the Roman Empire, just imagine the sheer volume of treasure that King Henry must have had at his disposal! All of that can't have just disappeared,' Fliss said.

Silently, Fliss retrieved a couple of glasses and a bottle of Kraken, a spiced rum, which she poured over ice for the pair of them. It crackled as they clinked their glasses. She tried to catch Kenny's attention to see if he wanted one, but the boy had put his head in his arms and was face down on the table, presumably asleep.

'It must have been pretty frustrating,' Fliss said. 'For the King I mean, having this huge treasure that he couldn't use. It would be like me putting a fortune in your bank account in the wrong currency,' she said.

The rum burned Ari's throat as he took his first sip, but the warmth that spread across his chest and down his arms took the edge off the pain of his wrist.

At that moment, Benny strode through the kitchen door. In his arms, he had more papers, and books, which he dumped unceremoniously on the kitchen island.

It was hard to tell whether his sour mood had ameliorated, but it was the most he had said to either of them since the early afternoon in the food store. Still, Ari decided to err on the side of caution by remaining silent.

'Nice of you to join us, Uncle,' Fliss said, grabbing a third glass and pouring a Kraken for him. He pulled up one of the three unoccupied high seats.

'Don't push it, Felicity,' he said. 'You two aren't out of the water yet. But you are on to something – or at least so it would seem.'

He tapped at the papers he had thrown down.

'These are a few pages from the *Vita Sancti Thomae* written by a guy called William Fitzstephen in the 12th Century. It's Thomas Becket's biography, and Fitzstephen was his biographer. I've been studying it this evening and, well... "Turbulent priest" is an apt description indeed,' he said heavily, taking a long sip of his rum. He poured a second then glanced at Kenny.

'Is he alright, by the way?' Benny asked.

'Really depends on what you mean,' Ari said. The trio grinned, but Benny quickly rearranged his face, momentarily forgetting he was meant to be grumpy.

'Anyway,' Benny continued soberly. 'Old King Henry appoints Becket in the role as archbishop of Canterbury and Chancellor in the hope that he would... *Cook the books*, so to speak. He was convinced that Thomas would take a practical view of the matter of the pagan treasure, and allow the King to use it to finance his wars without sparking a pagan resurgence. It seems, then,' Benny said, 'that the entire reason for Becket's appointment as archbishop was to cover up this treasure.'

He let his words hang for a moment. 'I was expecting a bit more of a reaction,' he said.

'Sorry Uncle, it's been a long day. We had sort of come to that conclusion ourselves. But it's nice to have the evidence,' she said, smiling weakly.

Benny made to start speaking, but Ari cut in ahead of him.

'So Henry has made a pretty colossal mistake, and probably realised quite quickly that his new archbishop-Chencellor wasn't going to let him use the pagan treasure,' Ari said. 'But where does that leave us? It still doesn't explain the curse tablet or the Cornish Choughs. I mean I think we can safely assume they weren't produced by the King. He - or someone - clearly discovered a way to move the treasure on from *aquae* in spite of Becket's appointment, but what good would it do to expose himself? And if it was Becket who left the tablet, why would he do that?' Ari asked.

'I don't know,' Benny said. 'Is it possible that the archbishop left the clues at *Aquae* as a means of implicating the King in a pagan treasure scandal? And perhaps, as a safety net, he inscribed the three Cornish Choughs into the bronze head as a way of directing someone toward the cathedral, where he knew – or hoped – that any archbishop would do the right thing if approached, and tell them about the King's intention for the treasure?'

No one answered Benny's questions. Instead, Cicero let out a loud meow.

'He needs feeding,' Benny said with a sigh. 'We should come back to this tomorrow.'

'Someone's changed their tune from earlier,' Ari replied, shooting Benny a playful look. 'But we can't hang around here looking at books and thinking about the motives and rationale of this nine-hundred-year-old King,' Ari said. 'We need to act. We know where we need to be, Canterbury cathedral. And you can bet your life that Ocean Pearl will be on their way there right now. They'll have found the half of the curse tablet I lost in the Drain, and they already had the second head. Benny, you said earlier that we should leave tomorrow, and I think you're right.'

'Absolutely out of the question!' he retorted.

'Benny, we-'

'Fliss, tell him,' Benny interrupted. 'He's injured for God's sake, and Ocean Pearl are looking for both of you now! They saw your face!' he exclaimed.

'Oh yes,' Ari said, pointedly. 'Forgot to leave that part out of your recap last night!'

Fliss looked sheepish. 'They were already looking for us, Benny,' she said. 'And Ari, yes, they saw my face, so I presume they know who I am by now. I didn't want you to worry,' she said. Ari believed her, despite not really wanting to.

'You know what they're capable of,' Benny said. 'They tried to drown Ari for God's sake!'

'But what if, right now, there's some Ocean Pearl agent breaking into a vault somewhere in Canterbury cathedral, discovering a priceless pagan treasure?' he asked.

'Well then you'd be too late anyway!' Benny said, although he knew in his heart he was beaten.

'True,' Fliss said, placing her hand on his wrist. 'But assuming that isn't the case, I think we have to try,' she said, gently.

'Your Mother would-'

'My Mother isn't here,' Fliss said, her tone one of finality.

Cicero meowed again.

'Damnit! I'm coming!' Benny snapped at the cat, making a move to lumber his massive frame off the high stool, muttering to Cicero to follow him to his food bowl.

'So, we're going?' Ari asked quietly. 'To Canterbury?'

'Looks that way,' she said, glancing back over her shoulder. 'But we should make a stop on the way.'

***

PART THREE

Chapter twenty-four

Canterbury, Kent, UK
Present day

James Prince stood with arms folded at the side of Tennant's hospital bed. His colleague was asleep having been sedated by Ocean Pearl's medical team after he had, somehow, been bested by the girl at *Aquae Sulis* and found unconscious.

Might be best you stay that way, Prince thought to himself, looking down at his partner who lay topless, bruised all over.

Otherwise, I'd probably kill you.

The sound of echoing footsteps approaching loudly from the corridor culminated in a nurse bursting into the room to check a few things on a chart.

'Will he be alright?' Prince asked her after a few seconds.

'Oh he'll be fine once he's had some rest. They had to do some reconstructive surgery on his jaw, and he needed some dental work, but otherwise...' the nurse said, tailing off without looking up from her chart, 'he might not be able to talk for a few days, mind.'

Prince muttered his thanks to the nurse who shuffled off to the next patient without further comment. *We'll get back at them,* he thought to himself bitterly.

Ocean Pearl paid hospital Trusts to have beds staffed by their own doctors and nurses at hospitals up and down the country, no questions asked, and this small ward, tucked into the corner of a neurology centre, was the Bath ward. A7.

A light pattering of rain tinkled down outside, and the dark rooms were illuminated only by long, circular tube lights that flickered every so often. It made for an eerie scene, and Prince jumped slightly as the door opened for a second time. Aurora had not betrayed her approach with the sound of footsteps.

'My secondment has been terminated,' she announced unceremoniously. 'I'm meant to ship back to Egypt on the next flight.' She had changed out of her Vantablack suit and now wore a pair of bell-bottom jeans and a blue, zip-up sports top. A baseball cap covered her mass of black hair, which she had tied up in a pony.

Prince raised an eyebrow.

'*Meant* to be on the next flight?' he asked.

She smirked. 'The next Business-class flight isn't for a few days, Prince. And I don't fly economy.'

It had been two days since *Aquae Sulis*.

Aurora had been more than a little frosty with him. And he could hardly blame her. The whole operation had been utterly shambolic. From the moment they landed and set the alarm off, to flooding the Drain unnecessarily, to Tennant's jaw getting smashed in and the unexpected arrival of Ondrej and his damn Bluebirds.

Prince should have terminated the mission. He should have intercepted Ari on the train in Lime Street and been done with it. But his pride had gotten the better of him, and in his eagerness to find something new at *Aquae*, he had tarnished his reputation further, sealing his status as a failure with his peers at Ocean Pearl.

How did the girl manage to overpower you? he asked of Tennant in his head. If Tennant had managed to bring her in, she could have spilt on her friend. Would that have still been a botched job?

Perhaps - but at least a botched success.

When Prince had told Ironmonger, she had screamed so hard down the phone the thing nearly exploded. He'd never managed to provoke a reaction like that before, but there was no sense of mischievous pride this time.

He'd simply listened sheepishly and taken his telling off as she had told him in no uncertain terms that he was to bring Ari in as soon as he was able... then they would talk about his punishment.

He suspected his future rested on how swiftly he carried out her instructions, and how valuable Ari proved to be to Ocean Pearl, who Prince still believed could be a useful asset to their operations. After the water had washed out of the Drain and they had inspected the treasure room, it became clear that Ari had found what he and Ocean Pearl had not been able to.

Another room, largely empty save the shelves and a pulley system for transporting items to and from the surface.

But it was imperative that they bought Ari in for other reasons now, too. His researchers had found part of a tablet, which they had assured Prince had come from the new room, and that Ari must have dropped it when he exited *Aquae*.

'What did Ironmonger say about it all?' Aurora asked having slid into an uncomfortable-looking armchair in the corner of the room. She looked at Tennant in a way you might look at a dog that was about to be put down.

'What *didn't* she say?' Prince asked rhetorically. 'She basically told me that if I didn't bring Ari in - and quickly - she'd have to "review my position" with Ocean Pearl,' he said heavily. The words lingered between the pair for a moment, the silence interrupted only by the steady beep of Tennant's ECG machine.

'What does that mean?' Aurora asked, apparently sincerely. *So naïve,* he thought to himself.

'I know way too much, Aurora... It's in the contract. You know as well as I do what would happen,' he said matter-of-factly. Aurora's eyes widened with genuine fear.

'Surely not?' she asked, aghast.

'You think they make those threats idly?' he asked.

Aurora said nothing, but her dark skin seemed visibly paler than usual.

'Any more information on the other guy who showed up? With his goons?' Aurora asked, changing tack. Prince gave her a furtive look and grunted.

'C'mon,' he said. 'Let's get out of this damn hospital. I'll tell you about it over a drink.'

Aurora baulked.

'I'm not going for a drink with y-'

'We can't talk here,' Prince said sharply. 'These doctors and nurses are all Ocean Pearl employees,' he said in a low tone. 'Now come on,' Prince said unambiguously, breezing past her and out of the door. He smiled to himself as he heard her follow him out into the corridor.

***

A short cab ride later, Prince and Aurora found themselves in *The Dark Horse*, a dimly lit but cosy cocktail bar in the centre of Bath. It smelled of craft ale and hardwood floor.

Midweek, it was quiet except for a few groups of students, all of whom turned to look at Prince as he entered. *I'm probably the oldest person they've seen all week*, he reflected. He gestured to Aurora to take a seat in one of the booths along the back wall and crossed to the bar, ordering a couple of large Macallan Eighteens. He paid cash.

As he approached the booth, he slid the whiskey across to Aurora and took up the space opposite her, soaking in the atmosphere. He took a healthy draught of his Macallan, which was spicy with a hint of vanilla. It burned his stomach, and he felt the slow but familiar warmth begin to spread to all parts of his body. He allowed himself a deep sigh.

'Why didn't you use the company credit card?' Aurora asked. She looked more on edge than he and had perched on the edge of her seat, unwilling to let her guard down.

'Eagle-eyed indeed,' he commented. 'I don't want a record of where I've been.'

'Why?'

'Because I don't want Ironmonger to know what I'm up to,' he replied simply.

She didn't flinch.

He hadn't told Aurora everything there was to tell from the last few days, but he decided that he wasn't going to be able to pull off the stunt he had planned alone, and he suspected Tennant would have a different role to play once he had healed. What he really needed was a partner that he could bounce ideas around with, rather than a partner who let ideas bounce back off him.

'Because you're not going to intercept Ari?' she asked with the tiniest trace of enthusiasm. Prince met her gaze.

'Ironmonger called me after *Aquae Sulis* and was, understandably, pissed,' he said as he took another swig of Macallan, nodding at her to do the same. She ignored him.

'As I said at the hospital, she will be "reviewing" my position in Ocean Pearl. It's not good, Aurora. Not only did I let Ari get away, but I flooded the Great Drain. I made the call to have Tennant release the water. That's a two thousand-year-old site over which I no longer have any jurisdiction, and they're not impressed. The Drain has been disused for twenty years, and my actions have caused an untold amount of damage. It'll cost the company a pretty penny to restore. Not to mention that I also flooded the treasure rooms - yes, both of them,' he said.

'You see, that room that we caught Ari exiting from was discovered - by me - several years ago. It was quite the haul, but it was obvious that the place had been emptied at some point along the line. What was left there was inconsistent with the size of the room and, what was more, it seemed to sort of just... exist. No one at Ocean Pearl could figure out why someone would have built a treasure room that you could only access through a drain, but no matter what we did we could never find anything more to it than that, and so the conclusion was drawn that perhaps it had been intended to be used as a treasure room, but a time the ancient Romans had found access too difficult, and so it was abandoned and the treasure was taken elsewhere. We didn't have any other way of explaining why there wasn't more to find in the vault, other than to assume the treasure had never been there in any great quantity in the first place.'

He paused for a moment to see if she would say anything, but she just continued to stare at him, her brown-eyed gaze boring into his. He continued,

'Until of course Ari went in there three nights ago and uncovered the connecting room,' he said bitterly. 'The remote sensing technology was - and remains - revolutionary for Ocean Pearl, it really is our greatest asset. But in the nineties it was still being refined, and it missed that in-between layer. No one expected the room to be there, because no one thought the ancient Romans had that kind of technology. They surprised us again,' he said with a degree of admiration.

'So did Ari find more treasure?' she asked.

'No, but it's as good as. It's a conduit room for transporting treasure between the site of the temple and the treasure room.'

'So you *did* miss something back then,' Aurora said, sneeringly. 'That wouldn't have happened on one of my sites.'

'It would seem so,' he said, albeit begrudgingly. 'In my defence, the new room comes out under what is now a modern piece of road. There was no way we could have found it.' She raised an eyebrow.

'And yet this Marius Nicander managed to do it on his own, in about twenty minutes,' she said.

'*In pitch black dark*,' Prince added pointedly, ignoring the attempt to rile him. Aurora said nothing, but he was surer than ever that he was right about Ari's abilities.

'Anyway,' Prince continued. 'We'll get to him and his little friend in a moment. For now, let's focus on the room. So, we now know that at one stage there probably *was* a much vaster treasure than we found at *Aquae Sulis* in the nineties. The question,' he said, dropping his tone and leaning in toward her. 'Is whether that treasure still exists, and, given that it was not and is not at *Aquae Sulis*, where it has been moved to.'

The candlelight between them flickered.

'So?'

'So… in the past few days,' he faltered, but resolved himself. He had to trust her. He had to trust *someone*. 'In the past few days, now that the water has been drained away, I've had a few trusted agents down in the Drain. I obviously can't go back there myself, and I've been cut off from a lot of resources until I bring Ari in, but I still have a few favours I can pull. The agents did a sweep of the Great Drain and found… this,' he pulled out his phone and loaded an image on the screen, passing it to her. She frowned.

'I know a lot of things, Prince, but I don't know how to read Medieval English,' she said, annoyed. Then, her eyes seemed to widen with realisation. 'Wait,' she said slowly. 'Medieval English? I thought this was a Roman site?' Prince smiled priggishly.

'Flick to the next image,' he said. She obliged, and this time looked even more confused.

'The bronze head of *Sulis Minerva?*'

'Not exactly,' he explained. 'When I first took over the site in the nineties and did a full excavation, we found that head that you're looking at now hidden in the treasure room - the treasure room we knew about, of course. You can't see it on the image, but etched into her left eye is three Cornish choughs; a medieval coat of arms of Canterbury.'

'Canterbury? Why Canterbury?' she asked.

'That's the very question we asked twenty years ago. Of course, at that time, the coat of arms was all we had to go off, and Canterbury is a pretty big place. The cathedral is one of many buildings there that would have been standing during the medieval period and seemed the most likely candidate to find another clue, but the bastards wouldn't let us in. The archbishop resisted Ocean Pearl with a vehemency I have rarely seen in anyone. He was adamant that we would not have been given access, and that is still the case today. We tried all of our usual tactics, but to no avail; no amount of threat would budge him. We did try a covert search but, bear in mind, we didn't even really know what we were looking for then.'

'Right. And still don't,' was all Aurora said. Prince laughed.

'Fair enough. Anyway, having not understood the meaning of the head or found what it was pointing to, we hid it away from the public until we could establish a connection and only displayed the first head, the one that was already on site when we arrived and bears no inscriptions,' he said.

'Yes, fine. But what does that have to do with that... scrap of lead you just showed me?' she asked. Prince sat back.

He felt almost triumphant.

'That "scrap of lead" is inscribed, as you say, in Medieval English. Well, Middle English to be more precise. Dates from about 1250 CE.' On the next table over, he spotted a beer mat emblazoned with Ocean Pearl's *laburum.* He lowered his voice even further. 'And it says: *Will no one rid me of this turbulent priest? Sulis*, with a few other random letters in what looks like part of a signature.' He paused to let it sink in. 'Do you know that expression?'

'I did my reading on British history before I came here, Prince,' she said.

'I'd expect nothing less,' he said. 'Don't you understand the opportunity I am giving to you? The reason we gave up the search at Canterbury last time around is because we didn't have enough evidence to establish where the treasure might have been moved to, what it was tied to, why a Roman site dedicated to a pagan goddess would bear any relevance to Canterbury, the home of the fucking Church of England. In the end, we gave in to the archbishop's stubbornness because there wasn't enough evidence to suggest that there was definitely anything to find at the cathedral.

'But now, not only have we found more evidence that the inscription in the head of *Sulis Minerva* isn't some anachronous mistake, we also have a literal direction pointing us to Thomas Becket - who was killed in Canterbury cathedral!'

Aurora nodded slowly. 'I understand perfectly well, James Prince.'

'And where did it come from this... this-' Aurora asked.

'*Desfixionis.* A curse tablet,' Prince said. 'As I already said, it was found in the Drain after we flooded it. I can only assume that Ari found it when he discovered the in-between room, then dropped it when we pulled the plug... But more importantly,' he said a little too enthusiastically. 'It answers the question of why they - Ari and his friend - went to *Aquae Sulis* in the first place. This inscription is clearly half of another piece. I'd *bet* you he had that other piece, and I'd *bet* you that when we rumbled him in Liverpool, he thought he'd better high-tail it down here before we intercepted him and foiled his chance to make a discovery!'

Aurora looked annoyed. '*More importantly?*' she parroted sardonically.

'Well, yes. Perhaps not... but anyway, we've got the first lead in a cold case for two decades,' he said in response.

Ocean Pearl had, over the years, become comfortable with the fact that sometimes ancient clues led nowhere, and clues would run out. Sometimes, a case could sit dormant for fifty years, and suddenly some archaeologist somewhere would make a Find that reignited their interest. *Although, Ari is hardly an archaeologist,* Prince thought, picturing his fight with Ondrej outside *Aquae.*

'Where would he have got that from? The other half?' Aurora asked.

'My best guess is that Ondrej, the thug we encountered at *Aquae,* leader of the Bluebird gang, gave it to him,'

Prince said darkly, twisting the name around his tongue as though it were sour to the taste.

'Bad blood?' Aurora asked. Prince hummed in response, and looked broodily over his glass at the groups of blissful students dotted around the bar, laughing, joking and playing board games. He wondered whether any of them had what it takes to be an Ocean Pearl agent. *Doubt it.*

'You could say that,' Prince said. 'Ondrej is a gangster. He used to be contracted by the Ocean Pearl to, in essence, make them as much money as possible by whatever means necessary. I don't know exactly how he and Ari came to be working together, but their names are all over each other's files. Ari was working for Ondrej for a long time, running jobs for him, extorting treasure, probably smuggling. It seems like he was one of Ondrej's favourites... Until Merchant's Lodge,' Prince said. Aurora lifted her head almost imperceptibly, which Prince took to mean her interest was piqued.

'A very dark day in the company's recent history,' he said. 'Four agents were tipped off about a lead at an Imperial property in Liverpool, and went to investigate... and that's about all we know, because by that evening three of the four agents were dead, and the fourth was nowhere to be found,' he said solemnly.

'Dead?!' Aurora repeated. She seemed to be genuinely shocked. 'How can that be possible?' Prince smiled and took another chug of his whiskey.

'We've asked ourselves the same question. Ondrej was found at the scene, unconscious and covered in blood, a Bowie knife in his hand. Dotted around the property were the three dead agents. Ondrej swears he was the only one there, but it seems physically impossible for

215

one man to overwhelm three trained Ocean Pearl agents and cause the other one to flee.

'Witness reports taken by the police say that they heard *two* motorbikes enter the road earlier that day, not one. And that another came speeding out long before any discovery was made... But Ondrej confessed to everything. Took the rap. And that was that, case closed. Of course there was no trial or court proceedings. I don't even think Ondrej lost his contract,' Prince said. 'Perhaps to avoid drawing unwanted attention. But he was much quieter after that.'

Prince's mind was once again cast back to Ari in the Williamson Tunnel, escaping in the dark. *Is that why he had proven to be such a valuable asset to Ondrej? Is that how they had overpowered the agents at Merchant's Lodge? In a dark room?*

'Clearly you believe this Ari was there too, at this Merchant's Lodge?' Aurora asked.

'As I say, he and Ondrej were thick as thieves until then, and Ari suddenly disappears off the radar? And now, when he comes back into our scope, Ondrej just happens to show up again? Make no mistake, Aurora,' Prince said, glowering at her in the dim candlelight. 'Ondrej may be old, but that man is highly dangerous.' Aurora was immovable.

'And does Ironmonger know about this?' she asked. Prince took that to mean she believed at least some of it.

'She doesn't know anything. I haven't told her that Ondrej was there at *Aquae Sulis*, and no one knows that I commissioned the search of the Great Drain,' he said.

'Well, it seems to me that Ondrej and Ari are nothing more than insignificant distractions. The real prize here is this Roman treasure. Seriously, I'm impressed, Prince,' she said. She seemed sincere.

'Save it,' he said curtly, guiding the topic of conversation away from the Bluebirds. 'We haven't found anything yet, and I need to know if you're with me,' he said, trying to keep any trace of doubt from his voice.

To Prince, the moment felt pivotal. His career, possibly his freedom, rested on this mission's success. The only way to secure his future was to finish what he started. Find the lost treasure of *Aquae Sulis,* solve a twelve-hundred-year-old mystery, restore his reputation and get Ari and Ondrej off the scene once and for all.

He would need Tennant, definitely, but he would need someone with him where he was going next, too.

Aurora, finally, seemed to relax and sunk into the emerald-green leather of the back seat of her booth.

'As I said earlier, I have a few days here,' she said coyly. She picked up her Macallan and knocked it back in one go. Prince raised an eyebrow and allowed his gaze to fall on the gold *laburum* of Ocean Pearl once more, this time etched into the wood of the bar, as it was in so many places. Prince felt exhaustion come over him like an illness, and he noticed quite suddenly that he was nursing an excruciating headache.

'Another round?' she asked, making moves to stand. 'Then you can tell me your plan,' she added.

For the first time in a while, Prince was smiling.

***

Chapter twenty-five

'You're absolutely *sure* he'll help us?!' Ari yelled.

He and Fliss found themselves on another train. To Oxford this time, but there was no first or second class to choose from, and the train was considerably less well maintained.

The upholstery on the seats looked like a Grandmother's carpet, and there were cigarette burns and empty bottles all over the carriage. The seats were uncomfortable to the point of disbelief, and it was so humid that Ari felt nauseated. But the windows couldn't be opened, because even when closed the noise in the carriage was such that Ari and Fliss had to shout to each other in order to be heard. The Pendolino they had enjoyed from Liverpool to Bath suddenly seemed like a veritable palace in comparison.

'He's your *Dad*!' Fliss shouted back. Ari mustn't have looked very convinced, because she added, 'he'll be happy to see you!'

Ari sunk back into his chair. Last night, he, Fliss and Benny had argued into the early hours of the morning about the merit of pursuing their journey further.

Benny was of the opinion that the pair should call it quits; they had managed to upset Ocean Pearl a little, and Ari had managed to make the agent who had accosted him in the Williamson Tunnel feel some embarrassment as retribution. He had told them they should wash their hands of the matter and be thankful they had escaped with their lives.

Ari and Fliss had vehemently disagreed, and consequently, their departure that morning had not been a friendly one. Benny had told them in no uncertain terms that he thought they were foolish and, if they were lucky, he'd see them in prison.

He didn't elaborate on where he thought he would see them if they were *unlucky*. The problem with Benny's argument, Ari thought, was that Ocean Pearl clearly were not going to stop chasing him down, even if he stopped chasing their treasure. Whether he liked it or not, he had reopened a decade-old can of worms, and he was convinced he would be reinvestigated for this role at Merchant's Lodge with Ondrej.

Ondrej.

He still hadn't had much chance to think about how or why Ondrej was mixed up in all this, but Ari was fairly sure his old mentor wouldn't be pleased to see him.

He had been very stark in his warning that Ari should steer clear of Ocean Pearl at all costs, get out of the treasure hunting world entirely and do something useful with his talents. Instead, Ari had started producing fake artefacts from antiquity and selling them right under Ocean Pearl's nose, which could hardly be classed as taking his advice.

A *tiny* part of him wanted to believe that Ondrej had, somehow, discovered that James Prince was after him and, knowing some of the nefarious tactics employed by Ocean Pearl, had raced to *Aquae Sulis* to save him.

Of course, this was nothing more than a child's fantasy.

Because Ari knew him, or at least *had* known him, Ari viewed Ondrej as some kind of protector. Even as a father figure, of sorts. When, in fact, Ondrej was a hardened gangster. A criminal, running a smuggling ring in Liverpool and commanding respect among some of the most notorious mobsters in the city, and outside it too. More than likely, Ondrej had gotten wind of Ari's involvement in some scheme from someone at Ocean Pearl and, because he knew about Ari's talents, he would have assumed there was money to be made, or something to be found.

And only then had the old Bluebird raced to *Aquae Sulis*.

'I can't believe this is a *tourist* train!' Fliss screamed from the seat next to him, breaking his concentration. She looked as though she wanted to cry.

The train was indeed a tourist train, designed for travellers who wanted to see the English countryside as part of their journey, and so it took a far less direct route from departure to destination. They had decided it would be prudent, in the small chance that Ocean Pearl still didn't know their destination. He regretted their decision now.

Ari had thought that the passengers might have been entitled to a cup of coffee as part of the service, but it didn't seem likely.

Oxford was their chosen destination because Ari's Father, also Marius Nicander, had agreed to see them at short notice after Fliss had called him earlier that morning.

She hadn't gone into much detail about the nature of their visit, only saying that they were "down that way anyway," and that she thought it might have been good to catch up. He hadn't asked why Ari wasn't the one calling, nor had he enquired as to his son's whereabouts. Ari's father had played a big role in Ari and Fliss' life as children, but their relationship had fractured beyond repair when Ari had started working for Ondrej.

Unable to talk to Fliss, he found his thoughts lingering on those years. The last time he had spoken with his father, despite how angry they had been with each other at the time, if asked to describe him Ari would have said he was principled, fiercely intelligent, loyal, and charismatic.

Ari would have told anyone who asked him that his father was the kind of man with a stalwart moral compass that would always point true when called upon. In hindsight, he often wondered why he hadn't seen that his father - and Fliss - had been right all along. He should never have been working for Ondrej.

Ironically, it was Ari's father who had - accidentally - introduced them to one another. At the time, Professor Nicander – his father - had been a curator at the Liverpool Museum, which had been in dire need of repair at the time the Professor had taken charge.

It had been largely forgotten as a place where exhibitors might think to display their work, let alone an investor might pump in some money. Of course, when he took over, he had been approached by Ocean Pearl almost immediately, and had almost as quickly refused their help.

"History belongs to the people," Ari remembered his father saying. "And this museum will not be privatised under my stewardship," he had said.

And, true to his word, his father had spent the next decade turning Liverpool Museum into an enviable attraction, filled with wonders and treasures gained from the far corners of the earth.

Enter Ondrej.

The Bluebird boss had posed as a simple collector, making regular donations to the museum, all of which he said he had sourced from overseas using his "network," and that he would be honoured if they could be displayed at the museum in his adopted home city of Liverpool. It was a mutually beneficial relationship that blossomed into a friendship and, eventually, Professor Nicander brought Ondrej on board with the team at the museum, and the pair had become good friends.

That was until, shortly after the first time Ari met Ondrej at an evening soiree to celebrate the opening of a new wing of the museum, an intractable rift grew between the pair.

Because by that point, Professor Nicander had figured out that Ondrej was in fact working for Ocean Pearl.

He had surmised that they must have seen Ondrej as something of a middleman; not someone they wanted working for them directly - they couldn't be overtly associated with criminal activity - but clearly someone that they believed aligned sufficiently closely with their interests that they could keep him on the payroll in a contractual capacity.

And in doing so, when the museum was in a sufficiently-well-off position, they had used their substantial legal resources to argue in court that they should be allowed to be shareholders in the business, given the amount of money "they" had generated in making it a success, by virtue of Ondrej's donations.

Professor Nicander, who had volunteered to represent the museum in court, had proclaimed proudly that he had demonstrable evidence that he had turned down Ocean Pearl's offer of support and produced a transcript of their email exchange confirming his position.

At which point, with a sneer that Ari suspected he would never forget, their lawyer had offered a contract between Ocean Pearl and Ondrej to do precisely the same thing.

The judge was left with little choice, although he did say that, "it was with a heavy heart" that he would have to rule in favour of Ocean Pearl, and agreed that the financial capital they had expended when weighed against the revenue generated by the museum as a direct result of this input warranted their share of ownership.

As the short, sharp smack of the gavel came down binding the judgement in law, Ari could almost pinpoint the exact moment at which his father's heart was broken.

And so Ondrej had, overnight, gone from a small-time art and antiques dealer to a major player in the market in control of a powerful museum with contacts, influence and a considerable amount of wealth.

It was also at that time that Ondrej reached out to Ari to ask him if he wanted to start working for him.

Desperate for a way into treasure hunting, Ari had accepted and had proven to be a gifted Finder for Ondrej, with a knack for identifying profitable items, unlocking puzzle boxes, seeing beyond the first layer of text on a tablet or overhearing titbits of conversation that led to Big Finds. Of course he had been using his heightened senses, which he didn't tell Ondrej about until some time later.

It was also at that point that Professor Nicander and Fliss voiced their considerable disapproval of his actions.

Ari and his father had fought bitterly, and his father had effectively ended their relationship by saying he could not condone his son working for a man on the Ocean Pearl payroll, not after everything he had done to build the museum, only to have it snatched away from him at the last moment.

Fliss, on the other hand, pointed to the fact that Ondrej was a criminal, and the "jobs" he had Ari complete were dangerous.

Ari distinctly remembered the angry words he had chosen in response and thought he had made himself perfectly clear. It was those words that replayed themselves in his mind as he hurtled toward Oxford, this time trying to undermine Ocean Pearl rather than aid them.

The train pulled into a rural station, and they were offered a brief respite from the deafening noise it made while in motion.

'Do we really need my father's help?' Ari asked, taking the opportunity to speak with Fliss while he didn't have to shout.

'Go on then, *you* tell me the significance of the second head of *Sulis Minerva*,' she said sarcastically.

'There's really no mention of it? Anywhere?' he asked.

'Nope. Checked all the websites, every book I could think of... *nada*. Zip. Zilcho.'

'So... the working theory is that this head, a pagan icon dating to - probably - pre-Christianity which bears the coat of arms of the *archbishop of effing Canterbury* was just chilling behind one of the other displays for twenty years?' Ari asked.

Fliss cocked her head and smirked.

'That's about the rub of it, yes,' she said.

'What will we do if my Dad doesn't know anything that we don't already?' Ari asked. Fliss took a moment to respond, before offering,

'We go on to Canterbury anyway,' she said. Ari rolled his eyes.

'I'm just as passionate about this as you are,' he said, holding up his bandaged wrist as a reminder. It was still sore. 'But Ocean Pearl already searched Canterbury in the nineties. We saw that in Benny's records,' he said. 'And it was obvious from having been there!'

Ari and Fliss had spent the morning going through Benny's library to see whether they might unearth something useful on Canterbury. They hadn't really had enough time to get into any heavy reading, but they had managed to establish one thing for certain: Ocean Pearl had taken a definite interest in the place shortly after they had finished excavating *Aquae Sulis*, but the cathedral itself seemed to have done a good job at resisting their efforts.

'Yes, and the fact that they're chasing us round an ancient Roman bath house only proves beyond doubt that they think there is more to find,' she said in a hushed tone.

'If my Dad doesn't know anything, there's nothing to find,' Ari said firmly.

This flip-flop of opinion had been the story of their time together so far. As one swung left, the other swung right. Inextricably connected to one another, but forever apart, like two balls at either end of a Newton's cradle.

Ari sighed audibly.

'Look,' Fliss said, 'we find *the head* of a statue with Canterbury's Coat of Arms inscribed into the eye and a tablet written in the Middle Ages pointing us to Thomas Becket - the archbishop of Canterbury who literally *lost his head* at exactly the same time this thing was written.'

'I know, and on the tablet, the King of England is telling *Sulis Minerva* to look after something and lamenting his "turbulent priest," and on the other a symbol of the church inscribed in the eye of a bronze head. They have to be linked... I'm just not convinced we'll like the answer when we find it,' he said, then fell into silence.

A sudden lethargy washed over him, and he found his eyes were beginning to droop, Ari sat back in his chair as the train pulled away, and within a few moments the rolling countryside was melting into the distance outside, a brown visage of Autumn offering a chilly view of the south-eastern countryside. The deafening roar resumed as the train picked up speed.

Who on Earth would pay for this? he thought to himself, lolling to one side and looking lazily out the window.

Gradually, the afternoon began to draw dark. Before long, the hills were no longer visible, and Ari was soundly asleep. Fliss had spread out across two seats on the train, and she too was drifting in and out of consciousness.

Neither of them noticed the well-groomed man in his early thirties join at the stop before Oxford, but even if they had, they might not have recognised him.

Tennant's reconstructive surgery had been successful, but the wounds were still healing, and the stubble that had lined his jawline was replaced with black and blue bruises.

***

Chapter twenty-six

Ari couldn't help but marvel at the streets of Oxford as he and Fliss meandered through the city toward Grove Park, where they had arranged to meet Professor Nicander. Ari tried not to dwell on the fact that Grove Park was strikingly similar to Grove *Street*, where Merchant's Lodge still sat empty.

The light had faded entirely now, and in the dusky twilight the University buildings seemed even more grand than he could imagine. The Gothic look of the city reminded Ari of places he had been to in Germany and Romania when he had been selling his fakes.

He didn't think he could do much better than the Victorian poet Matthew Arnold, who dubbed Oxford the "city of dreaming spires" after the stunning architecture of these university buildings.

The place seemed ancient, and yet simultaneously modern, as though it had been designed to look old as opposed to being genuinely old. And yet, Ari reflected as he and Fliss navigated the fairly small city centre, it was home to one of the oldest academic institutions in the world.

The pair soon found themselves at the site of the historic Magdalen College, where groups of bookish-looking students were still grouped outside, despite the late hour. It was clear but cold, and a few were gearing up to ride their bicycles home, donning scarves, gloves and hats in earnest.

Ari and Fliss passed the faculty building of the Department of Classics, where Professor Nicander worked, but didn't linger.

Ari wondered whether his Mother - who had long departed for her job in the Middle East – even knew her ex-husband had moved to the university. Or that Ari had been in touch for the first time in years.

'Not much further,' Fliss said encouragingly. Ari's pace had begun to slow, until eventually, he came to a halt entirely.

'I don't know whether I should see him, Fliss,' he said. She turned, her hood pulled over her face against the cold. The wind was picking up slightly, and for the first time that year Ari felt as though there might be snow.

'He's your Dad,' she said, softly.

'That was the same argument as the one you put forward on the train. Being my Dad might not be enough.'

'For heaven's sake,' she said. 'If we're not going to see him then what the hell are we doing here?' she asked, her temper straining. 'You're damn lucky your father is even alive. Not all of us have that luxury,' she said, turning away from him.

Only the third time he had ever heard Fliss mention her own father.

'Now you can either grow up and come with me, or stay here and freeze to death,' she said, looking back at him. 'Either way, there's a world-renowned classicist waiting for us on the other side of this fence who might help us to solve this mystery and get Ocean Pearl off your tail. So, I'm going to speak to him. Are you coming?' she asked firmly.

Ari stood frozen for a moment, weighing her up.

'Yes,' he said simply. He pulled his coat higher around his face and adjusted his rucksack.

'Good,' Fliss said, although she was clearly disgruntled.

A short walk later, Ari and Fliss found themselves approaching a figure on a bench in Grove Park.

The figure rose as they approached and, for a horrifying moment, Ari thought they had somehow been duped by Ocean Pearl. He felt his heart quicken, and the urge to flee came over him. But as the figure stepped into the glow of a lonely lamp, Professor Nicander's unmistakable countenance was illuminated.

His face had shrunk in the years since he had joined Oxford and he wore a scraggly, greying beard that hadn't been present when Ari had seen him last. His hair was thinning around the sides and his skin seemed more wrinkled than before but, otherwise, he looked exactly as Ari remembered him. Familiar only in the way a parent can be to a child.

The trio exchanged a brief but decidedly awkward hug.

A curt, 'son', was all Professor Nicander offered as a way of greeting. The word hung in the air like a nasty smell, until Fliss broke in.

'It's so good to see you, Professor Nicander.'

'You too dear,' he said, much more gently. 'How have you been?' he seemed a little on edge as Ari sat down in the space his father had just vacated on the bench.

Clearly not a reunion I need to be part of, he thought to himself bitterly.

Ari watched on like a mute child while the adults talked with one another.

His father and Fliss stood in front of him, chatting airily, as though not a day had gone by. He listened with vague interest as Professor Nicander explained where he was living in Oxford, how the faculty had treated him so far, and the flat he had recently moved into with the funny-shaped windows.

'And the countryside in this part of the world!' he exclaimed to no one in particular. 'Quite fabulous... but only if it ends with the pub,' he said, his veiled attempt at humour falling flatly against Ari's wall of petulance. 'Yes... we quite enjoy it here,' he said.

Ari's eyes widened.

'We?' Ari asked.

'Yes...' Professor Nicander said slowly, turning to Ari now. 'Janine and I... my wife.' A silence descended once more. Ari said nothing, but looked away from the pair, into the wind. He wanted to feel the pain of the cold on his cheeks. He didn't have a mirror, but he knew they would be ruddy red. His cheeks always coloured when the weather changed. Much like his father's.

'It's been years, son,' he added after a time in a tone that sounded almost pleading. Ari did not look at his father.

For the first time in a while, he felt the wetness of tears in his eyes. He hoped the wind would cover him.

***

Chapter twenty-seven

Professor Nicander's flat really did have funny-shaped windows.

They were hexagonal, and Ari suspected they would have offered a glorious view of the nearby deer park if it weren't so dark outside. The whole place was fairly small, with two bedrooms and an open-plan kitchen-cum-living room. The furnishings hardly stretched the imagination, and the colour scheme was uninspired at best but boring at worst.

But what did grab the visitors' attention was the human skeleton laid out on the coffee table.

Ari sat perched on the edge of the armchair, one eye fixated on the mangled skull of the clearly very ancient bones, the other on the clock.

'*Homo Habilis,*' Professor Nicander proclaimed proudly as he entered the room. 'A loan from the Archaeology Department. He's quite something, no?'

Ari and Fliss shuffled awkwardly in their coats.

'He's proven to be a bit of a paradox in my field,' the Professor continued. 'Anyway, perhaps a story for another time.'

'Just tell him what we're here for Fliss, and let's get this over with,' Ari said, sulkily.

And so Fliss did. She explained everything that had happened to her and Ari at breakneck speed, including showing the Professor the half-tablet on her phone and how they had uncovered the second half of the statement, as well as the missing head pointing them toward Canterbury. She kept her voice hushed despite being inside, and by the end, Professor Nicander seemed both stunned and impressed.

'How did you manage to find the room?' he asked Ari, 'in *Aquae Sulis?*'

Ari shot a meaningful look at Fliss in response. He had never told his father about his abilities, and he didn't intend for him to find out now.

'How did you manage to remarry without mentioning it to your son?' Ari deflected. Not the most tactful approach, but he was certain that his father would get the point.

'OK,' his father said slowly. 'Let's try a different question. Why are you *here?*' he asked, enunciating the question.

Fliss gave Ari a reproachful look.

'Well, Professor,' she said. 'We need to know what can you tell us about King Henry II, Thomas Becket... and paganism?'

Professor Nicander rubbed at his scraggly beard, then frowned at nothing in particular.

'Treasure hunting are we?' he asked.

Ari was instantly transported back to his childhood, to the days when he and Fliss would sit and listen to his father give one of his lessons, and he would always start with a similarly enigmatic statement such as that.

Each week they would cover different topics, debates, philosophies, and talk about mysteries and histories, sometimes into the early hours of the morning. Sooner or later, Ari's mother would come in and demand they all went to bed.

How things have changed, Ari thought to himself. He doubted he could hold a conversation with his father for longer than a few minutes now.

'Obviously,' Ari said. 'We're not doing this for a history lesson. I had enough of them as a child,' he said, more scornfully than he had intended. Professor Nicander looked hurt but didn't engage.

'Well,' the Professor started, thoughtfully. 'The tale of Henry II and Thomas Becket's dispute is quite infamous, you know. I'm surprised you don't know it,' Professor Nicander said, removing his scarf.

'We know bits,' Ari replied. 'Will Janine be making an appearance by the way?' he asked. It had actually been the only question on Ari's mind since they had left the park, but he hadn't been able to bring himself to ask.

'No, no. She's away with some colleagues. Field research. She's a marine biologist and-'

Professor Nicander cut himself short. 'Anyway,' he said. 'You don't need to hear my ramblings, suffice to say she won't be joining us. Shame. You would like her.'

Ari said nothing. Fliss cleared her throat - and the tension - then said,

'Perhaps stick to the King?'

'Yes, quite... well, Henry, Becket and paganism. It almost sounds like Shakespeare,' Professor Nicander mused. 'I think the first thing to say is that King Henry II was, as you may know, not a particularly pious man in the Christian sense. By today's standards he would be considered a veritable bible basher - but for the time...

'No evidence of any pagan influence?' Fliss asked.

'The Danish invasions of the British Isles had ended some centuries prior to Henry's time here in the twelfth century, and the Romans had departed a millennium beforehand... No, we can say with absolute confidence that the population of medieval England would have been wholly Christian.

'Now, King Henry II took the throne in England in 1154 CE - the first King of the House of Plantagenet, the royal house that originated in Anjou - where he was from. I suppose *how* he came to be on the throne is entirely irrelevant, but the point I am making is that his taking over the English throne was the start of a new line of Kings, with the potential for a new *dynasty*. And with dynasty comes the pressure of legacy,' the Professor said with a rueful smile.

Ari and Fliss looked blankly at him.

'It has long been the obsession of a monarch to create something that will outlive them. Some achieve it through building. The Colosseum in Rome, for example, so named because of the *colossus* that once stood outside it; a giant statue of the Emperor Nero - an attempt to be remembered for anything other than playing the fiddle while Rome burned. Others, try to create a legacy by reputation. Henry VIII and the dissolution of the monasteries, Cromwell and his reforms. Others create it through inaction, such as Queen Victoria who was the longest reigning monarch of her time, or Saladin who reigned in the Middle East during the crusades, and was famed for his mercy.'

Professor Nicander paused to take a cigar box from the cabinet beside his chair, which he lit with a match. The room quickly filled with the smell of musty smoke, and before long a light haze had settled between the three of them.

'King Henry II, made *his* legacy by acquiring territory,' the Professor said. 'A popular technique. When he came to the throne his lands only extended across England and - of course - Northern France, as was the custom since the Norman invasion. But by the time he died in 1189 CE, his territories included Wales and Scotland. He had in fact almost been successful in securing Ireland too, but again, a story for another time perhaps.'

Ari visibly rolled his eyes. 'Is there a point to all this, *Professor?*' he asked, emphasising the final word.

'Well... I suppose I could simply answer the question you asked me now. Is there any connection between King Henry II, Thomas Becket and hidden pagan treasure? No,' he said, sitting back in his chair and taking another puff of his cigar.

Ari looked at Fliss, then made as though he were going to stand.

'Well!' Ari proclaimed. 'That was useless, thanks for the history lesson Dad, but we have to be getting on-'

'Wait,' Fliss cut in. 'Don't be so nasty Ari, we have nowhere to be except a hostel bed.'

Ari sat back down, perhaps a little quicker than someone who had ever really planned to leave would have done. 'There must be more you can tell us,' she said to Professor Nicander. 'Please.'

Professor Nicander scrunched his nose.

'Fine, but I don't appreciate being *rushed,*' he said, glaring at his son. He sighed and watched the smoke curl from the end of his cigar.

'Look,' the Professor said, a little haughtily. 'When Henry II took the throne, the country was in something of a mess. I won't get into the why or how, but the country's finances had been decimated from years of civil war.'

'So how did Henry manage to take the throne at such a tumultuous time and, by the sounds of things, immediately start conquering new territory in France, Wales, Scotland and Ireland, if he had no money?' Fliss asked.

Professor Nicander smiled. 'A very perceptive question indeed. There is lively debate among scholars as to exactly how King Henry II financed his conquests,' he said. 'And an almost equally lively debate about why he made his childhood friend, a clerk with no religious training, the archbishop of Canterbury and head of the church in England.'

'Thomas Becket?' Ari offered. The Professor hummed.

'Becket. Yes. He really wasn't suitable for office, and it would have been a controversial appointment... the popular theory is-'

'That the King wanted someone he could trust?' Fliss interjected.

'But trust to do *what?*' the Professor asked, answering her question with another. 'It is possible that he installed Becket as a yes-man. Someone who, as his friend and a man not traditionally religious, would be pragmatic and not intervene too heavily. But to what end? Being archbishop also made him Chancellor, so he would take control of the country's finances, but if the country had no finances to begin with, it wouldn't particularly matter who controlled them. Not to mention that Henry had witnessed first-hand how religious men could prove to be tricky customers: his Mother's husband was the Holy Roman Emperor Henry V. He would have had plenty of dealings with the Pope's officials as a child, perhaps even met the man himself. Henry would have known that in order to be given the freedom to rule as he saw fit, the church's role would need to be diminished.'

'Not a popular opinion at the time, I shouldn't have thought,' Fliss said.

'Definitely not. This is a population of people whose religious belief was unswerving. You must consider the belief in God and God's power as nothing short of fervent in the minds of a medieval Briton... I think the idea that a King would be capable of ruling *without* direct influence from God would have been quite alien. There are practices from that time that showed a devotion only heard of in legend.'

'Anyway,' the Professor continued. 'If it was the King's intention that Becket, his childhood friend and ally, would give him an easy ride as archbishop, he was wrong. In fact, from the second that Becket swore his allegiance to the church, he was nothing but a pain in the King's Royal arse. The infamous "turbulent priest" quip - as your tablet there so states. No, very quickly a rift grew between Henry and Becket, which led to a series of conflicts, culminating in something we know today called the Constitutions of Clarendon, where Becket was officially asked to agree to the King's unequalled power as head of state, or face the... *consequences*,' he said gravely.

Ari and Fliss watched as Professor Nicander removed his glasses, wiping them clean with a putrid yellow handkerchief he had drawn from the top of his pond-green overshirt.

He sighed audibly.

'Did I teach you two nothing?' he asked, suddenly irritable. 'You should know all this already. King Henry II presided over the assemblies of most of the higher English clergy at Clarendon Palace and, in sixteen constitutions, he sought less clerical independence and a weaker connection with Rome. He gained consent from all but Becket who refused to formally sign the documents. King Henry summoned Becket to appear before a great council to answer allegations of contempt of royal authority and *malfeasance in the Chancellor's office,*' he said, emphasising the last part of the sentence.

Ari and Fliss looked at him blankly.

'I'm more confused than I was when I arrived. Tell us what you're getting at,' Ari said, matching his father's irritability.

'What I am *getting at,*' the Professor said. 'Is that there is another angle from which you can view Becket and the King's rift. It was Becket the *Chancellor* that the King had a problem with, not Becket the priest!' he said.

He let that simmer for a moment. Fliss' face was one of concentration.

'Is it likely,' the Professor begin, musingly, 'that Thomas Becket saw through the King's plan to install him as archbishop, accepted the post and then began a campaign against him? Possibly. But I think more likely he took office, then the King told him something he thought was unreasonable. Or dangerous. Something that caused him to do everything in his power to stop the King from gaining success in his endeavours... But in either case, Becket was convicted of financial malpractice and fled to the continent,' he said.

'But, unfortunately, the tale of Thomas Becket doesn't end there... and it's also where the details get hazy. But for reasons that aren't quite clear, Becket came back, the charges against him seemingly dropped, but very much in the mood to agitate. He immediately started disbarring bishops and undoing many of the laws that Henry had enacted while Becket had been away... and, well, the rest is history, so to speak. Hearing their King speak the very words uttered that are inscribed on your tablet, his desire to be ridden of this turbulent priest, four knights set out to Canterbury cathedral under the misapprehension that they were carrying out the King's orders. By morning, of course, Thomas Becket was dead. The world reeled as news of such a heinous crime could be committed on holy grounds, and Becket became a martyr in the name of God.' Professor Nicander finally paused and relit his cigar.

'Becket's death didn't impede the King?' Ari asked.

'No. If anything, quite the opposite. Rather than detracting power from the King, Henry was free to appoint a new archbishop - this time making absolutely sure it was a man who he could rely on for this meekness – and he carried on as though Thomas Becket was a mere blip. There's a certain irony about a man achieving sainthood only to have it used to diminish the role of the Church, but that is what happened to Becket. King Henry used his death as a money-spinner, by making Becket "England's saint", and people made pilgrimages there for another two centuries which, incidentally, is how Canterbury gained its fame and is the setting for Chaucer's *Canterbury Tales*. And it wasn't until the dissolution of the monasteries some centuries later that the altar at the place of Becket's death was destroyed,' he added.

'I can't help get the sense, Professor, that there's something you're not telling us,' Fliss said, shrewdly. Ari looked at her confused, then back at his father, who, suddenly, seemed fatigued beyond his years.

He sighed heavily.

'I want to believe in the purity of the story, I truly do. A fight between two men standing for what they believed was right, the death of one being the gain of the other. Each on two sides of history carrying their own merits and pitfalls, but both too principled to concede defeat. One dying honourably, the other ruling nobly. You see, the problem with the study of these ancient characters is that we are dealing in the ephemera of the spoken word. Few people could read or write, and a single decision or utterance at a single point in time can alter the course of history. Like in this example. Had Henry II said something other than, "will no one rid me of this turbulent priest?" who knows, perhaps those knights would never have set off on their quest and no one would have gone for Thomas Becket that evening, he wouldn't have died and we, eight hundred years on, wouldn't be having this conversation,' the Professor said.

'And yet,' he continued, 'there are those outside these walls who would exploit these points in history for all they're worth. Ocean Pearl are one such example. If they were to make this discovery, for example, I am quite convinced that they would, like Henry II, only seek to make themselves rich. To those who merely want to listen, I find that history exposes more of itself than it would otherwise, as if our ancestors are trying to keep us from making the same mistakes as they did...'

'Dad?' Ari asked. 'What discovery?'

Professor Nicander snapped back into the room.

'I worry,' he said. 'I worry that if I tell you more, you plan to go looking at Canterbury cathedral. And I don't want that,' he said. 'I don't want you to go to the site of Becket's death looking for clues to a pagan treasure, I don't want you to cross swords with Ocean Pearl. I may be a desk researcher, but I have heard things that would shock you about that company.'

'We've already lived it,' Fliss said.

'Yes,' the Professor said, rounding on Ari now. 'And those thugs you were running with a few years back, hm? What about them? I assume you owe them money or something?'

'Owe them money?' Ari scoffed, almost with a laugh. Taken off guard, he let his temper get the better of him. 'What do you take me for?! You don't owe those kinds of people money. They would have just taken it from me!'

'And that's supposed to bring me comfort, is it? I should be glad of the fact that "at least my son isn't in debt to the murderous gang of smugglers."'

'You know nothing about what they did! Or what I did for them. They took me in when I needed a home-'

'You had a home!' Professor Nicander shouted, standing as he did so. 'We had a home. We had a *life*!'

Ari jumped to his feet too, causing Fliss to react and get in between them.

'*Sit down,*' she spat.

Ari and his father eyed each other menacingly but, reluctantly, they obeyed.

'Ari, you'll get your wish; we'll leave in a second. But first, Professor, you said that "if Ocean Pearl had made this discovery," ... what discovery are you talking about?' she asked.

The Professor seemed ruffled, less reserved. He was breathing a little more heavily and his eyes were glazed. Suddenly, his entire demeanour changed, and he adopted a veneer of nastiness that Ari had never seen in him before.

'Alright then,' he sneered, goadingly. 'You want to go off playing treasure hunter? See if you can get one over on Ocean Pearl? Fine – I'll answer. What if the King never uttered those words? What if those knights were always going to kill Becket?'

'Wait... what are you-' Fliss asked.

Professor Nicander said nothing, but instead jumped up and grabbed a newspaper that had been lying on the vacant armchair. He thrust it at Fliss. It had yesterday's date on it. Fliss read the title aloud,

'*Underground secrets of an archbishop*,' she looked up at Professor Nicander. 'What is this?!' she asked, rising a little.

'Well, it's a newspaper article about a diary... A diary that, until *yesterday*, was hidden, and had been hidden for eight hundred years,' he said.

Yesterday.

The epiphany washed over Ari, and he felt as though he were dreaming.

'This is the discovery? You gave it to Ocean Pearl? How much did they pay you?!' Ari demanded, rising from his chair once more.

Any colour that had been left in Professor Nicander's face drained away, and the dark circles underneath his eyes had become more pronounced.

'You had that newspaper ready, you knew we were coming! A diary conveniently found yesterday, you told Ocean Pearl about it!'

Fliss recoiled as though she had been physically wounded.

'Then we're too late,' she murmured.

'Ocean Pearl are dangerous!' the Professor exclaimed.

'You're in their pocket!' Ari said.

'And what of it?! I work twelve hours a day, seven days a week for a paltry salary and a two-bed apartment, they offered me more money than I earn in a lifetime!' the Professor exclaimed.

'So you revealed to Ocean Pearl the existence of Becket's lost diary, a dairy which, I assume, explains how he and King truly came to loggerheads, that the King had asked him to hide the use of a treasure to finance his wars? A pagan treasure?!' he demanded.

'No!'

Silence hung between them.

'No?' Fliss parroted.

'No,' the Professor repeated. He seemed to visibly shrink in his chair, and he paused to take another long draw on his cigar. 'I didn't tell them everything,' he said, a little more composed. 'I couldn't bring myself to. This is history, and it belongs to the people... it makes me sick to think of the danger I have put Janine in—'

'Get to the point!' Ari roared, still furious.

'Damnit!' the Professor shouted. 'Damnit! They barged into my office asking exactly the same questions as you are now,' he said. 'When I declined the money and tried to remove them from the premises, they threatened Janine - that's where she's gone. She's not out doing field research, she's in hiding! I told them about the diary... but what I *didn't* tell them, the crucial detail, is about the tomb of Becket, buried underneath the cathedral, in the catacombs.'

'Oh come on, this is-'

'It's true!' he said theatrically, rising from his chair. 'It's true... the information I gave them yesterday has led them to make a find that will not show them to the treasure. The diary is a red herring. It has been kept secret by the church for very different reasons, nothing to do with this treasure. It was always thought that Becket's body was lost when his tomb was destroyed, but there is a tomb, I'm sure of it. It's in the catacombs at Canterbury, and there will be *something* there that ties all this together. The body has been lost, for many centuries, hidden by Henry VIII in his deranged attempt to undermine Catholicism-'

'Skip the fucking history lesson!' Ari roared. 'None of this matters! I don't believe a word that you say. If they have found that diary, they might have found the treasure already, which means they don't need us anymore and the next time we bump into them could well be the last!' Ari said.

'Stop! Stop... If they find out I didn't tell them everything...'

'So why *did* you tell us?!' Fliss asked, matching Ari's fiery temperament. 'Why did you agree to meet?'

'They told me to! They told me that if my son comes asking questions, I should tell you everything, but not to tell you they had called!' he cried, then stood up with swift dexterity that belied his age.

Ari and Fliss exchanged a glance of mutual understanding, and Ari made a mental note to warn Kenny.

Ocean Pearl meant business this time.

'You're nothing more than one of their puppets,' Fliss said, disgusted.

Ari's mind turned to Ruaridh McIntosh, his dog and the lady in Benny's office who had sold him out. "They never knew Ruaridh or his dog," he remembered Benny saying. Professor Nicander growled.

'If they lay a single finger on my wife because of some shit you're into, Marius. If you cost me another family—'

The Professor didn't see the punch coming.

Ari hit him square on the jaw with an uppercut, exploding through his core and legs. Professor Nicander fell backwards in a slump on the chair behind him, and Ari had to stop himself from following through with a second blow.

He stood panting for a moment, his hand still balled up in a fist.

'Fuck,' was all he could manage to say.

'There's no time,' Fliss said.

She put her finger on the Professor's pulse, then bent down and listened to near his nose. 'He's breathing, I expect he'll come round and have nothing more than a sore head. Ari, we have to get to those catacombs.' Ari hadn't taken his eyes off his father.

'We'd be putting him in danger, they told him not to tell me that they had been looking for me - but he did. What if they come back for him?' he asked.

'They won't,' she said in a tone as calming as she could manage. 'Trust me. The best thing we can do to help him is to get this over with. If they're not looking for a treasure any more, they won't be looking for him. We'll make a plan in the car... Now come on, the catacombs, the tomb!' she repeated.

Reluctantly, Ari made his way toward the door, still watching to see if his father would wake up. He had punched many people before, but it wasn't just his hand that hurt. The sickening *crack* of his father's jaw on his fist stayed with him as Fliss dragged Ari to the hallway.

Somewhere in his mind, he was fairly sure he had heard Fliss use the word "car."

***

Professor Nicander came to sometime later.

His apartment was dark, the low hum of his refrigerator the only sound to break through the silence. He blinked a few times. Like a delayed relay feed, his head burst into an agonising thump a few seconds later. He groaned out loud and tried to stand, but found he was unable to do so. He looked down at his body stupidly, his mouth open, his expression vacant.

'What the-' he started to say out loud.

'I see you're awake, Professor,' came a voice from the dark. Professor Nicander jumped and tried to scramble across the sofa, but found himself flailing around like a limp fish.

'You tied my hands?!' he asked, eyes wild and breathing hard.

'Just a precaution,' the voice in the dark replied. 'You told your son everything, as planned,' he said.

'Yes,' he spat.

'And your "wife"? I admit that was a nice touch, I hadn't expected you to invent - what did you call her - Janine?' he asked.

The Professor's heart rate was beginning to settle, and he found he was able to think a little more clearly.

'I did what I had to,' he said, calmly.

Between breaths, Professor Nicander pictured his son in the catacombs of Canterbury cathedral. *If he unlocked the secrets of Aquae, he can unlock this too*, he thought.

'Now loosen these ties,' he said, his demeanour entirely changed. 'And put the fucking light on, Tennant - you would do well to remember who it is you're talking to.'

'Yes, of course,' Tennant replied. 'Didn't know we'd found a diary,' he said as he worked on untying the Professor, who let out an audible sigh. For a moment, he wondered whether he should just kill the man and find another agent, but he calmed himself with slow breathing before responding.

'We haven't found anything, Tennant, you damn fool. We haven't found anything,' he repeated, bitterly. 'And that's the problem! We need a win. Me, you, Prince, Aurora,' he said. 'I told him we had found a diary to incite a sense of urgency. To make him think we are closer than we are,' he said, rubbing his newly-unshackled wrists. 'I've been helping you lot out for what, twelve years?' the Professor asked. 'And I've hardly seen a penny in return. Risking my academic career for promises from *James Prince*,' he said, rolling his eyes. 'If anyone can uncover the treasure hidden at Canterbury cathedral, it's my son.'

***

Chapter twenty-eight

The Ocean Pearl safe house in Canterbury was, much like the rest of the city, quintessentially English.

A two-floor, thatched-roof cottage, with ivy growing thick up the trellis on the outside and a small garden hidden behind a white picket fence and an iron gate that clicked shut at the end of the path. Interspersed among the autumnal colours of the brick and grass and ivy were specks of colour where perennial flowers grew wild and tall.

Beautiful, but chaotic.

And yet, much like the rest of Britain, the city of Canterbury was anything but "English."

James Prince recalled from his research that the walls surrounding the city were of Roman origin, and the place had been settled by Anglo-Saxons and then raided by the Danes. It wasn't until around the 1000 CE mark that monks started to build their monasteries here and a settlement began to form.

One of those monks was the famous St Augustine, and the ruins of the monastery he installed which can still be seen today in the grounds of the colossal cathedral. Prince thought there was something almost entirely religious about the place. Despite not being particularly secular himself, it was as if the goodness of Christianity emanated from its centre.

Prince felt contemplative as he reclined on the green-leather armchair underneath the wooden beams of the country cottage and the real oil-burning lanterns flickering on the walls. The log fire made the room nauseatingly warm, but still he leaned over and stoked it a little with the poker that hung around the oakwood mantle, among an assortment of other trinkets and items.

Outside, the day had fallen into evening, and Prince was enjoying another large Macallan over ice. Somewhere upstairs, Prince could hear Aurora shuffling about as she readied herself.

After leaving Bath, he and Aurora had travelled to Canterbury - this time with a plan.

Tennant had recovered swiftly thanks to some of the more experimental medicinal methods employed by Ocean Pearl and, although he was uglier than before, he was back in the field, and that was all that mattered.

Aurora appeared at the bottom of the stairs.

'Can't we just sneak in there ourselves?' she asked. 'This all seems extraordinarily risky. What if the Professor gets it wrong?'

'The company's reputation in Canterbury would suffer even more than it already has if we get caught snooping around in there, and their position would become even more intractable. The treasure could be lost forever. No, we'd only make it more difficult for ourselves.'

'That's if we were caught,' she said. He ignored her.

'I understand your concerns, Aurora, but Ari has proven himself a worthy Finder already,' Prince said.

'Assuming he falls for it,' she added. Prince smiled.

'He already has. Tennant just sent a message. The Professor came through.'

Aurora raised an eyebrow in response. A Father, sending his own son into an Ocean Pearl trap. Prince guessed if push came to shove, she wouldn't draw that red line.

Prince wore a black turtleneck jumper with light blue jeans and black Air Max trainers, his short, salt and pepper hair stuck up neatly at the front and a fresh scent of Armani Code lingering behind his every movement. Aurora wore similarly nondescript clothing, her hair tied up behind her head in a tight bun. Outside the window, a light smattering of snow was beginning to form.

Prince had instructed the Professor that he should tell his son the truth of anything he knew about a treasure at Canterbury cathedral linked to *Aquae Sulis* and the pagans, but he should also tell him that Ocean Pearl had visited him the day previously and prised the same information from him. Crucially, though, he had to make it seem as though was supposed to have kept that part a secret.

To make it *seem* as though he had made a mistake. That would add a sense of urgency to Ari's movements, and Prince hoped it would encourage them down to Canterbury swiftly. This was important, because what he had as yet been unable to ascertain were Ondrej and the Bluebird's movements.

But that aside, by the sounds of things, all had gone to plan. Prince glanced at his watch. If Ari and Fliss made the journey immediately, as he expected they would, they would arrive within two hours.

But that wasn't the reason he was smiling.

'You seem to be particularly gleeful,' she said, her sarcasm returning to her naturally.

'Well, that phone call with Tennant was useful in more ways than one,' he said.

'Drop the enigma, Prince,' she said warningly.

'I know who the girl is. And she has played an absolute blinder,' he said. His smile widened to a grin, then a laugh. Aurora looked disconcerted. 'Oh Felicity,' he said, raising his glass. 'An absolute blinder.'

***

Chapter twenty-nine

Ari and Fliss arrived in Canterbury at 03:19 a.m. and realised fairly swiftly that it would be almost impossible for them to do anything at that ungodly time of day.

Ari had been correct about the car; his father apparently owned a brand-new, black BMW 5-series, which struck Ari as odd for a man usually so infuriatingly frugal. *Perhaps he's having a mid-life crisis*, Ari reflected.

In any case, the car had proven extremely useful, because it had allowed the pair to make good time from Oxford to Canterbury and, if they were lucky, Ocean Pearl wouldn't have already found what they were looking for.

And at least this time we know what we are looking for, Ari mused.

"It's in the catacombs at Canterbury, and there will be something there that ties all this together," Ari heard his father's words repeat in his head.

He rubbed his knuckles, still sensitive from the punch.

They had retreated to the only B&B that would take them in the middle of the night, a homely place called Greyfriars's Lodge. Fliss paid for a room with a view of the canal. It seemed nice enough, and the matron had been kind enough to make a room up for them without asking too many questions.

They went to bed without saying a word to one another, and Ari had been asleep before his head hit the pillow. In the morning, went to the reception of the lodge to pay for another night, then did something he had not done for eight years.

He called his father.

Professor Nicander seemed to have forgiven his son, but said he would tell Ocean Pearl, "everything they asked him to avoid his wife being hurt". For once, Ari agreed with his father's position. Ari went back to the room to find Fliss awake and dressed, where he suggested they go for breakfast.

Sullenly, she had agreed.

Keeping Fliss' identity a secret from Ocean Pearl was no longer going to be possible, although to Ari she seemed unusually worried about revealing it. She gave furtive glances up and down the side street that housed Greyfriars Lodge when they left, the low sunlight blinding her to anyone approaching from the left.

'There's no one here, Fliss. It's 08:30 on a Saturday morning,' Ari said. 'The tourists are asleep.'

Fliss said nothing but stepped out into the street and breezed past him, heading off in the direction of the town centre.

Greyfriars Lodge sat squarely in the middle of the city of Canterbury, a stone's throw from the cathedral, and Ari thought that Canterbury had a wholly ancient feel to it. Or he would have, had he not been so too exhausted to notice.

The inexorable feeling of hopelessness in the pit of his stomach was almost too much to bear, and he wondered whether Fliss felt the same. Ondrej, Benny, his father.

Anyone who had ever told him not to get tangled up with Ocean Pearl had been right; they weren't really any closer to finding a treasure than they had been a week ago, and Ari suddenly felt quite foolish.

After what seemed an age, the pair found a café with a sign outside that read, *"All Day Breakfasts – Clue's in the name!"* and, as they opened the door to the jingle of a small bell and trudged inside, Ari noticed it was very empty.

They sat and ordered two large coffees from an octogenarian woman who looked almost as exhausted as Ari. She shuffled off to fix the drinks, and now Ari and Fliss were faced with the joyless prospect of conversation.

'Doesn't make sense, does it?' Fliss asked, bizarrely cheerily. Clearly he had misread her mood. It incensed Ari to the point of despair to hear her speak so airily.

'You mean the fact that my father lives in a flat in Oxford with a skeleton and his new wife that he didn't tell me about, drives a fancy BMW, and that he now-'

'You don't get to be angry with that man, Ari, not after what you put him through,' Fliss said. Ari acquiesced and fixed his attention on his coffee. 'He moved on with his life, Ari. You could have been a part of it, you chose to work for that gang instead,' she said.

'Working for that gang saved me from-'

'Saved you from what, Ari? This is your mess, you created it. You could have chosen a life that included your father. And me,' she added.

'Look,' Ari said, softening his tone. 'I know now that what I was doing with Ondrej all those years ago was wrong, and of course, it ended pretty badly.'

'Pretty badly?' she asked, turning to look at him disbelievingly. 'Pretty badly?' she repeated. 'Yeah Ari, I'd say-' she cut herself short unexpectedly.

Ari eyed her mistrustingly.

'Well, what *would* you say?' he asked. Fliss seemed to be lost for a moment, then her eyes regained focus.

'I'd say I lost my best friend! I thought you were dead, Ari!' she said in a hushed whisper, wary of others in earshot. 'My mother is a lunatic, my father is god-knows-where, and it wasn't until I took that *fucking* job at the Fruit Exchange that...' she trailed off.

Ari broke in with a change of subject.

'Will no one rid me of this turbulent Priest? Sulis, let it never be found. Henry,' he said aloud.

Fliss said nothing.

'You're right,' he continued slowly. 'This whole thing doesn't make any sense. Still all we have are rumours. Rumours that this treasure exists based on the financial records of a medieval king, rumours of a diary that will somehow link all this together, rumours of a body buried underneath a cathedral that might point us to a treasure.'

They were interrupted by the arrival of their breakfast, which improved Ari's mood almost immediately. They spent a few seconds eating in silence, perhaps both having underestimated the severity of their famine.

'Well, we do know one thing for certain,' Fliss said after a time, between mouthfuls.

'Oh yeah? What's that?'

Fliss mulled over her response for a second before answering. 'We know that that Ocean Pearl acted on your father's advice about the diary the instant they heard about it... and that means they think there is something to find. Perhaps a Big Find.' Ari raised an eyebrow at the use of the company jargon but hummed in agreement.

'Well then, let's hope these catacombs tell us where that "Big Find" might be,' he said, before shovelling another bit of sausage down his throat.

***

In the queue for evening Mass outside Canterbury cathedral, darkness had washed over them, and the Gothic stone of the medieval structure bathed in bright up-lighting, each and every detail of its wonderful decoration resplendent in an amber glow.

Ari's senses were almost overwhelmed as he stood in the throng of worshippers waiting for the colossal double doors to be opened. He focused his vision on different aspects of its facia, drinking in the splendour of the architectural work and allowing himself to imagine what it would have been like to have seen the cathedral in its infancy.

Perhaps most striking was, given its considerable size and length, that not a single inch of the building was left untouched, and the sculptors had clearly spared no expense in crafting their temple. Ari felt a pang of guilt for his and Fliss' plan, but talked himself around by convincing himself that if he didn't find the secret to this treasure, then Ocean Pearl surely would. And they would be far more disruptive than he and Fliss.

Or, even worse, Ari thought, *Ondrej.*

'This won't be easy,' Fliss muttered. He wondered if she too had let her imagination get the better of her.

'Should we abandon the plan?' he asked.

'No!' she squealed. 'If anything, my resolve is hardened. I'm just saying - it won't be easy. The fact that the cathedral is open for this Mass at all and hasn't been put into some kind of lockdown tells you that Ocean Pearl haven't tried anything yet, which means that somehow - we're here in time.'

'Yeah. Or we're springing their trap.'

To fight the cold, Ari had brought with him a long, dark overcoat with a matching scarf and gloves. His battered Chelsea boots weren't quite right for the temperature, but he wouldn't trust another pair of shoes if things got tetchy with Ocean Pearl.

Fliss too wore a winter coat and comfortable trainers. Much to her chagrin, her face was uncovered.

'They'll probably guess we're up to something if you don't show your face!' Ari had argued. It was unassailable logic, and she hadn't pushed the point.

The congregation of people queuing outside the main doors of the massive building shuffled without moving, and Ari's thoughts once again turned to his father.

'You can see why people made pilgrimages here,' he muttered to Fliss.

She had been on edge all afternoon, as though revealing her face had somehow broken the illusion for her that what they were doing somehow wasn't really happening. They had spent the afternoon going over the blueprints of the cathedral and hatching their "plan," if it could be called that. Ari's heightened vision allowed him to view the maps in a 3D render in his mind's eye, and it made it much easier for him to get to know a place if he was able to see the blueprints first, no matter how crude.

He glanced at Fliss who, perhaps unsurprisingly, looked white as a sheet.

People around him sniffled and coughed, speaking to each other in low voices in foreign languages as, finally, the mechanism behind the doors clicked and swung silently open, revealing the Dean of the cathedral stood in the entryway, surrounded by bright light that spilt out from the inside, giving him an almost angelic quality.

He was older, greying, and altogether unremarkable. But he smiled in a warm, grandfatherly way, as though he were inviting them into his home.

'Welcome,' the Dean said to the flock. 'Please, come in.'

At once, the crowd lurched forward toward the door, desperate to get out of the cold.

As they drew nearer, the overwhelmingly large face of the cathedral hung over him, Ari looked upwards and almost physically crossed himself, but refrained.

He found it to be a very powerful experience, walking through the doors of the episcopal seat of England, and his atheism threatened to abandon him as he felt himself being swept along in the religious current.

A moment of villainy in a place of pure sanctity, he thought to himself.

The cathedral had seen much worse, he thought, thinking of Becket's murder.

And he hoped that, on balance, the world would remember him better than the four knights who murdered the archbishop so many centuries ago. *If history remembers me at all,* he added, soberly.

Ari and Fliss took up seats quite near the altar. Behind them, the choir sang a soft, soothing hymn, and there was an air of anticipation among the churchgoers, as though the crowd were expecting the return of Christ at any given moment.

It was clear that no one present was a regular member of the flock, and they had all chosen to take in a Mass as part of a visit to England. *Each to their own,* Ari thought to himself, who couldn't imagine a worse way to kill time during a vacation.

Now that he was inside, though, nothing could have prepared him for the splendorous magnificence of Canterbury cathedral. No amount of videos watched or pictures seen could do justice to the deep shades of gold leaf that spanned the length of the walls, interspersed with a painted teal that clashed but worked.

Hung strategically around the cavernous nave were typically gruesome and vivid Christian paintings depicting various scenes from the bible, and Ari wished he knew more about their origin and representations. He focused his vision on a few, craning his neck to admire the detail of the brushwork. Many of these paintings were on the ceiling, inserted in a way that made the characters seem as though they could have stepped down and joined the mass at any time.

Eventually, the Dean reappeared at the altar, and the humdrum dipped to an almost eerie silence. The noise of the heavy wooden doors at the front of the cathedral being slammed closed reverberated around the nave. Ari looked at Fliss out of the corner of his eye. She gave him a meek smile in return.

'All rise,' the Dean said, his voice deep and saint-like. There was a cacophony of shuffling as everyone in the hall did as they were commanded. 'Praise be to God,' he said.

The crowd murmured it back to him.

'You may be seated.'

***

Ari's heart was beating out of his chest. He looked back at the corridor he had just sprinted down, but saw nothing, only the white outlines of the brickwork in his night vision, and the gentle sway of the blue curtain at the end, which led back to where the Mass had been held. He wondered whether he had been detected, and strained his hearing, but there didn't seem to be anyone with him.

Compared with the echoey Mass, it was bizarrely quiet.

He couldn't help but smile to himself. Fliss had played her part beautifully. Right at the moment when the Dean was about to start the choir on a new hymn, she had stood up, exclaimed something unintelligible and fainted dramatically. The ensuing chaos had been even more pronounced than Ari had expected.

The Dean, who had walked down the centre aisle toward the choir, spun in all directions looking for assistance, which a gaggle of churchgoers had leapt from their seats to provide.

In addition, a number of security personnel in high-vis vests had descended and were trying to disperse those who now encircled the incapacitated Fliss. Ari wondered whether the extra security had been employed as a result of Ocean Pearl sniffing around.

A crude plan, but an effective one.

In the midst of the mayhem, Ari had taken approximately three steps to his right and disappeared behind a blue curtain, which he suspected no one had noticed.

And, even if they had, he was sure they would have believed him to be allowed to be there. The corridor behind the blue curtain led him down a series of stone passageways that had, eventually, brought him to the room where Thomas Becket had been killed.

Despite his running, Ari was cold.

The room was vast, tall, and the exact spot where Becket had been struck down was marked by a plaque on the floor, which bore the martyr's name in dramatic, blood-red lettering.

Above, a sculpture of four swords, two of which had bloodied tips, pointed downwards to where he had been murdered. In all, Ari couldn't say he cared for the modern twist on the ancient site.

He stood with his hands on his hips for a moment, despite being very aware that the time he had to study it and potentially find a clue to any treasure could be interrupted at any moment. He focused his vision on the writing but saw nothing. Then too on the swords, but there was nothing there either.

Shit, he thought to himself.

Ari realised he was - again - woefully under-prepared. He had studied a few maps, had a haphazard diversion conversation with Fliss then headed off to unravel an eight-hundred-year-old mystery without the first clue as to where he should really start looking.

He scanned the whole room.

He spotted there was some Latin writing above the door, but all it said was that the room was the place of the martyrdom of Thomas Becket, some strange shapes on the floor - which told him nothing - and more examples of glorious but hideous Christian scenes, this time depicted by stained-glass windows.

He sighed audibly and looked down the corridor to his right. *Perhaps there's something behind, a set of stairs*, he thought to himself, very much unconvinced by his own chain of thought.

'You won't find what you're looking for here, son,' someone said in the darkness.

Ari nearly jumped out of his skin.

I didn't hear anyone approach?! he thought to himself, questioning his heightened hearing. Panicked, he spun around, wondering why he hadn't detected someone's imminent arrival. It wasn't often he was taken by surprise.

'Who's there?' Ari asked out loud, confident at first, then abashed. He felt foolish.

He strained his hearing down the corridor, beyond the curtain. In the hall of the cathedral, he could pick out Fliss' voice quite clearly, complaining of light-headedness. The rest of the hall sounded empty, and he assumed the sermon had been abandoned.

'Follow my instructions to the letter,' the mystery voice said. The Martyrdom was the name given to the spot where Becket had been murdered.

'Keep going,' the voice continued, 'and eventually it'll lead you to a section which gives access to the grounds. Cross into the courtyard there. Head for the archway in the furthest corner. There's a barrier. Hop over it. You'll be in a car park. *Don't* go to the front door of the building in front of you. Follow the path to the right. As you round the corner, you'll see a set of stairs leading down toward a large wooden door. Knock three times. Like this -'

There was a tapping noise that sounded like static. One, two in quick succession, then a pause of a count of one Mississippi and another knock.

Ari realised in that moment where the voice was coming from; a series of small white speakers mounted on the walls around the room, which he saw now that he was looking for them. His heightened vision was great for detail, but sometimes missed the big picture.

'Meet me there.'

The voice clicked off leaving Ari to stare disbelievingly at the Martyrdom.

Ari strained his hearing once again back to the cathedral hall, but couldn't make out Fliss' voice this time. Perhaps she had been so convincing in her acting that she had been taken to hospital. He felt a pang of guilt as he thought of leaving her, but couldn't see an alternative.

For a moment, he wondered whether this was some kind of Ocean Pearl ruse.

Perhaps they wanted to demonstrate that he was in over his head, and this was some elaborate way of upstaging him. If that were the case, he resolved himself that he would face up to his foolishness with at least a degree of humility. He gave one last meaningful look at the place where Thomas Becket had died. He wondered what the old Martyred archbishop would have made of his actions.

At a brisk pace, he set off for the courtyard.

***

Chapter thirty

Ari had followed the instructions given by the voice of the speaker as best as he could remember them. He wasn't sure whether he had managed to carry them out exactly, but as he looked around he was fairly sure that he was in the right car park the voice had described.

The temperature had dropped even further, and the cold stung his eyes and ears while the rest of his body was warm, protected by his winter coat. Mist rose from his mouth and nostrils.

The building in front of him was illuminated by a single, tall black lamp, which he suspected would have shown very little to a normal eye. He, though, could see evidence of some extremely old stonework in the buttresses protruding from the walls, and the faces of religious figures in an archepiscopal cartouche that he doubted the current occupier would have been able to make out even during daylight, as they appeared to him outlined in white.

He glanced around the car park and, quite certain he was alone, followed the face of the building until, almost to his surprise, he saw the set of stairs the voice had mentioned. Slowly, he descended, straining his hearing for any sign of movement. *Or Ocean Pearl,* he thought.

He could hear nothing of what - if anything - lay beyond the door at the stairs' base. He considered echolocating to find out what was behind it, but decided it to be a futile endeavour, given that he would almost certainly be going in anyway. When he reached the door he knocked three times, a count of one Mississippi breaking the second and third taps.

He felt sweat begin to form around his armpits that was unrelated to his winterwear. The door creaked open, and a hooded face appeared in its wake.

'Get in,' the figure muttered. Ari obliged, and the door slammed behind him.

'An undercroft?' Ari said out loud.

Centuries-old, clearly, but still a working pantry, the large underground space was filled with old wooden barrels that he assumed housed wine or whiskey, and the walls were lined with shelves whereupon there sat an immeasurable amount of food, herbs and ingredients.

The whole place smelled of ginger, which caught in his throat, but stopped short of making him cough. He turned around to face his unknown accomplice who, to his astonishment, had removed his hood to reveal a thin, bespectacled face. It wore a kindly smile.

The archbishop of Canterbury looked different in real life.

He was older than Ari would have envisioned, and somehow without the dazzle of his robes, he seemed a lot earthlier.

He was thin, spindly and a little sickly-looking. But there was an authoritative air about him that Ari suspected came from years of doing God's work. Not sanctimonious or unctuous, but a degree of self-assuredness that Ari didn't think was common for most people.

'Something the matter, son?' the archbishop asked. He removed his glasses and wiped them on the inside of his coat.

'I'm not particularly religious, but I know who you are,' Ari said, with all the gravitas of a child. 'I wasn't expecting-'

'The archbishop?' he asked. 'In the archbishop's Palace?' he smiled again. 'Don't worry. I get it all the time,' he said with a wink. He walked past Ari and retrieved two glasses from a nearby shelf.

'Drink?' he asked. Ari shook his head, and the archbishop gave him an almost penitent look. He shrugged.

'I'm having one.'

Ari said nothing as the archbishop twisted a valve on one of the wooden casks and a golden brown liquid slid into his glass. He filled what Ari thought was slightly more than a double measure, then flicked it off. Two chairs had been pulled to face opposite one another on either side of a barrel, and the archbishop gestured that Ari should sit down while he took the other seat.

'Maybe I will have that drink,' Ari said. He crossed the room and filled the other glass, then took up his place. 'Er-' he began awkwardly. 'What do I call you?'

The archbishop laughed out loud.

'*That's* your first question?!' he asked incredulously. 'Incredible... Gregory, will do fine I'd say. And you?'

He doesn't know who I am, then, Ari thought to himself.

Ari couldn't say that he had been entirely put at ease by learning the identity of the mystery voice - not after seeing how easy Ocean Pearl seemed to find it to get to people. But, if that were the case, the archbishop - *Gregory* - knew his name already, and this was a bluff.

'Ari,' he replied. 'Well, Marius, actually,' he added.

'Marius? Unusual name. I only know one other. But that's not important right now,' Gregory replied.

'I share it with my father,' Ari said.

Gregory ignored that comment, but instead said,

'Well then Marius Nicander... why are you here?' he asked, gazing at Ari with an unwavering stare.

Ari stared back.

'I'm-' he started to say, but the archbishop raised a hand and was now looking over Ari's shoulder, at the door.

'There's no one there, Gregory,' he said in an almost condescending tone. The archbishop shot him a reproving look.

'And you would know that how, exactly?'

Ari hadn't properly appreciated the extent of his fatigue until that moment. In his tiredness, he had almost given away a secret that he had held close to his chest - save for Fliss and Ondrej - for his entire adult life. He found himself wondering whether it would really be so bad to tell Gregory, the one man he had met in recent times who probably *wouldn't* try to exploit him.

But then again, if he's an Ocean Pearl man...

'Because I made sure I wasn't followed,' Ari said, deflecting. 'You asked why I'm here,' Ari said. 'I came to witness Mass in the cathedral,' Ari said.

'Interesting. You just said you're not religious,' he said. 'And I found you skulking around a backroom, far away from the altar.'

'I was, uh, lost,' Ari said.

The archbishop looked reproachful.

'Marius, I want to be honest with you when I answer your questions, of which I am sure there are many, but I can only do that if you have been honest with me. Right now, I do not trust you,' he said frankly.

Ari sighed deeply. He didn't enjoy being backed into a corner.

'I was looking at the place where Thomas Becket died,' he said after a short pause. Gregory raised an eyebrow that made the frame of his glasses shift on his face.

'One of my more infamous predecessors,' he said in response. 'And - stepping back slightly - you came here, to Canterbury, to do that this evening?' he asked.

'Yes,' Ari said.

'Excellent,' Gregory said, almost cheerfully. 'Then they were right: you were here to rob me.'

Ari's face dropped.

'No, you don't understand-' he started to say, but once more was cut short by the simple raise of a finger from the older man opposite him.

'Marius, I understand more than you give me credit for,' he said solemnly.

Gregory stood up from his chair, which scraped uncomfortably along the stone floor and began to pace. 'But I wonder whether you might be able to fill in a few gaps for me? You see, I was approached here - in the Old

Palace grounds - two nights ago by two Ocean Pearl people in the car park. I know they were Ocean Pearl because they wore those stupid wetsuits,' Gregory said. It was odd to hear an archbishop speak so disparagingly.

'Anyway,' he continued. 'I would like to know whether my suspicions about them are correct. They had a warning for me, you see, that my cathedral was under attack, that I would be robbed imminently, and that once I had apprehended the culprit I should do everything in my power to hold them here.'

Ari's heart sank, and he felt more than a little nauseated. *So it was a trap, luring us here.* His mind flashed to Fliss, and he wondered whether she had been apprehended. 'They assured me it was "Official Business",' Gregory continued. 'Not something I want to "dirty my hands with." Perhaps I shall decide for myself what should be dirtied and what should remain clean. But these people are dangerous and powerful. Canterbury has always resisted Ocean Pearl influence, but I may not be able to do so indefinitely. You understand now why I was watching the cameras while the Dean gave Mass tonight; something I do not usually do,' he said, sitting back.

He leant over the back of the chair in a way that, for some reason, Ari didn't expect of a holy man. 'Tell me the story of how you came to be here this evening,' he commanded.

Ari took a sip of the drink he had poured. It was sweet wine. He wondered whether it was the same wine served when they hosted guests in the refectory above, but decided that changing the topic of conversation in that moment would do little to deter the archbishop from getting to the bottom of the truth, and so he instead recounted the story from the very beginning. Once he started, he actually found it quite difficult to stop.

From his entanglement with Ondrej at Merchant's Lodge all those years ago, the Fruit Exchange, the Williamson Tunnels, Fliss showing him the tablet, *Aquae Sulis* and the second half of the message, what the message said, and his conversation with his father, although he left out the fact that their conversation had ended violently, and then high-tailing it down to Canterbury following his father's clues.

He omitted the exact nature of how he had made the discoveries using his heightened senses.

By the time he was finished, Gregory had poured a second glass of wine from the barrel.

'Well then,' he said, distractedly. 'That is quite the tale.'

'Tale? You don't believe me?' Ari asked, eyeballing the archbishop.

'What? Oh no, I believe you. It's just that I am... well,' he stood again. Then sat. Then stood once more.

'Gregory?' Ari asked concernedly. 'Are you OK?'

'Tell me... what are you *actually* looking for?' he asked. Ari felt his cheeks colour with embarrassment, but said,

'Treasure. The pagan treasure that King Henry wanted to use, but couldn't because of Thomas Becket.'

The archbishop hummed. 'And what are Ocean Pearl looking for?' he asked.

'Me. And the treasure. Both, really. The fact they warned you someone would attack the cathedral tells me that they are trying to get me to discover the treasure for them,' Ari replied.

The archbishop drained his glass of sweet wine in one gulp, then put his hands on his knees and leant forward, his head sagging toward the floor. When he looked up, it seemed as though there were tears in his eyes.

'Sorry, Marius, sorry. But you must surely understand the gravity of the tale you have told me?' he asked.

The archbishop paused for a few moments further, then asked,

'Can I interest you in a proper drink, perhaps somewhere nicer?'

Chapter thirty-one

Gregory was right, Ari thought to himself as he sank into the leather chair. *It is nicer here.*

The Shakespeare was one of the best-preserved fifteenth century houses in the whole of England, and Ari wondered how much trouble had been taken to ensure the place kept its "original" feel each time it had been refurbished.

The upstairs room was simultaneously modern and antiquated, each part of it likely to house a touchscreen menu as it was some medieval artefact. There was a marble fireplace with a real wood-burning fire that roared audibly over the gaggle of punters, all of whom were crowded around large, barrel-shaped tables. The walls were stone, the windows single-glazed and the beams in the roof looked as though they were about to collapse; the ideal spot for a clandestine chat with the archbishop of Canterbury about an ancient treasure, or so Ari thought.

Gregory had led him from the cellar through a series of tunnels, which had gone on for much longer than Ari had anticipated.

He had been surprised when they had come to the end of one of the passageways and had been greeted with a door. Gregory had knocked three times - in the same fashion as he had asked Ari to knock on the door to the undercroft - and a few moments later a hatch had slid open. The archbishop had mumbled something incomprehensible, and the door was unlocked from the other side. They were greeted by a large, bearded man who introduced himself as Phil.

'We've been hostin' archbishops here for o'er six hundred years,' he had claimed proudly, before showing them up a set of rickety, wooden stairs. The stairs had led to a back corner of the upper level and a table marked with a *G*, where he sat now.

Ari focused his vision and could see where a number of other letters had been etched in previously - a *J*, an *R*, perhaps another *G* - but it was difficult to tell much further back than that, even with his vision. *Justin, Rowan, another Gregory,* Ari thought, recounting archbishops.

A table reserved for them, Ari thought.

Phil reappeared. 'What'll it be?' he asked.

Ari removed his coat. He found it difficult to relax, but short of having a curtain pulled across the booth he thought it was as private as it was possible to be. And he suspected another drink might help his nerves.

'Do you have Kraken?' he asked.

'We certainly do!' Phil exclaimed over the hubbub of punters behind him. Ari asked for two large measures and, by the time he had finished ordering, the archbishop had an internet page open on his phone, which he pointed in Ari's direction. Ari frowned.

'The Parker Library?' he asked with genuine confusion. The Parker Library at Corpus Christi College, Cambridge, had a digital archive available on its website.

'Yes... it's there somewhere,' the archbishop replied. He snatched the phone back and frowned

275

concentratedly, the glare from the screen illuminating his holy features.

'Make sure you call me Gregory in here, by the way,' he added in a lowered tone. Ari nodded.

'Do those tunnels go anywhere else, by the way, Greg?' He couldn't keep a look of boyish mischief away from his face.

The archbishop smirked.

'Never you mind,' he said in an attempt at a stern tone. 'Now, where are we? Ah, yes,' he put the phone back on the table and slid it across to Ari, who was reminded of Fliss making a similar action with her phone when she had first introduced him to the tablet.

How things had changed since then.

He wasn't even sure he knew how long ago those events had taken place. Another waiter - not Phil this time - brought their drinks over, which Ari and the archbishop clinked together before Ari turned his attention back to the screen and frowned. He focused his vision on the detail. As with the tablet, it was harder to see on a pixelated screen.

'What is this?' he asked after a time.

'This,' Gregory said. 'Is the *private* archive of the Parker Library.'

Ari glanced at the top right-hand corner of the screen and noticed where it said: *You are logged in as TMR.*

'TMR?' Ari asked.

'The Most Reverend,' Gregory said with a roll of his eyes. 'They like their little jokes,' he added apologetically.

'Right,' Ari said. 'What am I looking at?'

Gregory removed his glasses and wiped them on his sleeve.

'The key to everything,' he replied, simply.

***

A while later, two more Krakens were delivered to the table. This time, it was Phil who brought them over.

'All good 'ere sir?' he asked. Ari smiled and waved him on, muttering his thanks. The Shakespeare had grown steadily busier as the evening had drawn on, and they had brought out more tables for punters to sit at. Even so, some people now stood by the fire, their drinks resting upon the wooden mantle as they leant, growing steadily drunker.

Otherwise, everything was the same, but the archbishop of Canterbury had been replaced with his childhood friend Felicity Candle, who sat in the archbishop's vacated seat.

Ari should have been exhausted, but he felt more alert than he had for days.

Ari had called Fliss the moment Gregory had disappeared down the staircase at the back of the pub. He wondered how many other people would have known where it led, but then almost immediately guessed that the answer was zero.

'Don't use the tunnel again, Marius,' Gregory had said just before he had left. 'I am sure *they* know it exists, they seem to know just about everything, but they mustn't know the information that I have given you here tonight,' he had said gravely.

'Do you understand what I am telling you? As we have discussed, if you must go off and find the treasure then so be it, but it will be given to the cathedral and we, as we have always done, will resist Ocean Pearl authority.'

'I understand, Gregory,' Ari had said. And he had meant it, too.

'They may have authority over treasure hunting, but this is a treasure that no one company should possess. This is a treasure that belongs to the people. This is the history of the goodness of Christianity personified, and Thomas Becket should - finally - be granted his wish,' he said. 'That the pagan treasure is used by the church to do good in the community.'

Ari wasn't sure he saw it like that, but he did agree with Gregory's sentiment; any treasure found as a result of their actions belonged to the people, not to Ocean Pearl. He smiled to himself. *I'm becoming like my father after all.*

Fliss had shown up shortly after he had called her. Phil had let them keep the booth.

'Great acting during the sermon,' Ari said, playfully.

'Never mind all that,' she replied promptly, taking her coat off and immediately starting on the Kraken. 'Tell me what happened,' she replied. Ari raised an eyebrow.

'Calm down,' he said. 'You're clearly shaken up.'

He inspected her a little more closely. Her nervous energy from earlier in the evening had given way to a more erratic way of holding herself, and for a moment it seemed as though she had taken some kind of drug.

'Are you alright? What happened after the cathedral?' he asked, genuinely concerned. She took a long breath and put her head in her hands. When she looked back up at him, she was smiling, and it seemed he may have confused her mania for exhaustion. Her well-groomed appearance was gone, but her kindly demeanour was back.

'I'm just shattered,' she said calmly. 'It has been quite the ordeal. They emptied out the cathedral and the Mass was brought to an early end. Some paramedics arrived and I was carted outside toward an ambulance. I managed to break free and run. They tried to catch up with me and spent a long time looking for me, but I was well hidden. Eventually, they must have called it a night, because the last I saw of the ambulance was the back of it, heading out of the city. So, I just stayed where I was and waited for you to call,' she said, taking a sip of her rum.

She scrunched up her face afterwards as the taste threatened to overwhelm her, then relaxed into a warm smile.

'Honestly, Ari, I'm fine,' she added. She wrapped both of her hands around his across the table. 'Tell me everything,' she said.

And so, for the second time that evening, Ari found himself explaining his actions. When he reached the part about the staircase and The Shakespeare, she looked enthusiastically around the side booth and let out an audible gasp at the sight of the banister.

'Incredible!' she exclaimed.

'Heh, wait until you hear the rest,' he said. He went on to explain everything that archbishop Gregory had told him about King Henry and Becket.

How King Henry II of England was not a particularly pious man. How he was more concerned with making sure that England's territories were shored up and her citizens properly protected from outside threats than anything else. How he had taken over at a time of civil war, and people's appetite for God was slim. How, when he took the crown, he would have been told of a vast fortune of pagan treasure that had been hidden underneath the temple of *Sulis Minerva* at the ruined site of the Roman Baths in *Aquae Sulis*.

How, in the main, it consisted of offerings that people had made hundreds of years beforehand, during the days of the Roman Empire, and how the hoard had been added to, rather than raided, by the Danes during their Viking invasions in the ninth and tenth centuries, because they worshipped the same pagan Gods.

Ari explained that Gregory had told him that these offerings ranged from a few coins to substantial sums of gold, weapons, heirlooms, altars etc. Usually, as Ari and Fliss knew, they were accompanied by a *tabula defixionis* - a curse tablet - which essentially asks the goddess Sulis Minerva to ensure that a rival business fails, a fight is lost, a family will have all girls etc. in exchange for the item offered. The bigger the ask, the more valuable the item. Over time, these votive offerings were collected by the temple priests and hidden in a vast room underneath the temple of *Sulis Minerva*, which Ocean Pearl had discovered in the nineties.

'How does he know all this?' Fliss asked, suspiciously.

'Well, so far it's not much more than we do,' Ari countered.

'True... but he has details of the treasure?'

'He said, and I quote, "I should remember this isn't the first time that Ocean Pearl have come sniffing around Canterbury in search of this treasure," and that in their attempts to persuade him to allow them to excavate parts of the cathedral in search of clues, they had tried to tempt him with the vastness of the fortune available,' Ari said. Fliss hummed her understanding.

'So, the claims may be exaggerated?' she asked.

'Possibly. I saw the room underneath *Aquae*, and it was large, and they had clearly been chronicling the items they found but... yes, I assume their estimate was nothing more substantial than just that - an estimate.'

Ari went on to explain that the archbishop had confirmed that Ocean Pearl had discovered the room using their remote-sensing technology, then had figured out the easiest way in was through the drain. Once they gained entry, though, they found it empty - clearly the treasure had been moved at some point in time, but the only clue to its whereabouts was-

'The second head of *Sulis*, with the Cornish Choughs,' Fliss interjected.

'Exactly,' Ari replied. 'And I think their renewed interest tells us that they found the missing half of the tablet, the one that I lost at *Aquae* and had the quote about the turbulent priest written on it. This would have been another sign clearly linking them to Becket, and Gregory seemed to think they must not have had a clear idea of what they were looking for last time, as they didn't press him as hard as he thought they might have done otherwise,' Ari said. He was reminded of Benny's words, "there was always a feeling that they had missed something at *Aquae*."

Ari went on to explain that Henry II was constantly fighting rebellions against his sons, and the years of war that had preceded him meant that the state coiffeurs were empty. The crown was wealthy, but not so wealthy that it could sustain continuously fighting these intra-familial skirmishes. And that was when Henry began dipping into the gold at the Temple of Sulis Minerva, selling individual items to wealthy tradespeople from the Far East for large sums of money. Fliss looked aghast.

'So... it's gone? Sold?' she asked.

'Not so fast,' Ari said. 'The Byzantine Empire was still going strong, and many of its citizens felt that these treasures - while relics of the West - still belonged with the Roman Empire in the East. Henry may not have been pious, but religion was extremely important around the world at the time, and he realised very quickly that the church was unlikely to take kindly to using pagan treasures to finance wars - especially ones linked to curses. We were correct in guessing that he was of the mind that if it got out, it could be perceived that the pagan goddess *Sulis Minerva* had helped Henry to defeat his sons and gain power over a united Britain, which could undermine the church and possibly undo the work that had been done to bring Christianity to the fore. Enter Stage Left: Thomas Becket,' he said.

'How did the Archb-'

Ari shot her a warning look.

'Sorry - *Gregory*,' she said, pointedly. 'Again I ask, how did Gregory know all this?' she asked, suspiciously.

'I'll come to that, I promise. Anyway, Henry had decided that the best way to circumvent this problem was to appoint one of his closest advisers - Thomas

Becket - in the role as Chancellor of the Exchequer - the state's chief financial advisor and accountant.'

'I think we failed to appreciate that before,' she said. 'That he was Chancellor *before* he was archbishop. I guess it makes sense... we know he worked as a cleric and all available sources single him out as being a gifted individual. No doubt he could have turned his hand to the Chancellorship without too much issue.'

Ari nodded his agreement and lowered his voice.

'Here's where things get interesting. Shortly after the King had made this appointment, the sitting archbishop - Theobald de Bec - died,' Ari said, in almost a whisper.

'That's hardly news, Ari. I could have told you that,' Fliss said, not bothering to lower her own voice for what she clearly deemed to be a trivial fact.

'Listen!' Ari urged in a shrill register. 'There was a lot of turmoil between de Bec and King Henry... de Bec had opposed him at a number of key points, had not intervened in key matters of state and had, in general, been a thorn in the King's Royal backside! He was still in post from King Henry's predecessor, with whom he had been - by and large - a loyal servant!' Ari exclaimed.

'So it's like we thought!' Fliss said, remembering their conversation in Benny's kitchen.

'Sort of,' he said impatiently. 'Thomas Becket was part of de Bec's patronage - the people who run the Archiepiscopal affairs and keep its house in order - and de Bec used his influence with the King to install him as Chancellor! He *wanted* Becket inside the Royal Court because-

'de Bec already knew about the treasure,' Fliss said.

Ari breathed and sat back in his seat.

'de Bec already knew about the treasure,' Ari repeated. 'Clearly his own King, King Henry's predecessor, King Stephen, had confided in him too. And presumably asked de Bec – as Chancellor – to use the treasure for war, much like King Henry would ask of Becket thirty years later. It seems that de Bec had resisted, and wanted to ensure that whoever was in place after him would show similar resolution in protecting the interests of the church,' Ari said.

'What are you implying, Ari?' Fliss asked.

'*I'm* not implying anything,' Ari said defensively. 'This,' he said, producing his phone and showing her the same image that Gregory had shown him, of the document in the Parker Library at Cambridge University, 'implies that King Henry took power, learned of the fortune, knew that de Bec had denied King Stephen access to the treasure, and so killed de Bec to create a vacancy for his Chancellor Thomas Becket who he thought he could trust-'

'But was actually de Bec and the Church's man all along. So, there was no "sudden" change of heart from Becket when he became archbishop,' Fliss said. 'And all the times it seemed like Becket was trying to get on the King's side-'

'He was in fact working for de Bec,' Ari said.

'So that's how Gregory knew all this?' she asked. 'That document on your phone?'

'Yes. It's a psalter, a book of psalms.'

'And I assume this is a particularly important psalter?' she asked, eyeballing his phone as though she wanted to climb inside the screen.

'Oh yes... this is Becket's psalter.' Fliss frowned.

'But... anyone can access that library... Are you telling me that this has been kept a secret from the world despite being hidden in plain sight?' she asked.

'Ah,' Ari said. 'But not just *anyone* can access that particular document in the Parker library. Gregory had to log in as the archbishop,' he said. 'These are just screenshots which he has made me swear I'll delete,' Ari said.

'Hmm. OK. Why?' Fliss asked.

'Well, Becket became Chancellor and eventually archbishop. De Bec had warned him that once he was installed as archbishop he would be told of the treasure asked to sanction the use of the treasure to fund his conquests for the good of the Kingdom. So when the King told Becket of the treasure, Becket acted surprised, then immediately suggested that it should all be melted down and sold, and the proceeds be given to the church.'

'A proposition that didn't go down well?'

'Not at all. The King apparently quite openly told Becket he wanted to use the money to finance his wars, but as we suspected, he knew that using pagan treasure so overtly would cause a religious rift and could very easily lead to an uprising from his people. They wouldn't want a pagan King,' Ari said. 'It hadn't been so long since the last pagans had invaded. The Vikings,' he said gravely.

The warmth from the fire was beginning to ebb, and slowly people were leaving The Shakespeare. The humdrum had simmered to a low murmur now, and Ari felt a little on edge as he approached the climax of the story.

'But still the King pressed Becket, threatened to move the treasure from *Aquae Sulis* and to start selling it as soon as he was able. Becket countered that poor people would flock to *Aquae* in the hope that they might gain access to some of the treasure. The treasure was vast, and rumours would spread - it would become to be seen as a place that gave riches to those who visited.

'It might even become somewhere to pilgrimage to. And those people might start to abandon God in favour of *Sulis Minerva*, the pagan goddess who had sprouted gold from the ground. The King was undeterred, but it presented an early and irrevocable impasse for the old friends. Becket was going to remain true to his word to de Bec - but more than that he became a thorn in the King's side from the get-go.'

'Yes,' Fliss said. 'And on the matter of the treasure, King Henry's hands were tied. He needed a way he could get access to the gold, and therefore the money, in a way that wouldn't expose him. But with Becket watching his every move and unwilling to give the go-ahead, there was nowhere to turn.'

'Exactly,' Ari said. 'And that is why he asked me to delete the screenshots. And why very few people have seen the Psalter. You see, it contains a very detailed record of what happened, and would give anyone with half a mind access to the last purported location of the treasure. You see, according to the story in this psalter, the King struck upon an ingenious idea. He would move the treasure to-'

The alarm on Fliss' watch beeped.

Ari cut himself short and frowned at her wrist.

'What's the alarm set for?' he asked, confused.

'Ari,' she said. 'Whatever you do, don't tell me where that treasure was moved to.'

Before he could reply, he felt his eyes very slowly start to close. His vision blurred, and he flailed his arms in front of himself as he fell forward, unable to control his actions. His glass hit the stone floor, and its dark-liquid contents splashed across the room. A few punters turned to look in their direction, but Fliss was already gathering their coats.

He fought to hold on to consciousness.

'What... is... happening...' he managed to force out. 'You....'

'I'm so sorry, Ari,' she said. She sounded sincere.

And that was the last thing he remembered.

***

PART FOUR

Chapter thirty-two

When Ari came to, he was lying face-down in an uncomfortably small single bed.

His surroundings were entirely alien to him. His face was dripping with sweat, and it was swelteringly humid. He felt groggy, and his first attempt at standing led him to vomit into a bucket that had been placed strategically next to his bed.

He groaned out loud and tried to calm himself, the familiar feeling of panic beginning to wash over him. He breathed in a controlled manner and managed to calm himself. He doubted he would be able to do so a second time.

He was sick again.

After a little time, he found he was able to sit himself up on the floor next to the bucket, and stretch his legs out in front of him. His head lolled onto his shoulder unnaturally, and his eyes were open but unfocused. Looking without seeing, he guessed that the room was no more than ten feet long or wide, and the walls seemed to be made of metal.

There was a sink in one corner and a few of his personal effects left in a heap in the other. At the head of the room was a large, metal door, which was raised slightly and accessed via a small set of stairs. There was no bolt or handle.

There were also no windows, he noticed. The only light source came from a small lamp affixed to the ceiling.

The light was bright, particularly so to Ari's sensitive eyes, but for a moment he enjoyed feeling uncomfortable. At least he felt something.

He let out a long breath and closed his eyes again, feeling the gentle roll of the floor.

Wait, he thought to himself. *Am I moving?* Slowly, like a shadow creeping across a hallway, it dawned on him.

Is this a ship?

With more moaning and groaning, he hoisted himself up and rubbed his head. The cramped ceiling was barely enough to house his frame, and he stood slightly in a slightly stooped fashion.

On the side of the sink basin was a small radio, which crackled noisily. In his haziness, he had hardly noticed it, but much like the movement of the floor, now he couldn't unhear it. He switched it off and rubbed his forehead aggressively. The space in his brain that the noise had occupied was promptly filled by an unearthly headache, and he groaned once more. Nausea threatened again, but he swallowed hard and steadied himself. He looked down and realised that someone had changed his clothes.

What the hell is going on? he thought.

He felt the panic begin to set in again, and his breathing started to become heavy. Then, he heard a tapping sound. A metallic noise echoed around in his mind. He managed to focus on it and allowed the noise to consume him.

He closed his eyes.

The noise stopped, and there was a scrape of metal on metal as the deadbolt on the door was pulled from the outside. It swung open.

'Hello, Ari. Turned the radio off I see,' James Prince said.

He stood in the doorway, his frame filling its frame.

He wore the same odd wetsuit that Ari had become accustomed to seeing Ocean Pearl agents wear, and it seemed to drink in the light from the ceiling.

At that moment, the ship lurched, and Ari was thrown forward, landing hard on his knees. He made to stand, as though he were going to throw himself at Prince, but the sound of a light *click* stopped him in his tracks.

'Don't try it,' Prince said. Ari felt the cold tip of the barrel of the gun press into the nape of his neck. 'Do you know where you are?' he asked.

Ari's arms trembled under the weight of his body, and he didn't answer.

'Do you know where you are?' Prince repeated. Through gritted teeth, Ari said,

'I'm on a boat.'

'Very observant,' Prince remarked in a dulcet tone. 'I meant in a more... geographical sense?'

Ari frowned at the floor, racking his brain. He felt Prince's arm lift, as though he were going to hit him with the gun.

'Wait!' he cried out, raising his arms above his face. 'Wait... I think I remember.'

Like the warmth of a sip of Kraken spreading from his stomach to the end of his fingers, his mind was flooded with his memories of the last few days and weeks, and he felt as though he had managed to return to a dream he had been having.

'So, you do know where we are, then?' Prince asked again.

***

Tintagel Castle, in Cornwall, South-West England, is one of tremendous beauty.

During the day, it cuts an imposing figure atop a sheer clifftop, and offers dramatic views over the neighbouring ocean and coastline. Archaeologists have found evidence of a settlement at Tintagel that dates back to the fifth century, but nothing in stone was built until the twelfth.

Today it is in a ruinous state, having ceased to operate as anything other than a tourist attraction many centuries ago. To the modern visitor, the castle appears to have been built across two islands, however historically these were part of the same rock.

The ravages of the weather and the Atlantic Ocean have resulted in that land falling away, and what remains is connected by a man-made bridge. To stand on the edge and look out at the hair-raising drop to the ocean from the height of the castle atop the cliff is electrifying, but a fall would not be survivable. The ferocity of the waves of the Ocean beating and crashing into the cliff would sweep anyone who entered the water away as though they didn't exist.

Beneath the spot where the rock has fallen away is a sandy inlet, where the waves wash in a little more gently, and visitors can enjoy a nicer time, exploring the natural caves and enjoying the view of the medieval castle high above them.

Unfortunately for Ari, he had not been brought to Tintagel to enjoy a leisurely stroll and take in the history. He had been smuggled on a merchant ship in the dead of night by a deranged Ocean Pearl agent who - probably - had only kept him alive to exploit his abilities.

Ari had changed into a neoprene wetsuit that Prince had thrown on his bed, eaten the measly meal of porridge and water he had been given and taken a little time to reflect on the gravity of his situation. On the camp bed in the room below deck, he had prayed for the first time in his life.

Prayed to *Sulis Minerva,* the first God that had come to mind.

Now, standing on deck, he stood in a small circle of Ocean Pearl agents. And Fliss.

He had so far avoided her gaze. Out in the open air, when he looked over the railing, he saw nothing but the inky blue of the night sky, and the white outlines of froth from the tide. Even with his night vision, there was little to observe. He assumed they were quite far out to sea, and nowhere near another shipping lane. The more he looked, the more he realised there was nothing.

Must be a big ship, he thought. It was still moving.

'What did you give me?' he asked through chattering teeth, wondering what had been put in his drink to knock him out.

'Nothing that won't wear off,' James Prince replied.

'A sedative?' Ari asked. He didn't really expect an answer. The other man was there, the one from the train to Bath, which seemed like a lifetime ago. Tennant. He assumed the dark-skinned woman was the one who had been present with James Prince at *Aquae Sulis* the last time they had physically seen one another. The sight of them all together with Fliss made him feel a little ill.

'We need to have a little chat,' Prince said.

You better believe it, Ari thought.

He risked a glance at Fliss, who was looking down at her feet. The agents all had torches clipped to their suits, and it was only as Ari looked closer that he realised they all wore the same wetsuits he had seen Prince wearing in the cabin below. He focused his vision on them each in turn, which drew some funny looks, and he could see in the fabric of the cloth where a mysterious material was weaved into the fabric of the cloth in a strange way. He didn't have time to ponder what it might have been.

'They know everything, Ari,' Fliss said, meekly, as though she were warning him not to bother lying. Her voice sounded shaky, but Ari didn't think she appreciated the gravity of her betrayal. Fliss, working for Ocean Pearl, the whole time. It made him want to be sick again.

'I'm sure they do,' he said, icily.

'I don't expect you to know precisely where we are, Ari - even with your incredible vision. This place was built to be hidden, after all. In fact, if it weren't for the psalter that you so kindly photographed for us, we may never have found it at all,' Prince said. His smile was delectable. Ari instinctively touched for his phone. It was gone. Ari's shame was almost audible.

'I know where this is,' was all Ari said.

Prince's smile widened.

'Well,' he said. 'I'm sure you do. You can see in the dark, after all. But I didn't need young Felicity here to tell me of your extraordinary abilities,' Prince said. He took a step closer to Ari, who shuffled uncomfortably. Underfoot, the boat rose once more with the swell of the water. 'I have suspected that ever since our little altercation in the Williamson Tunnel. That was quite impressive, the way you managed to escape. I almost lost my job,' Prince said.

'But I was able to track you to *Aquae Sulis,*' he continued, 'a place I'm sure you know I am familiar with,' he said with a sneer. 'And in fairness, what you did there, the way you located something that even we had been unable to find with our remote sensing technology... I'll admit, I was impressed. Of course, you're not infallible. You dropped this.'

Prince threw the tablet that Ari had found in the treasure room at *Aquae Sulis* on the table in the middle of the group. The man, Tennant, looked at it as though seeing it for the first time, while the woman looked thoroughly bored.

'Cool, well if you're quite finished monologuing-'

Ari didn't see the punch coming. Prince struck him squarely in the stomach. He doubled up and wheezed heavily, which turned into a heaving cough. He spat.

'I'll try to keep it brief,' Prince continued, as though nothing had happened. 'As I'm sure you're aware, I knew where you were going after *Aquae Sulis* because this thing was pointing you in that direction. We didn't have that twenty years ago. All I had was the second head. The one with Becket's coat of arms. It didn't seem like it was *enough*,' he said, emphasising the last word.

Clearly a regret, Ari thought.

'But with this, I was certain. I *knew* that fucking archbishop had hidden something from me then, and I knew there was a reason that damn cathedral was so resistant to Ocean Pearl's advances... we offered them so much money... Anyway, he had continued to hide it from me until - well - until you spilt your guts to Felicity,' he said, placing a hand on her shoulder. 'And what a tale you had to tell! Imagine Thomas Becket engineering his martyrdom to protect his own church. How principled, how dignified! What. A. Death,' he said, enunciating the last few words.

Ari's breathing became easier and the pain in his stomach began to subside. For a moment, Ari felt a deep sense of regret for Gregory.

'Is there a point to all this?' Ari squeezed out, then tensed up in anticipation of another blow. It wasn't delivered.

'Oh yes,' Prince said. 'The point to all this is that, having led us here, you're going to need to use those uncanny abilities of yours to finally help us to find this goddamn treasure,' he snarled.

Ari laughed out loud.

'What on Earth makes you think I'll do that?!' he asked. Prince laughed back mercilessly.

'I am glad you asked! Two reasons. Number one. Tennant, if you please.'

The man on Prince's right picked up a television remote control and flicked it toward a large screen on the wall. It was slow to come to life, but eventually, the image displayed shaky footage of a dark room. The feed came through like a nightlight, and Ari was put in mind of some kind of badly-made hostage video. Then, with alarm, he realised-

'Dad!' Ari said out loud, taking a step toward the monitor.

He peered into the dishevelled face of his father through the screen. The Professor had clearly been beaten. He was tied to a chair, and his head hung low between his shoulders, dropped onto his chin. But it was definitely him.

Unmistakably familiar.

'You bastard!' Ari snarled, turning back to Prince. This time, it was the woman who lashed out. She hit Ari in the kidney, and once more he found himself doubled over, the pain radiating from the side of his midriff.

'What the hell has my father got to do with this?!' Ari managed to squeeze out.

'Nothing, particularly,' Prince said wearily. 'But life is all about leverage, Ari. You of all people should know that by now... Speaking of which!' he said. 'Aurora!' he nodded at the woman who, quite unexpectedly, grabbed Fliss by the arm.

Fliss had clearly been hiding other things than her identity. She reacted in a way Ari thought only a professional would. Fliss tried to wrap herself around the woman and get her left arm in a lock, but Aurora was too quick for her, and she had the momentum.

As she stepped forward, she aimed a sharp punch into Fliss' stomach, who let out a yelp. In a nanosecond, Aurora had pulled her arm up behind her back and was leading her out of the control room, back onto the deck. Prince nodded at Ari as if to tell him to follow and, not for the first time, Ari found himself unable to take his eyes off his father as he was ushered out of a room.

On deck, it was somehow much darker than it had been only twenty minutes earlier. Ari looked up. The sky had vanished, and all he saw was the white outlines of a rocky outcrop above him. He swivelled and realised that the ship had pulled into some sort of cave.

Only behind them could Ari make out the open water beyond.

'Turn some fucking lights on!' Prince called out, seemingly to no one in particular. A second later, four large, halogen lights shot up with a whooshing sound, and the cave was illuminated. Ari had been right - in the light, the space was enormous. And only now did he appreciate the true vastness of the ship.

They must be expecting a large treasure, he thought to himself.

In front of him, Fliss had been led to the edge of the starboard railing by Aurora, and Prince was strolling leisurely in their direction. Ari glanced back over his shoulder to see if he could see his father, but Tennant - who had remained behind - had turned off the screen.

Prince stopped a few feet away from Aurora and the struggling Fliss.

'Tie her,' he commanded.

He turned and faced Ari who, over Prince's shoulder, could see Aurora wrapping a length of rope around Fliss' wrists. 'This one,' Prince said, jamming a thumb over his shoulder, 'is quite the silky operator. She has played us all for fools from the get-go. But what a dangerous game she was playing,' Prince said. 'Isn't that right, Felicity?' he called out in a comically sarcastic tone. Fliss could only squeak and hum her protest, as a piece of duct tape had been firmly affixed to her lips. Her eyes were wide with terror and, despite everything, Ari found himself longing to go run to her.

'You see, she has been working for Ocean Pearl for some time. She went through basic training in Liverpool and has worked a number of low-level assignments since. But, slowly, she has risen her status and she is seen as a safe pair of hands who can carry out most rudimentary fieldwork with a degree of competence not displayed by everyone,' Prince said.

'Nevertheless,' he continued. 'Our paths have never crossed in a professional capacity. I only ever knew her as the compere at the Fruit Exchange, and even then, only in passing, never by name,' he said. 'Now I know, of course, that it was she who stole that damn tablet from the VIP auction. She *knew* it would pique my interest because of my association with *Aquae Sulis*, and she must have also known that I was tailing you for all those fakes you were producing because, of course, the night I tried to intercept you, she whisked you away before I could ever get close, and even at *Aquae Sulis* she kept her identity well-hidden. It wasn't until your father sang like a good little bird that her identity was actually revealed to me. I was very impressed. She had successfully managed to goad us all into meeting at *Aquae*, and she had invited your friend Ondrej along. And what a debacle that was. I think what she has failed to appreciate, perhaps, is the level I am willing to go to in order to get what I want. I don't think she expected me to take Ari's father hostage, and I don't think she expected me to be waiting for her outside Canterbury cathedral after you had gone off on your little fact-finding mission,' he said.

Ari could feel his face going numb with the cold.

'But there is another thing she doesn't know about me. And that is that I am as indifferent as to whether she lives or dies as I am the changing of the weather. So, you ask me how I'll get you to find my treasure? Well, as I said, number one is if you don't, your Dad dies. Pretty simple,' he said unequivocally. 'But *just* in case that isn't enough to persuade you... Aurora?'

Ari's eyes widened in horror as Prince stepped aside. There was a short struggle before the female agent, Aurora, managed to throw Fliss, wriggling in her bonds, overboard. Ari saw the fear in the whites of her eyes as they met his, and he couldn't help but let out a squeal.

'You see, *Mr Nicander*,' Prince said, his voice much louder now and filled with unqualified grandiose.

'I was listening to everything she said to you in that pub. Canterbury cathedral might not be on Ocean Pearl's payroll, but Phil and I - you know, Phil, from The Shakespeare? Well, we go way back. So, when I asked him to personally deliver your drinks, he also stuck a small microphone on the underside of the table. It was all going too smoothly, until she had to go and say that last line. She had to let sentiment compromise her standards. "Whatever you do Ari",' he said, mocking her tone. '"Don't tell me where the treasure is!"' Prince laughed again.

He was laughing now, and Ari could feel the blood boiling underneath his skin. But there was no time to argue. Fliss was in the water.

Ari set off at a sprint.

'Do get in touch when you know what's down there!' Ari heard Prince say as he reached the starboard railing.

Without stopping, Ari flung himself overboard.

Freefalling, he snatched his arms in a cross over his chest and snapped his heels together, then braced hard. His eyes were closed. When he hit the water, the sudden jolt of icy cold that enveloped him threatened to defeat him, but he fought off the dizziness that reeled in his head and opened his eyes. Underwater, even in the depths of the dark water, he could see quite clearly.

The underside of the boat, the anchor, and the rudders gently swaying against the current to hold the giant ship in place, all appeared to him in familiar white outlines.

There was a surge in the water as the tide washed in and out of the cave.

Frantically, he scanned his surroundings. He focused his vision on the rock below him, searching for Fliss.

He saw her as her head hit the seabed floor with a gentle *thud*, disturbing the bedrock. Ari watched the ensuing stream of sand dance away toward the surface as he kicked his legs, swimming down as hard as he could toward her.

Come on, Fliss, he prayed as he swam toward her. *Please still be alive.*

The cavern was large and deep, and Ari had only taken one breath before plunging into the water. As he kicked, the biting cold began to wrap itself around his muscles, and he felt his arms and legs begin to go tight as the lactic acid began to build up. The deeper he went, the more he felt the pressure begin to build behind his eyes and ears.

He wanted to scream, but he managed to push through the pain.

Still, as he swam, his thoughts lay not with his own safety, but only concern for his lifelong friend. He couldn't imagine any situation in which Fliss, level-headed and sensible, could have come to be at the mercy of Ocean Pearl. He thought they must have something over her - or she has something over them, perhaps. Either way, as he approached her lifeless form lay supine at the bottom of the ocean, the white outline of her body coming into focus, it was his childhood friend he pictured, lying asleep on his couch with their first hangover at sixteen, not the Ocean Pearl agent in the black suit who had punched him on the ship.

Ari was on the seabed himself now, and he was a long way underwater.

He wasn't exactly sure how far, but even the bottom of the hull seemed a long way away, never mind the surface. In a panic, he began to untie Fliss' bonds, which had come a little loose during the descent. Once they were off, he looked at her face to see if she was conscious. Her eyes remained closed. Ari felt himself running out of air. He knew he would never be able to drag her to the surface before he passed out, and it didn't seem as though she would regain consciousness any time soon.

He swivelled and scanned the wall of rock behind him. It was his only option. If he could find a crevice or a fissure-

There!

There was a small opening in the rock face ten metres to his left, invisible to a normal eye, but clear to him.

With a sheer effort of strength that he could not explain if he tried, he swam behind Fliss' inanimate body and pushed her along the seabed. He considered going for air and then coming back, but he had no idea how far into the gap he would need to swim in order to find the air, and no idea whether Fliss was already dead.

After a struggle against the water, the tide, his screaming lungs, bones and muscles, Ari pushed Fliss through the aperture in the rock and prayed once more to *Sulis Minerva*.

Let us live, and I swear to you I'll return your treasure.

A votive offering.

***

Chapter thirty-three

Ari's chest heaved as he lay flat on the wet-black rock side.

Fliss lay next to him. He had managed to drag her out of the water, but was too exhausted to try to bring her around. He sat himself up and put his hands on his knees. The pool through which he had exited was only a few metres wide, and the pocket of space they now occupied in the rock was equally tiny.

The cave was echoey, and the gentle lapping of the water and dripping sound from the ceiling belied the dramatic events that had unfolded only moments previously. That was arguably the closest Ari had ever come to death. He had felt the life in him begin to fade as he had swam through the narrow channel, and only the glimpse of the surface - and air - had allowed him to force himself to carry on. He couldn't help but mutter his thanks to the pagan goddess who had delivered him safely.

A second later, Fliss began to cough. Ari had almost forgotten she was next to him, but he scrambled and knelt at her side, peering down into the paleness of her face, which bore a cadaverous look.

'Fliss?!' he asked. She was still coughing, and she vomited a large amount of seawater. She cried out in pain, and Ari wondered what lasting damage she might have done to her lungs.

'Are you alright?!' he asked, shaking her slightly. The coughing subsided and her eyes opened. She looked up at him.

'Ari,' she muttered, 'is that you?'

It was only then that he realised the cave was completely devoid of light. It hadn't even registered to him that he was seeing his surroundings in white outlines, or that the black was really midnight blue, a rare but true darkness that only Ari saw.

Fliss would have been entirely blind.

'Yes,' he breathed. 'Yes Fliss, it's me.'

She let her head drop back onto the rock and lay silent for a moment. She slipped back out of consciousness for a time, and Ari listened as her breathing stabilised.

It was some time before she came round again, by which time Ari was lying on his back next to her.

'Ari,' she muttered. 'I don't know what to say.'

Ari sat up and looked at her, her white outline sprawled on the rock. She seemed to be OK.

'Well, "thank you" might be a start,' he said.

She laughed, which produced more coughing.

'Don't make me laugh,' she said. 'It hurts. But yes, thank you. What a fool I was.'

'We have both been foolish,' he said, conciliatorily. 'We have been led by Ocean Pearl from the beginning, each of us as greedy as the other. I was only in this to find a lost treasure, make a fortune, become rich and famous and powerful. While you...' he tailed off.

'I was in this to become something at Ocean Pearl that I had never been in the real world. I wanted to make a Big Find of my own. When I heard that James Prince was tailing a counterfeiter called Marius Nicander? How could I turn down the opportunity to... intervene,' she said.

'So, you did get me into the Fruit Exchange auction after all?' he asked, sheepishly.

'Oh yes, Ari. I got you into it. And what's more, I helped James Prince along the way. I know about Merchant's Lodge, Ari. Prince really did only start chasing you because of these fakes that you produced. But he's seen your file. I've seen it. They know someone was with Ondrej that day. Three Ocean Pearl agents dead and one missing. And you're never seen again?'

Her words hit him like a blow to the chest. So Fliss had known all along.

'But what Prince said up there was true, I don't know him, as in we have never worked together,' she continued. 'But I know people who do. All it took was a few whispers in the right ears about your Finding ability. From there it was fairly simple, and the only question was how I would bring you on board. Another element of truth in the entirety of the ruse was that I genuinely believed Ocean Pearl had missed something at *Aquae Sulis*, that curse tablet was a real clue, and so I used that to gain your interest. It came up at auction at the Exchange, so I nicked it, photographed it and hid it,' she said nonchalantly. 'No one suspected the compere of the event. And you haven't changed, Ari. You can't resist treasure.'

Ari felt numb, but not just because of the cold. He couldn't help but wonder whether this was all fabrication too, and that in fact, Fliss intended to double-cross him again. Looking at her, though, he doubted it. It seemed to be taking a sheer effort to simply hold a conversation, never mind anything else.

'Why steal the tablet? Why not just photograph it but leave it to be auctioned?' he asked.

'I was trying to create traction. Trying to bring James Prince on board with tracking us, because I needed a way to generate impetus. You wouldn't have had any reason to follow me all this way without good reason. I needed them chasing us to spur you on, to ignite in you a spark that would fuel your ambition,' she said.

'Seems like a high-risk strategy,' Ari said.

'It was. But it worked,' she replied simply. Ari couldn't argue. Only one week since the VIP auction, they were now present in the last-known location of the pagan treasure of *Aquae Sulis*, and Ari couldn't deny that he wouldn't have followed her there without Ocean Pearl having chased them, and certainly not as quickly.

'So in the pub, you told me not to tell you that I knew where the treasure was hidden so that they would need to keep me alive?' he asked.

'Yes. And to ensure they brought you with us. Seemingly Prince saw fit to do that anyway. But it was a genuine attempt; I didn't know they were listening to our conversation in The Shakespeare. I should have, though. It's what I would have done,' she reflected gravely.

'Thanks.... I think,' Ari said. Fliss laughed and wheezed again.

'I thought you would be angrier than this,' she said. Ari allowed a few moments of silence.

'So did I,' he said. 'But I of all people can understand the allure of Ocean Pearl.'

Neither of them spoke for a while. Ari lay in the darkness, his thoughts wandering from Ondrej and the Bluebirds and Merchant's Lodge, back to *Aquae*, Benny and his Father. He let out a sigh.

'So I assume they told you everything?' Ari asked. 'About the Psalter?'

'No. I have literally no idea why we're down here, they didn't really trust me after I tried to stop you from spilling in the pub. Fill me in. What's in the psalter?' she asked.

'Ah,' Ari said, glad of an opportunity to change the subject. 'Well. Inside is an eyewitness account of the day of his death written by a monk called Edward Grim,' he said. 'It tells in detail of what happened that day, what was said between the knights and the archbishop, how many blows it took to kill him. It's widely considered to be a reliable source, given that Grim had no real reason to lie one way or another; he was only visiting Becket, and they didn't have a personal relationship. He just happened to be there the day the archbishop died,' Ari said.

'I sense there's a "but" coming,' Fliss said.

'Quite a big one. The pages the story are written on aren't really part of the psalter at all. A psalter is a book of psalms or prayers, whereas these pages are part of Becket's biography. And part of the story was inserted by Grim with a short note, asking the Parker Library to house the psalter and only give access to its contents to the archbishop of Canterbury,' Ari said. 'And it's this short excerpt that details the steps that the archbishop had taken in the days *preceding* his death - as well as the account of his relationship with the King and his archbishop predecessor de Bec, which I already told you about in the pub.

'Gregory told me that Grim's account of the day of Becket's death is accompanied by two documents, the importance of which only became transparent to him when I told him about the tablet and the head of *Sulis Minerva* with the coat of arms in the eye. The first is a small excerpt from Grim's account of his days at Canterbury which seems to imply that Becket was preparing to die. He had taken steps to get his affairs in order, spent time away from Canterbury, written letters to people he hadn't spoken to for a long time... Actions of a man preparing for his final days. I think they thought it was a coincidence. Until... well, the second item.'

'What is it?' Fliss asked.

'It's a receipt. Well, more like a book of accounts, which the archbishop assumes was inserted by Becket himself, rather than Grim. It shows large quantities of tin suddenly being sold from a mine here, at Tintagel, Cornwall,' Ari said. 'Becket was trying to point to the place he thought the treasure was being housed. I suspect his intention was that someone would discover the treasure and it would be claimed in the name of the martyred St Thomas Becket, and the glory would go to the church.'

'Right,' said Fliss. 'What happened to it instead?' she asked. He suspected she simply wanted to lie down and sleep. The physical strain placed on her body from nearly drowning would have been quite significant.

'Well, two things. Or three, depending on how you look at it. The first is that Becket died having only told Grim about the treasure and psalter. In the absence of a known successor, it was the best he could do. To tell someone entirely impartial visiting, and so would be least likely to be implicated. The second is that Edward Grim died the day after the archbishop, without having had a chance to tell anyone of the plan,' he said.

'No!' Fliss exclaimed, her cry echoing around the cave.

'Yep,' Ari said. 'Pure coincidence apparently, no evidence of foul play. The only other person who knew about the treasure – apart from the King - dead. And so now, whoever was appointed as archbishop after Becket would have had to find the psalter in order to uncover the treasure and expose King Henry for his possible hand in the assassination, and they had to do that without Grim there to tell them it existed at all,' Ari said.

'I sense that was not what happened,' Fliss said matter-of-factly.

'Well, no. Without Grim, the psalter was buried with Becket,' Ari said simply. Fliss swivelled her head around.

'It was *buried with him?!*' she asked, incredulous.

'Yep,' Ari repeated. They started giggling, which descended into a laughing fit. The noise of their uproarious guffaws echoed around the cave.

'Well, someone made a monumental cock up there!' Fliss exclaimed. This sent the pair back into hysterics. Once they had finished laughing, there was silence again, occasionally punctuated with a titter from one or the other.

'I just can't believe that the key to all of this, the psalter that contained the biography and the location of the treasure, the very thing that was meant to tie the tablet with the King's name on it and the crest of arms at *Aquae Sulis* was buried with the archbishop. Incredible.'

'Isn't it just?' Ari asked rhetorically.

'So, when your Dad said that finding the tomb of Becket would link all of this together, he was right? The psalter would have been with the body,' she said. Ari didn't even have the energy to worry about his father. He felt numb, as though he were talking about characters in a show.

'I assume that is why he wanted us to go to the catacombs, yes,' Ari said.

'Wait,' Fliss said. 'When was the psalter added to the library at Cambridge?' she asked. 'If it was buried with Becket?'

Ari smiled.

'In the sixteenth century, King Henry II's Great Grandson, King Henry VIII – you may have heard of him, he's quite famous,' Ari said, jokingly. 'Destroyed the tomb of Thomas Becket as part of his religious upheaval in Britain. The details are shaky at best, but Gregory's best theory is that someone loyal to the Church found the psalter, saw the note from Grim asking it to be placed in the Parker Library and only be seen by the archbishop of Canterbury... and took it there,' he said. 'My Dad could never have known that,' Ari said.

It was moments like these that Ari found himself marvelling at the spinning wheel of history, and how seemingly small events, such as who found what, or who died when, could alter the path to the future entirely. In another universe, it is a man loyal to King Henry VIII who finds the note, takes it to the King and, believing the treasure to belong to his Great Grandfather, takes it and uses it.

'The problem with all this,' Ari said, 'is that once Becket was out the way, and King Henry II was sure that he could use the treasure without interference from the Church... there was nothing to stop him doing just that. So the treasure was definitely here in the thirteenth century, but there's a damn good chance that it ain't any more,' he said.

'And it doesn't answer the question of who left the tablet or the inscription in the head of *Sulis Minerva* at *Aquae Sulis,* she said. 'It seems as though his attempt to expose the treasure was the Psalter,' she said.

'No, it doesn't,' Ari agreed. They were silent for a short while as the prospect of having gone through everything they had gone through could, ultimately, be for nothing.

'Ari?' Fliss asked.

'Yep?'

'That's all well and good. But how are we going to get out of this cave alive?' she asked. They glanced at each other again which once again brought on a fit of laughter.

'I don't know!' Ari yelled.

'Me neither!' she replied. 'Back through there is Ocean Pearl, and this cave is-

'Wait,' Ari said, interjecting.

'-sealed in from all angles. It's a cliff, after all-'

'Wait!' Ari repeated.

'What is it?' Fliss asked.

Ari began to whistle, echolocating. For the first time, he stood up and surveyed the wall behind him. White lines on a blue background. Same as always, the cliff was outlined to him, clear as day. And yet, there was something different about a section of the wall directly in front of him. A small, rectangular nook was clearly marked against the rest of the side of the cliff.

'It's a crawl space,' Ari said. Fliss rose too and grabbed onto him. Unable to see anything, she relied on him to act as her guide, as she had in the Williamson Tunnel.

'Thomas Becket's teenage diary isn't down there, is it?' she asked. Ari giggled, but the adrenaline was beginning to wear off now, and his composure was returning.

'I'm serious, Fliss,' he said. Their brains must have put them through something of a roller coaster in the aftermath of their ordeal. Between nearly dying and a lack of oxygen, he was surprised he could even function.

'Well I never!' someone said. Both Ari's and Fliss' hearts nearly leapt from their mouths. Ari thought he had perhaps overestimated his cognitive functionality and had started hallucinating.

'Who the hell said that?!' Fliss called out, spinning out of Ari's grasp. Ari watched her white outline as it spun close to the water. He grabbed her and pulled her back in.

'Me,' the voice repeated. Ari realised it was coming somewhere from his wetsuit. There was a small badge with a speaker pinned where a lapel would usually sit, atop his left shoulder. 'James Prince.'

The pair said nothing.

'I've heard everything you've said already, no use in going quiet on me now,' he added. Ari sighed and wondered how he hadn't predicted that they would be listening. Again.

313

'Fine, what do you want?' Ari asked.

'I want you to stay exactly where you are,' he replied. 'And I mean, precisely. *Don't* try anything,' he said warningly. 'Keep that radio on your suit. Remember, Marius. We still have your Dad.'

The voice clicked off.

Ari and Fliss were silent for a moment. Then Fliss, unable to stop herself, let out a small laugh. Ari giggled in response. Within a few seconds, they were beside themselves once more, cackling like they had as children.

***

Chapter thirty-four

After a while, the pair had sobered a little. Ari had laid back down on the rocky floor, while Fliss had gone back to the water's edge. She had dropped her legs in, and sat with her back to Ari.

'How long do you think it'll take him to get down here?' Ari asked, staring at the white-outlined curvature of the ceiling.

'They'll need to suit up. We probably have twenty minutes,' she replied.

'What are those suits Ocean Pearl wear anyway?' Ari asked, remembering the odd-looking black sheen of the agents' suits.

'Oh,' Fliss said. 'They're pretty nifty, eh? They're like superlight neoprene, but they're infused with this material called Vantablack. It's really dark, and it absorbs light rather than bouncing it off.'

'Ah, so that's what that stuff is,' Ari replied, thinking of the material he had seen woven into the fabric of Prince's suit when he focused on it. 'I think I remember hearing about it on the news,' he said. He sat up. 'How long have you been working for them?' he asked the back of her head.

'A while.'

'*Why?*' Ari asked. 'Ever since I awoke on that godawful ship, all I have been able to think about is why on Earth you would want to work for this gang of crooks,' he said.

Fliss sighed. He watched as she ran her fingers over a smooth piece of rock, caressing it as though it was comforting to her. The white outline of her hand moved lazily.

'I might ask the same of you,' she said, pointedly, clearly referring to Ari's time with Ondrej and the Bluebirds. 'But it's a fair question,' she admitted. 'Honestly? They're good employers,' she said. Ari snorted.

'Ha!' he exclaimed.

'And power is quite something. You heard the stories Benny told, of his friend. Not just anyone can exert that kind of influence, Ari.'

'I don't believe you,' he said, flatly. She sighed again.

'When we fell out because you were working for that gang, you thought it was because I didn't have the stomach for it, right?' she asked. Ari recalled the day of their last conversation before reuniting at the Fruit Exchange. She had been so angry with him. He remembered thinking she was like a wasp, and he had rattled her nest. She buzzed at him for hours, threatening her with her stinging tail, until eventually, she had given in. Her beating wings had flown her elsewhere.

'Yes,' he replied, honestly. 'You know that.'

'Well... that's not the reason, Ari. It wasn't that I didn't have the stomach for it, it was that on some moral level I thought we should be operating legitimately. I didn't want to be smuggling things, doing illegal stuff for some random gang. I wanted you and me to hunt treasure all around the world, to use the knowledge your Dad had imparted to go off and hunt down ancient mysteries. That gang, the shady stuff they were into... I had the stomach for it, but I didn't *want* to live that way,' she said.

Ari mulled her words over, unable to decide whether he was irritated or ashamed.

'Why didn't you tell me?' he asked.

'You wouldn't have listened,' she said with a shrug. 'You were... you are, so stubborn, Ari. You're headstrong and conceited but, above all, fiercely loyal. You'd have told me you owed that gang your life, and me telling you that they would destroy yours wouldn't have made a blind bit of difference,' she said.

She's probably right, Ari reflected.

'And...' she said. 'And I never told you what happened to my own father,' she said solemnly.

Selfishly, the mention of Fliss' father caused his thoughts to turn to his own once more, and now he could think a little more clearly, he wondered how Ocean Pearl even managed to get to capture him, then realised almost immediately that it would be a simple task for anyone, never mind a company with the seemingly limitless resource available to them. He was fairly sure they wouldn't hurt Professor Nicander as long as Ari did what they asked.

The problem, really, was that he was unsure how long he would continue to do that.

'My Dad was a great man, Ari,' she said, bringing him back to reality. 'He was funny and kind, and he had a big mop of curly hair that was beginning to thin at the back. When I was little I'd climb on the back of the sofa and tell him that a bird had laid an egg up there, and he'd get me on his shoulders and tell me that it must have been a pretty ugly bird,' she said, smiling. 'He had a great sense of humour, too,' she added.

Ari remained silent. These few sentences were essentially the most she had ever uttered about her father, and he didn't want to ruin the moment in the same way he had last time, when they were drunk and teenagers.

'We were happy when he was alive,' she said. She sounded choked. 'Me, him and Mum... She wasn't the way she is now. But after he left, she did her best, but you know better than anyone that she never really raised me. I was raised by you,' she said. 'And your family.'

'What happened to him?' Ari asked, unable to contain his curiosity. She turned around to look over her shoulder, although he knew she couldn't see him. He, however, saw her in clear detail. The white-lined streaks on her face, the puffy eyes. She sniffed.

'I don't know,' she sobbed. 'We never found out. He was a lorry driver, and he'd taken on some long-distance work to make some extra money. One time, he set off for Europe on a Saturday morning. He kissed me on the head and said, "I'll be back, little birdie," gave me a wink and got in his car to drive to the lorry depot... and that was it. I never saw him again.

'We got a call a few days later to say that he had been killed in some kind of argument over drugs... Drugs, Ari! Whichever poxy organisation they had investigating the case told us he had been smuggling drugs over the border, and had likely been picked up by a rival gang. According to their assessment it, "probably wasn't the first time he had done it," given where he was found and the route he was taking... We never got a body, there was no funeral... My Dad was just... gone. And no one ever asked any questions or did any digging. That was it. I was just a little girl with no Dad, and a Mum who needed more attention than I did.

'And now I'll never know, because when he's done with us, James Prince is going to shoot us both and leave us in this cave,' she said, angrily. She turned around to face Ari more fully. 'Now do you understand why I didn't want you smuggling, working with Ondrej?!' she asked. 'And now do you understand why I might have wanted a bit of power?! To be the one calling the shots as opposed to being told to swallow my fate and accept it?!' she asked.

'Fliss,' he mumbled. 'I'm sorry.'

She sniffed and wiped away the last of her tears.

'Yeah well, as I say it's too bloody late now,' she said. 'You did work for that gang and we did lose touch, and I did end up working for Ocean Pearl. I was *so* furious with you, Ari. That feeling never dissipated. You were working for these criminals and every time my phone rang I would get sweaty and think it was some agency or other calling to tell me you had been found dead, like my Dad' she spat.

An unpleasant silence followed, and Ari turned her story over in his mind. He almost couldn't believe she had kept that bottled up for so long, and he wondered whether he had done her a disservice by never broaching the subject previously. But then, how could he have done it? Any other times her father had been mentioned she had shut down.

'A touching story,' someone said. Ari jumped again, but this time at least knew where the voice was coming from;

it was Aurora, the Ocean Pearl agent on the boat. Her voice was coming through the radio in his suit.

'What do you want?' he demanded.

'I have Daddy issues too,' the voice said, sneeringly.

'I swear to God-' Ari started.

'Calm yourself, Mr Nicander,' she said, soothingly. 'Prince is on his way. I hope you didn't go through that crawl space?' she asked.

Ari frowned.

'You've been listening, you know I haven't gone anywhere,' he said.

'You think I listened to all that?' she asked. 'I had to turn it off when the crying started. I have no time for the weak,' she said with a snarl. The speaker clicked off, and Ari stayed motionless, thinking about what they were about to do.

'Are you ready?' he asked Fliss.

'Ready for what?'

'To die, probably,' he said.

***

Chapter thirty-five

James Prince arrived.

He clambered out of the small pool onto the rock side and sat for a moment to catch his breath. For a fleeting instant, Ari had a wild urge to try to incapacitate him, but the thought passed almost as soon as it occurred to him.

Prince was fitter than he looked.

He hopped up and threw a torch at Ari, who followed its white silhouette through the dark and caught it in one hand.

'Don't need it,' he said coolly.

He flicked it on and handed it to Fliss who, he now noticed, looked awful. Her dark hair hand tangled and stuck to her forehead, and her skin looked as pale as he had ever seen it. Her eyes were bloodshot.

'You two are friends again, then?' Prince asked as he lit his own torch.

Ari ignored him, not wanting to further provoke Fliss' emotions.

'Where's your diving gear?' Ari asked.

'That, boy, is the difference between you and I. You don't know how to push the body to its limit,' he said. 'If I had brought equipment, I'd have had to somehow try to take it through the crawl space with me. I travelled light. Makes it easier to keep an eye on you two,' he said, shooting Fliss a glance.

'I'm on your side,' she ventured, meekly. Prince actually laughed.

'Don't even bother,' he said. He dropped a small, waterproof knapsack off his back and opened the drawstring. He pulled out a gun, a radio and a watch, which he attached to his left wrist. His Vantablack suit seemed to - somehow - have dried already.

'You brought a gun?' Ari asked. 'Really?'

Prince didn't answer him but instead picked up the radio.

'Tennant, Aurora, do you copy?' he asked. Ari rolled his eyes.

'Loud and clear, boss,' came the crackled response from Tennant. *'She's here too, she just doesn't feel like talkin' right now,'* he added. This time, Prince rolled his eyes.

'Aurora, grow up. Are you in position?' he asked. There was radio silence, then finally she said,

'Yes,' and that seemed to be good enough to Prince. He exhaled through his nostrils sharply, then dropped the radio back into the knapsack and pulled the drawstring tight. He kept the handgun out.

'Well?!' he said, as though Ari had been keeping him waiting. 'Lead on!' he said, brandishing the gun in the general direction of the back wall of the cave.

Ari gave Fliss a concerned look, then dropped down to his knees and shuffled over to examine the crawl space. He tapped at it gently. The board of wood that covered it practically disintegrated in his hand. He peered through the hole.

'It's a tunnel,' he said. 'It's tiny.'

'Lucky we're all so thin, then... In,' he commanded.

Ari shuffled forward onto his arms and did as he was told. He focused his hearing, and somewhere down the line, he could hear wind rushing through a large, echoey chamber. And now, with his head in the crawl space, he could faintly make out an entirely unexpected sound, too. Something he had never heard before.

'What's in there?' Prince asked.

'Shut up and I'll tell you!' Ari turned and snapped.

He popped his head back into the hole and listened once more, shallowing his breathing and allowing himself to relax.

In that moment he felt entirely serene, as though he was meant to be there. He had heard it said that the moment before drowning is one of complete calm. Your brain has shut down, your mind is willing to live but your body has given up, and you agree to make a deal with your mortality. It tells you that its end of the bargain has been upheld, and now it's time for you to uphold yours, and pay it back what it let you borrow. But in these moments of calm, of tranquillity, the boundaries between living and dead are blurred, and the past might just speak to someone who is listening hard enough.

For a moment, Ari thought he was dreaming, but he focused his hearing on a faint sound, and the more he allowed it to fill his mind the more distinctive it became.

The noise was of people in the castle keep. Vendors, soldiers, Lords and servants. It seemed his hearing had taken on a new dimension.

***

Chapter thirty-six

'How's that, my Lord?'

Ari was on his stomach doing an army crawl through the tunnel, trying with all his might to drown out all other noise and listen to the ethereal voice. Prince and Fliss were behind him, in that order, and he wondered whether they were as uncomfortable as he. The tunnel was barely large enough to fit through, but the further they crawled, the more confident Ari became that they were in the right place.

He knew the tunnel ended somewhere, he could hear the cavern, but the voices had grown louder as they had made their way deeper into the rock.

But there were competing sounds to deal with. The drips of the tunnel, the whooshing of the wind in the cavern up ahead, the shuffling that he and his companions made, the occasional grunt from one of the two of them. All of it interfered with the voices as he amplified the voices in his mind. Incredibly old voices, in fact. And he suspected they were strongly tied to this location.

'How's that, my Lord?'

They continued crawling for what felt like a long time, but the pace at which they had moved made it difficult for Ari to judge how far they had come.

When they emerged, they did so into a small hallway, with the remnants of a door at the end. Ari stepped through the doorway into a wide, circular chamber, with a shaft that stretched high above. Fliss and Prince joined him and pointed their torches upwards, but even Ari couldn't see the top. Prince's watch beeped.

'Point seven miles,' he said.

'We just crawled nearly a mile into a cliff?!' Fliss asked.

'It seems that way,' Ari muttered, peering up the shaft. He whistled into it, trying his echolocation, and waited for a few seconds. 'That's a bloody long way up,' he said. He whistled again but got nothing.

'What's at the top?' Prince asked as he slowly moved around the outer edge of the shaft, shining his torch in different places. He stopped to examine the bottom of an ancient wooden staircase, which only rose a few steps before disintegrating into nothing.

'It's hard to tell,' Ari said. 'I'm sure it's closed off up there, though. As in, the hole doesn't open to the sky.' Prince hummed in response.

'And the stairs?' he asked. Ari strained his vision upwards, searching for any white lines that might indicate what lay above.

'I don't think there's anything up there,' Ari said, flatly.

The trio converged in the centre of the shaft and spent some time gazing upward, the lights from the torches dancing into the dark before becoming nothing. Ari saw only the white outline of an abyss. It was Fliss who broke the silence.

'So?' she asked. 'What do we do? Go back outside, swim to the surface, regroup and do some remote sensing?' she suggested. The flawed technology that Ocean Pearl had used to uncover so many treasures in its recent past, but had failed to show them the secrets of *Aquae Sulis*. 'See if we can't get in through the top?'

'This place has already been remotely sensed,' Prince admitted. 'It's not anymore, but Tintagel used to be an Ocean Pearl site. The company let it go after a while because... well... it didn't seem like there was anything left to find,' he muttered.

Fliss and Ari exchanged amused glances.

'Well then,' Ari said, much more cheerily. 'Perhaps it's time we resorted to more old-fashioned methods.'

Ari walked over to the edge of the wall where some of the wood from the old staircase jutted out. The haphazard nature of the brickwork meant that opportunities for foot and hand grabs were plentiful and, as Ari studied the wall, he mapped out a route as far up as he could see, using the white outlines of the brick. Ari put his foot on the wood and leaned his weight on it, testing its resolve. It held.

'Last one to the top is a martyred archbishop,' he said, flashing a grin over his shoulder. Then, he was off.

He wasn't an expert climber by any stretch, but he had done enough bouldering and rope work to know his way from the bottom to the top of a wall. Still, the climb was dangerous, and it involved a lot of trial and error. He had a map of where he wanted to place his hand next, where his foot should go, and as long as he could comfortably get them into those positions, he could hoist himself upwards, set himself and find the next move.

The problems arose when there was no obvious next step.

Because the three climbers all chose slightly different routes, they all ended up on different paths to the top.

Fliss and Prince had switched to head torches that – presumably – Prince had brought with him, and before long they found themselves separated around the shaft, beams of light streaming upwards in separate streams.

Ari looked back down over his shoulder. Fliss, it seemed, had tracked quite close to him, and she was only a few metres behind him to his left. Prince, on the other hand, had managed to find a route that had let him overtake Ari, but he was on the opposite side.

Ari tried to guess how far up they were. Then abandoned it and just kept going.

It was some time before he started to worry that the surface still hadn't yet appeared. The trio had found a resting place at a similar height. Ari's hands and fingers screamed at him in pain, but he held on as tightly as he could, breathing hard. His wrist was still sore from *Aquae*, but it had healed well enough that he didn't feel like he was going to immediately fall.

'How far to the top?' Prince called, his gruff voice echoing around the chamber. 'It's not even getting any narrower!' he said. Ari tried to picture the cliff from the outside. Conceivably, the shaft could be just as high.

'I still can't see it,' Ari admitted. Prince let out an exasperated gasp.

'I need to rest,' Fliss said. Ari looked back at her and saw her face contorted in agony. Ari looked up.

'There!' he said, not daring to remove a hand to point. 'Above us!'

Fliss and Prince shone their head torches into the sky, which revealed the underside of some sort of platform. 'If it holds, we can rest,' he said. 'Come on!'

He started to climb again and could hear Fliss and Prince had done the same. A few moments later, he was pulling himself up and over the lip of the platform. It was smaller than he had anticipated.

Ari surmised that whoever had built the shaft had left strategic points of natural rock, presumably to increase stability and make it less likely to cave inwards. Perhaps the others had since crumbled away.

He peered out over the edge and saw that Fliss was right beneath him. He grabbed her hand and hoisted her up, where she collapsed into a heap and lay panting. She was studying her hands underneath her torchlight, and Ari didn't need heightened vision to see that they were cut to shreds.

Ari thought they had a bigger problem.

'The wall on this side,' he said. 'We can't climb it any further.'

Fliss stood up, rubbing her fingers. Somewhere through history, someone had smoothed this side of the shaft, and there were no more natural hand or foot holds.

'Shit,' Fliss said. Opposite them, Prince was not stopping for a rest but was continuing to climb up his side of the shaft.

'We'll have to launch to that side,' Ari said. They were too high now to consider going back down.

'There's a bit below us where the rock juts out,' he said. 'We can make that. Once you hit the rock, anchor your feet to the wall. You should be able to pull yourself up onto the lip of the brickwork before the cliff starts again,' Ari said.

Fliss, who seemed not to have been listening, suddenly sprung from her position. Ari called her name, but she moved lithely, and Ari was plunged into darkness as the light of her torch went with her. He watched her white silhouette with his heart in his mouth as it flew across the chamber and landed hard on the rock. To his amazement, she stuck to the wall, and then hoisted herself up.

She looked back and smiled. Ari gulped.

'Sorry!' she called out. 'All that thinking, I'd have never gone.'

'It's here, My Lord.'

Ari had been hearing the spectral voices more clearly the higher they climbed.

'Jump!' she called. 'This ledge is big enough for two, I can help you!'

Ari reset himself and focused on the piece of stone. He counted backwards in his head.

Three... they'd best not hurt my Dad...

Two, if I die, I hope Fliss finds the treasure and uses it to bring these bastards down...

One...

He jumped and, miraculously, landed on the rock. He hung for a moment and looked up at Fliss, who was beaming at him.

'Well done,' she said, stepping off the ledge and back into a climbing position. 'Pull yourself up-'

There was a sickening crack. The stone he was holding came loose, and Ari's eyes widened in fear as he felt himself start to fall backwards.

He couldn't stop himself. His legs flailed wildly, and his arms grabbed out for the wall, but they only found the air.

'Over here, My Lord?'

Ari jerked to a halt. He cried out in pain as his shoulder was whipped up and over his head unnaturally. He dangled for a moment, then managed to scramble himself onto the wall.

Ari looked up to see James Prince moving away.

'*You* saved me?' he managed to squeeze out. Prince simply kept climbing.

***

The rest of the climb was agonising because of his shoulder, but Ari reached the top. Fliss helped him up onto the uppermost ledge, and he dusted himself down with his good arm. Her torch was still strapped to her shoulder, and he smiled at her as the light lit his face.

'We're doing a good job at this near-death thing today,' he said with a smirk. Fliss only shook her head in response, a grave expression pasted across her face. She stood out of the way and allowed him to pass. His vision drifted into the familiar white outlines, and he saw they were in a small, cramped enclosure.

In front of him was a man-made door.

The masonry was unlike anything that they had encountered at *Aquae Sulis* or on the rock they had just climbed. The paintwork was much neater and wasn't flecked or spayed. Clearly, it had been devoid of contact with the outside world for a number of centuries.

A lion was carved into the centre of the door. It was massive, and its mouth was open as it looked to the heavens, roaring. If Ari blinked, he was convinced it might have jumped out at him and tried to catch his jugular with one of its menacingly large talons.

It quite clearly marked an entrance. *This is the porch, then,* Ari thought with a smile.

To the left of the lion, etched into the spandrel, was a short inscription written in Middle English. Ari quickly translated in his head. It read:

Here is the entrance to the mine of Tintagel, opened in the year of our Lord 1168 by His Royal Highness the Second Henry, King of England.

The door had survived remarkably well. It looked heavy and thick, and sat on a rudimentary hinge, which Ari thought might be one of the earliest examples of that kind of technology ever found.

Ari allowed himself a moment to drink it in. 'Incredible,' he muttered out loud. 'Where's Prince?' he asked.

'I don't know,' Fliss started to say. 'He got here well ahead of me-'

She was interrupted as the door swung open from the other side, and the image of the lion was replaced with the lithe figure of the Ocean Pearl agent.

'That climb was nearly ninety metres,' James Prince said abruptly. He was fiddling with his watch. 'The cliff face leading to the castle at Tintagel is about ninety-five.'

'So, we've climbed through the centre of the cliff, and now we're at the top?' Fliss asked.

'Seems so,' Prince said. 'But for some reason, I can't get a proper signal down here. Tennant or Aurora would be able to get a read of the landscape if I could. But there's...

something interfering with the equipment...' he said tailing off, returning to his watch with a frown.

'Are you pleased with the mine, My Lord?'

Ari heard again in his head. He said nothing. Looking past Prince, he could see there was a tunnel with a gentle, downward slope.

'Well?' Ari asked. 'Are we going in?'

Prince looked up. 'I don't like to go places without radio contact,' he said.

'Doesn't seem we have much choice,' Fliss chimed in.

Prince grunted. 'Fine. How's your shoulder?' he asked. Until he had mentioned it, Ari had almost forgotten about the searing pain coursing through his left arm, all the way down to his wrist. He had unconsciously been holding it tight to his chest, as though it were in an invisible sling.

'It's bloody sore,' Ari replied. 'I'm surprised you care.'

'I saved you, didn't I?' Prince asked. And with that, he turned heel and trotted off down the passageway, beckoning the pair to follow him.

It wasn't a long way down.

As they approached the end, Ari could feel a chill beginning to descend on the tunnel and, although there was no natural light, the torches started to fill a bigger space than they had previously. It was widening, and the smell of saltwater that had been quite unmissable during the climb was leaving them. *We're heading deeper into the cliff,* Ari thought to himself.

'My Lord, we have moved it here, as you asked.'

Ari felt his breathing was becoming erratic.

'Some items are sold, Sire. To the East. But a vast treasure remains below.'

His heart rate increased.

'My Lord? I'm afraid I have news... from Lundene...'

And he was sweating. *'My Lord?'* he heard someone say, and the sound filled his head like a balloon expanding inside his skull.

It pushed all the way through his brain and to the backs of his eyes, and he wasn't sure if he cried out as he fell. He knew he'd tried. The last thing he remembered as his eyes closed was a gurgling sound that filled his soul with dread.

***

Chapter thirty-seven

The man wasn't exactly good looking, but he seemed more powerful and strong than most, no doubt about that. He had a stockiness about him that meant, in spite of his small stature, he carried himself well and appeared taller. He wore scraggly clothes and blended in well in the courtyard.

To the average passer-by, they might not have even recognised that he was their King.

'Ari?!'

The sunlight reflected off his pale features giving him a ghostly look, and all around him the Castle keep at Tintagel was alive with shopkeepers, vendors and traders.

The King leant against the side of a large well. In the distance, the smell of the seawater washed over the scene like a salty blanket, and Ari could taste the waves on his lips, each gust of wind bringing with it a renewed flavour.

Oh yes, Ari thought to himself, this is as real as anything else I've seen.

As he watched, another man approached. This man wore a long, fine coat and had his hair pushed back into a knot.

The King looked uneasy, and kept an eye on the sky, as though he were expecting some harbinger to bring news from above. As the man in the long coat reached his King, he said,

'Sire?' in a tongue that Ari knew no longer existed. Middle English. Once more he thanked his father for his lessons. The King looked up at the tall man, squinting into the sunlight. His countenance suggested he knew he was being brought bad news.

'What news?' the King asked. There was an uncomfortable pause. The King picked up a rock near his right hand and passed it between his fingers, waiting for the man's response. A vendor cried out across the Keep. The King smirked.

'Sire, it has all been brought here,' he said.

'Yes,' The King replied, dutifully. 'I decreed it,' he said. 'What more?'

'My Lord. It is your archbishop,' he said. The King moved the stone in his hand a little more quickly.

'Well?' the King asked.

'He is dead, My Lord,' the man squeaked.

Ari watched the King's reaction very closely, but nothing was betrayed. No twitch that gave away his feelings on the matter, no squint in the eye. Nothing more than a bead of sweat upon his brow. He clenched the stone, then placed it down.

'Flood the mine,' the King said unequivocally.

'My Lord,' the man in the long coat responded, aghast. 'This is... forgive me, did I hear you correctly?' he asked. 'Flood the mine?'

'Ari?!' It was Fliss' voice. Ari heard it from somewhere else. Somewhere he both was and was not. It made him feel nauseated to try to be in both places simultaneously.

'You heard me. Flood the mine, keep this castle open long enough to build in a failsafe-

'Sire this was not what we agreed!' the man in the coat snapped.

The King raised one, fat, ginger eyebrow, and the man corrected himself immediately.

'Forgive me, but My Lord... Henry,' the man said, pleadingly, quietly. He glanced around the courtyard then took a step closer and lowered his tone. Ari strained his hearing. 'This castle is my life's work. To close the mine would mean to close the fort. I thought if I hid the treasure here it would add to our coiffeurs, not force them to be emptied!'

King Henry returned his gaze to the heavens.

'Richard of Dover,' the King said, not unkindly, but not friendly either. Ari recognised the name as the man who had succeeded Becket as archbishop. The "yes man" that Gregory had told him about. 'Thomas Becket has just changed the course of the future. You are a good man now, and I have no doubt in my mind that you have the capacity to become a great man and leave a long-lasting legacy in future,' the King said, Ari translating roughly from Middle English, but the sentiment was clear.

'If you do not assist me, if you don't trust *me,' he said, emphasising the word "trust". 'Then tomorrow I shall be deposed and hanged for murder by accessory,' he said. Henry might have been talking about the changing of the weather, and it struck Ari that to the King, death would*

have been as natural to him as walking into another room would have been for him.

'But, if you do help me,' Henry continued. 'I can make sure you fulfil your potential. All you have to do is follow this one, extraordinarily simple instruction,' he said. 'Flood the mine. You will of course need to leave this place, forever. By the time you hear of it again, it will be destroyed.'

Another vendor screeched something, and Ari felt his stomach lurch again as he was pulled between the land of the living and the dead. The King leaned in closer and whispered something hotly in Richard of Dover's ear. Ari focused his hearing as hard as he could, concentrating on translating.

For a brief time, Ari was one of past and present.

***

'Ari?!' Fliss said, shaking him. When he opened his eyes, he found he was staring directly into the light of a torch. He made a groaning sound, and Fliss pulled him to his knees.

'Ari!' she said. 'We don't have time, the cave... I don't know what's happening to it!' she exclaimed.

Ari rubbed his eyes. The gurgling sound he had heard as he collapsed had grown louder, and now there was a tremor in the floor that had not been there before.

'I do,' he said. She gave him a peculiar look. 'And there's absolutely no time to explain how,' he said. 'Where is Prince?' he asked, delicately getting to his feet. He held on to his childhood friend for support for a moment.

'He's gone into the cavern,' she said. 'He said he needed to try to get in touch with the team and wanted to hunt for a better radio signal. Can't say I believed him, but what was I meant to do?'

'Nothing,' Ari said. 'You weren't meant to do anything. We're not "meant" to be here it all,' he said cryptically. 'But we need to get down into that cavern,' he added.

Fliss hoisted his arm over her shoulder, causing him to cry out in pain. He - and clearly she too - had forgotten about his climbing injury. He shrugged her off.

'There's no time!' he said, echoing her own words.

'I know!' she wailed. He raised his voice against the now distinctive gurgling sound. Behind the walls, he could almost feel the flow of water rushing all around him, and for a moment he was transported back to the Great Drain at *Aquae Sulis.*

'We've got to find a way out of here!' he shouted.

***

Chapter thirty-eight

'He opened this mine, Fliss,' Ari was saying as they hurried down the tunnel.

'He, King Henry, opened this mine and claimed there was a new tin reserve in Cornwall. He claimed it had provided the State with untold new fortune. Cornwall was already tin-rich anyway, and the discovery of a new depository would hardly have been a surprise. He thought no one would bat an eyelid because there were already countless mining operations in this region,' he said. 'But it wasn't tin they were mining here,' he said, excitedly. 'In fact, they weren't mining anything. Not after it was brought here,' Ari said. Fliss grabbed his good arm and stopped him dead.

'After *what* was brought here?' she asked.

'The treasure!' Ari exclaimed. 'They brought the *Aquae* treasure here on the King's orders and were selling it off to the East. And they were concealing the proceeds as profits from the tin industry so as to not alert the Church!' he said. Fliss didn't question this information.

The pair jogged down the rest of the tunnel, Ari being careful not to move his shoulder too much and entered the cavernous space that Ari had expected to be there.

The room was huge. It was decidedly devoid of treasure, but it was clearly man-made. The noise of the gurgling was quieter than it had been in the tunnel and somehow seemed less pressing, but Ari didn't think for a second that the danger had passed.

'It's empty?' Fliss asked as they entered from the downward slope of the tunnel, the pair slowing to a walk. 'Is this the treasure room?'

'Yes. Look even if I am wrong about the exact details of how or why it happened are wrong, the pagan hoard *was* moved here, we know that much. And this,' he said, 'is the "mine" opened by King Henry the Second. The King had already decreed that a settlement be built here, and had the foresight to give the site a holy-sounding name - 'Tintagel - Tin – *augellus*', ' Ari said. 'The angels of tin.'

'Clearly Becket hadn't fallen for it then. The King's ruse. Do you think he knew what was going on? That this "mine" was a front for the selling of the treasure?' she asked.

Ari waved his hand deprecatorily. 'You've missed the most important part of what I am saying-'

'I didn't,' said Prince, who had approached them silently, and Ari was so distracted he had failed to notice his approaching footsteps.

'You said he started selling treasure,' Prince said. 'Which means he had to get it to and from the surface, which he certainly didn't do through the entrance we have just used,' Prince said. 'Which means-'

'There's another way out,' Fliss said, cutting him off.

'Exactly,' Ari said distractedly, studying the ceiling. 'After the King learned that Becket had died, he instructed the Lord of this land, Richard of Dover, to flood the mine. To move the treasure out of its new hiding place and to sell it as quickly as possible to the

East. He told Richard of Dover that if he did this, he would make him archbishop after Becket,' Ari said, craning his neck upwards.

The ceiling was extremely high, and Ari wondered just how much treasure there must have been. He couldn't help but lament its loss.

'And, what's more, the King knew about the clues Becket left in his psalter to implicate the King in the murder of an archbishop. Clues that were written in a book that was buried with his body,' Ari said, not taking his eyes from the walls and roof of the cavern, desperately searching for the white outlines of a way to the surface.

'Buried with his body by a man who was about to lose his land at Tintagel and would relish the opportunity to become archbishop next. Buried by a man who suddenly had next to nothing to lose. Buried by the man who, at the King's request, flew to Canterbury as fast as he could to take charge of the body, which no one else would touch for fear of consecration,' Ari said. 'Buried, not accidentally, but very much purposefully, by Richard of Dover, the next archbishop of Canterbury after Thomas Becket. All on the King's instruction.'

Ari allowed the words to hang for a moment.

'And the King was very thorough. Even though Tintagel was gone and the psalter safely buried, he couldn't rule out the possibility that Becket had told others sympathetic to the cause, who might go snooping at *Aquae*, looking for treasure. Hence he had clues planted at *Aquae Sulis* that pointed toward the archbishop of Canterbury which, if followed, would lead them to Richard of Dover. The King's new yes-man,' he said.

There was a louder gurgling sound than any they had heard previously. Ari tore his gaze from the ceiling and squared himself up to Prince.

'What happened when you opened that door?' Ari demanded, pointing over Prince's shoulder, back toward the tunnel they had entered through. Prince stammered while Ari continued to point. 'What happened?!' he demanded. Another gargling sound, followed by a tremor that shook the floor, causing the trio to lose their footing. Some loose rock fell from the ceilings, and the trio looked at one another, wide-eyed.

'I- it, there was a-'

'There was some kind of trip or switch behind it, wasn't there?' he asked, angrily. 'You activated a goddamn *failsafe*,' Ari said. 'This place was never meant to be found, and the King wanted to make sure of that. So after it was flooded the first time, he instructed Richard of Dover to seal it and had it boobytrapped. This whole place is a basin. The water the ship is currently floating on outside is flooding into the walls as we speak, and very soon it will penetrate this cavern!' Ari shouted.

Prince took a step back.

'And if we don't get up there!' he added, swinging his finger round and pointing back up to the ceiling. 'We're going to drown in here in the next fifteen minutes!'

'The water's rising!' Fliss said. 'Can't we just float up?' she asked.

At that moment, a door came down and sealed the tunnel leading into the room. There began a slow hiss.

'What's happening?!' Fliss asked. A jet of water broke through the wall to her left.

'The failsafe doesn't just flood the mine, it's going to collapse on itself. We'll be crushed!'

More jets of water were appearing now, and bits of stone were beginning to break away from the walls.

'We're out of time!' Ari exclaimed.

***

Chapter thirty-nine

'What's up there?' Prince asked, stupidly. Ari realised that, for the first time, he saw real emotion in the Ocean Pearl agent's face. For everything they had been through, it took the prospect of his death to show his humanity.

Water was beginning to pool at their feet. It had taken a few minutes of hard searching, but Ari had managed to find a route to the surface that had been used to transport treasure to the surface.

'There's a hatch,' Ari said. 'It's been bricked in and sealed in the same way the treasure room at *Aquae Sulis* had been,' he said. 'It's the way treasure was passed from here to the surface, and it's the only bloody way out of this room,' he said.

'When will it collapse?' Prince asked. Ari skipped over to the nearest of the four pillars that supported the room. He tapped on the bottom. It was hollow.

'I imagine these pillars will give under the weight of the water when it gets to about halfway, and the roof will come down not too long afterwards, along with the rest of the cliff!' Ari exclaimed. Prince immediately started pawing at his radio, desperately trying to get the signal back.

'Can you get through to them?!' Ari asked in response.

'Nothing yet,' Prince said. Ari suspected the agent was feeling a little panicky, and he let out an exasperated groan to air his frustration.

'Keep bloody trying!' Ari said. 'If you get through to them, tell them to get to the top of that cliff and find a way through, that hatch must lead somewhere!' he said. Ari peeled off and made his way across the room to where Fliss was studying the wall furthest from the tunnel entrance.

'What do you reckon?' Ari asked as he approached her.

'It'll be tricky,' she said without looking at him. 'And I heard what you just said to Prince,' she added. 'How long?'

'If it stays filling at this rate? Ages. But I suspect we're in for a bit of a surprise-'

He was cut off by a loud, rolling boom. For a second, Ari thought a thundercloud had somehow descended into the chamber with them. Fliss spun around, her face a picture of horror. The bowels of the cliff were churning as though they were hungry. The floor began to shake more vigorously, and Ari gave Fliss a grave look.

'Well, this is an invidious position!' she exclaimed. The rumbling and the sound of water came closer and closer.

The only saving grace seemed to be that Prince, finally, was talking into the radio. He must have got hold of someone on the surface.

'Tell me you-' Ari started to say to Fliss, but was cut off again. The door that had come down to cover the tunnel they had come through burst open, and a torrent of frothing sea water came in its wake. Ari watched in panic as a geyser opened, and the foaming, freezing chimaera of water was swiftly pushed around the room. The small pool of water began to threaten their ankles within a matter of seconds. *We do not have long.*

'Come on!' Fliss said. 'There's not much we can do but climb again!' she screamed.

The noise was deafening as the water gushed in. The room was sealed, leaving little room for the errant sound to escape. Ari looked at Prince, who was still talking on his radio, then back at Fliss.

'Forget him!' she shouted. Ari called Prince's name, but he couldn't hear them over the din of the water. Ari made a pained expression, then made to run back to Prince's position.

Fliss screamed Ari's as he tore off.

'Climb!' he shouted back over his shoulder.

Running was quickly becoming more difficult as the water started to lap at his lower shin, his Chelsea boots fully submerged. It was penetratingly cold, and Ari didn't like to think how long he would survive at this kind of temperature if he were submerged. *Not very long*, he thought, morbidly.

'Prince!' he screamed as he reached the Ocean Pearl agent, who stood with the radio to his ear. The man was paralysed. What Ari had mistaken for an in-depth conversation on his radio was in fact just a man frozen in fear.

'James Prince!' he bellowed, waving his hands maniacally in the agent's line of sight. Prince seemed to snap around and looked at Ari with boring, frenzied eyes.

He grabbed the tops of Ari's arms and his radio fell into the water.

'Is anyone coming?!' Ari wailed. Prince didn't answer but kept Ari locked into his grip, and the two men must have looked as though they were about to start wrestling.

The smell of saltwater was becoming unbearable. Ari broke free of Prince's embrace.

'Come on! We've got to get to the top!'

With some difficulty, Ari lumbered back to the wall that Fliss had climbed, dragging Prince with him. The water was at his knees.

'Climb!' he shouted again, this time at Prince.

Ari didn't wait around, heaving himself onto the wall and climbing as nimbly as he could, using the gaps between the large, dark stones as foot and handholds. He made his way to Fliss' position near the top, the pain in his shoulder conceding to the adrenaline.

He looked around and saw that Prince had made good progress too.

'Where's the hatch?!' Fliss screamed. The noise of the rising water was beginning to give way to a taunting creaking sound, and Ari could have sworn he saw some of the pillars begin to move a little.

The trio clung to the wall in a line, almost directly below the outline of the hatch, that still only Ari could see.

'Directly above us!' he called. 'If we die down here,' Ari said to Fliss, panting. 'I want you to know that I'm sorry for ever working with Ondrej. We're a team. We should have stayed as one,' he said.

Then, Ari turned to Prince.

'God damnit!' he roared. 'You fucking coward! Did you manage to get through to them? Is anyone from Ocean Pearl coming on the surface?!'

In response, Prince only nodded to the ceiling. Ari spun around to where, miraculously, a small hole was beginning to appear.

In amazement, Ari watched as it became larger and larger, until eventually the head of a large drill came poking through, and bits of rubble cascaded into the icy waters below. Ari almost screamed with delight but faltered.

'We'll never make a jump from here!' he called out.

'They'll lower something down!' Fliss said.

'Even so! We'll only get one shot at this! If we miss, those pillars about to give out and we'll be drowned... but if we were on *that* platform, we'd be much closer!'

Ari had noticed it from the ground but hadn't realised there was a gap large enough to stand on. Near to the ceiling, there was a stone platform near to the hatch which, he assumed, had been designed as a place to put treasure that was due to be moved to the surface. Presumably there had been a staircase or lift of some kind at one point in time. It was close to the hatch.

'You've got to be joking!' she screamed. 'We can make it from here, Ari!'

'I don't want to take that chance! Spend now, save later!' he shouted and, on his final word, he began shimmying away. He paused for a second to make sure he had judged the gap correctly, then pushed himself off the wall with all of his might.

Mid-air he felt a moment of panic as he thought he was going to fall short but, to his relief, he landed on the platform and stood up, testing its weight.

'It'll hold!' he bellowed. Ari looked down. The water was nearly a third of the way up the pillars. 'And those pillars are about to give! This cavern is on its way out!' he screamed. His gaze followed the nearest pillar to him upwards to the top of the room, and he could see it was beginning to shake.

Shit. It's now or never.

He looked back at Fliss who, as expected, had managed to get into a jumping position. He waved her over, and within a few seconds, she too was safely on the stone platform. She stood, and the pair looked at James Prince, who still clung to the wall.

'PRINCE!' Ari screamed.

The hole in the ceiling was, all of a sudden, a proper hole.

A stream of light flooded through, and Ari could see the stone beginning to fall away from the pillars all around them. He felt tiny as the huge pieces of rock began to fall, and the cave was shaking him around like he was on a roller coaster. He gripped the wall. They had seconds.

In the wake of the stream of light came down what looked like the metal arm of a crane with a metal grid attached to the bottom. Oddly, Ari thought it looked a bit like a giant, mechanical fly swatter – but with a flat base that was – thankfully - easily within jumping distance. It wouldn't have been had they stayed where they were, Ari noted with a sense of satisfaction. He and Fliss stepped back two paces. He grabbed her hand, and they jumped across.

Prince was still on the wall.

In his heart of hearts, Ari hadn't wanted it to end this way.

'Prince!' Ari and Fliss called out in unison.

But it was futile. Their fly-swatter crane was already beginning to hoist them upwards to safety, and the climb was insurmountable.

James Prince looked haggard.

No longer a white silhouette in the dark, Ari could see every sinew of his being desperately trying to cling to the rock.

'The treasure!' Prince shouted. Ari was incredulous.

'Don't be ridiculous!' Ari yelled back. 'Prince this place is about to collapse! Get onto the platform and-'

At that moment, the first of the four pillars gave way. It was perhaps less dramatic than Ari had expected. There was no loud noise, no build-up, no crumbling or gurgling. As it had been designed to do, the pillar simply fell away, and the far corner of the cave began to collapse too.

Then came the noise. There was a great booming sound that filled Ari's sensitive ears and made him cry out. The cliff was collapsing.

Their crane surged toward the surface.

Ari dropped to his knees as he and Fliss lurched through the hole and out into the light. Beneath them, the ancient mine sliced in on itself.

Fliss let out a sob, and Ari was sure he heard a scream. They were hoisted up and away, and dropped unceremoniously a few seconds later.

Ari lay face down on a stone floor, blinking. Like a snake, he felt the vibrations in the ground, and knew he was feeling the death of James Prince through his fingers. He allowed himself a final prayer to *Sulis Minerva*.

'My Lord?' Ari heard some distant voice say. It almost made him jump. *'It is done. The castle at Tintagel is flooded.'*

Silence followed. Then,

'Good work, Richard. You will do well.'

The King's voice slipped away for what Ari knew would be the last time.

He pulled himself up and looked around. Ari blinked a few times. Fliss was next to him.

He was in a room filled with treasure.

In a strong Eastern European accent, someone said, 'Mari-oos'.

***

Chapter forty

The cool wind lapped at Ari's face.

It was a mercifully calm morning at Tintagel Castle. He sat near the cliff edge at the surface, where the view of the coastline was quite stunning as the sunset rose on the horizon. He was wrapped in a blanket that had been given to him by one of the paramedics, and he chugged on a hot coffee in a travel mug. There was general chatter among the groups of people spread out about the grassy plain.

Somewhere behind him, if he listened carefully, he could hear Ondrej and his crew explaining what had happened to some police officers.

How they were Ocean Pearl employees who had been working at the site and had heard the commotion.

And lucky they had, because clearly the two mountaineers had gotten quite lost, and would have wound up dead were it not for their arrival in the nick of time. Ari wondered whether the police would believe them, then almost immediately decided he didn't care.

Fliss sat with him too.

On the grass with a large rock behind them. She had her own blanket and travel mug. They didn't say anything for a while and simply watched as the sun slowly crept upwards. Ari was suddenly struck by how long it had been since he had slept and found himself longing to be back in Benny's spare bed in Bath, with Cicero the cat curled up on the windowsill.

Ari was struggling to process what had happened, his brain almost refusing to allow him to believe that he had just been as close to death as he had ever been, or was ever likely to be again.

'I can't believe we found it,' Fliss said, shaking her head. 'Literally, can't believe it.'

'Reckon you'll go back to work? At Ocean Pearl?' he asked her, breaking the silence with a wry smile. The paramedics had put his arm in a sling, but the pair were waiting for their turn to be questioned before they were taken to hospital for further checks. Fliss laughed.

'Absolutely not. I think I'll be taking a period of indefinite leave...' she said. 'If they'll let me, that is,' she added.

Ari looked at her sideways.

'Ah yeah,' he said. 'I had almost forgotten, they don't take kindly to deserters. We'll sneak you away,' he added. They were quiet again until Fliss said.

'Your Dad, he's OK?'

His Father had been Ari's first thought when they had come out of the hole, and he had called him as soon as he was able from one of the police officer's phones. He was fine, so Ari only nodded in response.

'And Benny?'

Fliss had called him as soon as they had come out too. She nodded. 'Fine. And Kenny.'

The sound of heavy boots on gravel made Air look up.

He covered his eyes with his hand against the morning sun until the person was close enough to block out the glare. Ari felt the breath leave his lungs as the man's face came into full view in the shade.

Ondrej looked even older than he had when Ari had caught a glimpse of him at *Aquae* just a week previously.

His gait had taken on a slight limp in the intervening years since Merchant's Lodge, and there was a streak of grey that washed through his hair and beard that gave him a sort of half-and-half effect. Ari could see the youthful vitality of a man who had lived life to the full battling against the inevitable creep of age and, with it, an equally inevitable slowing down.

Age appeared to be winning, as it did with everyone. But there was some fight left in the dog yet.

Ondrej flashed Fliss a toothy grin. Prince had revealed that the pair had already met, or at least spoken. Neither showed it.

'Marius,' Ondrej said, overpronouncing "oos" as he always had done. 'You're one fucking lucky idiot.' Ari couldn't stifle a laugh.

'What are you doing here?' Ari asked with a genuine fondness for his old mentor.

Ondrej popped his rusted tobacco tin from the inside pocket of his bomber jacket, the same he had used when Ari had known him. He struck a cigarette and took a long draw, then pointed out to see, over the cliffs.

'We followed you, and them, here. I *knew* that if you were mixed up in this, it would be worth it,' he said. 'And boy were we right.'

Fliss rolled her eyes but managed to hold her tone in check when she spoke.

'And?' she asked. 'What is down there?'

The treasure room had been hastily emptied by Ondrej's men before the police arrived and loaded into the back of a transit van, which had long since disappeared down the single-track road leading away from Tintagel castle. Ari had watched it as it meandered around the cliffside and out of view, and in his heart he had known he was watching his fortune disappear forever.

'What is left of a pagan treasure,' he said unequivocally. 'Quite priceless. A mix of Roman and Viking artefacts. It will keep me in business for many years,' he said with a smile, taking another draw on his cigarette.

Bitterly, Ari remembered hearing about the sale of the Loch Arkaig treasure. How he had thought that having helped Ondrej to find and sell it would clear his name with the gangster, and there would be no bad blood between them. He had been right, but that success had led him to follow Ari to treasure once more, and had been rewarded.

'You don't even know its history,' Fliss said, a little more venomously this time.

'No,' Ondrej said. 'And I don't need to. All I care about is the sale value.'

Fliss fell silent, her face stony.

'I promised the archbishop of Canterbury that if I discovered any treasure I would give it to the church,' Ari said, flatly. Ondrej took another draw on his cigarette, weighing up the comment with what was clearly significant amusement.

'I will make a donation,' was all Ondrej said. *Guess that'll have to do,* Ari reflected.

'What did you do with the Ocean Pearl agents... Tennant, and Aurora?' Ari asked, wondering if they had met the same fate as the agents at Merchant's Lodge. Ondrej raised an eyebrow.

'Why do you care?' he asked.

'There has been enough blood shed for this treasure. I was hoping to avoid more,' he replied. Ondrej made an odd face, as though that kind of empathy didn't compute with his brain.

'They are probably fine,' he said. 'Once my men had commandeered the ship, we made them tell us where to look for you. They seemed to think you were somewhere on the surface, so we stuck them on a lifeboat and pushed them in the direction of land,' he said with a shrug.

The image of a lifeboat gliding silently across the water in the dead of the night filled Ari with an almost palpable sense of dread. But he didn't spare them too much thought - he was sure they wouldn't have given him that luxury – but he was genuinely glad that they had survived.

Unlike Prince, he thought with a pang.

The image of the hole collapsing in on itself replayed in his mind like a bad dream. All he could hear was Prince's final words. *The treasure.*

'Well,' Ondrej said, flicking his cigarette away as if making to leave.

'What will you do now?' Ari asked.

Ondrej stopped and turned back to the pair, looking down at them with a confused expression. Then, a smile tugged at the corner of his mouth, and within a few seconds, he was chuckling. It was an odd sight, as Ari knew him to be the kind of man who only laughed out of schadenfreude.

'Marius, this may be the end of your biggest adventure, and probably feels like a pivotal moment in *your* life. To me, it's just another day of business,' Ondrej said, with a smile that seemed legitimate. 'I'll see you next time,' he added, then turned and walked away, leaving Ari and Fliss sitting on the rock as though none of it had happened.

As though none of it has happened.

Ondrej was right, of course. As had Benny been when he had warned them about Ocean Pearl. *No one else cares.* On the news, there would be a tiny segment dedicated to a new treasure having been found. In a few weeks, once it had been sold off and Ondrej was richer than he might be already, some historian somewhere might use some of the treasure to make a determination about Roman Britain, which also no one would care about.

The dramatic, life-defining events for Ari and Fliss of the last few hours and days would be inconsequential to the perpetual passing of time and turning of the world. And no one would even blink an eye.

'Oh!' Ondrej said when he had taken a few paces. 'I almost forgot,' he turned and pulled a long object wrapped in brown paper from the inside of his jacket. Ari felt his blood run cold. Ondrej tossed it to him unceremoniously, and Ari caught it as though he were expecting it to be hot. He didn't need to open the paper to know what was inside. His old Bowie knife. He held it on his lap like a child and looked up at Ondrej.

'Thank you,' he muttered.

'They're a pair, remember. One of us should have them both. Who knows maybe one day they'll lead you somewhere,' Ondrej said, this time turning and leaving for good. Ari frowned at his back as he stomped across the grass. *Lead me somewhere.* He smiled delectably to no one in particular. *The knives are a pair... A clue?*

'I don't think you'll hear much more of this,' Fliss said, the reference lost on her. Ari decided not to mention it for now. 'The treasure will, I'm sure, make Ondrej and his goons a fortune, but that will be it,' she said. 'Ocean Pearl certainly won't be making anything public. This is a humiliation for them.'

Ari shot her a sideways glance.

'Should keep me off their radar then,' he said with a wry smile. They fell into a comfortable silence for a few moments, staring out at sea. Ari clutched his Bowie knife like it was a priceless heirloom.

One hundred metres away, near the now-collapsed hole they had been pulled from, Ari could see Ondrej talking calmly to a police officer. On the road nearby, another officer was packing away the cordon. They were making to leave.

'How did you know all that stuff?' Fliss asked, quietly. 'Down there, in the cave? What *happened* to you, when you fell unconscious in the mine?'

Ari shook his head.

'I don't understand it yet,' he said. 'But the place... Tintagel castle. It *spoke* to me... I heard... voices. From the past,' he said. 'I'm not crazy, I wasn't hearing things. It's not speaking to me now. But it was like I was there, in the thirteenth century. When I collapsed, I *saw* them.

King Henry, Richard of Dover – the man who owned Tintagel at the time and Thomas Becket's successor. Just recordings from a time gone by, channelled through me like an aerial. Nature is capable of powerful things,' he said with a sigh. 'And for some reason, I am particularly finely-tuned.'

Ari hugged his knees to his chest. The sun had risen to a mid-morning point on the horizon, its shine beginning to pull away from the surface of the dark waters.

'I've told you before,' he said after a time. 'All I have is heightened senses. I think I'm more in tune with the signals that nature puts out for us to experience. These "powers" – as you call them – are nothing to do with me,' he said. 'I just respond to the signals.'

'So,' she said, lowering her voice. 'What did happen? Why is that treasure here?' she asked.

Ari sighed. It had been a long night.

'Thomas Becket engineered his own martyrdom, as we know,' he said. 'But what Becket had failed to appreciate was that the King had anticipated that move. Somehow, he had known that the four knights would go to Canterbury with the intention of taking the archbishop's life. Perhaps,' Ari said, gravely. '*Perhaps* the King even ordered the killing. I don't know, his face was difficult to read.'

'Wait when you say you saw him... you mean you actually *saw* him?!' she asked, her face a picture of incredulity. Ari could tell she wasn't disbelieving, just surprised. This was new for both of them.

'Yes, while I was unconscious. I literally saw the conversation between the King and Richard of Dover. And Tintagel as it looked back then. A full and working castle, not the ruins it is today. The last thing I heard before I woke up was King Henry whispering to Richard to go to Canterbury to take hold of Becket's body. The King told him that he should bury any evidence of the treasure with Becket, and that would be the end of it. And to an extent, it was. Until now,' Ari said.

Fliss hummed her agreement.

'And the treasure that Ondrej has just taken?' she asked, unable to keep the bitterness from her voice. 'Is that all of it?' she asked.

Based on the tiny glimpse Ari had managed, it really would be priceless.

'That's just another holding room, like the one at *Aquae Sulis*,' Ari said. 'Which incidentally is why it was never found. Again, like *Aquae Sulis*, that remote sensing technology Ocean Pearl use will be revamped after all this I suspect. The larger cavern underneath the smaller one masked its presence,' he said.

'Crazy how it came out, though. Through a well? That's a big miss from Ocean Pearl.'

The well that Ari had seen King Henry leaning on was, as it turned out, the access point that Ondrej had used to rescue them from the mine.

'Yes... and when James Prince had finally managed to make radio contact with the surface, it must have been Ondrej's voice that he had heard,' Ari said, not realising the revelation until he spoke it aloud.

'So *that's* why he stayed,' Fliss said. 'With his agents gone, he knew if he came to the surface he would be killed by Ondrej. Or worse, handed back to Ocean Pearl.'

'Yes...' Ari said. Something else dawned on him too. 'And he must have given Ondrej our location for the rescue to be successful,' he said. Fliss remained silent.

James Prince, a martyr? Hardly. But at least his final act had been one of redemption.

'Anyway,' Ari said, continuing the recounting of his vision. 'That treasure is simply part of a must vaster collection. The treasure room here at Tintagel was flooded and sealed. Either they forgot about the few items that were in the conduit room, or – more likely I think – Richard of Dover didn't fully trust his King, and so left himself a little reserve he could come back for should he ever need it.'

'Not a bad plan,' she said. 'Anything about who wrote the curse tablet?'

Ari let out a barked laugh. 'I'd forgotten all about it!' he said, genuinely. 'Unfortunately not. I don't suppose we will ever truly know who wrote it,' he said. 'But the only person I can think of who had the means and motive is Beckett himself. I am less convinced he would have had the opportunity,' Ari said. 'As we know, *Aquae Sulis* is pretty far from Canterbury.'

Fliss hummed her agreement.

'So, what will you do now? Do *you* have a little reserve somewhere?' she asked, playfully.

Ari hadn't had much time to give his future a lot of thought, but he knew one thing for certain. He wanted to try to stay away from Ocean Pearl for as long as possible. And yet, simultaneously, he wanted more treasure.

'Well,' he said. 'The first thing is to not go to jail for wrecking an English heritage site,' he said, flashing her a grin.

'None of the castle was damaged,' she said in a sympathetic tone. 'None of it that they knew was there, anyway.'

'Good point,' he said. 'After that, I think I want to go home and have a shower. Then... who knows?' he said. 'Might join Ocean Pearl,' he said. Fliss punched him gently on the arm.

'No more treasure hunting?' she asked affectionately.

'Oh no, *definitely* more treasure hunting,' he said with a grin. 'We've proven that even Ocean Pearl can be beaten at their own game. I don't know about you, but I fancy doing it again,' he said.

'Well, as I mentioned earlier, I'm pretty sure I'm out of a job. And, as of this moment, on the run from my previous employers,' she replied. 'My main concern is that we don't have any leads,' she added. Ari closed his eyes and pictured the other Bowie knife. Ondrej's Bowie knife.

'That may not be entirely true,' he said, cryptically, running his fingers along his knife through its wrapper.

Before Fliss could respond, she was interrupted by one of the Police Officers calling their names. The officer was waving at them, letting them know that they were packing up and about to leave.

'Will you guys be OK?' she called, her voice travelling clearly over the flat land of the cliffside. Ari and Fliss shot each other a knowing look.

'We'll be fine Officer!' Fliss called back. 'Absolutely fine!'

***

Epilogue

In the dead of night, Thomas Becket brought his horse to a stop.

The cool evening wind blew gently across his balding head, and he couldn't shake a feeling of unease that gnawed at his soul.

He glanced over his shoulder nervously, not for the first time since he had embarked on his treacherous journey to *Aquae Sulis*.

He steeled himself as he slipped off his horse and tied the reins to a short fence post. With a final glance around, he crossed himself and headed toward the large outline of the baths, knowing in his heart that if he were discovered, he would have some extraordinarily difficult questions to answer.

What is the archbishop doing in England, when he is supposed to be banished to the continent?

What is the chaste archbishop doing at *Aquae Sulis*, a bath house that was at one time used and enjoyed by some of the richest and most powerful people in the land?

And why, of all things, does he have with him a pagan curse tablet, seemingly signed by King Henry II?

***

Printed in Great Britain
by Amazon